THE LOOKED AFTER CHILD

by

K.C. Dowling

Grosvenor House
Publishing Limited

This book is published by
Grosvenor House Publishing Ltd
Link House
140 The Broadway, Tolworth, Surrey, KT6 7HT.
www.grosvenorhousepublishing.co.uk

A CIP record for this book
is available from the British Library

ISBN 978-1-78623-994-5

Also by K.C. Dowling

A Man of Insignificance

The Red Hat Guide to Manchester City Centre

Acknowledgements

Thank you to Debbie, Geoff, Elaine and Marilyn.

Thank you to Jennifer and Sarah Armstrong, two lovely women, both of whom tolerated my impromptu readings with spontaneous smiles, grace and good humour.

Thank you to Luciano Braga for creating the cover.

Thank you to many of my guests at The Springfield Hotel in the glorious town of Marple.

Contents

Chapter 1	Back Piccadilly	1
Chapter 2	Monday Morning	13
Chapter 3	The Trefor Family	33
Chapter 4	Committee Room Two	42
Chapter 5	At Home with The Kinders	68
Chapter 6	Parkhurst Lane	82
Chapter 7	A Life of Emma	97
Chapter 8	Winton Kiss and The Death of Jason Dunphy	108
Chapter 9	Allegation	126
Chapter 10	The Stonemasons Arms	136
Chapter 11	Strategy Meeting	151
Chapter 12	Hypothesis	164
Chapter 13	Disruption	186
Chapter 14	Archie Hamilton	195
Chapter 15	Panel	210
Chapter 16	Camille and Justine	225
Chapter 17	Trensis Station	240
Chapter 18	Threesome	257
Chapter 19	Doctor Maxine Wells	268
Chapter 20	Chic Conway and The Bar of World Opinion	279
Chapter 21	The Travellers' Oak	297
Chapter 22	Phone Day	311
Chapter 23	Names and Initials	326
Chapter 24	Rosemary Gilmartin	335
Chapter 25	Sunday Lunch	346
Chapter 26	Sisters Under the Skin	358
Chapter 27	Diana	369

Chapter 1

Back Piccadilly

Even, after they had given thought to the facts, which were; it was the city of Manchester, it was Wednesday evening, it was well into the month of March and there had not been one single droplet of it, since half way through February. Even after many of those "experts," who were supposedly "in the know," had forecast it and everybody was expecting it, even with all this understanding, warning, prophesy and promise, the people of Manchester still expressed surprise, or perhaps they feigned it, when eventually at 6:22pm, it had finally arrived, it was happening and it was happening now.

This predicted event was torrential, hard, heavy rain. It was hurtling across the city skies, like a previously uttered convulsed threat, that was now in complete fulfilment. As well as this, the wind was up and the conditions were icy cold, causing the rain to bite and swirl as it teemed down from up above. Each drop seeking out and piercing unprotected skin and bone, like a tiny, blunt needle.

Everybody was indoors, sheltering from its pervading, invading, wetness. Even those who had gone out, were in. They were in the pubs, restaurants, cinemas, theatres, shops, the houses of others, anywhere they could think of, that could offer them shelter from the rain, as it swirled and swished, descending upon the roofs and roads, cascading down the tiles and slates and falling into the gutters. From there it plummeted the downpipes, before disappearing on its directed way, by method of fall and camber, into the kerbside channels, before disappearing altogether down the street gullies, only to be replaced by more rain, in what seemed to be an endless torrent of spiteful water, which meant good to none, and harm to all.

Just on the edge, of what is deemed by many, to be central Manchester and opening for the first time as Store Street in 1842, renamed Manchester London Road in 1847, then finally after some reconstruction given its present name in 1960, Manchester Piccadilly is known to all Mancunians, without any argument, to be the principal railway station of Manchester. Its current offer contains 6 train operators and 14 platforms and approaching 4 million passengers use its services every year.

Known to virtually all Mancunians and just on the edge of the city centre, beyond the 'S' bend of Manchester Piccadilly Station Approach, is Piccadilly itself. This thoroughfare bends its way out of the Approach and then runs on bullet-straight, for about five hundred metres, in a slight north-westerly direction towards the city centre. During this journey, it trundles past an assortment of workaday bars and shops on one side, and posh hotels and offices on the other. It crosses some nondescript streets before cutting through some better-known ones such as Lever Street and Portland Street, then more bars and shops, before finally coming to a dead stop at Oldham Street. After fifty paces it then changes its name to Market Street and finally disappears towards the completely devoid of distinction, soul-lacking, Arndale Shopping Centre.

Running alongside Piccadilly, virtually all the way in parallel and no more than twenty metres away from it, at any given time, is what can only be described as a back-alley. This back-alley though, is no ordinary back-alley, for this back-alley is known as Back Piccadilly. In confirmation of this street name and just to make it official, there are two street signs fixed either end of it, by Manchester City Council. Save for the different coloured plastic skips of litter and locked up, alligated back entrances, standing along either side of it, Back Piccadilly, finds itself, these days inactive, mostly empty and in a condition of gentle dilapidation and desertion. This was not always the case, for Back Piccadilly has experienced a chequered history throughout its almost two hundred years existence. Its most colourful period was probably in the post-World War 11 days of the 1950s/60s and 70s. During this thirty years plus span, Back Piccadilly played landlord to the Manchester Barrow Boys who lined its then cobbled streets along the side of the then C&A Store. On the face of it they sold fruit and veg, but it was well known to Mancunians that you could purchase, anything from a rowing boat to an electric guitar from these apparent purveyors of apples and oranges.

The barrow boys, the cobbles and C&A are long gone, but Back Piccadilly remains. Today, it is not completely deserted, for about half-way down its length and at the little-known junction of Little Lever Street stands a public house, Mother Mac's.

As the rain swirled around in Back Piccadilly on this Wednesday evening, the keen observer, had there been one, would have noticed that that there was some movement in the alley. Whosoever was there, was under the cover of night, still, silent and sheltered, in an empty doorway, several doors down from Mother Mac's and in the direction of Lever Street.

Inside the pub was a small band of straggling early-evening drinkers. There were ten in number, two standing at the small bar in low conversation, another six, sitting around the small lounge in comfort enjoying the blaze of the open fire. Sitting apart from both groups were two men in their sixties. Even sitting down on the low, green-upholstered furniture, it could be seen that both men were tall and well dressed. They had obviously been drinking together and judging by their verbal coherence, quite heavily. They were discussing their day in general and their arrangements for getting home.

'How many stops have we had today, nine, ten, maybe, how many drinks?'

'I've not been counting Geoff, but probably, as you say nine, ten stops and at least one drink in each, two in some. Three in *The Vine* but that's where we started off, we always linger in the first one, wherever it is.'

'I don't know how you do it Deacon, on those Scotch-fire-water-chasers that you down-charge, one of these days you'll just burst into flames, like the character in that book?'

'What book?'

'I can't think of the name now, my literary recall has gone backwards with each drink, it was written by Charles Dickens, you know the one, have you ever read it?'

'If you told me the name of it, or what it's about, I might be able to tell you, Charles Dickens wrote a lot of books?'

'He didn't Deacon, not if you compare him to say, Enid Blyton. It's just that every book he wrote was as thick as a kerbstone, and took you the best part of a year to read it, so it just seemed that way.'

'Go on then Geoff how many did each of them write?'

'I don't know exactly, Charles wrote about ten, eleven perhaps, let me think, there was: David Copperfield, Oliver Twist, Bleak House...'

Deacon interrupted, 'Please don't go through them all. I couldn't stand it, I've not got the patience for it, I'll take your word for it, let's agree to agree on ten. I've come out for a drink, not a lesson in English Literature.'

'Whereas Enid must have written hundreds, with all that "Secret Seven" and "Famous Five," stuff.'

'I can't think of anybody else, only you Geoff, who would compare Oliver Twist & David Copperfield to Noddy and Big Ears.'

They both laughed.

'Oh yeah, I'd forgotten about Noddy,' Geoff continued, 'anyway this man, the one that burst into flames, was played by Johnny Vegas on the tele.'

'Geoff, you said it was a book.'

'It is a book, by Charles Dickens.'

'Charles Dickens wrote about the condition of England in mid Victorian times, he had nothing to do with modern America, anyway Vegas hadn't even been invented when Charlie was alive.'

'Deacon, what are you talking about, why are you bringing America into the conversation?'

'You said that it was set in Vegas.'

'Las Vegas, eh? No! I said that this character from the book was played in the TV drama by Johnny Vegas. He's an actor on television.'

'I know who Johnny Vegas is Geoff, I like him, he's a good actor, but what has he got to do with somebody bursting into flames.'

'It doesn't matter Deacon, forget it now, what I meant to say was that we've had a good drink and a good day.'

'I know, I think I'll walk up to Piccadilly and get the 8:14.'

'Are you sure that you want to walk up to the station in this weather, it's a bad night out there, then there's all those steps from the platform to the exit at the other end, you'll be blown away. Why don't you take a taxi home or at least from here to the station, it's not as if you can't afford it?'

'It's got nothing to do with money Geoff, and I've walked up and down those steps a thousand times. No, I'll be fine, it's only a quarter of a mile to Piccadilly and it's sheltered along the way, I've got my hat and coat, anyway, it isn't that bad, I don't know what everybody is going on about, it is only a drop of rain, and in Manchester of all places. It isn't as if it hasn't been seen before. I've been out in much worse, when I was working, and so have you and all night too. You remember the Shudehill Shootings? It rained for a whole week, twenty-four-seven, never stopped, nobody said anything in those days, they just got on with whatever they had to do. Weather was just weather, it was just there, now they talk about it all the time as if it is some new kind of scientific phenomena. The newspapers have headlines about the weather, I saw one recently it read; "Arctic Blast, Coming Soon." It is just to get a story. I've bought a return train ticket from Heaton Moor, I got a third off with my rail card and I'm not wasting it, also I need the exercise and the journey will bring me round a bit. If I get in the back of a taxi, I'll just fall asleep. We've been drinking since one-o-clock and I'm just about done now.'

'I'm just about done too, but I'm not going home until I'm completely done, good and proper, so I'm going to have another one or maybe two drinks. I don't get out much these days, so I'm going to make the most of it. After that I'm going to phone a cab and the taxi driver can concern himself with getting me home, right from this front door to my own front door.'

'When were the Shudehill Shootings Geoff, nineteen-eighty-eight was it?'

'No, Deacon it was more like, nineteen eighty-two!'

'Was it really, yes it was, you know you're right, it was eighty-two, thirty odd years ago, where has my life gone?'

A silence ensued and Deacon finished the remainder in his glass.

'Right then Geoff, well I'm going, I'll ring you, and we'll do it again next month.'

As Deacon said this he stood up, put his scarf and raincoat on, then his cap, then silently and deliberately he shook Geoff's hand, braced himself for what the night had to offer and staggered out of the side door. Geoff walked over to the bar and after a few minutes conversation with the pub landlord he returned to his seat with yet another drink.

Geoff thought about Deacon and his own relationship with him. Their association went back a long way. Geoff considered that he had known Deacon longer than he had known his own wife and he had married when he was twenty-two years old. Deacon had been the "best man" at his wedding and godfather to Harriet, his eldest. Deacon himself, had never married, he had remained a bachelor all his life and had lived with his mother all that time until she had died last year. Both he and his old friend were the same age, and they had first come across each other when they were both sixteen years of age. They had met when they were sitting opposite each other in a draughty corridor in Bootle Street, Manchester, in October 1969. Both were awaiting interview by the Police Selection Panel for the position of Police Cadet in the Manchester Police. Both were successful in their interviews and ever since then, their lives had intertwined. They had worked closely together as serving Police Officers, often on the same case and over a period of thirty plus years. By the end of their careers both had achieved the rank of Inspector. Geoff had retired as early as he had been allowed to and Deacon had stayed on as long as he had been allowed to. In their respective situations, this meant retirement at 54 years of age for Geoff and 62 years of age for Deacon. Legally, Deacon could have gone on longer but he had confided in Geoff, that his ideas were based on old fashioned policing and the new, much younger, senior management wanted him to change or leave, he couldn't change, he had no idea what he was expected to change to, so he left.

Since Deacon's retirement the two ex-police officers had met up regularly, usually once a month for their pub crawl and reminisces, as Geoff's wife called it. There was a certain amount of irony in his wife's statement, as Geoff and Deacon didn't really reminisce. When they were on their pub crawls, they rarely discussed their time in the Police. They always met on a Wednesday as it 'broke the week up,' always on the second Wednesday of every month, they didn't know why, always at 1:00 pm and always in one of the old Manchester city centre pubs which they both knew well. There was certainly plenty of them still around, all frequented by both men in their police days: *The Britons' Protection, The Peveril of the Peak, Vine Inn, City Arms, Shakespeare, The Unicorn, The Abercrombie, The Nag's Head;* there were many to choose from, but wherever they started their crawl and they always tried to vary it, they always ensured that they finished it in Back Piccadilly, in *Mother Mac's*.

Recently, Geoff had become a little concerned for his old friend. Albert (Deacon) Bailey had always been a bit of a loner, but it wasn't just that. Geoff knew of a younger brother, Cyril, who lived in New Zealand and had done for over thirty y ears, but Deacon rarely mentioned him and as far as Geoff was concerned, Deacon and his brother were not close, they were out of touch, if not estranged altogether. Apart from Geoff himself and Cyril, Geoff knew of no other friends or family that Deacon had. He had taken up with a few girlfriends in his younger days but these relationships had never lasted long and it must be ten years since the last one. His life had always revolved around his job, his drinking and his 'Ma,' as he called her. Since Ma had died last year, Deacon had become more withdrawn than normal. He had graduated from being a loner to a recluse. Geoff surmised that it was only natural, when you were close to somebody who you had known all your life and then one day she just wasn't there anymore, it was bound to influence you. Although she had been well into her eighties. Deacon's mother hadn't been ill. She had enjoyed good health. Right up to the day that she died, she was still doing the shopping and the cooking and she went swimming a couple of times a week and she walked everywhere. She had just declared that afternoon as she often did, that she was going for a 'bit of a lie down.' This was exactly what she did, only this time she didn't wake up from her afternoon snooze, she died 'from natural causes' in her sleep. Deacon repeatedly told Geoff that '…it was the best way to go,' and he was right, it was better to go like that than to have to suffer through some pain-ridden debilitating illness. However, Geoff knew that despite Deacon's seeming acceptance of the situation, it had all come as a complete shock to his old friend and it had upset him deeply. Before his mother's death, Deacon, although a solitary man had been active and involved. He was an avid reader, a regular hill walker and in the summer months he played for his local bowling team, but he'd stopped all those activities and now all he did was rattle around in that big old house in Heaton Moor. Another thing that Geoff had deduced, was that Deacon had started smoking again. He hadn't said anything to Geoff about it and Geoff hadn't said anything to Deacon. Geoff though, had been a dedicated non-smoker all his life, he had never smoked. Even when it had been fashionable in the 60s and 70s, he had always hated it. He could smell a smoker at ten paces and he could smell it on Deacon. He could smell the stale tobacco smoke and he

could also smell the petrol fumes from that ancient cigarette lighter that Deacon still carried around with him.

At the same time as Geoff raised the glass to his
lips, sank into his thoughts, inside the cosiness of the
pub and warmed himself by the fire, the excesses of the
day's drinking were finally taking their toll on Deacon,
who leaned in the pub doorway, in a state of advancing
drunkenness, outside in the alley of Back Piccadilly. He
walked ponderously up the alley towards the railway
station, sometimes seemingly taking as many steps to
stand still as he did to move forward. Soon though, he
found his rhythm and began to make steady progress.
The rain was heavy as he approached Lever Street. He
looked up at the darkened sky and then he looked down
at his wristwatch. He had 24 minutes before his train
was due, which he reasoned was more than ample time.
He decided that he'd have a cigarette, he'd not had one
since this morning. Manchester pubs, like all pubs now
were a no-smoking-zone these days, some pubs did have
smoking areas but he'd just spent the whole day with
Geoff and if there was anything that Geoff hated more
than smoking then Deacon was yet to discover it. Geoff
would have gone on and on about it. It was far easier to
abstain, than face a whole afternoon being lectured on
the subject, so that's what he had decided to do, abstain.
Rummaging around his clothing he found his cigarettes
and his lighter. He dangled the cigarette from his lips.

Just as he was holding his old lighter to his cigarette, his mobile phone rang. It was probably Geoff, he
thought, calling from the comfort of Mother Mac's,
making sure that he was all right. He decided to ignore
the call, then he decided that he would take it. As he
fumbled for his phone he dropped his lighter in the dark

alley. When he placed the phone to his ear he heard a voice which he didn't recognise say,

'Inspector Deacon Bailey?'

'Yes.'

Answering that call was probably the last act that retired Police Inspector Deacon Bailey carried out. For what happened next was incredible by the stretch of anybody's imagination. Had there been anybody around to witness this event, then they would have found great difficulty in believing what their eyes saw; nobody though, did witness it.

What occurred was extremely easy to describe but extremely difficult to explain, as Deacon Bailey's whole being from the tip of his toes to the top of his head set alight. He instantaneously burst into flames. Within a matter of seconds, he was engulfed in red, orange and yellow, upward-searing-fire. The flames licked and dashed all around him and gave off a ferocious heat. His on-fire flesh gave off a terrible burning stench. His screams went unheard on the wet, wild night and in less than the space of half a minute he was burned alive to his horrible death, in Back Piccadilly. Even his blood boiled and bubbled away in that raging human inferno. All that remained of him, in the drenched back alley was a smouldering skeleton, an old petrol fuelled ciga-rette lighter which he'd dropped a minute earlier and a mobile phone which fell to the ground, as his bones did.

Chapter 2

Monday Morning

It was evident and not in any doubt, it was indeed a fact, that on occasions, Councillor Danny Senetti was jaded. On some days and at certain times he was less jaded than others. This manner and demeanour of his was really a given, and all who had even the remotest connection to him knew it. However, if the observer could select the part of the week, perhaps even the part of the day, or even the hour when there was a likelihood that he would be at his most jaded, perhaps even to the point of numbness, then it would certainly be, providing he was awake that is, between 9:30 am and 10:30 am on any Monday morning. He was completely unheeding to this perception, but the observer, had indeed there been one to see him around this time and on this day, which there invariably wasn't, would have noticed.

With none of this in his mind, Senetti gingerly extricated the polystyrene beaker of lukewarm, white coffee from the vending machine which was in the small corridor which in turn led off the room from Norford Town Hall's main reception area. He raised the beaker to his mouth and sipped the contents slowly and as he did this he thought about two things simultaneously.

Firstly, he considered his own reflection, which looked blurred and mockingly back at him, from the polished stainless-steel case of the coffee vendor. He appeared to himself, to inhabit the look of man who had done everything hurriedly this morning, which of course he had. Secondly, he considered what the Council Leader Karen Spencer could possibly want him for at 10:00 am on a Monday-morning?

It wasn't her words, the ones which he had played back three times on his telephone answering-machine, just to make sure the message was real, no it wasn't those actual words, '...element of urgency, 'utmost importance...' for everything was *important* and *urgent* to people like Karen Spencer, and she threw those particular adjectives away, with the same abandon a standing politician throws out promises. Conversely, in Senetti's opinion, she seemed to have little regard for the issues that really were genuinely important and urgent. Somehow, she didn't seem to recognise those. Throwaway adjectives aside, people like her, just didn't understand anything that wasn't running at full pelt, giving it your all. She didn't understand the strategic benefit of slacking around on a Monday morning in a state of negative capability and composed demi-lethargy, reading the morning newspaper and waiting around for the pubs to open at midday.

Anyway, who was it who decreed that the working week should start on Monday-morning, who said so? He didn't know, it could probably be traced back to some old time agricultural reason or to religion. Well he wasn't agricultural and he certainly wasn't religious, old time or any other time and his working week, as a rule, didn't include anything before midday, on any day. His working week normally started on Tuesday at midday, rarely did it include mornings. If it really had to, then it would be Wednesday or Thursday morning, and his week ended on a Thursday evening at around five-o-clock. Rarely did it include any part of Friday and it never, ever included Monday-morning.

Back to Karen. No, once Monday-morning came around, even worse it was probably Sunday-evening with Karen Spencer, she wanted to be 'up and at 'em,' and if you were with her, she wanted you, as she often put it to, 'either lead, follow or just get out of the way.' He wasn't particularly receptive to doing any of these things at the best of times, and he was particularly unreceptive to all of them on any Monday-morning and particularly on this, Monday-morning.

As far as cosmetic appearance was concerned, he was unshaven, his tie was fastened loosely around his neck, the top button of his shirt was missing altogether and the second button was unfastened. All this was minutiae to him and he was oblivious to it. His mind was totally occupied with the fact that he was feeling a little groggy. This was mainly because of his late Sunday night lock-in, in the tap-room of the Black Swan, or was it an early Monday-morning lock-in, he couldn't quite remember which and to clarify to himself, he tried to remember what time he had eventually poured himself into the taxi that had taken him on the short journey home. However, like most of these occasions, his memory deserted him and he couldn't make an accurate recall. He glanced again at the stainless-steel reflection of his dark uncombed hair, his hooded eyes and his crumpled, cheap grey suit, draped over the even cheaper, light blue shirt he'd put on, one-handed and over his head, without unfastening the buttons and straight from the bedroom floor, an hour or so earlier.

He reached for his inside jacket pocket and came out with a pair of heavy, dark blue-rimmed spectacles and put them on. They weren't so much for optical purposes but more to hide himself behind, at least for a bit more of the morning.

He continued with his contemplations on the Council Leader.

No, he was mad at and puzzled about Karen. What perplexed him about her actions was this. It was Monday-morning and she knew enough about his bad habits to know what *his* Monday mornings were for, or at least what they were *not* for, and if she was to get the best out of *him,* then they were not for attending meetings with *her,* and Karen was always concerned about *getting the best* out of everybody. After all she would have almost certainly, at the tax payers' expense been on one of those *educationals* that she kept racking up by the tens. She'd probably been on twenty or thirty of them by now. No doubt this course would have been run by some Local Government Association department in London, and its content would have explained in full, in three days, *how to get the best out of people.* Why was it always *three days* for those courses, why was it never two nor four, why, no matter the subject, was three days always the optimum number? If they ran a course on teaching *Mandarin Chinese*, and they probably did, they would no doubt claim fluency in *three days.* Furthermore, why were they always run by a 'facilitator?' A facilitator who always seemed to be two years either side of eighty years of age, who had come out of retirement specifically to teach this course and one who didn't need to wear glasses; where did they find all these octogenarians with perfect eyesight, and what was a 'facilitator,' anyway?

Upon reflection, he was almost sure that he'd seen something with that very title, not *Mandarin Chinese* but *Getting the Best out of People;* it was probably on one of those round-robin e-mails that followed him around throughout every aspect of his civic life. The ones that he just spontaneously deleted without reading them, almost everybody did. Everybody that is except people like Karen, which was why nobody, except people like Karen, ever went on those courses, nobody ever knew about them, because they all deleted the emails without reading them, everybody knew that, everybody that is except Karen and the people who kept sending the emails. Then, what did the people who sent you the emails do? They called you by telephone and asked you if you'd received the sodding thing. You just said, 'no, sorry I haven't seen it', and for chrissake! What did they say when you said that? 'I'll send it you again,' that's what they said, and they weren't laughing either, well, they weren't able to laugh, well not any more. Let's face it, if you spent all day, every day, telephoning people about emails, well it wouldn't be very long before you lost the ability to laugh. Anyway, that was exactly what they did, they unlaughingly sent the email to you again, and you deleted it again, without reading it, and so it continued. This after all was local government.

As well as this, Karen had telephoned him person-ally which was a rare occurrence indeed. Combine the personal with the Monday morning, and the reason for this whole appointment was a complete mystery and entirely without precedent. He leaned slovenly in the corner and threw the remaining contents of his coffee cup into the wash basin. He casually dropped the empty beaker into the provided bin, as he did this, he took a small bottle of antiseptic mouthwash from his jacket side pocket. He unscrewed the top and gulped some of the liquid, swilling it around his mouth for a few seconds. He leaned over the wash-basin and spat the gargled slops into its stainless-steel bowl. Now he was as ready as he would ever be on a Monday-morning.

He walked along the corridor before passing through two security doors. Then he looked up and saw the heavy timber door with the slender, reinforced glass panel running vertically through the centre of the door. At the top of the door was a black plate, which was inscribed with white lettering. It read, *Leader of the Council.* As Senetti came through the door and entered the outer office he noticed that sitting behind her desk as usual like a vigilant sentry, her flame red hair piled high upon her head like an upended, exotic, giant unsliced loaf, was Karen's secretary, the formidably-natured and formidably-named, Araminta Rock.

Araminta and Senetti had long since formed a mutual understanding. It was based on the shared recognition that they both disapproved of each other and that he knew exactly what she was about and that she knew exactly what he was about. In short, she didn't trust him in her way and he didn't trust her in his. This unspoken of, but shared acceptance, worked well and they rubbed along nicely by accepting the premise that unless there was no alternative whatsoever, they would exclude each other from everything that they could possibly think of and by leaving each other alone.

'Good Morning Araminta, how lovely to see you, you look well,' he tried to sound sincere.

'Good Morning Councillor, you look well,' she tried to reciprocate with the same degree of sincerity and hoped it came over that way. She eyed his dishevelled state with the combination of a faint whiff of suspicion and more than a distinct air of disapproval. It was Araminta's role, at least she thought that it was, as secretary to the council leader, to have a little outside intelligence on all the councillors. Because of this, she knew all about Senetti's drinking and some of his other wayward ways. She also considered that she couldn't remember when she had last seen him or even heard of him being in the Town Hall on a Monday. He had certainly never been in the Leader's Office before, on a Monday, at any time of the day and certainly not on a Monday-morning. She couldn't even recall him being seen in the building or come to that, anywhere else in the borough on *any* morning. All her information on Councillor Danny Senetti informed her that he was not a Monday person nor was he a morning person and he most definitely was not, a Monday-morning person.

'Please go right in, she is expecting you.'

As he entered the room, Senetti saw Karen seated behind her desk. There were also two black leather covered chairs in front of the desk, one of them was empty, but the other was occupied by someone who had their back towards his front. Despite this he could see that this person was a woman. She had long, curled, shiny, black and brown hair, tied behind her. She was wearing a dark blue trouser-suit, with a white shirt, he could see the white collar above the lapels of her jacket. He could see little else, but he could smell her perfume and amazingly, at least for him, he recognised it. It was called *Tom Ford's, Oud Wood*. It wasn't that he had any expertise in ladies' perfume and he certainly didn't have a penchant for remembering the names of any, if anything the contrary was true. However, as far as *Oud Wood* was concerned, Charlotte used to wear it, and he recalled that some years ago, he'd spent almost all of one day immediately before Christmas Eve, trawling the shops of Manchester city centre, desperately looking for it. If his recall was accurate, he remembered that it was very expensive, but then again it would be if Charlotte wore it.

Karen stood up, 'Thank you for coming Danny, especially at such short notice and on a Monday morning,' she said knowingly.

'Let me introduce you to Officer Alberta Curtis-Brightland, she's from the Home Office, Child Commissioner's Office to be precise. Alberta, please meet Councillor Danny Senetti.'

Officer Alberta Curtis-Brightland rose from her seat, turned around and smiled, showing perfect even and white teeth. She looked straight at Senetti and shook his hand, gently, firmly and in silence. He joined in the hand shake, but not the smile, he couldn't smile, how could anybody smile? Leastways not now, on this day and not without looking like a grinning jackass, not that he had the remotest idea what a jackass looked like or even if there was such an animal, grinning or otherwise, he'd never actually seen one. He'd just heard the phrase somewhere in the dim and distant past. He wasn't on his own in not smiling. He'd read somewhere or possibly heard it on the radio, that in the U.K. the average time the average person first smiled on a Monday morning was 11:14 am. Anyway, whether it was true or not, he made no attempt to smile, he thought it was best left that way.

Senetti pondered on his newly introduced colleague in general and on her name, *Alberta Curtis-Brightland*, he mulled the name over in his head. Although your name was always said to be yours, on most occasions, you very probably couldn't really do anything to either assist or resist its acquisition. It was usually your parents who bestowed it upon you when you were very young and as a helpless baby, you had no faculty for either acceptance or refusal. By the time you realised any implication that went with your name, it was all too late, you had become known by it and stuck with it. Whatever you tried to do to it; modify it, change it, deny it altogether, there was no going back. It was just as that Stevie Wonder song said, it was all: 'Signed, Sealed, Delivered and Yours.' So, all in all, your parents were to blame. So even if your name said nothing about you, what did it say about them? What was that poem by that great post-war poet from Hull and what was his name, how did it go?

They muck you up your mum and dad
They do not mean to but they do
They give you all the faults they had
And add some extra just for you

Senetti pondered, he wasn't sure that he was recalling the verse verbatim, he thought that there might be a four-letter word in that stanza. Nevertheless, he was content that he had recalled it with more accuracy than error and he'd just thought of the poet's name, *Philip Larkin.*

Anyway, take the name *Alberta,* ostensibly a woman's name, but really it was a man's name, a man's name which had been modified, well, one letter added on to the end of it, to alter its gender, and to be precise it had started life as *Albert.* So maybe Alberta's parents wanted a boy, so they could name him after his father or his grandfather or his uncle. Then, when she came along and she was a girl, they were disappointed, but, not to be out done, they just feminised the name *Albert.*

Furthermore, what about the double-barrelled bit, *Curtis-Brightland?* Why did people do that? Give themselves two names, when one was enough. It wasn't so much the burden itself, it was more to do with the way that people who had double-barrelled names didn't realise it was a burden in the first place. The contrary was true, they thought that having two surnames was in some way a social advantage, when it was actually a social disadvantage. It was a bit like one of those personalised number plates on your car whereupon the owners of such plates thought that by having one, it elevated their status and gave them kudos. As anybody who has ever owned one could have told them, the opposite is true. For gradually the owners of such plates come to realise that their own presence is now espied, recognised and commented upon, as it appears in all the common locations, the ones where everybody else visits. Whereas before, it was often considered that you were too important, or in control of your life, or too intelligent, or too healthy or too moral, to go to such places. Places like the launderette, the cheap booze shop, the

Chinese takeaway, the doctor's, the pizza shop, and if you were unlucky, your number plate was seen parked outside the nearest rub and tug shop! Before you had the number plate, nobody even noticed your car with its nondescript registration, wherever it was parked.

Senetti looked Alberta Curtis-Brightland in the eye. She was black, probably Afro-Caribbean antecedence and she wore spectacles. She was tall for a woman, probably two or three inches shorter than his midge's short of six feet. He couldn't tell whether she was wearing heels or not. Even beyond the spectacles, he could see that she had clear brown eyes. She was slim, trim, and toned, he estimated that there probably wasn't one single kilo of flesh on her that wasn't there because she wanted it to be and wasn't in the exact place that she wanted it to be in. He also concluded that she had that face and body scrubbed, clear-skinned, strict diet, gymnasium, three circuits a week, steam-room look. He now got the front view of the immaculate white open-neck shirt under the dark blue trouser suit. All put together she was physically a very attractive woman. He guessed her to be in her mid to late-thirties. The most noticeable aspect about her, to him though, was not a feature but a general absence. She wore no jewellery of any kind, her face, hands and body were completely devoid of it, there was not a ring, bangle, broach, neck-lace, pin, stud nor even a watch to be seen anywhere about her; he considered this unusual for a woman, par-ticularly one who had a taste for expensive perfume.

He summed her up to be: unmarried, unattached, childless, career driven and even though she hadn't yet spoken a word, he decided that he probably wouldn't like what she had to say when she said it. He also knew that it was as an absolute certainty that she was going to say it, and whatever it was she was about to say, he wasn't looking forward to hearing it. He was also now aware that she was undoubtedly the reason for his interrupted Monday-morning.

Alberta Curtis-Brightland looked upon Danny Senetti. She thought that she'd heard the name somewhere before, but she couldn't quite remember where or why. She half recalled that it was to do with some scandal, but she couldn't recall any more. She supposed him to be in his mid to late-forties. He was nothing original, she had seen his type, many times before. Local Councillors, they came in all ages, physical shapes, sizes and all genders too, but there was little else difference between most of them. Danny Senetti, she thought, probably cared for nobody and nothing, except his partner if he had one, his children if he had any, his mother if she was still alive and the success or failure of his next election, whenever that was, and those people and that event were not necessarily in the assumed order of priority.

On reflection she now thought, probably in his early fifties. He looked to her, as if he'd been drinking last night, which he probably had. In evidence of this he absolutely reeked of antiseptic mouthwash, always a dead giveaway. He was scruffy and unshaven and his shirt was all creased, it was probably the one he had been wearing yesterday. She thought to herself that he had the appearance of somebody who bought his clothes from charity shops or perhaps had them given to him and today he had got himself up and gone out in a hurry. She glanced down at his shoes which were scuffed and unpolished. His clothes were crumpled, as indeed he seemed to be. In contrast, she was drawn to his hands.

They were scrupulously clean, his fingernails were perfectly and expertly manicured, and this finish had not been accomplished by him and although she only caught a glimpse of it, under his shirt sleeve, he wore what appeared to be an expensive wristwatch, possibly a Rolex, she thought. The watch didn't quite go with the rest of him and she wondered about it. Apart from the watch and the nails, the hands in general, his overall appearance was one of being ragged and crumpled.

She decided, as most official people did, on first meeting Danny Senetti, that whatever the situation, no matter how important or unimportant it was, that he was just not to be trusted with it, nor was there anything about him that gave the impression he had any of the characteristics which could be seen to be virtuous or that another person could rely upon. There was more than that, for her overall perception of him depressed her. Just then she received an impromptu insight into his personality. His mobile phone rang in his trouser pocket, he fished it out and without even giving it a glance, disconnected whoever was trying to reach him, switched it off completely and put it back from where he'd drawn it. Alberta thought that whosoever was calling and whatsoever it was about, mundane issue or life or death situation, as far as Councillor Danny Senetti was concerned, then they were invisible! Looking across at Karen Spencer and as if to justify his recent action with his phone he said, with what Alberta thought was more than a hint of sarcasm.

'Well whoever it was, first thing on a Monday morning, it can't be as important as this can it?' He said it more as a cynical statement than a question.

The three of them sat down around Karen's desk, Karen was the first to speak.

'Danny, Alberta is up here carrying out a very important investigation and I'd be grateful if you'd co-operate with her.'

'Naturally, why wouldn't I? I'll do what I can.'

Alberta detected that sarcasm again.

'What exactly are you investigating Ms Curtis-Brightland?'

'Call me Alberta please, can I call you Danny?'

This was the first time she had spoken, she spoke in a clear but slow drawl and he immediately realised from her accent and with an element of shock that she was an American. He didn't know why this revelation should shock him but it did. It was probably because an American in Norford Town Hall was indeed a rarity. He tried to work out which part of America she might be from, but she'd said too little at this stage, as well as that he would only have been guessing.

Karen Spencer interjected, she seemed impatient and on the move. Senetti thought the tone of her voice seemed to raise an octave and that she almost screeched as she said:

'This is probably not the right time nor place for you both to swap notes. As I said before, Alberta is up here with a brief from the Home Office. We've agreed to assist her, that's where you come in Danny. I don't have all the details myself and I don't need them, nor do I want them, at least not at this precise moment.'

'Karen, we've moved on very quickly from co-operate to assist, setting aside, that they are not exactly one and the same. I need to have some idea what I am co-operating or assisting with.' He emphasised the word 'assisting' in such a way as to demonstrate his dislike for it.

'I know that Danny, but right at this immediate moment you don't need chapter and verse, do you?'

'Chapter and verse no, but a throwaway paragraph might be helpful, even just one sentence would be enlightening.'

Alberta could see that patience was not one of Senetti's apparent attributes, nor did it seem to be Karen Spencer's either. Although in Senetti's case you could add both irritability and cynicism, particularly she calculated on a Monday-morning. She sensed that he wanted an argument of some kind, just for the sake of it, and if there wasn't one to be had *au naturelle,* then he was going to do his utmost to bring one about. Her first impressions confirmed, she began to dislike him and she began to think that she didn't want to work with him. Nevertheless, for her purpose she most certainly needed somebody with local knowledge and official standing. Preferably though somebody who was a little more docile, a little more compliant, perhaps even obedient and these were words that just didn't spring to mind when she thought of Councillor Danny Senetti. Despite her thoughts, she thought that she would go through the motions, so she said.

'I'm up here on a special investigation that's been initiated by the Children's Commissioner. It's to do with looked after children and their connections who have died in unusual circumstances. I will brief you in due course but right now it is all ultra-confidential and there is no point in divulging such information just for the sake of it. I'll be frank, right at this moment. I'm not sure that you're the right person for this, I'm not even sure that you want to do it.'

"I'll brief you in due course," "I'll be frank," Senetti repeated her words over in his head. Why did people who had jobs like hers, always speak in cliché like this? They were never 'frank,' and *they* briefed *you* in what *they* wanted *you* to know. The other bits they left out. So really, they weren't being 'frank' at all.

'That's fine by me, I'll be frank also, shall I?' He said in deliberate parody.

He added, 'I'm happy to leave you before I start, I'm happy to leave right now and as we are being confidential let me confide in you, I may even be able to save you wasting your energy on your 'due course' briefing. If there is one thing that makes me nervous, it's people I've just met, telling me that they'll take me into their confidence. So please don't feel compelled to do that. As for my part I can live without all aspects of secrecy and intrigue, the absence of either of them makes life much simpler. I'm neither sensitive to, nor offended by, rejection of any kind and I'm willing to accept that the only harm done so far, is that I had to turn in a little earlier on a Monday than I normally do. So, if that is what you want, shall we just cut our losses and as the man says, include me out!'

Karen Spencer considered the irony in Senetti's words. There was a lot of intrigue and secrecy in local politics. Norford was no different than any other council in this respect and contrary to what he'd just said, she'd often found Senetti to be right at the hub of it, it would be fair to say that he created his share of it – no, more than that he thrived on it. Also, again typical of a lot of things that Senetti was involved with,

Karen Spencer could see that he was creating conflict, when there actually wasn't any to be had. What should have been a simple introduction was becoming something more complicated, apart from anything else it was taking up more of her time than she could afford, she now realised that she'd erred in judgement arranging this meeting on a Monday morning, but she'd done it to draw a line under what she'd thought a routine issue. Alberta looked as if she was going to say something dramatic and final, which would have just played into Senetti's hands, as far as his *include me out* statement was concerned. His exclusion would have still left her with the problem to solve, albeit later, so to manage the situation, Karen interceded once again.

'Alberta, even with the little you've told me about your investigation, it is obvious to me that you will need somebody who knows their way around the Local Authority network over here. Now, as admirable as Councillor Senetti is in many ways, I would be the first to acknowledge, that just like the rest of us, he is not without a few shortcomings. However, what I can assure you of, is that he has a very original way of looking at situations and when it comes to knowledge of local government, particularly in North West England, you won't best him, by a long way. None of this really matters though, you see we don't really have the luxury of options. The overriding factor at this moment, the one that supersedes everything else, is that there is nobody else who is even available let alone remotely qualified, so it's either Councillor Senetti or the alternative which as far as Norford Council is concerned means that you are on your own.'

Senetti seemed to groan silently when she said this and Alberta in turn had a look of despair upon her face.

The three of them then fell silent, Karen paused and then continued, it was now her turn to demonstrate some Monday morning tetchiness.

Karen continued, 'As for me, I received all three, an email, a text and a telephone message from the Commissioner's Office on a Sunday afternoon of all days. These communications asked me to find somebody who matched a certain profile; well I've done my bit and the closest match I can find is Councillor Senetti. Now I can't make you love each other, but you don't really need to, so can I suggest the next best thing, which is that you both go and find somewhere to have a discussion and then decide between yourselves, without my input, whatever you are going to decide and take it from there. Please don't come back to me personally about any of it. In the meantime, I've got a council to lead and a train to catch in precisely thirty-nine minutes.'

As she said this she glanced up at the clock on the wall. Senetti followed her gaze, '10:14, God help us!' She said.

As Karen finished speaking, she stood up, came from behind the desk and walked purposely to the doorway. Senetti thought that her voice had screeched up yet again as she addressed, "loaf head."

'Araminta,' she said, 'Can you please find somewhere for Councillor Senetti and Ms Curtis-Brightland to hold a confidential meeting? Danny, Alberta, if you need anything more from the Council in relation to this, then Araminta is your contact. Now that I've discharged my responsibilities, I will say good Monday-morning in equal measure to both of you.'

Accepting the instruction, Danny and Alberta simultaneously left their chairs and walked the few paces to the secretary's office. As they entered it, Karen Spencer's door closed soundly behind them.

Araminta Rock, peered over the top of her glasses and handed Senetti a large, bright orange key fob with a large old brass key on it.

'Committee Room Two,' she said. 'The Dogs on Trams Scrutiny Committee,' have booked it for midday, but it is free until then, please leave in good time before then and lock it after you, can I have the key back please, when you've done?'

Senetti knew where the room was, he led the way and Alberta followed him there. They had to pass the coffee vending machine again and Senetti stopped outside it and turned to the woman.

'Coffee?'

'Thank-you, what's on offer, any Cappuccino?'

Senetti pondered: Cappuccino, for chrissake! Why did people ask things such as this? It wasn't the Roastery or the Exotic Coffee Company that they were considering here, it was Norford Council's coffee vending-machine, what did Alberta Curtis-Brightland expect was on offer, Monsoon Malabar, Orange Pekoe Tea? He'd drunk many a cup over the years and whether it was tea, coffee, it didn't matter, they all tasted the same, like a cross between lukewarm dish water, drawn from a farmyard trough and chicken soup. Ah, chicken soup! Almost everything that you received from that vending machine, whatever it was described as, had a taste of chicken soup, that was of course except for the chicken soup itself, which tasted like the farmyard trough dishwater, only without the chicken soup.

'As far as coffee is concerned you can have black, white or decaf,' he said, 'There is hot chocolate, but I'd advise against it, Councillor Peggy Letter-Hough drinks the decaf stuff permanently, she must go through gallons of it each week and it doesn't seem to have harmed her in any way, except that she is completely barmy, but that's nothing to do with coffee. She is Chair of Licensing and Tenancy and doing that job for even a short period would send anybody off the head. There is also some stuff that claims to s Chicken Soup, which I've never seen nor heard of anybody drinking more than once, even Councillor Peggy.'

'Thank-you, I'll have the black decaf please.'

Chapter 3

The Trefor Family

In 2011, the government of the United Kingdom carried out its most comprehensive population census to date. From information gained from that census, the population of the United Kingdom, which comprises of England, Scotland, Wales and Northern Ireland, was sixty-three million people. This figure is a minimum approximation, as the census, however thorough it claims to be, cannot hope to capture everybody, but it is a close approximation. Of the sixty-three million people recorded in the census, fifteen million were defined as, 'children and young people.' This category at that time, was descriptive of people up to and below the age of eighteen.

Most young people in the U.K, are both born into and brought up in, what is universally accepted as the best social unit for their personal nurture and development. This social unit has evolved naturally through time and is known as, a *Family*. Family make-up today, particularly in the western world is no longer as nuclear as it once was. There were always exceptions, there will always be exceptions to everything, but in the main and not too long ago, a *Family* consisted of two adults, a man and a woman who were married and their offspring, who were their children, usually biological to at least one parent and often both.

In the United Kingdom, even considering the changing face of the family through the years and all the arising implications, there has been for some time and still is, many children who at an episode in their lives cannot be raised in their own family, nuclear or otherwise. There can be a multiplicity of reasons for this. Sometimes it can simply be that the parent at that time is temporarily incapacitated. A typical example would be if a parent became ill, had to be hospitalized and there were no other family members or friends to look after the child. In this example, the local authority would intercede and take over the parenting of the child until that parent had recovered. Once recovery had been established then the authority would seek restoration with child and parent.

In extreme cases though, children can be at risk of harm, neglect and abuse within their own parental setting. Sometimes the source of this harm, neglect and abuse is from members of the child's own family. In these situations, once again the government in the shape of the local authority, is forced to intervene and offer parenting advice, guidance and support. Often this support works, and there are many families who thrive and prosper because of outside support. Sometimes though this doesn't work. In the most extreme cases the authority has no alternative, other than to take over the parenting of these children themselves, and where children are at risk, from the conduct of their own family adult members, the authority may remove the children from the custody of these adults. All children looked after by the local authority in this way have for a long time been known as *children in care* and current professional jargon describes them as being *Looked after Children*.

At the year ending 31st March 2015, there were a total 69,540 Looked after Children, in England alone.

Some of these children are only 'in care' for short episodes and many of them are returned to their families after only a singular brief episode in care. Some though are in care for longer periods and some drift back and forth between the care system and their birth families all their lives, until they reach adult, independence.

Extremely, there is a significant minority of children who are in care continuously. It is sometimes judged, for their own safety that they are forbidden from free unsupervised contact with their families throughout most of their lives, some of them from birth to adulthood.

However, happiness is defined, some Looked after Children go on to find it and make a success of their lives.

Some Looked After Children go on to find neither happiness nor success. It is a known fact that looked after children who have had prolonged stays in care, reached adulthood and have left the care system are inordinately represented in many of the negative aspects of adult life. Such aspects as: prison, mental health, substance abuse, alcohol abuse, violent crime, premature death, suicide, divorce. It is also well known that the experience of being a looked after child can be passed on from one generation to the next. It would be untrue to state that it is common, but neither is it unknown and there are too many examples today, within families, where the children, their parents and their parents in turn, have all had experience of being in the care system as children. There are even rarer cases of several generations of the same family who have been raised throughout all their childhood years, wholly in the 'Care System,' since all the family members from birth through to adult independence have been throughout and continuously, a Looked After Child.

Such a family are the Trefor family and their story spans three generations.

It begins with Gwendolyn Ellen Trefor who was born in Manchester, England in 1951. In April 1969, after a lifetime of being looked after in the care system, Gwendolyn Ellen Trefor, at the age of 18 years was discharged from this system. Immediately on discharge, she transferred her life from that city to the boisterous, seaside town of Prestatyn, North Wales. For some inexplicable reason upon her arrival in Wales, Gwendolyn stopped using her Welsh forename and began calling herself 'Diana.' It was by this name that she would be known for the rest of her life.

Like most aspects of her life, Gwendolyn's or Diana's journey to Prestatyn and her aims when she arrived, were speculative and without any plan. Exactly what was she was searching for: work perhaps, adventure possibly, love maybe? Nobody really knows. However, she found none of these and lacking the basic amenities of money, food and shelter and all the consequences these absences bring with them, she very soon came to the attention of the local degenerates in Prestatyn and was rapidly inveigled into their nefarious circle.

Diana dabbled for a while in petty dishonesty, prostitution and drunkenness. The petty dishonesty and prostitution were activities that were not really in her nature and she soon abandoned them. She did though maintain the drunkenness and added to it a life of welfare benefits, sex and drugs. In 1970 and accompanied by a male partner she travelled the sixty miles from Prestatyn to the relatively quiet Welsh town of Criccieth, which sits sedately on the beautiful Llyn Peninsula. That year, she became pregnant for the first time, but suffered a miscarriage early in the pregnancy.

Later that year she became pregnant again. This time, the pregnancy was successful and a baby girl, Angharad Ellen, was born in Bangor Hospital, Wales, in May 1971. Diana really loved the little girl, this was never in doubt, but Mother and her partner had long since come under the scrutiny of the local Social Services department. Despite valiant effort over a sustained period, various social care professionals had been powerless to halt the catastrophic descent of the mother's life. They were though determined that Angharad's situation would be different. With all this in mind they removed Angharad from Diana's care when she was little more than a few months old. It broke the mother's heart and in despair, she returned to her former life of pointless self-destruction. In little more than twelve months' after the birth of her daughter, she would be dead. Her demise the subject of a coroner's enquiry, convened after her expired body was found in the corner of an old, empty dilapidated house, in the Welsh town of Port Madog. Her vital organs had gradually been subdued, then eventually overpowered and snuffed out by pills and booze.

The young Angharad lived in foster care for the first five years of her life. First in Pwllheli, latterly in

Caernarfon. Then at the age of five, she moved to Manchester, England, to live with a 'maternal cousin' who had been identified and who was living there. It wasn't long before the relationship with the cousin disrupted and Angharad, the little Welsh girl became A Looked After Child in Manchester. Throughout the 1970s, there became the possibility of her being adopted and as a young child she went through a formal introduction process with two separate couples, who were viewed as prospective adopters. Nothing came of these meetings and as she became older, like most looked after children, her opportunities of being adopted gradually diminished then disappeared altogether. Throughout what was left of the 1970s and in the early part of the 1980s, she drifted from one foster placement to another. By the time she was twelve she had attended six different schools and had been accommodated in twelve different foster placements, one for each year of her young life. Each one of these schools and foster placements had different adults, different children, different habits and different rules and boundaries. It was little wonder that she became confused, damaged and emotionally battered. It wasn't as if any of the placements ended in a positive way for Angharad. Without exception they all ended in disruption. This was usually because the foster carer lost patience with the child's behaviour and as Angharad became older, her behaviour became more wilful, less compliant and her conduct became worse and not better. It came to be that the duration of her placements was determined by the duration of the foster carers' tolerance level as the child violated each rule or boundary that the adult tried to impose. It finally came to the stage, where her wild reputation preceded her and there was not one foster carer in the whole of Manchester who would accommodate her. So being out of options, she was placed in the care of a Residential Unit. The point of realisation for a young girl not yet in her teenage years was that nobody wanted her. 'Ann,' as she was now calling herself, considered that at least in a foster placement, you were in a family wherein both the children and the adults were living the same life. If you had a problem when you went to bed at night it was still there for all to solve in the morning. In the Unit though, it wasn't a family situation at all, it was staff on one side and kids on the other. These two sides weren't necessarily in opposition. In fact, there was much dedication on offer from staff. It was just to the kids it was their lives whereas to the adults it was their job. When their shift ended for that day, they just clocked off and went home to their real families, they left their pretend one in the Unit.

However, the die was cast for young Ann and in the Unit, she remained.

School made little impression upon Ann and she in turn made little impression on school. By the time she had stopped attending permanently, of her own volition, at the age of thirteen, her academic status would have been best described as illiterate and innumerate. What she lacked in scholastic achievement she made up for in physical attraction. Even as a teenager she was very beautiful with advanced looks for her years. These looks attracted the attention of men and Ann did nothing to discourage these attentions. These men gave her gifts and money and introduced her to the world of drink and drugs. She became a drug addict. Once she acquired the habit she didn't make any kind of attempt to shake it off. She just accepted it and just carried on with it, as if it was part of herself and as such, part of her own unhappy life and inevitable destiny.

At the age of sixteen she gave birth to her first child. The only questions from those professionals who had known Ann for most of her young life was sourced in cynicism and it was to ask themselves…'Why had it taken so long?' Amazingly Ann would go on to have five children in total. Each of them had a different father. In descending order of age their genders were: girl, boy, girl, boy, girl. Even though there were five of them in total, there was little more than nine years between the eldest and the youngest. Ann gave all her children Welsh forenames. Bethan was the oldest followed by Dylan, Glenys then Gethin and finally Lowri who was the baby of the family. When it came to their surnames she registered three of them: Dylan, Glenys and Gethin with their supposed individual father's names. Bethan and Lowri she registered with the same surname. It wasn't because they both had the same father. In fact, Ann did not know who Lowri's father was, she reasoned that it was one of several men but which one she was unsure. So, she registered Lowri with the surname of 'Trefor' which of course was her own surname. As for Bethan who she also called 'Trefor,' nobody was quite sure why. Because although Ann would not divulge his identity she did know who Bethan's father was. Furthermore, in an uncharacteristic aspect of behaviour and for reasons known only to herself, Ann lodged some information about Bethan's father with the firm of Manchester Solicitors: Knapp, Snodgrass and Knapp. This information was to be made known to Bethan when she attained a certain age.

As far as her children were concerned Ann made several half-hearted attempts at parental responsibility with each one individually. Addicted to drugs, alcohol and adversity these attempts at motherhood all ended in swift failure as each child for their own safety was quickly taken into care by whichever local authority she was residing in at the time.

In the summer of 1996 at the tragic young age of twenty-five, Angharad 'Ann' Ellen Trefor daughter of Gwendolyn 'Diana' Ellen Trefor died all alone in a dingy bedsit room in Oldham, Greater Manchester. Her death was caused by a self-inflicted drug overdose, which was probably accidental.

Like their mother before them, her children in the ensuing years were destined to become the victims of the old adage about history repeating itself. Each of them would be bounced around the Children's Safeguarding system of whatever Social Services Department they individually found themselves under the protection of. It seemed that depending upon their own ages at any precise time, all these children in their own different ways were at various stages of their own mother's life and that their own present lives were mirroring her now expired one. As time progressed throughout the 1990s, towards the millennium and beyond, the future for the third generation in care of the dysfunctional and disjointed Trefor family was quite frankly, 'just not up to much.'

Chapter 4

Committee Room Two

Polystyrene cup in hand, followed by Alberta Curtis-Brightland, who also had a polystyrene cup in hand, Danny Senetti walked down the narrow corridor that led away from the council leader's office. Then he walked halfway around a quarter landing, into a spacious timber panelled hallway, adjacent to Norford Council Chamber. He came to a halt outside a large, thick timber door. A brass plate fixed across the centre of the door, announced that behind the door was 'Committee Room Two.' After unlocking the door and opening it, Senetti made an 'après vous' gesture, with his hand, Alberta entered the room and he followed.

Inside Committee Room Two, was a long wooden table and ten wooden chairs with maroon leather seats and backs. For some strange reason, there was a map of the African Continent on the wall, with all the countries in different colours, each different colour depicted the African country's European colonial master from a bygone age. Senetti noticed that the only other objects in the room were an empty glass flower vase which was in the middle of the table and a small, solitary stainless-steel pedal bin which stood alone in one corner. He non-chalantly depressed the pedal with his foot, the lid gaped open, he stared into it gormlessly and it stared back at him, as he expected, it was empty. The room smelled of waxed furniture polish, its odour completely overwhelmed the subtle fragrance of Alberta's *Oud Wood*.

Senetti and Alberta took seats at opposite sides of the table with their beverages. Senetti sipped his coffee in silence and ran his fingers through his hair a couple of times. Last night's drink was wearing off, this morning's coffee was kicking in and he felt a slight act of contrition coming on, to atone for his previous irritability. Alberta took a writing pad and a pen out of a large blue shoulder bag that Senetti had just noticed she had with her; he spoke first, he thought he might try a little icebreaker.

'Whereabouts are you staying, whilst you're in town?'

'Some place in Manchester city centre, I've forgotten the name of it now, I only arrived there late last night by taxi, it was all arranged for me, as I said it was late and I wasn't paying much attention. No, I've just remembered it, Malmaison, Hotel Malmaison.'

'All right, is it?'

'Well, yes but you know, it's a hotel, they are all pretty much the same, there is no place like home.'

'Where is that then, home?'

'Currently, West London.'

'Currently,' he thought, the word *currently* and the word *home* didn't seem to go together, one suggesting the latest in a sequence whilst the other should at least have some longevity and permanency to it. Nevertheless, he thought that he would not pursue it and instead he would turn to the business at hand.

'Well, as Karen said, the choice is, me or nothing, I admit it's evenly balanced, there's not much to choose between the two and if you decide to go for the nothing, I promise you that I won't take offence.' As he said this he half-smiled and looked at his wrist watch.

She thought, at least he seemed to have a sense of humour, albeit a sarcastic one, but nevertheless, a sense of humour. She realised that what she really needed here, was time to think, only she didn't have anything like that luxury. She knew what she had to do, she was in strange territory, in another man's land, it would be hopeless on her own, and she wouldn't know where to start looking and who to start looking for and that was a dangerous situation to be in. She also knew that this slightly, dishevelled, sarcastic hack of a councillor was a long way short of the calibre of person she was used to working with. She thought that at best she might be able to use him as a leg man. Then she asked herself, with his lack of enthusiasm and his lackadaisical atti-tude, what would he achieve. The answer that she came up with was nothing. Yes, the worst or best, he could achieve was 'nothing' and nothing wouldn't be so bad after all, as a result, nothing would be all right. She sus-pected Karen Spencer's endorsement of him. Karen was probably just glad to rid herself of him for a few weeks, so she'd foisted him onto her.

Alberta knew that people like Senetti could be a handful of trouble, if they set their mind to it. The truth of it was though, in the last analysis, if she didn't have a real insider, to tell her who was who, and where was where and just as important an official one, to refer to in her report, then she might as well shut up shop and go home now. At this moment in time, going home as an option seemed like much more than a good idea. She had never actually wanted this case in the first place, it had just complicated her situation. The reality though was that it existed, it meant that she had no choice but to chase it. She had been sent up here by others, others in London and they wouldn't think going home was a good idea. Anyway, they would only send somebody else up here and that could make things worse. The last thing she wanted was an investigation into her investigation. If nothing else, she needed to make a show at least for a month or so. One way or another she thought that she was stuck with Senetti and one way or another she was going to have to try and find a way to get what she wanted from this wayward councillor. She thought that she'd try a bit of sarcasm of her own.

'Right, I've decided, you're right, it's not an easy choice, as you say it's either you or absolutely nothing, I'm afraid I must tell you, that you just about shade it. You beat absolutely nothing but only just. I mean if it was a race between the two of you, you or nothing, the difference would be in micro-seconds.'

'That's the way I feel too, I'm only doing this because I don't want Karen Spencer sulking, holding a political grudge and bearing down on me like some angry ex mother-in-law, for the next twenty years. Political grudges are not like ordinary ones, they last forever. You will just write your report and ride out of town, but I've got to live here and work with her.'

'All right, I understand.'

'Let's leave it at that and let us also a have a few ground rules here. Whatever it is you're investigating, I need to know everything that you know, nothing held back or hidden, agreed?'

'Agreed,' she mumbled.

'No not agreed, agreed,' he repeated. He mumbled the first one and pronounced the second clear and loud.

'All right agreed,' she said, loudly and clearly.

'Just one more observation.'

'Only one?'

'I can do civility but I don't do subservience or servility. There are no bosses in this partnership, my electorate puts me in office, not you or even Karen Spencer, they are the only ones who I really answer to, so as far as our partnership goes then that is exactly what it is, equal - equal, even Stephen, yes?'

'Oh, so it's a partnership then?'

He ignored the comment.

'What exactly are we investigating here, where do we start?' he asked.

'The first point to accept in this, is nothing, we have absolutely nothing that in any way can be deemed to be conclusive, there is no substantive evidence about anything, we are not sure of anything, we're not even sure of what we are doing or to some extent why we're doing it and where we are going to go, to do it.'

Senetti laughed, 'Sounds absolutely spot on for the council. But come on Alberta, we must be investigating something, I know that we are hapless but we can't be totally hapless, give us a bit of a clue.'

'We are investigating untimely deaths.'

'Untimely deaths, well that's a start I suppose, but aren't they all that?'

'Aren't all what, that?

'Aren't all deaths untimely?'

'Already you've lost me, in what way do you mean?'

In all this, he was still trying to work out what part of America she was from. Her voice was cultured and refined, her diction was clear. He'd already discounted all the southern states and she didn't sound anything like a New Yorker; no, he decided, she was from the North West, perhaps Washington state or maybe Montana. He could just ask her outright, but he didn't want to, he just thought he'd let it unfold naturally.

'Well, nobody really wants one do they, a death I mean, especially their own. Nobody looks at the calendar, checks their watch and says, hmm, I think it's about time I died, I'll just check with the timekeeper. So that's why they are all untimely.'

'Senetti, your cynicism is boundless, although I have to admit, it's a good point you make, but these deaths are untimely for specific reasons.'

'What kind of specific reasons?'

'Well some of them are in similar circumstances but all these circumstances are not normal and these deaths are premature.'

'Here we go again, surely, all deaths are premature, nobody shouts, come in number seven your time is up, people die all the time, not everybody can die in their bed, in their sleep, of natural causes at ninety–nine years of age.'

Alberta was beginning to feel a little exasperated by what she considered to be Senetti's cynical interjections. Nevertheless, she resisted the temptation to enter challenge mode, she drew on the depths of her inner patience and smiled as she said.

'Karen said that you had an original way of looking at situations, I now understand what she meant, only original isn't the word that I would have chosen. Yes, people do die all the time, but these deaths were not the subject of natural causes, they were all caused by unnatural causes, none of the deceased in any of these cases was known to be ill and not one of them was anywhere near ninety-nine years of age.'

'What sort of unnatural causes, suicide, murder? Were these deaths deliberate?'

'Well, there are always these possibilities. But there have been no suggestions, at least no suggestions that I have come across about suicide. There has not been any suggestion whatsoever of murder. However, everything and anything is a possibility.'

'Aren't possible suicides and murders something that should be left to the police?'

'All these incidents have had police involvement and it has left us none the wiser. I engage with the police a lot and there is a misconception about them, especially amongst the public and with people who have little or no contact with them and that is most people.'

'What is the misconception you speak of?'

'The misconception Danny, I can call you Danny, can't I.'

'Yes, we've done that one Alberta, yes.'

'The misconception is that the police always do a great job. Well, that isn't always the case, sometimes it is, but just as often they do an awful job and often they do an average job. As well as this, they have a constant resource problem to attend to just like the rest of us. As I've just said, most people never meet the police in their whole lives. The only contact that most people have with the police is second-hand and fictional, through television detective shows or books and on those shows and in those books, the police solve everything. Well in real life it doesn't work that way. It's a well-known fact that even though reported crime is going down, the police are solving less and less of it.'

'That's surely true. I have had plenty of involvement with police over the years and they can be quite brilliant but they can also be rather hopeless as well. It seems to me, it depends who you are dealing with.'

'What's more, in these incidents, after what seemed a brief investigation in each case, a coroner's verdict was reached and all the cases were closed. My office has made a polite request to the police to reopen them but they say that they don't have the resources and there are no grounds for doing this. In each case they cite absence of evidence. All of which by the way may be completely reasonable.'

'I don't see what little old me and you can do if the police with all their resources have been forced to close the cases.'

'I don't think that it was as much that they were forced to close the cases as they wanted to close them. Of course, it may well be that there is nothing to investigate and we cannot rule that out. Anyway, I'm not the spokesperson for the police and we are not looking at these cases from a criminology point of view, or even to see if there is any foul play, in the way the police would be looking at them. Our stance is more to look at the individual circumstances and our own systems and to examine anything we have done that could have contributed to these deaths and to see if anything could have been done to prevent them happening in the first place and more importantly to try and prevent them happening again.'

'Sounds like an odd case for the likes of you and me. By our systems, you mean your systems, the ones used by the Children's Commission. Anyway, it all sounds like council speak, you know the one where we all trot out that worn out clichéd sentence, about much being done, much to be done and lessons to be learned along the way. Only we never seem to do it and we never seem to learn them. You see it time after time, year on year. We all wait knowingly for the horse to bolt the unlocked stable door, then when he's gone we fasten the door up so securely that even if he decides to come back, he can't get in at all. I agree with a lot of what you've just said about the police but surely the fact that the police have closed their investigations must be indicative of something.'

'Danny, we are going around in circles here, just tell me are you in, or are you out?'

'Erm, eh, in, you've convinced me, definitely in, accidents, incidents, possible suicides, haven't got a clue, don't know what we're doing, don't know why we're doing it, don't know how we're going to do it, don't know where we are going to do it, this is right up the street of a local councillor, this is exactly how local council's work, and being a local councillor, this is exactly how I work most of the time! So yes, I'm in.'

She said, 'Right then, let's get this police involvement out of the way, once and for all. The police closing their investigations is irrelevant as far as we are concerned. It is indicative of one thing and one thing only, it's indicative of the approach the police have, but that's all, nothing more, it just doesn't help us, because it means the trail is a bit cold. Just changing the subject slightly Danny, not that it really matters to me, but what political party do you belong to?'

'Alberta, why do people say that? If it didn't matter to you, you wouldn't ask. It isn't an original question, everybody asks it. That's the very first question they ask you, when they find out you're a politician, it's all a bit disappointing really, they don't ask you if you've got a wife or kids or if you feel good about yourself, or how your mother is, or where you are going for your holidays, or what you are having for your tea. In contrast, they ask you all that when you are having your haircut, but they don't ask you any of it when they realise you're a politician. They just ask you what party you're in. Then when you tell them, they categorize you in accordance with their own knowledge and their own opinion of your party and the party leader, they don't seem to realise that no individual and no political party could ever be completely reconciled with each other, but that's what they think you are, a clone of what they know about your party. Especially if your party is not the party that they normally support. Anyway, it's all a bit disappointing for them, when they ask me, because, I'm completely party less, a party of one, independent, The Winton Kiss Party.'

'Why doesn't that surprise me, Winton Kiss, what's that, Winton Kiss?'

'It's where I live, it's the name of my political ward, there's a story to it, but not for now, maybe later.'

'Does being independent give you a better understanding of the electorate and does it give them a better understanding of you?'

'I don't know about them understanding me, but as far as anybody understanding the electorate, it's just not possible. That's why these pollsters get their predictions wrong year after year.'

'Yes, they do seem to, don't they?'

'I don't understand the electorate, I don't under-stand them at all. Then again, I don't really try to get into the politics of it, certainly not the party politics, some of my fellow councillors can be very childish in the debating chamber, I often feel embarrassed when some of them are calling each other names and the only reason they are doing it, is because of party politics.'

'Why did you go into politics then, the money?'

Senetti laughed a little, 'The money! Where is it? When you find it, let me know. There are an endless number of situations where you could earn much more money for doing a lot less in terms of productivity and responsibility than you must do to discharge your responsibilities as a local councillor. As far as money is concerned, being a councillor is hard work, big respon-sibility and comparatively scant reward, and those people who say differently, all have one thing in common.'

'What is that then?'

'It is, that between all of them, Alberta they have not got one day's experience of being a local councillor. Like any occupation there are a few wonderful council-lors, a lot of very good councillors, a few very bad ones and some in between. Some might do it for the status, some might do it out of civic pride, perhaps vanity comes into it, even altruism maybe. If you asked a group of councillors that question, then there would probably be as many individual reasons as there would be individuals, but I've never met one, not yet anyway, who said that they did it for money.'

'Why do you do it then?'

'It sounds a little unoriginal, but I do it because I thought that I could make a small difference and put something back into the community where I've lived for a long time. I suppose there was a bit of a status thing as well but only a bit of one. As far as my constituents are concerned, whether they voted for me or not, if they come to me for help and they ask me in the right way and sometimes even when they don't, then if I can do something to help, then I will. I think that it is important that some part of the life you lead should be of some use to others. It's that simple, for me anyway.'

Alberta didn't respond, she was a little surprised by Senetti's revelation, almost shocked. Somehow it didn't seem to fit in with the rest of him. Then she noticed how he seemed to switch off completely from the subject he had been engaged in and revert to its predecessor.

'How many deaths, sorry incidents are we talking about in total and over what period?'

'Danny, you've already asked me that.'

'I know and you didn't answer me the first time either!'

'Sorry, I thought that I did, you probably distracted me. There's been three of them over an approximate twelve-month period.'

'Three, that's not really an excessive amount, is it? Is there any connection at all between any of them?'

'Three doesn't seem many, I agree, but it's three from the same area of occupation, three from the same geographical area and three over a short time span. Three is enough for my office in London. There could be more, it's just that they've not been identified yet. As far as the connection is concerned it could be stronger, but it's there, that's where you and I come in. If there is more than three or a stronger connection, we'll be expected to find out what it is.'

'What does all this have to do with The Office of the Children's Commissioner?'

'You asked me that one before.'

'I know and you didn't answer that time either, you're good at this.'

'Sorry it isn't intentional. I become engrossed in the task of it all. The vague connection mentioned, is as we said, that these three people, the deceased victims, all have a connection to looked after children in the North West of England. Their deaths are all in a small-time frame and the way that they have died has similarities.'

'When you say, looked after children, all children to an extent are looked after, do you mean in the sense of what we know as The Corporate Parent or the Safeguarding Board.'

'Exactly that, yes.'

'So, to repeat, the victims of these incidents are all connected to looked after children, children who were being safeguarded, to use the old term, kids in care. Were any of these victims, children themselves?'

'No, none of the victims are looked after children or even children themselves. All the victims were adults, even more they were adult professionals.'

'Well then, is that the only connection and what exactly do you mean when you say that their deaths had similarities?'

'We don't really know if there is another connection, other than as I keep saying they all had a *connection* to look after children but in different ways. The victims are a social worker, a foster carer, and a councillor, it's a mixed bag really. All working in different capacities, but all had that involvement with safeguarding. The foster carer and the councillor were both run over by a train and a tram respectively, the social worker was run over by a car.'

'The first part Alberta could be just coincidence, there are a lot of looked after children in the North West of England and a lot of people have a connection to them, but did you say that all three of them were all run over, two of them by trams and the other by a car, are you making it up?'

'No, I said that they were run over by a tram, a train and a car, but that bit doesn't matter and of course I'm not making it up. I agree, it is all unusual but it could just as easily be coincidence and that may turn out to be our finding. I don't wish to make up a case if there isn't one there to start with, that is just counter-productive. I only came up here last night. I've not spent twenty-four hours on the case yet. I can't report back with a finding of coincidence within twenty-four hours. I am expected to put in a few weeks investigating at least.'

'All right I understand, you said that there was a councillor amongst the victims, who was that?'

'Councillor Jason Dunphy, from Oldham, did you know him?'

'March 17th, last year.'

'That's the date of his death yes, I'm impressed, did you know him?'

'I wouldn't say that, I've been in his company over the years, twice I think and I've been in the same chamber as him at various council meetings. He was the Executive Member for Children and Young people at Oldham Council for many years and he was also Chair of the Greater Manchester Regional Safeguarding Board and he will have probably been on a few other committees, connected to those areas. So, as you say, a straight-line connection to kids in care. As I said, March 17th, last year, that date is significant for certain people, do you know who and why?'

'It's their birthday?'

'No Alberta, it's not because it's their birthday, not in this case anyway, and we are talking about a significant number of people here, the world over.'

'I give up Danny?'

'No, you don't Alberta, you can't, we are not going to make much of an enquiry team, if you give up at the first challenge. Think of the name, his full name was Jason Declan Dunphy, so what comes into your mind?'

'Well Jason, sounds fairly straight forward, Declan and Dunphy sounds Irish, is it Irish, was he Irish?'

He said, 'Yes, Councillor Dunphy was Irish. Now think March 17th.'

'Doesn't mean much to me.'

'Oh, you surprise me, I always thought America was big on celebrating this particular day. I've seen the celebrations on the TV. It's a big event in New York.'

'America? What has America got to do with this Danny?'

'You Alberta, you're American, aren't you? I've been trying to work out which bit.'

'Oh yes that old one again and which bit have you decided upon?'

'I thought perhaps Washington or somewhere along that coast.'

'Not bad, right coast but wrong country.'

'You're Canadian, apologies, forgive my assumption, I don't know why I made it. Saint Patrick's Day, it falls on March 17th, every year, that's how I remembered the date. Councillor Jason Declan Dunphy was Irish, he was on his way home from a St Patrick's Day celebration in Failsworth. He lived in Oldham, it was only a short journey and he was travelling on the tram, he'd been drinking heavily when he fell off the platform at Failsworth Station, into the path of a through tram. It was headline news in the local press. It was a tragic accident, he was forty-five years of age and had a young family, wife and two kids, if my memory serves.'

'Your memory does serve, it serves you well.'

Danny looked downwards, he could see into the woman's blue bag, she had left it unfastened, inside it was what appeared to be a paper file with a pink cover.

'Is that the file connected to this case?' he asked.

'It's *the* file, well the only one I've got, there isn't much in it, but it's all the information we've got.'

'I'd like a copy of it,' he said.

'I'll see that you get one.'

'If you give your file to Araminta Rock, she'll see to it.'

'Is that really her name, Araminta? I've never heard that name before.'

'No, it's an unusual name Araminta, it's a hybrid name, from Arabella and Aminta, Aminta is Greek, means defender. Speaking of names, what about yours?'

'Greek defender, you're a mind of information Danny, I'm impressed. My name? Oh yes, of course, that other old one, people always think that I was named after my father or at least a male relative who was a man named Albert and that my parents were expecting a boy and instead they got me.'

'And isn't that it?' he asked.

'No, it's not, it's nothing like it, although it is all to do with my father.'

'Most children's names are, if not their father, their mother and often it's both.'

She couldn't quite figure out if he was being serious or if it was the Senetti sarcasm again. She responded by saying; 'No, I don't mean it in that way, my father was an unusual man.'

'I'm sure he was, most children feel that way about their parents, it is all to do with self-worth.'

'No, I don't mean that either.'

'What exactly do you mean Alberta?'

'My mother is English, Penelope Curtis, you can't get much more English than that. The name Curtis has its origins in Norman England, 1066, and all that, as they say, but my father, was a black French Canadian. He worked for the Canadian foreign office and he travelled around a lot. I suppose he had to go where he was sent. Mum and Dad eventually settled in Canada but before they did, they travelled around with dad's job. They named their children after the places they were in at the time the children were born. They had three children. I've got a brother and a sister, there has never been anybody called Albert anywhere near my family, so now it's your turn for detection, where I was born?'

'Don't know. Give up,' he said.

'No, you don't Danny, we're not going to make much of an enquiry team if you give up at the first challenge.' She parodied his earlier statement to her. 'Think places.'

'Alberta, is this a quiz or an investigation?'

'Come on Danny put your mind to it.'

'Albert Square in Manchester.'

'Is that the best you can do, maybe I should have gone for the nothing after all.'

'Well, you said that your dad was French Canadian, so what about Alberta, Canada?'

'Excellent, Alberta, Canada, I think we're going to make a good team.'

'What about the Curtis – Brightland bit, doesn't sound very French Canadian to me?'

'Well, it is all very simple. My dad was called Brightland, that was his family name. My mother is Curtis, so we put the two together, Curtis-Brightland, simple. One from my mother and one from my father. As I said a few moments ago Curtis is an old Anglo-Norman name. It originally came from the French word "curtois" which translates as polite or courteous. What about you, Danny Senetti, what's that Irish, Italian, where is that from?'

'My mother is Irish and my Grandfather was Italian, but let's leave the names for now, let's not do the Senetti family today, one set of names is enough for one morning. I'm sorry I brought it up. Alberta Curtis-Brightland is a fine name, it certainly isn't one you would forget in a hurry, anyway what's in a name, what's more to the point 'what's in the file?'

'Everything is in it, or at least everything that we've got, which as I said isn't that much. Consists of names of the deceased, their dates of birth, dates of death and a bit of background information on the circumstances of their deaths a bit on them and little else, nothing more. If we want more then we'll have to find it out for ourselves.'

'Who else is in it, you said there were three, who are the other two, besides Jason Dunphy?'

She removed the pink file from her bag, 'I'll get this to Araminta for copying, then you can read it for yourself.'

'I will do, but just give me another name for now.'

'Alma Alice Spain, age 44, died'...

'November last year, Social Worker for the City Council,' Senetti interjected.

'You knew her too?'

'Once again, very slightly. I did know her yeah, worked with her on a couple of issues, perhaps in her company for an hour on each one. Apparently, she was standing on a quiet path, minding her own business one winter's eve in Didsbury. A car ploughed right into her, killed her instantly then drove off. The speculative view, at least in the newspapers was that it was a boy racer, apparently, they race that road. He lost control, then panicked and drove off. There was an investigation but nothing came of it. There was an appeal for witnesses but none came forward, no CCTV, nothing. There was one small but odd thing though, I remember thinking about it at the time.'

'What was that?'

'Well it happened in Parkhurst Lane and Parkhurst Lane is just not really the type of Lane you'd be standing around on. You would have to visit it, to understand what I mean. It's out of the way, you would have look for it to find it. The only reason I know it, is I canvassed it for a friend a few years ago.'

She noticed he looked puzzled.

'There was something else, I remember they found her car parked up at her office, it's a short distance from Parkhurst Road?'

'How short?'

'Perhaps a fifteen-minute walk at the most.'

'I don't really understand your point. What's wrong with that?'

'Why park your car, half a mile away from your destination, why not park on Parkhurst Lane.'

'Maybe she wanted to walk.'

'Maybe she did, there was also something else that was significant about that car, her car I mean but I just can't bring it to mind right now. Maybe it is in your file.'

'I've not read it thoroughly, but there isn't that much of it and I don't remember seeing anything about her car. I don't think it was mentioned.'

'It's odd, Parkhurst Lane doesn't go anywhere or really come from anywhere, there's only a few houses on it. The bus doesn't stop there, nor the train nor the tram. There are no pubs, shops or restaurants nearby, so unless you were visiting somebody, or you had already visited somebody in one of those houses, then you've got no reason to be there on a November night.'

'Well perhaps that's it, she was visiting.'

'If she was, that person never came forward and identified themselves. The witness appeal was in all the local papers and on local TV, it wasn't a secret in any way whatsoever?'

'People do what they want to do, they don't always follow the patterns that others think they should.'

'Very true, although I've just thought of another reason why she might have been stood there.'

'Why?'

'It's conjecture and it's got very little to do with our systems, which as you say, is what we should be looking at.'

'Danny, virtually everything we have apart from names and dates is conjecture, so don't let a bit of speculation stop you.'

She paused for a moment as she looked at him in earnest.

He said, 'Alma Alice wasn't visiting somebody who lived in Parkhurst Lane, she was waiting for somebody who didn't live there. Parkhurst Lane was just the rendezvous point. In addition to which, once she had met whoever she was meeting there, she was leaving with her date in their vehicle and that's why she left hers in the staff car park.'

'Possibly, but why not just drive your car to the rendezvous point, as you call it, leave it there, go off with your date, then pick it up when you returned.'

'I don't know, it's a good point that you make, I'll have to consider that one, but there is another one, that has just leapt into my mind.' he said.

'Go on.'

'If Alma Alice was meeting X, at Parkhurst Lane and she was the subject of a hit and run fatality, then where was X in all this?

'What do you mean?'

'Well, did he arrive before the incident, during the incident, after the incident? Who is he and where did he go? Surely, he would have been a material witness, yet as far as I'm aware there was no mention of any witness of any kind. That was part of the problem - unless...'

'Unless What?'

'No, I'll leave it there for now Alberta, I'm getting into speculation on speculation.'

Alberta Curtis-Brightland began to think that she was impressed with Senetti's recall and his power of deduction, she began to think that there was a bit more to Danny Senetti than the ragged, haphazard portrayal that he presented. She wasn't sure if this realisation was going to be beneficial to her or not.

'I think you're right Councillor, we've made enough supposition. What we need to do now, is get you a copy of this file. Then once you've read it, we can compare notes and we can plan our next move.'

'I've already planned that,' said Senetti.'

'Go on, let me know please, I'm impressed.'

'You said that there had been three incidents, let's just take the two we've got, Jason & Alma Alice and let's have a look at their cases. Let's not muddle the whole situation just yet with the third case. Let's not try to force connections into the situation that aren't there. We need to keep an open mind as well, it is very easy to make a given set of circumstances fit a theory. As we've said people die all the time, and sometimes in unusual circumstances. Unusual just means that, it doesn't necessarily mean anything else.'

'No, you're right, I agree yes, it's a good move.'

'How many people Alberta, do you think die, in just Manchester itself each year?'

'I've got absolutely no idea Danny.'

'It's about three thousand five hundred.'

'How do you actually come to know this stuff?'

'Council meetings.'

'Council Meetings?'

'Yeah, I have to attend these various meetings, committees for this and committees for that, they give this sort of stuff out regularly and I have to sit there and listen. You try not to absorb the irrelevant bits, but it's impossible, some of it just goes in anyway, have you ever wondered why most councillors are boring?'

'Well, no not really, I mean I don't know that many of them, to say whether they are or not.'

'A very diplomatic answer, but trust me they are, I should know. None of us actually start out that way, many of us begin as a force majeure, but after time, being fed a constant drip- stream of banality and futile statistics, we become overwhelmed with it all, and in the end, we succumb to communicating that way ourselves and gradually we turn out to be as boring as a Romanian algebra lesson.'

Not for the first time that morning, she laughed at his blatant cynicism.

'All right but what relevance to us and this case does the number of deaths in Manchester have?'

'The relevance Alberta is, that out of three thousand five hundred deaths, the vast majority I can safely say, took place at home or in a hospital bed. Because of the large numbers involved, then statistically there are bound to be some that didn't take place in such an environment and your incidents will be amongst them.'

She wasn't quite sure that she followed his convoluted logic, but she said. 'All right Councillor, you've made your point and I actually agree with it.'

'As I'm a councillor, I'll go over to Oldham and see what I can find out about Councillor Jason. I'll visit the scene of death and I've got a few contacts in Oldham. I'll talk to some of them, see if they have anything to say about the late councillor. Where is Alma Alice Spain from, City Council isn't it?'

Alberta looked through the thin file.

'She was actually working for Manchester City Council, the address where she was killed is in Didsbury, where's that?'

'Yes, as I said Parkhurst Lane. That's where she was at the time of her death. Didsbury, it's the posh part of Manchester, all trendy bars and bistros. Ideal for someone like you, you won't be out of place there. If I showed up in Didsbury, they'd follow me around all day until it got dark, then they'd escort me off the premises. It's all Lib Dem territory over there, the pubs have odd names for pubs, there are sushi bars instead of chip shops and you can get lemon sole on the bone. As soon as I show up, they'll have me down as somebody who takes their fish in fingers. I'll speak to Araminta and we'll get you an introduction to a local contact out there, somebody who knew Alma Alice. You can get a tram from Piccadilly, which is close to your hotel, to the edge of Didsbury town centre. I'll do Failsworth and Jason and you do Didsbury and Alma, we'll both keep completely open minds and meet back here, on Thursday, what do you say? Not at ten-thirty though, let's make it midday.'

'I can't do it Danny, I'm back in London tomorrow and Wednesday, which means I've got to travel back down on the train tomorrow morning straight after breakfast. I'm sorry, it's just burden of work, I've still got some things to mop up from previous cases, you know how it is. Once I've done that I can focus on this case, I only came up last night for this meeting with you this morning.'

'I'm honoured, but I wasn't expecting that. I'm supposed to be the sidekick around here, you're the lead.'

'Danny, I understand what you are saying, but I am afraid that's the way it is, at least for the next week.'

'O.K. let me think, I can probably do both, Alma Alice tomorrow and Jason on Wednesday. Then as we said, meet back here on Thursday.'

Half an hour later Danny Senetti and Alberta Curtis-Brightland walked out from the Town Hall entrance together, Senetti walked ahead whilst Alberta headed for the nearby railway station. She watched Senetti, he cut an odd figure with his crumpled appearance, further enhanced now by the sight of his shirt lap, hanging out beneath his jacket, as he ambled casually down the hill, carrying a slim, pink coloured, pristine conditioned file. She realised that he was a complex and contradictory character. She wasn't sure that she was happy to have him foisted on her by others, the way he had been, but she realised she would now have to manage him the best way she could. She also realised that being in the company of this apparently bedraggled councillor, with his opinions and his speeches, even if it was only for a couple of hours was an experience, and almost instantly she felt mentally drained.

As Senetti continued down the hill, he pondered on his new temporary partner. She was a complicated person, for sure. By nature, she was questioning and challenging, yet she was all too ready to accept the possible coincidences of this case. Perhaps it was her way of being open minded. He looked at his Rolex Oyster Wrist Watch; it was precious to him, not because of its monetary value, he placed no importance on such things, it had been a present from his friend, Doctor Maxine Wells, there was a simple, six-word inscription on the back, it read: *To you for saving my life*.

The Rolex Oyster face, read four minutes past midday. Senetti stood outside the Town Hall Tavern, his plan was to go inside and read Alberta's file over a drink or two.

Monday morning, he thought to himself, it was usually a time of recovery, an uneventful period, and one of negative capability, this one had been anything but, anyway it was all over now, at least for another week.

Chapter 5

At Home with the Kinders

In life, as many of us know, things can seem to be moving irrevocably in one direction and turn out to be entirely another. After almost a lifetime in care for all the five Trefor siblings, over a comparatively short period of time a situation developed for them, that had the potential to transform their lives. This situation was in the form of Geraldine (Gerry) Kinder and her husband Martin. Gerry and Martin were both ex-teachers in early retirement. Martin himself had been a Head teacher. In retirement, they had both become foster carers for The City Council. They lived in a big old house in Chorlton-cum-Hardy, which is an agreeable part of Manchester. Initially the Kinders fostered Bethan and her alone. Bethan, was the oldest sibling, who at the time of entering the placement was just fourteen years of age and although the insecurity of the system had not inflicted as much damage upon her as it had done to her mother a generation before, Bethan had still bounced around it and had not escaped completely unscathed. One of her teachers (Mr Ledstowe) had written of Bethan on one of her previous school reports, the puzzling but intuitive comment,

"...seemingly, naturally, highly intelligent and obviously very capable - but, apparently not."

From their first meeting with Bethan, Gerry and Martin were determined that the inevitable direction described in Mr Ledstowe's prophetic conundrum, would be halted and even reversed.

The critical difference between Bethan and her mother Ann, both as teenagers, was that whereas there was both the *illiteracy* and *innumeracy* factors as far as the mother was concerned, as far as the daughter was concerned the opposite was true, for Bethan was highly intelligent and naturally academic to the point of being gifted. It was just that apart from being subjected to a lot of preaching, throughout her young life, from a succession of adults, and apart from her attendance at several different schools, she had never been in any environment which placed any value on academic education and thus her true potential had not been encouraged. All this changed when she moved in with the Kinders.

An immediate bond formed between Gerry, Bethan and Martin. Gerry was a Mathematician and Martin was an English specialist. When these two ex-teachers began to take an interest in Bethan's education they began to coach her, on a one to one basis. Where others had failed, the two teachers succeeded by examples of gradual and gentle conviction to show Bethan herself, the value of education. The outcome of all this was that in the space of less than two years, Bethan went from hovering around the middle of the lower class to sitting emphatically on top of the upper class. She excelled at her chosen subjects and gained top grades in all her examinations. When Bethan's examination results were announced, all ten of them were top grades. The whole Safeguarding Children's world sat back in amazement. This amazement turned to self- satisfaction.

Bethan and the Kinders were held aloft in high example of what this system could achieve if only it wanted to. Looked after Children, the system said, were as good as anybody else, in some cases even better. This of course was true, it always had been, but now here was the proof.

Although they had not been brought up as a family unit and each one of them had always lived at different addresses from each one of their siblings, the Trefor siblings kept as close as they could. Throughout the years they had regular monthly 'visits' arranged by professionals at different venues. It couldn't be compared to growing up together as a family but for five looked after children, all living in different locations across the North West of England, it was the best that could be done. During these visits, they would eat biscuits and cake and drink tea and coffee, enjoy each other's company and chat about their lives. These family 'visits' were the highlight of their individual lives and the common ambition of all the siblings came to be a dream. This collectively shared dream came to be for all of them to live in the same place and all grow up together as a family. This dream, of course, was just that, it was going to be extremely difficult to bring about, perhaps even impossible. There were some though who refused to accept the impossible.

If this familial aspiration of the Trefor siblings was ever to move anywhere near reality then there were four identified and formidable obstacles to overcome.

The first, was an operational one, to do with the care system itself. As all the children were born in different political boroughs, each sibling came under the jurisdiction of different councils. This also meant that they all had different Social Workers. These individual Social Workers had statutory responsibility for the individual children's lives and of course over the years the identity of these Social Workers changed. It was therefore difficult to obtain a cohesive thought process throughout these changes.

Secondly, was the matter of budgets, or in simplified terms money. It was expensive to look after, looked after children. For a family of five the cost was horrendous, and it was seemingly a lot less expensive if that cost was being shared by four local authorities than if one was bearing it whole upon themselves. Of course, the total cost was no different, it was just the share-out of it that was, but no single authority was about to step forward and volunteer to take the whole cost on.

Thirdly, Child Protection Legislation dictated that foster carers could only accommodate up to four children. Under special circumstances an *exemption* could be applied for, so in theory at least, the Trefor siblings could be brought up together in one family setting, but where was such a place to be found, where was this setting, where indeed? For, even if the administrative, budgetary and legislative obstacles could be cleared, there was one more practical obstacle.

The fourth obstacle and this one appeared to be truly insurmountable. It came in the form of an unanswered question, and that question was.

Where was there a foster carer who was prepared, experienced, trained and willing to take on five children let alone five children who were siblings?

As far as anybody could tell there was no such person across the length and breadth of the United Kingdom, let alone within the confines of the North West of England. Furthermore, every child protection textbook that was still in print denounced such a placement as very poor practice indeed and the commonly held view was that any such placement was bound to end up in disruption, and as everybody involved in any way with safeguarding children knew, disruption caused even more damage to be inflicted upon the children. The phrase that was used to describe such a course of action was 'setting all up to fail.'

All these negative reasons though, did not consider the tenacity, creativity and belief of four people. Those people were: Gerry Kinder, Martin Kinder, City Social Worker Rosemary Rowntree and not by any means least, the young Bethan Trefor.

It was Bethan herself who first raised the idea one Saturday morning as she was having breakfast with Gerry and Martin. By this time, she had been in the care system, sixteen years and she knew most of what there was to know about it. She had been living with the Kinders, for about two of those years and for Bethan they had been two phenomenally, successful years. Latterly, she had thought up a scheme in her mind to bring all her siblings together, but she knew this would be no easy task and if this scheme had any chance of realisation, then it would have to be done gradually. She was aware of the cross-boundary issues that existed between different local authorities but she was also aware that as far as she herself and her youngest sister Lowri were concerned, there were no cross-boundary issues, as they were both being looked after by The City

Council. In addition, both she and Lowri had for many years been represented by the same Social Worker, Rosemary Rowntree. Bethan liked and respected Rosemary, she thought that Rosemary was on the side of the children and unlike many other Social Workers she had met, was not on the side of the budget.

She could never really understand why some people became social workers or why they went into any kind of caring profession in first place, when the way that they spoke and acted they would seem to have been much more suited to accountancy. Looked after Children called such social workers 'budgeteers' and Bethan was glad that she didn't have a budgeteer for her social worker.

This morning Gerry and Martin were sitting around the kitchen table, Gerry and Bethan sat next to each other and Martin was sitting across from his wife and his foster daughter. The radio was playing softly, Bethan was listening to the lyrics that came out of the speaker.

'Oh, yeah, yeah.
And you're so innocent,
Please don't take this wrong 'coz it's a compliment,
I just want to get with your flow,
You gotta learn to let go
Oh baby, won't you....'

Bethan had an open book on the table, which she glanced at occasionally between eating mouthfuls of toast and marmalade and keeping an ear on the music. Martin looked across at Bethan then down at the book.

'New book,' he said, 'What is it, anybody I would know?'

'Martin, seeing as I've never in my whole life, come across a book in the whole world that you don't know something about, I'd say yes. It's called *The Big House*, it's by an American writer who lives in a house with eleven bedrooms, hence the title.'

'Sounds interesting,' said Martin.

'I think that it is going to be, but I've only just started it, I am on page twelve.' She paused for a moment, 'Speaking of big houses, how many bedrooms are in our house?'

'You know the answer to that, six.'

'And downstairs we've got the lounge, family room, dining room, conservatory, this huge kitchen, your study Martin and I've not even mentioned the cellars or the huge garage, or the summerhouse.'

'You're not trying to evict me from my study, are you? Sometimes that's the only place left where I can get some peace.'

'No, absolutely not, not at all. Gerry and I quite like it sometimes, when you lock yourself in there. All I'm saying is that it just seems a lot of rooms for a small number of people.'

'Are you thinking of becoming an estate agent Bethan?' asked Gerry.

'No, that is the last occupation I wish to consider, no disrespect to estate agents.'

'What exactly is the observation,' said Martin.

'That this is a very big house for three people.'

'Are you suggesting that it is too big and that we should move to a smaller one,' asked Gerry.

'No, of course not, I love this house, it's fantastic.'

'You've lost me, said Martin.'

'It fills up a bit more when Michael and Melanie come to stay.'

'That is true Gerry, but it isn't much more, is it, and it isn't very frequently either? Michael and Melanie only take up one-bedroom, you and Martin one, and me one, that still leaves three empty bedrooms and anyway Michael and Melanie live in Vancouver, Canada and they're not likely to be coming over here every other weekend, are they? In the time I've been here, they have only been here once.'

Gerry looked at Bethan, 'Bethan you know that we always try to be forthright and honest with each other. If there is something that you need to say, then go on say it, don't feel that you have to go all around the house to say it.' She laughed softly at her own unintended pun, which both Martin and Bethan didn't get anyway.

Bethan decided to be as Gerry had suggested, she liked Gerry and she owed her a lot. In the last two years, she felt that she had known stability and contentment and she knew that Gerry and Martin had played a big part in that. She said, 'Fair enough then, I think that this house would be better if it had more people living in it.'

'Did you have any particular people in mind?' Gerry teased.

'I know that this is a lot to ask but I was just wondering if Lowri could come and stay with us, after all, we've just established we have got the room.'

The older woman looked across the breakfast table at her husband, 'By Lowri I take it you mean, your sister Lowri?'

'Yes, sorry I should have made it clear, I was talking about her.'

Gerry looked across at Martin, she said, 'What do you think Martin?'

'I can't see why not, when were you thinking of Bethan and for how long?'

'Gerry, you said that you wanted me to be forthright and honest.'

'Yes, always, it's almost always the best way, although there are times when it is best not to be as forthright or assertive as others, but even in those times you should always try to be honest.'

'Well, to be honest, I was thinking of, as soon as possible and forever.'

'Forever, that's a long time,' said Martin.

'You did say that you were thinking of looking after another young person.'

'We did,' said the man, 'But we were thinking of an older young person, somebody a little more independent, more your age. Somebody like Emma's age, the age was more for you, than for us, somebody that you could relate to.'

'Emma, is the right age, that's true but she doesn't like school, she used to play truant although I think that she's stopped that now and she was always losing points at the unit for missing lessons.'

'I thought she wanted to be a nurse.'

'She does, she recognises the ambition and she recognises the aspiration, she just doesn't want to do the bit in the middle that gets you to be one.'

'We would work with her on that,' said Gerry.'

'If she can't get her own way she kicks off.'

'We would work with her on that too.'

'It's not always easy to explain things to Emma.'

'She isn't unique in that, it's not always easy to explain things to anybody sometimes.'

'I know but Emma can be more difficult than most.'

'Bethan, Emma has had a difficult time and she is very deserving. I thought that she was your friend, I thought that you and she were close.'

'She is Gerry, we were, we are.'

'Well you don't seem to be doing a very good job of representing her case in her absence.'

Bethan could see that the argument that she was pursuing was not helping with her objective; she thought that she would change tactics.

'It's all a bit more complicated than Lowri or Emma or even me or even you Gerry or you Martin.'

Martin said. 'You've never said a truer word, but what's your understanding of it.'

'The way that I see it, is this, it is not about who is the best person or the most deserving individual, I'm not saying that these aspects shouldn't be considered, but you could say that everybody is as deserving as everybody else and it wouldn't be untrue. Emma has had a difficult time but so has Lowri, neither of them are where they want to be. It's a bit like a football manager, it's no good having a fantastic individual player, if he destabilises the rest of the team.'

Martin laughed, he never ceased to be amazed by the teen-age girl and her often originality of argument. 'Bethan, what do you know about football?' he said.

'I've been reading about it, well more the management side than the actual sport itself, anyway if we think of Emma as that player and us three as the settled team then that's what will happen if Emma comes here, she will destabilise everything, she won't mean to but that's what will happen. I've seen it all before with her. It is all histrionics. She will put the spotlight on herself and it will reflect darkly upon us.'

'Very poetic,' said Martin.

'So, what should we be considering then?' Asked Gerry.

'We should be taking what Mr Sharma at my school calls a holistic approach, and thinking about what is best for the family and which placement has the best chance of success both for that young person of course, but also for the rest of the team, which as I've just said is Martin, you and me.'

'You obviously think what's best for the team is Lowri, I can fully understand you wanting a sister or brother here, but why Lowri, she's a lot younger than you, why not Dylan or Glenys, or even Gethin, they are all closer to your age group? You are the oldest and Lowri is the youngest,' Gerry interceded.

'They are, it's true but it wouldn't be possible now because of all these cross-boundary issues within social services across the county. Dylan is with Bolton, Dilys is with Rochdale and Gethin is in Oldham. All three have different Social Workers, whereas, both Lowri and I are with City Council. We've both got the same social worker, Rosemary, and I've already spoken to her about the situation, more to find out her opinion really.'

'What did she say, what is her opinion?' asked the older woman.

'She said, that she thought that it might just work, she said the final decision would have to be yours and Martin's, but if you are half-interested, telephone her, I've got the number here,' as she said this, Bethan produced a small notebook and set it down on the kitchen table.

Martin said, 'Bethan, if, and I only say *if*, Lowri was to come and stay with us, there would need to be some preliminaries agreed upon.'

'What kind of preliminaries.'

'We would want some assurances from you and from Lowri as young as she is.'

'I would give them.'

'I don't doubt that you would, but would you keep them.'

'I promise that I would.'

'What about Lowri, can you promise for her as well?'

'No, I can't promise for somebody else, only that person themself can do that, but I spoke to Lowri about it on Tuesday at the visit. It isn't the first time that we've spoken about it. I've been giving her little tests over a longer period. I didn't say anything to her about her coming here until Tuesday when I made everything very clear to her. I feel sure that she really wants to and I feel sure that she understood what she will have to do to make it work.'

'What about Rosemary, she would have to support the move?'

'As I said, I have spoken to her as well, like all of us she has her reservations, after all nothing is guaranteed but she is supportive and she is prepared to give it a go. That's all I'm asking of you, that you be prepared to give it a go.'

'You have been busy,' said Gerry.

'I'm only doing what you've taught me to do.'

'How is that?'

'You always say, proactive beats reactive.'

'How very true.'

The older woman once again looked across at her husband and said to Bethan, 'You are doing well at school, there is every chance that you can be anything that you want to be. I've been in your position many years ago, it is difficult and it is so easy to be deflected off course by your own problems let alone the problems of others, especially others that you care about.'

'By others Gerry, do you mean others such as young sisters?'

'I mean especially young sisters.'

'Gerry, I worry about Lowri, she doesn't fit in where she is, she's only eight years old and I feel protective towards her.'

'That's right and understandable but as far as Martin and I are concerned you are our priority and it would be irresponsible if we put distractions in your way.'

'I'm determined to make something out of my life and shouldn't Lowri have the opportunity to make something out of hers.'

'Of course, she should, everybody should have that opportunity, what do you think Martin?'

'What do I think, I think that there is a risk, but then again I think that there is a risk with everything. You never make any progress without risk.'

'Does that mean that you'll agree to it?'

'Not exactly.'

'What does it mean then?'

'It means, that Gerry and I will have our own discussion with each other and then we'll talk to Rosemary.'

'When will you speak to Rosemary?'

'I don't know, sometime next week."

'Yes!'

So, it was, Gerry and Martin had their promised discussion with each other, after which they spoke to Rosemary Rowntree. They all agreed that they should see if Lowri could come and live with the Kinders and after a gradual introduction, involving several stop-overs, Lowri moved into the big house in Chorlton-cum-Hardy with Bethan, Gerry and Martin. Lowri had to change schools as her old one was too difficult to get to from Chorlton-cum-Hardy. There were a few teeth-ing troubles at first but they were just that, mainly to do with settling an eight-year-old into a new school and very soon everything settled down.

There was much more to come for the Trefor sib-lings and the Kinders, for over the next six months, the various local authorities, mainly due to some creativity by Rosemary Rowntree, the relative success of Lowri's placement with the Kinders and by no means least, the Kinders kindness and willingness to help the family, the professionals found ways around their administrative and financial issues. By Christmas that year all five Trefor siblings were united under one roof. They all lived with Gerry and Martin Kinder. The five-sibling placement was unique and although it was accepted by everybody involved that it was very much 'early days,' the signs were good. To the Minister for Social Care, 'early days' was overlooked, if not completely ignored altogether and to him it was a success, a complete success, no it was more it, was a raging success. It was such a success that he referred to it in a speech that he gave to conference delegates in Brighton.

Chapter 6

Parkhurst Lane

Alberta had a light breakfast of *one* poached egg, on *one* slice of brown toast with, *one* 'sliver' of smoked salmon and *one* glass of still water, with *one* slice of lemon in it. She was very particular in stressing all the 'ones' to the young waiter in the Hotel Malmaison dining-room; she added a comment just to ensure that he fully understood, 'Please don't bring me two of anything as I will only eat it and then I will dislike myself all day and probably all day tomorrow.'

The young waiter smiled back and said. 'The last thing we want Madam, is you disliking yourself for any part of the day let alone all of it.'

When her breakfast did arrive, she could tell that the young waiter had fully understood her request, she smiled at him and once again he smiled back.

An hour after Alberta Curtis-Brightland was smiling at the waiter in the five-star breakfast room at the Malmaison Hotel, Danny Senetti was climbing on board the number 42 bus at Manchester Piccadilly Bus Station, some five hundred yards from the Malmaison. Today he was investigating the death of Alma Alice Spain. He thought in view of his conversations yesterday with

THE LOOKED AFTER CHILD

Alberta, that perhaps the word 'investigating' was a little too official, but he couldn't really think of a more suitable one. Then he thought of one, 'examining.' Yes, that sounded better, it was a little more relaxed.

In advance of his examination he had asked Araminta Rock to obtain some background details for him on Alma Alice. Senetti deliberately didn't want anything too detailed, as he found that too much detail could be distracting and it often gave you preconceptions, which turned out to be false and he believed that an open mind should be kept on all cases. Experience had taught him, that in these situations it was far too easy to pick up all kinds of fantastic theories and guesses which if allowed, assumed the identity of facts. Once this happened then everything could be falsely represented. No, haste and assumption were the enemy of deduction, he would take his time on this one. He expressed this wish, although not the concern to Araminta and told her that all he wanted was a nine / ten-line bio and this was exactly what he had received. He studied it, it read:

Alma Alice Spain, aged 39.
Address, Flat 22, Heathfield House, Wilmslow Lane,
*   Didsbury.*
Marital Status, divorced. Children, none.
Occupation, Social Worker.
Graduated, Salford University.
Employer, City Council.
Hobbies/Interests, Walking, Amateur Dramatics.
Date, Time, Place of Death: November 14, 2016,
*   recorded time 20:34 hrs. Parkhurst Lane,*
*   Didsbury Park, Didsbury.*

There was also a little analysis which in summary supported the theory that Alma Alice had died from injuries which were consistent with her being struck by a motor vehicle moving at speed and that despite a police investigation and an appeal for witnesses, throughout the local media, nothing of significance had been discovered and no witnesses from anywhere had come forward at any time.

There was also a small photo-copied black and white photograph of Alma Alice Spain, paper clipped to the inside of the pink coloured file cover. Senetti studied the photo, as if he was looking for some inspiration, it stared back at him giving none. Photographs could be deceiving, he knew that, but from the photograph, Alma presented as a dark haired vivacious, attractive woman.

At Danny's request, Araminta had arranged for him to meet a colleague of Alma Alice's, another Youth Offending Team (YOT) Officer, Jim Bigelow, at the Didsbury Office. Jim had worked closely with Alma Alice in the YOT and was effectively her professional partner. Senetti thought that Jim might contribute to events. However, before he met Jim at 1:00pm, he was going to visit the scene of Alma Alice's incident. He had decided that he would travel to Didsbury by bus, travelling by bus would give him the opportunity to sit there and focus on the case.

The sky was a little grey but the climate was dry and mild. He sat upstairs on the back seat, the morning, rush-hour traffic had dispersed and most of working Manchester was by now in front of their computer screens or safely behind their desks, counters and steering wheels. There were only three other passengers upstairs on the number 42, two young women and a young man, the women were seated next to each other and stared in silence at their own mobile phones throughout. Occasionally one would prod the other and offer her phone up to her friend, as if in ritual sacrifice. The man sat there almost completely motionless, with his earphones in, occasionally his head nodded slightly from side to side. The bus journeyed south through Manchester City Centre, onto Rusholme, through what is known locally as 'The Curry Mile,' then Fallowfield, Withington and finally Didsbury. He observed how each area seemed to be gaining affluence with every passing bus stop. As the bus journeyed along, one of the young women extended her arm with her phone in her hand and took a selfie. Senetti pondered: he wondered why anybody would wish to take a photograph of herself sitting on top of a bus? Furthermore, he knew that such people posted such photos on social media and he wondered why anybody would choose to look at such a posting. It seemed to him that such an activity was sinking mundanity to even lower depths than it already deserved to be in.

Alighting the bus outside the library, he noticed all the trendy bars and restaurants that he had teased Alberta Curtis-Brightland about. Parkhurst Lane, he thought was roughly a mile on the other edge of town. He decided to walk there. Twenty minutes later he came upon it. It was a little bit hidden and he almost went past it, but then he noticed the big church on the corner, the one he'd seen on the screen when he'd logged on to the street scene the previous night. The church itself was a magnificent stone building, but he deduced from some new signage that it was no longer a church and was now being utilised for commercial purposes.

Parkhurst Lane, he discovered, was a narrow lane with a narrow entrance. Just before the entrance is a sign that reads: *no entrance except for access.* The lane itself is about seven to eight hundred metres long, just wide enough to accommodate two cars and has a narrow footway running down one side of it. As the carriageway progresses away from the main road, it widens a little and Senetti thought that where it widened, it could probably accommodate three cars. It was a cul-de-sac and even though only a short distance from Didsbury centre, it was isolated and quiet. It wasn't the sort of street or the sort of place that you would accidentally find yourself in. It wasn't even the sort of street that clandestine lovers would park up in, due to its narrowness. Down the opposite side to the footpath side and running for about half the length of the lane was a well-built ten-feet high brick wall. As the wall came to an end, then a pretty little municipal park came to a beginning. Adjacent to the park was a small hard standing area which obviously served car parking. He reasoned that this area could probably accommodate five or six cars but now it was empty. There was a sign inside the park railings, '*Didsbury Park.*' Opposite the little park was an elegant terrace of expensive looking, three-storey, town-houses, six of them in all. These were the only dwellings in Parkhurst Lane. Alma Alice had died in November, Danny knew this and he confirmed it with another glance at Araminta's memo. He could fully understand why somebody would take a pleasant walk around here on light nights and in pleasant weather but he was puzzled as to the reason why anybody would want to visit Parkhurst Lane on a November evening.

There was only one exit and one entry, the same one for both, so it was unlikely that you would be passing through, anyway there was nowhere to pass through to. There was of course a multiplicity of reasons why people pursued all manner of strange actions and you could never apply common logic to individual eccentricity, but if you *were* applying it, he could think of only four possible reasons why you would be in Parkhurst Lane in November! You lived here, you were lost, you were visiting somebody else who lived here or you were meeting somebody here. As far as Alma Alice was concerned, Senetti discounted the first two as being incorrect and unlikely, respectively. Through this mental process of elimination, he settled on the third or fourth as the probable reason. If this logic applied to Alma Alice as the victim, then surely the same logic applied to the driver of the car who ran her down. Surely even the most superficial police enquiry would have both established and eliminated whether the car driver lived here or was visiting somebody who did. After all, the investigating team would have only had to make house-to-house enquires of six addresses. If this had been the case and he or she was a resident or a visitor then the culprit would have soon been discovered. Working on the theory that the driver of the car that killed Alma Alice didn't live in Parkhurst Lane and wasn't visiting somebody who did, what was left? He could of course have taken a wrong turn and in his attempt at correction had accidentally caused the fatality. Senetti also considered the physical aspects of Parkhurst Lane. He thought that the lane did not in any way lend itself to careless speeding, nor did it lend itself to losing control of your car. As he stood outside the park and surveyed the lane from end to end, it was arrow straight, carpet flat and there wasn't a bend or undulation in sight, not even a slight one to lose control on. He thought about the 'accident' and he considered that whatever the reason you were in your car on a November night in Parkhurst Lane, the balance of probability suggested that you were present more as an act of deliberation than by accident.

He withdrew a small notebook from his bag and made a rough sketch of the lane and some brief annotations of his own reflex thoughts. Then he decided to walk the short distance to the YOT's office to meet Jim Bigelow.

Fifteen minutes later he arrived outside a single storey ugly brick building, with aluminium windows. There were metal guards on the windows and the whole building was surmounted by a flat roof. He thought how the building looked out of place in the posh suburb of Didsbury. He signed in at reception as requested and almost immediately, Jim Bigelow came through a grey painted door to him. Jim introduced himself and ushered Senetti politely into a small side office, which had a sign that said, *interview room* fixed to another grey coloured door.

Senetti observed Jim Bigelow, he was a tall man, probably about six feet two, athletically built, and altogether a handsome man around forty-five years of age. He had a nattily trimmed dark beard and moustache, and his hair still retained most of its original dark brown colour. He had soft brown gentle eyes and was dressed casually in jeans and shirt. Senetti had met

YOT's officers before and knew that the male ones, at least in day to day activities favoured casual dress. It was considered that this dress code helped break down the barriers that more formal dress sometimes presented to the young people whom they were working with. He also observed another thing about Jim Bigelow. He noticed how he was a little flirtatious and forward with the receptionist who had signed him in. This wasn't in a contrived way but in a way, that seemed second nature to the officer and as if he just couldn't help himself. It came into Senetti's mind that Bigelow had a bit of a reputation with the ladies. He now recalled that Jim Bigelow in some circles was referred to as 'Bigelow the Gigolo.' After the initial pleasantry exchange Senetti spoke first.

'Thanks for seeing me, I've just come to see if you can help me in relation to Alma Alice Spain.'

'I'll do whatever I can, although I thought that business was all over by now.' We've had the police investigation, coroner's enquiry and all the other stuff, it was a tragic business and an ill wind, everybody knew Alma. It shocked all of us, we're just about over it now. Don't really know what I can tell you that I haven't told everybody else, and I really can't see what good can come out of opening it up again.'

'That seems an awful lot of resistance Jim, I've hardly said anything yet. We're not really as you say opening it up again, we are just re-examining some aspects of the case. Alma Alice Spain's death is a small part of a much bigger internal enquiry being carried out by the Children's Commissioner's Office, that's who I am representing at this moment.'

'The Children's Commissioner's office, I can't see what they have to do with this. What sort of bigger enquiry do you mean?'

'The Children's Commissioner's Office is involved because the YOT works with children and young people and your colleague Alma Alice worked for the YOT team. More than that, I can't really tell you because of the confidentiality aspect, you know how it all works Jim, you've been around long enough.'

'I suppose so.'

'How well did you know her?'

'She was a colleague, we worked in YOTs together, that's it really.'

'How many years have you been colleagues?'

'Six, no seven.'

'So, you knew her well then, professionally?'

'Yes, I'd say so.'

'Did you know her personally at all?'

'That was a different issue altogether, Alma was a keep yourself to yourself person. She came to work and then she went home.'

Danny had learned from experience that when people were trying to distance themselves from others they always referred to the other person as 'keeping themselves to themselves.'

'What about social events, those at work?'

'Events?'

'Come on Jim, you know what a social event at work is, special occasions, birthdays, weddings, people leaving, people arriving, Christmas, that type of thing?'

'I personally don't go to Christmas Parties, I don't know about Alma. I did occasionally go to the others that you mentioned, we both went to them, but I only turned up out of courtesy and I think that Alma did the same. One drink, two maybe, pay my respects and I headed off home. Alma Alice was the same. She used to say that when you had been with your colleagues all day in the stressful situations that you find yourself in, in this job, that when you were off duty you wanted to be completely off duty and that meant off duty from them.'

'What about her domestic life?'

'Again, she didn't speak about it much, she had been married some years ago, before I knew her, but it didn't last long, didn't work out, there were no children, she was divorced and lived alone, moved into a flat in Wilmslow Road, after the divorce and stayed there. I met him once, the ex-husband, twice if you count the funeral, what was his name now? Alexander that was it. I think they called him Alex for short. Alma and I were on a case together over in Bury and he became involved in it. He's a doctor, GP, I think and he has a practice over that way. Seemed nice enough to me, then again so was Alma but I wasn't married to either of them.'

'Did Alma Alice have anybody who didn't like her, anybody who disagreed with her, anybody who wished her harm?'

'Councillor, we all have people who disagree with us. It's the nature of this job. We are dealing with delinquent youth. There is always a school of thought that wants to kiss them and another school that wants to kick them. Often the YOT's officer is in the crossfire and Alma got herself in as much crossfire as the rest of us. As for doing harm, that's a different thing altogether. There is nobody who I'm aware of, she wasn't that sort of person. So, no, not that I can think of, no.'

'Did she have any family, relatives, you know parents, siblings?'

'Yes, her parents were at the funeral, they made all the arrangements. It was a horrible emotional day, at least that's how I found it. I'm not aware of any brothers or sisters.'

'Did she have a boyfriend?'

'None that I'm aware of, she never mentioned any and I certainly didn't see any.'

'You seem very sure about that Jim, she was married once, she was an attractive woman, she was only young, why not?'

'I don't know Councillor, the only thing that I do know is that at one time she was doing online dating.'

'How do you know that?'

'Is it relevant?'

'I don't know, it might be.'

There was a pause in the conversation.

'If feel as if I'm breaking a confidence.'

'Jim, it might be helpful.'

'I heard her discussing it one day with Jean Fortescue. They didn't realise that I'd entered the room, when they did realise they stopped talking about it. If anybody knows anything about Alma, then it is probably Jean.'

'Do you remember what they were saying?'

'No, not really, I didn't take much notice at the time.'

Is Jean another social worker?'

'She is yes, her and Alma were quite friendly, in a professional way, if that's not a contradiction.'

'I know what you mean.'

'I think they confided in each other, if anybody knows anything about Alma it's probably Jean.'

'Is Jean here, do you know where I can find her?'

'No, she's not, she left here about six months ago, went to manage a team for Kensington and Chelsea Borough Council. As far as I know she is still there. It should be easy enough to contact her.'

'You people must get involved in some fairly dangerous stuff, was Alma Alice working on any sensitive cases?'

'They are all very sensitive Councillor, but none of them are what you would call dangerous, we don't really get involved in the dangerous stuff. Most of our offenders are too young to be involved in anything like that. There are some exceptions of course, there always is with everything. If it starts looking like that, then we hand the case over to others. Others who specialize more. Our objective is to stop young kids re-offending or even offending in the first place. Most of them are just misguided, mixed up kids. Occasionally we do come across a real 'wrong un' who usually ends up in prison but most of the time we are not dealing with bad people, they're just kids who don't get much guidance at home and have been led astray a bit by people who are looking out for that kind of vulnerability.'

'Jim, what cases was Alma Alice working on at the time of her death, was she involved with any 'wrong uns' as you call them?'

'As I recall, it had been an uneventful caseload for quite some time, I mean there was plenty to do, there always is, but it was mainly kids, involved in kids' stuff, it was all routine.'

'What sort of stuff do you call routine, kids' stuff ?'

'Shoplifting, breaking into cars, possession of drugs, sometimes dealing, vandalism, those sorts of things.'

'What about Alma's private life, was there anything happening in there at the time?'

'As I recall she was probably at her most un-talk-ative about that, she really wasn't saying much about anything.'

'She didn't say much or she didn't say anything?'

'Obviously, we spoke, but she didn't say much.'

'Did she have any cases in Parkhurst Lane?'

'No, she didn't, nobody did. You know Councillor it's a funny thing about Parkhurst Lane.'

'Yeah, why is that ?'

'Well about a week before she was found there, Alma and I spent the morning together in the Juvenile Court. We were both on separate cases and most of the time we were just hanging around in the corridor, waiting to be called. She asked me about Parkhurst Lane, well not so much about it as where it was.'

'She didn't know where it was?'

'No, she didn't, but that didn't surprise me, a lot of people don't, it's tucked out of the way and most people don't have any reason to go there. Anyway, I explained it to her, gave her some directions.'

'So, she was obviously planning to go there at least one week before she actually did?'

'It would seem so, yes.'

' Jim, did Alma know anybody in Parkhurst Lane?'

'If she did, she certainly didn't mention it to me.'

'Why would she be in Parkhurst Lane on foot and at that time?' Senetti asked.

'I honestly don't know.'

'What about her car.'

'What about it.'

'Where was it?'

'It was found here in the car park.'

'Jim, why would she leave her car here and presumably walk over to Parkhurst Lane on a November night?'

'I don't know for sure, but she liked her cars Alma, always had nice cars too, expensive cars, always changing them. You'd look out the window and see a new car, you didn't recognize, then you'd see the number plate AAS30.'

She had a personalised number plate that read 'A.A.S.?'

'Yes, she did A. A. S, Alma Alice Spain.'

'What about the thirty, what did that represent?'

'I don't know, I didn't ask her. I only know about the letters because it was so obvious. Personally, I would never have one myself, everybody knowing where you are, when you are, but she loved the idea. She changed her car on a regular basis but she kept the plate.'

'All right, thanks Jim, that's it I think. If you think of anything that you consider might have any relevance then call me please.'

As he said this he placed a business card into Jim Bigelow's hand.

'Sure.'

Later that day as Senetti sat on the top deck of the 42 bus, on the return journey back to Manchester he considered his time in Didsbury. He had only just scratched the surface of the circumstances that surrounded only one of the cases he was considering and already something didn't seem quite right.

As for Alma Alice Spain, standing on a remote lane, a lane that she didn't know the whereabouts of the previous week. Run over accidentally by some boy racer who lost control of the car, then lost control of himself and fled in panic. Nothing that Senetti had seen or heard today seemed to support this explanation of her death. He thought about his interview with Jim Bigelow. He thought that Jim could have been more forthcoming with his answers, but probably that was just the way he was.

His thoughts then drifted back again to Parkhurst Lane itself. He considered that he might be making one of those hasty assumptions that he was so guarded about making and he tried to dispel the theory from his mind, but it just wouldn't keep out. If you were the victim of a hit and run accident on a dark November evening, then the location of Parkhurst Lane ideally fitted the bill. As well as this though, if you were going to select a location to kill or injure somebody in a pre-meditated way, by running your car at them and then escape into the night, then where would you find a better time or place to do it, than on a November evening in Parkhurst Lane.

He thought of Alberta Curtis-Brightland by now on her train to London. He also thought about Councillor Jason Dunphy. He would tackle that case tomorrow.

Chapter 7

A Life of Emma Luckhurst

Emma Luckhurst didn't like to spend any time at all thinking about her life, not even a few seconds, because, when she did, it hurt her head and she hated everything about it. She hated where her life had come from, she hated where it was right now and she hated where it was going. The answer to all these questions about past, present and future could always be answered in one word, nowhere!

All her life, for as long as she could remember, she had been in care with the City Council. She had forgotten exactly how many faceless foster homes she had lived in and how many pointless schools she had attended. She could remember very little about any of them nor the names of the people associated with them. All she could remember was that they all had lots of different rules. They each had their own different sets of rules and regulations. One foster carer, she remembered his name, he was called Anthony and he referred to them as '...The Regs.' There were dozens of these 'Regs,' no not dozens, more than dozens, hundreds of them, and when you found one, you could always find another one to contradict it. She no longer knew which rules were right and which ones were wrong. Sometimes, when she thought of her past and tried to gain an accurate recall about some part of it, she didn't know if this recall was true or imagined. It had got to the situation now, where there was no difference in her life, in the way that she felt, everything was always the same, day on day, week on week. There were no highs and no lows anymore, just levels. The only thing that she could recollect was that when she was very young she used to cry a lot and now she didn't cry at all. She didn't know if she felt better when she used to cry, or since she had stopped.

Now, she was seventeen years of age and she disliked where she lived more than anywhere else she had ever been. This place was called The Acorns Children's Residential Unit and it was run by City Social Services. She didn't particularly dislike the staff nor the other kids, there wasn't much to dislike, neither was there much to like, she just didn't care about them one way or another. The other kids were all younger than her, the oldest of them was only fourteen and the youngest was eight and they all behaved and acted like babies. It was the same with the school she attended, she didn't care about any aspect of it, the teachers, the other students, the subjects, she just sat through each lesson until it ended, then she went onto the next one and did the same. At one time, she had been ambitious to be a nurse, but recently she had lost all interest in this. The teachers didn't ask her questions anymore, after all she would be leaving school soon and the teachers had just given up on her. She didn't want to feel this way, she couldn't help it and it was the best she could do. All she was interested in now, was getting her weekly allowance on Friday, going into Manchester over the week-end, getting drunk and hooking up with that boy Leroy, who she'd met last month. Leroy had been in care too, but he was now discharged and on an aftercare programme. He was going to St Albans College, where he was learning to be a plumber. He had his own council flat in Longsight and he played the guitar. Today though was Tuesday and she would have to wait for the week-end to come. Even though today was Tuesday, it was not to be an uneventful day. For Emma Luckhurst, it was to be a monumental day, for today was the day that she was going to execute her revenge on the person who she really did hate, she hated her more than anybody else she could think of. This person wasn't a teacher, wasn't a student, wasn't a member of staff in the unit and wasn't one of the kids in the unit either, this person wasn't nameless or faceless, Emma knew exactly what she looked like and who she was, it was Bethan Trefor, and Bethan Trefor had betrayed and hurt Emma. Bethan had hurt Emma, more than anybody else in her life had hurt her and she wasn't going to get away with it.

Emma hadn't always hated Bethan; the opposite was true because for some years they had been the best of friends. Emma and Bethan had spent four years of their lives together in The Acorns, and they had been inseparable. After all they had experiences in common. They had both been in care almost from birth. Unlike Bethan, Emma had a Grandmother who was on the scene but that was all, neither of them, Emma or Bethan had ever had birth parents who had played a significant part in their lives. Bethan's mother was dead and she didn't know who her father was. Emma's father was dead and nobody knew where her mother was, she had disappeared years ago. Both girls were the same age and were both the eldest of two separate sibling groups who were all being brought up in care as looked after children. If you totalled all the children in both families there was eight of them altogether, Emma was the eldest of three whilst Bethan was the eldest of five. Emma's family were the Luckhursts, but Bethan's brothers and sisters all had different surnames. Bethan had explained it more than once to Emma and identified them individually and told her why they all had different names, it was all to do with their fathers, but it was confusing and it made your head ache, when you thought about it. So, Emma didn't think about it and therefore she didn't understand it.

Bethan was very clever, she was good at school, Emma knew this and she had always been in Bethan's shadow as far as that was concerned. Bethan was also very pretty, Emma wasn't, and Emma knew this too. Bethan and Emma attended different schools. Bethan was in one comprehensive school whereas Emma attended another one, two miles from Bethan's. Emma knew that Bethan was very popular at her school with everybody: boys, girls and teachers. However, Bethan wasn't really interested in doing well at school, she told Emma this. More than anything both girls wanted the same thing, to be out of the care system altogether, they both wanted to be care leavers and make their own decisions about their own lives. Nothing good ever came out of the care system, nobody ever prospered in there. The best that you could do, was to get through it and out of it as soon as you could. Emma had learnt over the years and she knew that no matter how bad things were, no matter how poor they were, no matter how dysfunctional they were, you were always better off with your own family than in the care system. Even if you had no money and you went hungry, there could never be any substitute for being with your own family.

Like everything else in this world, there was a pecking order, a league table even amongst the kids in care. Those who were with their own family in a stable, long-term foster home, with a long-term foster mum and dad were at the top of it. There were other stages along the way, being in foster care on your own was not as good as being in foster care with your family but it was o.k. Being on your own in a unit, you were classed as a 'Unit Kid,' and as a Unit Kid, you were at the bottom of the league.

Emma and Bethan had spoken to each other, they had told each other all about their lives. There wasn't anything that Bethan didn't know about Emma and there wasn't anything that Emma didn't know about Bethan. They were going to leave care when they were eighteen, nobody could stop you once you were eighteen. Once you were eighteen, they gave you a National Insurance number and a passport of your own. Your National Insurance Number was unique. It was called your N.I. Number, there were no two the same, and there couldn't be any two the same. Nobody could steal it, like they stole all your other stuff, your clothes and your make-up and your tunes and anything else they could find, it was impossible to steal your N.I. Number. It would be like stealing somebody's identity. Once you had your own identity and once you got your passport as well, you were a complete bona fide adult. You could go wherever and do whatever with whoever. When they were eighteen, Emma and Bethan had planned to get a flat together in Blackpool, they were going to get jobs there, save some money and do some travelling. They were going to go to the United States of America. They'd watched DVDs about America in the unit. They had talked about it a lot together, it was all planned. Emma and Bethan loved each other, just like sisters.

Then three years ago everything changed.

Rosemary Rowntree, Bethan's Social Worker came to see Bethan at The Acorns. She told Bethan that she had found an 'ideal' foster home for her in Chorlton-cum-Hardy. At first Bethan said that she was settled in the unit and that she didn't want to leave, but then she agreed to a trial period of one week with these carers. She told Emma that she was just agreeing to it to please Rosemary and that she would be back in the unit in a week. After a week Bethan did come back to the unit, but not to stay, only to visit and to pick up the rest of her things. She came to see Emma, she told her how wonderful the foster placement was and she said that the house was lovely and that it was big with lovely gardens, she said that she had her own room, and there were lots of spare rooms in the house, and that if Emma wanted to, then after Bethan had established herself, she was going to try and get Emma in there. Emma was overjoyed, she couldn't contain her own excitement and that night, alone in her room she couldn't help it, she cried for the first time in years.

Bethan had been in the foster placement about two months when Emma was invited for a sleepover one Saturday night. The big house in Chorlton-cum-Hardy was just as Bethan had described and the foster carers, who were called Gerry & Martin, were lovely and very nice to Emma. After the sleepover, the two foster carers took Emma back to the unit in their car, Bethan came with them and they were all chatting about Emma's life. Emma was excited, she couldn't sleep that night. Then a month later Emma was invited again. This time only Martin Kinder took Emma back to Acorns in his car, Bethan and Gerry stayed back at the house. On the journey Martin and Emma were once again chatting about Emma's future. Martin asked her about her ambition to be a nurse. It all seemed to be going just as Bethan had said it would.

Then, that was that! Everything just stopped, 'it was all over before it had begun,' as Emma's Nan used to say.

After the second sleepover Emma was never invited back again and gradually Bethan stopped visiting the unit and Emma saw less and less of her, until eventually she didn't see her at all. Emma tried to get some information on Bethan from Rosemary Rowntree, but Rosemary just brought down that usual social worker's blind of 'confidentiality.' Rosemary said to Emma, that Bethan was ...'getting on with her life and you need to be getting on with yours.'

Then the months just went by, then a year went by, then two. Even after two whole years, Emma just couldn't stop thinking about Bethan and her betrayal. Amongst the other students at Emma's school, was a boy called Jack Wyche. Jack lived in Chorlton-cum-hardy close to Bethan's new foster parents. His mum knew Bethan's foster mum, she used to see her at the shops, they went to the same church and Jack's dad occasionally played golf with Bethan's foster dad. Jack told Emma that slowly over a period, all of Bethan's brothers and sisters had moved into the big house and now they were all there, Jack could even recall all the sibling's names, which was more than Emma could. They were called: Dylan, Glenys, Gethin and Lowri. Jack hung around with Dylan sometimes and Dylan had told Jack that this was the best time of his life now that all his brothers and sisters were together as one family. Dylan also told Jack that next year the whole family, kids and foster carers were going to Vancouver in Canada, they were going to visit the carers' grown up son who was a doctor and lived out there.

So here was Emma, stuck in Acorns all alone until she was eighteen, with no future and her own brother and sister miles away. She had to be content to have some supervised visit with them, when the social worker could be bothered to arrange it. On the other hand, there was Bethan, safe and secure in the big house with her new foster parents and her whole family in the placement, a placement that had been promised to her. She had loved Bethan, she had been her soul sister, they had made all these plans together and this is how Bethan had treated her, she had been betrayed, she was devastated and after devastation came anger and after anger came an obsession for vengeance.

Emma thought to herself, why should Bethan get away with everything and have everything, just because she was pretty and clever? It wasn't that you worked hard to be pretty and clever. Pretty and clever wasn't anything you deserved, you didn't earn being pretty and clever, it wasn't anything at all to do with you, it was just an accident of nature. She determined that Bethan wasn't going to get away with it, not this time. She would disrupt this happy family, she didn't know how, but she would find a way. She lay on her bed hour after hour, night after night, week after week, month after month, thinking of ways that she could achieve this.

She had been around Social Services all her life and she knew what their 'red buttons' were. It didn't have to be true, it just had to be something that was impossible to be disproven. Two people, no more, the word of one against the other. 'Abuse,' that was the word Children's Social Services were terrified of, 'abuse'; the mere mention of the word sent them scattering, running for cover, cover for themselves that is, not for anybody else. That didn't matter though, it didn't matter who they were trying to protect, because she could turn all that to her own advantage. Any abuse would do: physical abuse, emotional abuse, mental abuse, as long as it was abuse, but by far the worst kind of abuse, worse than any other, was *sexual abuse.*

Sexual abuse, Children's Social Services were terrified of even the mention of it. When the term came up, they fled rooms, huddled in groups, spoke in whispers, made crazy decisions, broke whole families up, called the Police in. Sent people on extended leave. It didn't have to be true as long as it could not be disproven. Social Services departments didn't do proper investigations for sexual abuse, the way they did for other allegations, they didn't try to get to the truth, they were too fearful of the allegation itself. They were too fearful of the consequences of any blame or responsibility that could come to rest at their door. If the child care professionals, mistakenly found just one perpetrator innocent and it turned out he or she wasn't, then they were in big trouble, they could even lose jobs. In an extreme situation, they could find themselves in court, only this time as the defendant and not the expert witness. Once you were dismissed as a Social Worker, there was no way back, so why lose your living, your reputation and possibly even your liberty just for the sake of a bit of truth. So, what they did with allegations of sexual abuse, they worked on the basis of, it might be false it might be true, 'I don't know, I wasn't there,' but just in case it is true, this is what we'll do anyway.

In the event, they always carried out the same procedure; they removed the children from the alleged abuser. So, some innocent people got hurt, but innocent people often got hurt, that's life, she'd been innocent and she had been hurt all her life. The allegation itself didn't have to be too serious, she wouldn't cry rape or anything like that. If she did, the Police would be involved and they looked for evidence and questioned you. You could even end up in court. She didn't want that and she didn't want anybody else in court either. No, she'd keep it simple, trivial and simple – but abusive. That way, she didn't even have to speak to the Police, she wouldn't speak to them, even if they wanted to speak to her. All she wanted was disruption to Bethan Trefor's cosy family and she knew that if she came up with a scheme, Social Services would do that for her. There was a word for something or somebody who was supposed to do one thing and often did the opposite, what was it, she couldn't think of it? Social Services were supposed to keep families together but as far as Emma knew, every time they got involved, the family was torn apart. *Irony,* that was the word. Finally, she had come up with a simple scheme that she knew would work and give her the disruption that she deserved. Simple is best, she thought, that's the sort of thing her Nan would say.

She glanced over at the clock on her bedside cabinet, 10:50 am. She felt determined about two things. One was that from this moment on, her life was going to change for the better and secondly, from this moment on she was going to take her revenge on, Bethan Trefor.

Chapter 8

Winton Kiss and The Death of Jason Dunphy

Winton Kiss is a small town, or, a large village, depending upon your own perception in these debates. Most residents though, refer to it as 'Winton.' It has approximately three thousand five hundred inhabitants and sits at the start of the Peak District National Park foothills. The Peak District became the United Kingdom's first national park and was designated in 1951. 'Kinder Scout,' the Peak District's highest mountain can be viewed quite easily from some Winton Kiss streets. The Winton River runs just along the edge of the village and it is said, that it 'poetically kisses it slightly,' hence the name. Chasing the river and running alongside it, in parallel, is the village's main street, unimaginatively perhaps, but appropriately named, River Street.

River Street is probably no longer than two hundred metres end to end and is just wide enough for two cars to pass each other side-by-side. Nevertheless, River Street has: three pubs, three trendy wine-bar-café type places, a post-office-cum-general store, a baker, four hairdressers, a bridal gown shop, a book shop, a fireplace shop, a beauty therapist, a chiropodist, a chemist, a fish and chip shop, a dentist's practice, a doctor's surgery, a bookshop and two or three other shops that keep changing what they have to offer. Winton Kiss is in the political ward of Malton, which in turn is in the Metropolitan borough of Norford. Winton Kiss sits on the main Manchester to Sheffield rail line and is a minute or two over twenty minutes by train from and to Manchester and around a minute or two less than an hour from and to Sheffield.

Many years ago, the village had been in the parish of High Peak, Derbyshire and the 'Kissites,' as the residents sometimes like to call themselves, were pleased with this and liked the sound of it. Then, because of the never-ending boundary changes, which are usually drawn and redrawn for political reasons, it found itself in Cheshire. The Kissites didn't appreciate this as much as 'High Peak,' but it was marginal in their eyes and they soon got used to it. Latterly though, or to be precise in 1974, a major travesty had taken place and Winton Kiss changed its address once again. It had become part of the Metropolitan borough of Norford. There was even worse to come, for it was now addressed as: Winton Kiss, Malton, Norford, Greater Manchester. It was the word *Manchester* that was the problem. Residents did not appreciate this at all. It should be said, there was an element of hypocrisy in this stance as many a now 'Kissite' originated from this city and a significant number of these 'Mancs' still earned their living there, and commuted between the two daily.

Even though many of the residents were too young to remember when Winton Kiss had been in Cheshire and not even one of those who remembered it being in

High Peak was still alive, they still complained in the bars and cafes about their now *Manchester* address. Some of them, still stubbornly referred on any correspondence to 'Winton Kiss, Cheshire,' and a small few still referred to it as, 'Winton Kiss, High Peak.' In support of this denial, some of them had specially printed letterheads and business cards to prove it. The village may only be a short journey to Manchester city centre but to the residents of Winton Kiss, that industrially, revolutionised metropolis, which surely now had become England's second city after London, was considered by Kissites, to be a whole world and a half away from their own habitat and they were firm and eloquent in their disassociation from it.

There were young families in Winton Kiss. To educate their young children, the village contained three primary schools and in Malton there were two secondary schools for the same purpose with the older children. Originally, the village had been an Anglo-Saxon settlement, before it trundled its way meekly through history until by the time of the 17th century, it had become something of a canal town. Later, it was a Victorian mill village, but its growth and prosperity since the 1960s owed much to its previously mentioned location along the main Sheffield to Manchester rail line. To elaborate on this, throughout the 1950s, 60s and early part of the 70s, and as part of a plan to make the national railways more cost effective, the government of the day closed various lines and the attending stations with them. The Manchester to Sheffield line, via Edale, was one of those lines under threat, along with Winton Kiss Station. At the last minute, due in part to a campaign conducted by residents both were reprieved. Winton Kiss then became a place whereupon commuters could travel quite easily to Sheffield or Manchester for business, and live in semi rurality in the village. Therefore, the developers moved in, new houses sprung up and young families moved in. This is in seeming contradiction to the demographics of today as many of the residents seemed to be of a certain age and local government statistics recently stated that fifty-two per cent of Kissites were over the age of fifty-five.

The consensus though, is that Winton Kiss and indeed Malton altogether, is a very good place to live and its inhabitants are seen by the rest of the county, whether it is thought of as being in High Peak, Cheshire or Greater Manchester as being very fortunate to live there.

Winton Kiss was home to Danny Senetti, he'd lived there for the twenty-two years since he'd come out of the army, whereupon he'd married Charlotte. She'd lived there before him, but she'd since moved out after their divorce. He had stayed, well he had nowhere else to go for one thing and for another, for the last fourteen years he'd been the locally elected councillor for the area and as such was expected to live in his own ward by his own constituents, and more than anywhere, he now thought of the place as home.

He was seated at the kitchen table in his house in Winton Kiss, staring gormlessly into space. He was attired in a scruffy black and white dressing gown and a pair of bright red-carpet slippers, with the emblem of a robin wearing a scarf and a bobble hat embossed upon each one. They were quite frankly ridiculous, but his mother had bought them for him as a Christmas present last year and he had promised her he would wear them.

As well as this he didn't own any others. On the table in front of him was a mug of tea which he'd now let go cold, an open jar of marmite, a half-eaten piece of toast on a white napkin, his mobile phone and the pink coloured file that Araminta Rock had compiled for him the day before yesterday. He'd studied this file again during his breakfast and he now reflected upon its content. He heard the door of his outside post box squeak open and then squeak shut, as his postwoman delivered today's mail. He made no attempt to retrieve it, he didn't even think about it. After all, it would still be there, when he returned, later in the day, from the journey that he was contemplating, but had not yet embarked upon. You could lock his outside mailbox if you wanted to, but he didn't lock it. He left the key in it, all the time, so he didn't lose it. Nobody had ever stolen any of his mail, he didn't expect them to either and if somebody decided that they wanted to, they could have it with his permission. There was never anything interesting in it anyway and even less by the way of cheeriness. He considered that his mail fell into two categories. It was either somebody complaining about something *to* him or somebody demanding something *from* him.

This morning he'd made two separate telephone calls to two Oldham Councillors who he knew and who had known Councillor Jason Dunphy. Councillor Barney Croft and Councillor Jackie Jacobs. Both councillors had recited the same story, which was that Jason Dunphy was a well-respected, well liked person and that he was a happily married family man, who was not experiencing anything unusual, either personally or professionally. They had also both said that he liked a drink but he was comfortable with it.

Just then his mobile phone rang, now it was his turn to be the recipient. He looked at the screen which displayed a name, "Steve Fedeczko."

Senetti had left a message for him yesterday and Steve was obviously returning his call. Senetti and Fedeczko had known each other for many years and the latter now worked as the Health and Safety Director for Manchester Metrolink. Senetti knew that part of Fedeczko's role was the investigation of accidents on that service.

'Hello Steve, how are you, thanks for getting back to me.'

'Councillor, sorry I missed you yesterday, how are you, what are you up to these days. Are you still resident in The Black Swan? I must come over and join you for a few hours sometime.'

'Just say when and we'll arrange it, although I don't seem to get in as much as I used to, you know, usual council stuff gets in the way.'

'Sounds like a bout of self-delusion to me.'

'What, the council stuff?'

'No Danny, your attendance in the Black Swan.'

'In what way?'

'In the way that you think you don't get in it, as much as you used to.'

Senetti laughed, but ignored the remark, 'Anyway, I'm well, how are Coleen and the children, is she still freelancing?

'No, she's staffing now for The Evening News. Oh, the kids, they are not children anymore, but everybody is doing fine, Dominic is at Uni in Sheffield and Maeve is starting in September, not Sheffield though, she's got a place at Oxford no less, although what she plans to do with a degree in *philosophy and journalism* is anybody's guess. Their dependency though doesn't seem to have decreased the way I was told it would, it just differs. Anyway, can I be of some help?'

'Oxford eh, bright girl, obviously takes after her mother. I'm currently on a secondment with the Children's Commissioner's Office, well it's not so much a secondment, as a commandment from Karen Spencer, you remember Karen?'

'Yes, I remember Karen, does she still speak with such brutal candour?'

'She, does yes. I'm working with a lady called Alberta Curtis-Brightland, we're looking at several incidents which may be connected, although I've yet to make the connection myself. It's all to do with safeguarding children. One of these incidents is the circumstances surrounding the death of Jason Dunphy.'

'Alberta Curtis-Brightland, I think I've heard that name at least, the Curtis-Brightland bit.'

'Really Steve, where?'

'Oh, I don't know, in circles, you know how you hear things or overhear things or read them, half the time, they don't even register and you can't recall the reason why, but I remember the name, well you wouldn't forget a name like that would you?'

'No, it is a little striking.'

'I take it you mean *Councillor* Jason Dunphy,' he said.

'That's the one.'

'What do you need to know?'

'Whatever you know Steve, without breaching any confidentiality, of course.'

'There isn't any to breach Danny, there never really was, it's all in the public domain now, has been for some time.'

They both paused momentarily, then the officer continued.

'Last year, 17th March, Saint Patrick's Day, or night to be precise. As you probably know Jason Dunphy was Irish.'

'I did know, yes, Republic or Northern?'

'He was originally from a place called Letterkenny which is in County Donegal, I'm not quite sure if that's Republic or Northern, this bit didn't come up in the enquiry, I know it's the most northern county in the whole island of Ireland, but despite that, I think that it might actually be in the Republic.'

'You're right, both times Steve, Donegal is the most northern county, despite that though, it is actually in the Republic.'

'Well, thanks for the Irish geography lesson Danny, but I think I'm even more confused now. It's only to be expected, that's the Irish for you, I've been married to an Irish woman for nearly thirty years and I've not worked her out yet, so what chance have I got with the geography of the place?'

Senetti laughed, 'with that homespun philosophy Steve, you could almost be Irish yourself?'

'Yeah, what branch of the Irish would the Fedeczko's be? Would they be Republic or Northern?'

Both men laughed.

'Let's get back to Jason Dunphy, Councillor. As both a true Irish patriot and as part of his council duties, he'd been to a Saint Patrick's night celebration at the Stonemasons Arms.'

'Where is the Stonemasons Arms?'

'I'm shocked, a pub in the city region that Danny Senetti doesn't know. It's a pub around the corner from Failsworth Metrolink stop. It's been there for years. The pub that is, not the Metro stop. After his celebrations in the Stonemasons, which I understand were enthusiastic, he walked the couple of hundred yards or so to the station. He was waiting there to catch the tram home to Oldham when he fell off the platform into the path of a through train, killed him instantly.'

'Does that happen a lot on the Metro?' Senetti queried.

'It's not a regular occurrence, but it isn't unique either. It's the first incident we've had at Failsworth. Across the county network, we probably have two or three incidents a year, they're not all fatal. Statistics show, travelling on the metro is much safer than driving your car in the City Region or riding your bike or even walking.'

'Do we know what caused Jason to fall onto the line?'

'With these incidents, we never know for sure, but God rest his soul, it was probably the drink. According to witnesses and the medical experts he was well over the legal limit for driving'

'Yeah, but he wasn't driving was he Steve, he was minding his own business waiting for a tram.'

'Danny, you've seen how a drunk sometimes loses his balance and falls in the street, then just gets up again, well that was the consensus as to what the

councillor did, only this time he w...
he fell onto the tram line, which is
drop plus a tram was hurtling through
precise moment he did this. It was ve...
waste of a life, he was only a young man, n...
all accounts, a very good councillor who h.   ...ung
family and all his life in front of him.'

'I take it there was an investigation and an
inquest?'

'Yes, both of those took place. All the usual statutory procedures were invoked but it was open and shut,
it was all so obvious what had happened. The Coroner
made a recommendation about safety rails on the platform, which we've since looked at. It was recorded as
accidental death. Which if you ask me, is exactly what it
was, an accident, a tragic one but nevertheless an
accident.'

'Steve, you mentioned witnesses?'

'I did use that word yes.'

'You mean some people were actually there and
saw him fall onto the line.'

'No, nobody actually saw the incident. There was
nobody else at the station, it was deserted. Failsworth
station is hidden from view and is not a well-used
station, it's a dismal stop at the best of times and this
wasn't the best of times. It was late at night, it was dark
and the weather was foul, it was the middle of March,
so you can imagine. What I meant by witnesses, was in
The Stonemasons Arms. The councillor was well known
in that pub and there was a pub full of people who witnessed his drinking. He was well known for taking a
drink, he was celebrating after all.'

'What about the train driver?'

As is often the case he was oblivious to it all until it happened, he saw nothing. As I said before Danny, it really is open and shut, tragic, but open and shut.'

'Well, thanks Steve, appreciate it all.'

'No problem Danny, oh, one more point, I almost forgot. I've got a case file, wafer-thin mind you and apart from a couple of rough sketches I made at the scene and a couple of photos, I don't think there's much more in it than I've already told you, but you are welcome to it.'

'Might be helpful.'

'Right, I'll get Roxy to email it to you now.'

'Roxy, is she still with you?'

'She is yes, you've still got Christine Harris?'

'Yeah, I have.'

'We must inspire loyalty Danny. When we eventually do get to that meet in the Black Swan, we'll have to swap loyalty tips.'

'Good idea, don't forget, and don't forget to tell Coleen, I was asking after her. On that note Steve, I'll say thanks and bye.'

Two hours passed since his phone with Steve and Senetti had finished his breakfast and dressed. He left his house and walked down the hill to Winton Kiss railway station, where he boarded the train to Manchester Piccadilly. During the journey, he studied the emailed file that Fedeczko had sent him.

Manchester is truly the place where the railway age began for the whole world. It was the service established between Manchester and Liverpool which first demonstrated the use of rail as a viable public and freight transport system. The opening of 'Piccadilly Station,' in 1842, or 'London Road,' as it was then called, was a key milestone in the prosperity of Manchester. The main feature of the station was that it made direct travel from Manchester to London possible in just under ten hours. Prior to this, the swiftest method of travel between these two cities was by stagecoach, which unreliably took around twenty-four hours. This could be a very uncomfortable, even hazardous excursion. As well as this and much more importantly for the sake of commerce in general, and in relation to the carriage of freight, the stagecoach had obvious limitations, which were immediately eliminated by the advent of the railway and the train. Piccadilly Station has been progressively and extensively upgraded since 1960. The last refurbishment in 2002 saw the station made more leisure and consumer friendly with the addition of cafes, bars, coffee shops and retail outlets. Today, if you wished, you could probably do your weekly shop there. People use Piccadilly as a rendezvous point and meet up and socialise there.

It was at Piccadilly Station that Senetti alighted his train from Winton Kiss in completion of the first leg of his journey to Failsworth.

In English history, shortly after William IV died, the 18 years old Alexandrina Victoria, daughter of The Duke of Kent and Streatham and Princess Victoria of Saxe Coburg–Saalfeld ascended the throne of Great Britain and Ireland as Queen Victoria and was crowned at Westminster Abbey. Around the same time, approximately two hundred miles north of that magnificent building, the Brooks family, a prosperous local clan were energetically buying up large parcels of land in Manchester. One of those family members was a banker named Samuel Brooks who in his spare time, when he could find some, was Vice-Chairman of Manchester & Leeds Railway. Samuel purchased such a plot, known as Hunt's Bank, close to Manchester Cathedral and presented it to that railway company. This land was later developed and a building originally designed by George Stephenson the railway pioneer was built there. In July 1839, this building, after gaining royal assent was opened as Manchester Victoria railway station.

Today, Victoria railway station operates both a Metrolink service and a train service. As well as this a recent development has seen a Metrolink connection open from Piccadilly to Victoria.

As the tram pulled out of Victoria Station, Senetti gazed out of the window then he looked up at the electronic destination board. It showed the stops in sequence of arrival: Monsall, Central Park, Newton Heath & Moston, and finally Failsworth. He looked around the carriage, it was smartly liveried in yellow and grey which he rightly assumed were the corporate colours of the Metrolink Company. Sharing his carriage were the usual assortment of people. Senetti pondered on his fellow passengers. There were about ten of them altogether. He noticed in particular, a workman who was asleep, probably an early shift worker, on his way home. There was also an elderly gentleman, facing him but hidden behind an uplifted newspaper, Senetti could see the man's reflection in the carriage window. There was a young woman breast-feeding her child. It was altogether a conventional, content picture of modern society.

Then to his dismay he spotted them, the 'Clackers.' Two young female social media junkies. They were staring trance-like into their hand-held devices. He wasn't sure if it was the same two who had been on the number 42 bus yesterday as clackers all seemed to look the same to him. Each one of them had both thumbs on their individual devices and they were clacking and scrolling ferociously and almost in unison to some unknown exclusive rhythm. He wondered if they were communicating with each other, even though they were only inches apart. His disappointment never ceased when he came upon this sight and witnessed first-hand this negative addiction of 'clacking' which now permeated every corner of modern life. Wherever you went, shop, park, library, pub, anywhere these days, there always seemed to be at least one clacker who had managed to sneak in before you arrived and was sitting there lurking.

It occurred to him that clacking and scrolling was now the human epidemic that had established itself as the real alternative to human communication. It was contributing to a breakdown in community and family and was also fuelling a deep sense of loneliness which was sweeping through the world's society.

It wasn't the technology itself he was against, the contrary was true, he wasn't against that at all. He could clearly see benefits in the technology. What was wrong with sending a picture to Grandma in England of her new born grandson in Australia or sending an old friend a happy birthday message, absolutely nothing? Messages and images like these he could understand. He was also aware that mobile phones had saved people's lives and he certainly wasn't against that. He had a mobile phone himself and an ipad and he used them, he thought, to good effect. He made and received numerous phone calls, the same with emails and he also communicated via the occasional text message. What he was against was the apparent frenzy and totality with which many vulnerable people embraced, succumbed and conformed to this epidemic and without knowing it, had become addicts. These addicts in pursuit of satisfying their habit, intruded into the lives of others who weren't so addicted. There were some people who just could not be without their mobile phone or some such device. He had heard of people who placed their phone on their bedside cabinet at night. He had witnessed himself people who could not converse without using their mobile phone to show some kind image in illustration of what they were saying. He knew of people who were on so many social media sites, and did so much texting, image posting and reading that they just couldn't be doing anything else, they didn't have the time. As far as he was concerned, scrolling and clacking was for people who had nothing else to do, for some of them it seemingly had the same effect on the brain as opium and as such was a complete waste of a man's life. He wondered what intelligent reason there could be why you would post an image of yourself to somebody who had known you all your life, he couldn't come up with an answer.

Of all the trillions and zillions of texts and images that are sent to whoever they are sent to, how many of them actually mattered to the recipient or the sender? Has there ever been one text, just one image, whereupon, if you hadn't sent it or received it, then it would have had a significant impact on your life? He supposed that there probably were a few. Yet clackers behaved as if their lives depended upon all of them. All-day texting and posting seemed to be their life blood, which sadly, it very probably was.

Less than ten minutes later Senetti had escaped the clackers and alighted at Failsworth Station. As the tram moved off and on to Oldham, he was left completely alone on the platform. He recalled Steve Fedeczko's words, 'It's a dismal place at the best of times.' Senetti thought that conversely, this was probably one of the best of times to visit Failsworth Station. It was the middle of the day, it was light, the atmosphere was still and the sun was trying to peep through the sky, albeit without success. Even when all this was considered, Fedeczko's description seemed appropriate.

As he looked around Failsworth Station, he thought that it was probably like dozens of other stations dotted around the Metrolink network. It consisted of two concrete platforms both about fifty metres long and about three metres wide. The corporate colours were in evidence again and he thought how well the grey of the finished concrete blended in with the colour scheme. There was some overhead lighting which obviously should have been switched off during daylight but for some reason was still on. Oddly this artificial light seemed to add to the place's feeling of desolation. The only other thing worthy of mention, Senetti thought, were the two elevators, one on each platform, they were there for carrying passengers from platform to street level and back again. The doors were made of cold stainless steel, yet in paradox they exuded the only warmth on the station as they represented a connection to the outside world which was not present anywhere else in the station. He could see the part of the platform where Councillor Jason Dunphy had tumbled to his death and the thought saddened him. He walked up and down the platform a few times and observed that it did not seem to be over-looked. Then he walked down the ramp back onto the street and ascended the other ramp that led to the Victoria bound platform. Having stood on both plat-forms and surveyed the station, he walked over to the lift and entered it. A few seconds later he found himself at street level as he walked out onto the street. Immediately to his right, he observed the pub Fedeczko had mentioned, The Stonemasons Arms. He looked up at the sign on the wall. A convoluted thought came into his head and he wondered why they didn't put apostrophes in pub signs.

He thought that he might call in the pub. He glanced at his wristwatch. He didn't really expect anybody to be in the it, at least not at 2:04 pm on a Wednesday afternoon. It was mid-week and probably too late for lunch-time drinkers and too early for early-doors drinkers. Nevertheless, he thought that if he went inside for a drink for half an hour or so, he might soak up some second-hand atmosphere that might give him a better idea about the period prior to Jason Dunphy's demise. He didn't know what he was expecting to find, nothing probably. He told himself that he was only using this as an excuse to go in a pub. On the one hand, he was taking this too serious but on the other he was just being conscientious and doing what he said he'd do in his conversations with Alberta Curtis-Brightland. He thought that he should go in the pub anyway. He looked upon the pub building. It was a strange looking building with its frontage at an angle and over two streets. From the outside, it looked like a typical working man's pub in a typical working-class area. What is now known as a community pub.

He observed the licence plate over the door in the name of Ava Anna Gardner. He thought that the practise of placing the licensee's name over the pub doorway was obsolete but obviously not, at least not in The Stonemasons Arms.

Chapter 9

Allegation

Today at 11:00 am was the date and time of Emma's annual appraisal visit with the Independent Assessor. The Independent Assessor was just another name for yet again another social worker. There were lots of social workers, they were everywhere. There was a social worker for everything you could think of. So, for there to seem to be less of them, whoever oversaw them all, just gave them different job titles. There were Social Workers, then there were Family Placement Officers, Senior Practitioners, Independent Assessors, Youth Offending Officers, After Care Officers, Caseworkers, Project Managers, the list was truly endless. That way there didn't seem so many Social Workers, but whatever they called themselves, they were still social workers. Emma's Independent Assessor was a man, his name was Max Edwards. She'd met him a long time ago, he was O.K. the way social workers go and she knew exactly how to play him. She left her own room and made her way towards the room where the interview was to take place. Emma had made her mind up that today would be the day that she would put her plan into execution. Today, would be the day she would make the *disclosure,* that's the term that Social Services used for it *disclosure.*

She wouldn't make it straight away, she would wait for the right time during the interview, she had it all worked out in her head.

Max was running a little late, he was always late, he never gave a reason why, he would say '...apologies for being late, unfortunately I had a late call upon my time.' Nobody knew what he was talking about and they didn't care anyway, he was just late. He'd phoned through to Carol Tipley to say so. Emma thought that if Max hadn't taken the time out to make the phone call to Carol, then he probably wouldn't have been late in the first place. Carol was Emma's caseworker, she'd been allocated throughout Emma's time in Acorns. When Max eventually did turn up the big white clock on the wall said it was at 11:16 am. The three of them: Emma, Carol and Max went into the interview room and Max put the 'occupied' light on.

They sat around the open room, facing each other from their chairs. There was no table, it was all *unrestricted* as Social Services call it. Max had a large buff file on his knee and a pen in his hand. He went through the formalities as he always did which were really to establish Emma's identity. After this Emma had to sign a form to establish who Max was and then Max had to countersign it, to establish who Emma was. It was all a bit silly as Max and Emma had known each other for many years and he knew exactly who she was and she knew exactly who he was.

Max said, 'Apologies for being late, unfortunately I had a late call on my time which caused the delay. Emma, how long have you been living at Acorns?'

'Max, you ask these questions at every interview, every year, the same ones and you know the answers to all of them, it's all in your file.' Emma knew that she also said this at every appraisal, but she determined to keep everything as normal until the time of the disclosure.

'What do you like about being in Acorns and what do you dislike?'

'Max there is nothing to like, there is nothing to dislike either, I'm here, this is where I am and that's it.'

'Emma, why are you here, why are you in Acorns?'

'That's easy, I'm here because I've got nowhere else to go. That's the reason why everybody who is in here is in here. When you've got nowhere else to go, when nobody else will take a chance on you, that's where they put you, in here, in Acorns, it's the end of the line.'

'Have you ever thought about leaving here?'

Emma began to laugh, 'Max you're funny you are, have I ever thought about leaving here, that's what I think about all the time. Anyway, it won't be long now, only a few months to go.'

'Have you thought about what you want to do, when you do leave Acorns, are you planning to stay in the area?'

'Max, my life isn't exactly brimming over with choices and as far as staying in the area, I think that I'll get as far away from Acorns as possible.'

'Did you have anywhere in mind?'

'I thought that I might go to Blackpool Max.'

'What is the attraction there? can we talk about your future?'

She ignored his Blackpool query.

'Why, have I got one, a future?'

'Of course, you have Emma, it is all in front of you.'

'If you want to yeah.'

'Don't you want to Emma?'

'Whatever, yeah, I don't mind Max.'

'All right Emma, is there something that you *do* want to talk about?'

'I don't mind Max, I'll talk about whatever you want to talk about.'

There was a lengthy silence, then Max said.

'It isn't me that's important right now, you are the one that matters here.'

'When can I leave this unit?'

'How are things going at school?'

'It's all right but it's boring, I don't see the point of it anymore. I just go because it gets me out of Acorns.'

'You've not mentioned Ryan and Amy.'

'I was just about to. There's two things that I'd like to talk about and Ryan and Amy are one of them.'

Carol Tipley said, 'What would you like to say about them, you keep in touch, don't you? You've still got your phone haven't you, you telephone Ryan, don't you?'

'I do telephone Ryan yes, but he's not really inter-ested in talking on the telephone, it's a boy thing, and he lost his phone last month and he's only just got around to replacing it, and Amy hasn't got a phone, she's too young so she's not allowed one and phone calls are not the same as meeting-up, are they? So, can you set up a visit, that's what I wanted to say?'

'We can set up a visit in the next three or four weeks, can't we Max?'

'Yes, we will do that.'

'Thank you, that means a lot to me.'

'Have you seen Ryan and Amy recently Max?'

'Yes, I have, I saw Ryan last month, he's doing very well, especially at school and I saw Amy about two months ago, she's been having some trouble with her weight but she's over that now.'

'Is it her anorexia again?'

'It's just some idea that she gets into her head Emma, that's all, just some idea, anyway she's over it now.'

The small group then fell into silence, it was Carol who broke it, 'You said there were two things.'

'Two things?'

'Yes, you said that there were two things that you wanted to discuss. You said that Ryan and Amy were one of them, what was the other?'

'Oh yes, the other thing, 'It's a bit embarrassing, I don't know now if I want to discuss it at all.'

Max, looked up from his file, Carol spoke, 'That's fine if you don't want to discuss it, then you don't have to but there is no need to be embarrassed in front of Max and I.'

Max said, 'No, Carol's right, if you don't want to discuss anything Emma, you don't have to.'

He closed his file and tapped the edge of it on his thigh, he looked as if he was thinking of ending the session and going. That was the last thing that Emma wanted, so she almost blurted out.'

'It's about child abuse, sexploitation.'

Max Edwards fell silent and signalled with a slight nod of his head for Carol Tipley to take over the conversation.

'Emma, I didn't even know you knew that word, what is it about this subject that you want to say.'

'I'm not sure that I do want to say. I'm not sure that anybody will believe me.'

'Take your time Emma, we'll believe you, won't we Max?'

'We will, we absolutely will.'

'Do you know of somebody who has been exploited in this way Emma,' the woman said.

'Yes.'

'Do you want to tell us about it?'

'Yes.'

'Take your time Emma, just say whatever it is, you want to say.'

Emma bit her bottom lip nervously.

'Is it somebody in here Emma, is it somebody in Acorns?

'It's me Carol, I've been sexually assaulted Carol.'

Emma began to cry and as she did, Carol moved herself and her chair next to the tearful girl, then she held Emma's hand. Both social workers realised that this had now become a much more formal interview

Carol said, 'It's all right Emma you are safe here with Max and me. You don't have to say anything more if you don't want to but if you do, we're here to listen and to help.'

'I do want to, I want to tell you, I want to tell you today, I want to tell you here.'

'All right Emma, we're here, we've got plenty of time, we'll just wait until you say what you want to say, is that all right Emma?'

'Yes.'

The small group remained still and silent, then Emma said, 'You will believe me, won't you?'

'Of course, we will believe you.' Carol said.

'What will happen to this person?'

'What person?'

'The person who assaulted me, do you want to know who it is?'

Carol said, 'All I want you to do Emma is to tell me what you want to tell me, in any way you want to tell it.'

'What will happen to the person?'

'They will be held accountable.'

'What does that mean, 'accountable'?'

'The woman answered, 'It means that there will be some questions asked and there will have to be some answers provided.'

'What kind of questions, what kind of answers?' Asked Emma

'Questions and answers that will find out the truth.'

'I don't know.'

'As I said Emma, it is all up to you, you just say whatever makes you feel best.'

'I want to tell.'

'Emma if somebody has hurt you they may hurt somebody else.'

Emma paused and bit her bottom lip again.

Carol said, 'Emma, if I ask you short questions and you give me short answers will that help you to speak about it.'

Emma nodded in agreement.

'When did this sexploitation take place?'

'It was two years ago, when I had the sleepover.'

'Where was this sleepover Emma.'

'It was in Chorlton-cum-Hardy.'

'Who was at Chorlton-cum Hardy?'

'It was when I went to stay at Bethan Trefor's, foster home.'

'Bethan Trefor.'

'Yes, Bethan Trefor.'

'What happened at Bethan's?'

'It wasn't at Bethan's

'But you just said it was, Emma.'

'No, I didn't Carol, I didn't say that, you're not listening to me, I said it was when I was at Bethan's not that it happened at Bethan's.'

'All right Emma, I am sorry, we are listening to you, but it's very important that everything we say here is absolutely correct. Where did this assault take place?'

'It was inside a car.'

'Do you know who this car belonged too?'

'Yes.'

'Emma, were you in this car?'

'Yes.'

'What were you doing in the car in the first place?'

'I had been staying at Bethan's foster carers, they are called Gerry and Martin Kinder. I stayed overnight twice, it was all agreed and official and all logged. After the first sleepover, we all had breakfast together, Bethan, the carers and me, then we all came back to Acorns in the car, nothing happened that time, but after the second sleepover, there was just me and Martin Kinder in the car, the mum didn't come this time and neither did Bethan. He stopped the car before we got to Acorns and that's when he assaulted me.'

'What about Bethan and the foster mum didn't either of them come with you in the car?'

'No, I've just said, the first time both the foster carers and Bethan were there and nothing happened, but the second time, there was just me and him.'

'Didn't you think about getting in the car with him on your own?'

'No, why should I? I didn't think about it at all, he was Bethan's foster dad and he was a head teacher, I wanted to go and live with them, I trusted him, it never even crossed my mind, he just stopped the car and made me do things.'

She stopped speaking.

Carol said, 'Emma what sort of things?'

'I don't like to say.'

'Emma, it's all right, you can tell us, you're safe, what sort of things?'

'You know, sexual things.'

'What sort of sexual things?'

'Touching and stuff, things that I didn't want to do. I don't want to explain them in detail, not just yet anyway. I'll tell you later Carol, when we are on our own. I don't like to talk about in front of Max.'

'Did you say anything to anybody, after the incident, did you tell anybody?'

'No, I've not told anybody until now.'

'Not anybody.'

'Nobody.'

'Why Emma, why did you not say anything at the time?'

'I don't know Carol and it's no use asking me because I just don't know.'

'Emma, we need to be absolutely sure who we are talking about here, who is this person.'

'I've told you.'

'I know you have Emma but we need you to say his name.'

'I don't like to, it upsets me.'

'We really need you to say it Emma.'

'I'll get in trouble.'

'No, you won't Emma, you have done nothing to get in trouble for. I promise you.'

'It was Bethan's foster dad, Martin Kinder, that's who, it was Martin Kinder!'

'Are you absolutely sure Emma?'

'I am, I am absolutely sure.'

Max said, 'We need to write something down now.'

'Will Martin Kinder get into trouble, Max?'

'That's not really for me to say.'

'Will I have to speak to the Police? I don't want to speak to the Police.'

'You won't have to speak to anybody you don't want to.'

'Will I have to speak to Martin Kinder?'

'No, Emma you won't have to speak to Martin Kinder.'

'Is this the end of it then?'

'No, I can't say that, but you have told the truth Emma, that's all you can do. You've done the right thing and Max and I are here to protect you and that's what we'll do.'

Chapter 10

The Stonemasons Arms

As he walked through the revolving doors of the Stonemasons Arms, he saw her. She was seated on a stool at the corner of the bar. Probably in her early sixties, she was tall for her generation, with blond hair, cropped short. Even though she was sitting, he could see she had a full figure. She was wearing a red blouse and a dark pair of trousers. He observed she wore dangly gold earrings. He also noticed that she had unusually large hands, with long fingernails expertly painted bright red and her fingers were heavily adorned with several expensive looking rings. She got up from the stool and positioned herself behind the bar. He could tell from her demeanour that she was without reservation, completely in her comfort zone. She turned towards Senetti and fixed him with cloudy blue eyes.

'Good afternoon sir, what can I get you now?'

'Pint of local beer please.'

Even in that brief verbal interchange and because of it, Senetti could tell that she was unmistakably from Northern Ireland. He also considered that for some odd reason he seemed to be having an Irish day with reference to Jason Dunphy, Coleen Fedeczko and now Ava Ellen Gardner. He thought of his mother who is a

County Mayo woman, Margaret Higgins and he made a mental note to visit her soon.

'Stranger here aren't you, I know most who come in here and I've not seen you in here before, am I right?'

'You are, yes you are.'

'What brings you in here on a Wednesday afternoon?'

'Oh, you know just stuff and nonsense.'

She registered his reticence.

'Stuff and nonsense, secret, then is it? If it's a secret, I won't push you, I don't want to know anybody's secrets. There are enough secrets coming across this bar and most of them do little to improve the life of either the teller or the listener.'

'Sounds like texting.'

'Texting?'

'Oh, it's not important, it's just something I was thinking about earlier.'

Senetti pondered on the word 'secret.' He thought of that old-fashioned cliché, what was it, oh yes, 'There's only one thing that can't be sold and that's a secret. Unless of course you are a spy.'

'No, it isn't a secret I'm over here invest...his word trailed off, he paused then resumed. 'I'm over here re-examining the death of Councillor Jason Dunphy, do you know about it?'

'Are you Police?'

'No, Children's Commissioner's Office.'

'Children's Commissioner's Office, I don't think I've heard of them. They sound like they are in London.'

'I agree it is a bit of a mouthful. If it makes it easier to understand, I'm a local councillor.'

'What's your name, have you got any I.D?'

Senetti handed her his councillor badge which up until her request, had been hung around his neck fixed to a black ribbon lanyard.

She scrutinised it and handed it back to him

'Councillor Danny Senetti, pleased to meet you, I'm Ava, Ava Gardner.'

'Is that really your name, was your mum a film fan?'

'She was, yes, but in those days, I was Ava Nevin. Later, I made the mistake of marrying Billy Gardner and that's how I got the full name. After five years of marriage, I had two children both named Gardner and I wanted to keep the same name as my children, so here I am, Ava Gardner.'

'What happened to Billy?'

'Oh him, that was a bad decision of mine. He once accused me of having no regard for his two hobbies. When I asked him what hobbies he was referring to, without a flicker he said, 'boozing and womanizing.' Easter Tuesday, 1987, we'd only been here a month, he went to the bank to deposit the Easter takings. Thirty years later we haven't seen him or the takings. It's a long story Councillor, not a very interesting one and you haven't got time. As for knowing about Jason Dunphy, of course I do. The whole community knows about it, the whole town knows about it. It happened a few hundred yards from where we're standing. Had a terrible effect on this pub, no much more than just this pub, it was for miles around, lasted for months. Still not completely gone away. You think that it has and then you are reminded of it, your presence here now is evidence of that.'

'Yes, I see what you mean.'

He gave his best smile. She warmed to what she thought was his casual candour.

'Do you know much about the actual incident?'

'Only the same as everybody else knows, and what we subsequently read in the newspapers. Councillor Jason Dunphy, was well known around here and well liked as well. He did a lot for people around here. He was in my pub, this pub, standing right where you are. He'd been drinking since early evening. It was Saint Patrick's Day: all the local Irish community were in here. It's their day, they work hard all year they are entitled to a day, to a drink, a bit of relaxation, wouldn't you say?'

'Oh, I would, most definitely.'

'Councillor Dunphy left about 9:35 to catch his tram home, nobody expected what happened after that, he fell onto the tramline and was hit by a through train.'

'Did anybody in the pub have anything to add or alter?'

'As I said Jason was well known in here, and he's caught that tram on numerous occasions after a session and he's never come to any harm before, he was a capable drunk. but I suppose that there is always a first time, or a last time as the case turned out, did you say add or alter?'

'Look Ava, this is a pub, I know pubs, you know pubs, they will have been talking about something like this for months, embellishing upon it, subtracting from it, changing it, giving opinions on it. Did anybody have any credible or even incredible alterations that you heard about?'

'Not credible ones no. Unless you include Magoo.'

'Magoo?'

'He was one of my regulars. He was in here, on the night in question, but it got too crowded and noisy for him, and he'd had a lot to drink, he always had a lot to drink, so he went home, about ten minutes before the councillor left.'

'Senetti made a motion to interject but Ava raised her open right hand and said, 'Danny, I'm only at the comma, I've not yet reached the full stop.'

This gesture coerced Senetti into silence whereupon she resumed.

'Did you see the little run of terraced houses as you came into the pub? There's five of them, on the other side of the road, opposite the entrance to the tram station.'

'Yes, I half noticed them, I think so.'

'Magoo lives in one of those houses, the end one, the one nearest the pub and furthest from the Failsworth platform. His house overlooks the entrance to the station platform on this side of the bridge, it's the only one that does.'

'And he saw The Councillor walking to the platform?'

'No, he didn't see the Councillor at all.'

'What then?'

'He was standing outside on his front step smoking, he always has a cigarette before he goes to bed and his wife won't let him smoke in the house. It was 9:46 pm, Magoo has this thing about time and if he says it was 9:46 then you can rest assured it was. It is only a two or three-minute walk from this pub to the station plat-form, five at the most, if you've had a drink. By 9:46 Councillor Dunphy would have been on the platform.'

'Ava, is any of this relevant?'

'Danny if you are going to be a good detective you need to develop a little less boldness and a little more patience Trust me, I watch all the best detective shows on the television.'

Senetti gave an almost imperceptible nod.

Ava continued, 'As Magoo looked out into the night he claimed that he saw two men get in the lift.'

'Did Magoo give a description of these men? Did he say what they were doing?'

'The only thing he said, was that he thought they were black, apart from that, he didn't have any kind of description. As for what they were doing, according to Magoo, they weren't doing anything. They were just entering the lift to the platform. You asked for any alterations, you said credible or incredible and Magoo's is the only one I know about.'

'Did Magoo mention this to the Police?'

'He did, the two detectives who interviewed him came in here after, they bought a drink and sat down over there, I could hear what they were saying about Magoo's sighting. They weren't too impressed and they were basically saying, two men entering the lift, in a metro station, so what? But more than that, they didn't believe Magoo's sighting. They didn't think he was lying or anything like that. One of them said that he probably imagined it and the other one said that he seemed half crazy when he was sober, so god forbid when he was drunk. They said that he was not a credible witness, he could offer virtually no description of either man, by his own admission he was half drunk at the time, visibility on the night was bad, in addition to which, where were these men, emergency services were on the scene in minutes and both men had just disappeared and there is of course the obvious issue about Magoo.'

'The obvious issue, what's that?'

'Why do you think we called him Magoo?'

'Because that's his name.'

'Well in a sense you're right, it is, or at least it has become his name. I've just realised, most people probably don't know his real name, which is Bartholomew Topp. He's been coming in here since I've been here, everybody calls him Magoo and he answers to it. It's not used in a disrespectful way, if anything it's a term of endearment.'

'Ava, if his name is Benjamin Topp then why do they call him Magoo?'

'The reason we call him Magoo, is because he's half-blind and he looks like the cartoon character of that name. He's got a round face, a rubbery nose, a bald head and he wears glasses with lenses as thick as goldfish bowls. Obviously, the detectives had registered all this, when they interviewed him.'

'So, we have a possible sighting, with no description, on a night of poor visibility, in the dark, from a half- drunk half- blind witness'

'That's about the strength of it, yes.'

'Nevertheless interesting, where can I find Mr Magoo, I'd like to talk to him?'

'Right now, he's in Philip's Park.'

'That's very precise.'

'It is, because earlier this year, about a year after Councillor Dunphy's accident, Magoo went home after an afternoon and evening session in here, had his usual cigarette on the step, sat in his armchair and just died. His wife found him cold at two-o- clock in the morning.

142

Natural causes, I've never really understood what that means, I thought we all died of them. So, since then he's been in Philip's Park Cemetery. However, in those intervening months between the incident with Jason Dunphy and his own passing away, he drove everybody mad in here with what he called the mystery of his sighting.'

'The mystery, what mystery was that, what is so mysterious about two men getting into a lift at a tram station platform?'

'Mystery was his word not mine, but the way Magoo saw it, was different. He used to say, nobody passes through a tram station. If you go to a tram station it is for a purpose. It could be to catch a tram itself, or meet somebody who is getting off one, or see somebody onto one but whatever it is, it's purposeful.'

'Sounds like a reasonable assumption.'

'Magoo did some amateur detective stuff on the tram times and on what happened in those minutes between his sighting of the men and the arrival of the Emergency Services.'

'Did he come up with anything?'

'He was like a child with a cake, he wouldn't let go, and he just kept talking about it. His main point was - where did these men go? Because by the time the whole thing blew up and the Emergency Services arrived, they had both disappeared without trace!'

'Perhaps they caught an earlier tram or changed their minds and left the station altogether.'

'Not according to Magoo. He checked all that, there wasn't an earlier tram. The next one due was the one Jason Dunphy was waiting to catch which was scheduled at 9:58 pm. The through tram was expected before that at 9:53 pm, but it stopped at Failsworth, because of the accident with Jason. The accident disrupted the whole network and the next tram along with many others that night was cancelled. According to Magoo, his mystery men were on the platform at the same time as Jason Dunphy and if they had left the station between those times they would have either had to come down the steps or come down in the same lift that Magoo saw them go up in. In which case, Magoo was still on his doorstep smoking and he would have seen them. Magoo also reckoned that the mystery men must have been on the platform when the accident happened. So why didn't they raise the alarm or do something instead of just disappearing.'

'Maybe they left by the other exit, on the Victoria platform, could Magoo see the other exit from his house?'

'No, he couldn't, the rail bridge is in the way and it blocks your view. That's what Magoo thought they did, leave by the other exit. He said that was the only other possible explanation.'

'To leave by the other exit though, first you would have to get to it and the only way you could do that would be to walk across the tracks, and why would you do that, what possible reason could you have for doing that?'

'That's what Magoo used to say.'

'What did you think Ava?'

'Well on the one hand it was Magoo, most of the time he was half-drunk, half-blind and I won't say half-crazy, that's unfair and untrue, but he was certainly a little eccentric.'

'And on the other hand?'

'As Magoo was fond of saying, that was a very event packed few minutes. In that short time, Councillor Dunphy walked up to the platform, the two men entered the lift, the councillor fell on the tracks and was hit by a train, then everybody else arrived, Police, Ambulance, Fire Brigade. In the meantime, two men, not one but two, disappeared. As Magoo used to say, how could these men avoid seeing the accident? They must have been on the station platform at the same time as Jason Dunphy. Yet, neither of them was anywhere to be seen after it. Again, as Magoo used to say, if you'd just witnessed an accident like that, would you just walk off into the night? Even if you did and you had a genuine reason for doing so, even though I can't think what a genuine reason would look like. The police put out an appeal for witnesses; local radio, newspapers, but none came forward. Although Magoo developed another wild theory as the months went by, only he didn't openly speak about this, but he told me one night when he was in his cups.'

'Are you going to share it with me Ava?'

'I will, but you have to understand Danny, it isn't my theory, it's Magoo's.'

'I understand that, Ava'

'All right this was Magoo's theory. These men weren't there by accident but they didn't figure on anybody being out on a night like that. They also knew that the Councillor would be on that platform on that day at that time and he would be alone. Just as they were getting into the lift, Magoo reckons that one of them momentarily looked over at him and realised he'd been seen. They obviously didn't know that Magoo was bat-blind but they weren't taking any chances on somebody being able to recognise them later or in giving a description about anything. So that's why they crossed the platform and came down in the other lift. They didn't so much leave the scene as flee it.'

'Why would two people who were going to catch a tram be concerned about being recognised?'

'That's just it though, isn't it?'

'What's just it though, isn't it?'

'Those two guys were not just going to catch a tram.'

'What were they doing then? What other reason would you go to a tram station for? I suppose as we said earlier you could be meeting somebody who was actually getting off the tram.'

'No, they weren't doing either of those things.'

'What were they doing?'

'As I said Danny, this is Magoo's theory, it isn't mine, I'm not saying he's right and I'm not saying he's wrong.'

She paused momentarily and Senetti waited patiently.

'They were following Jason Dunphy.'

'Following him where, home?'

'No, not home.'

'Where then?'

'To the station platform.'

'Why were they doing that?

'So, they could push him onto the tracks as the through train arrived.'

'What you mean deliberately, as in a murderous act? Why would anybody want to do that?'

'That's where Magoo's theory comes to a halt. I can honestly say, that I've got absolutely no idea.'

'What did Magoo say?'

'He had absolutely no idea either. But just because neither Magoo nor myself have absolutely no idea why anybody would want to do such a thing, that doesn't mean it's impossible does it.'

'No, it doesn't Ava.'

Senetti looked pensive, 'Just refresh my memory, I don't want to get this wrong, I have been in Jason Dunphy's company on more than one occasion but sometimes your memory plays tricks on you. How would you describe his physical build?'

'He was short and slight about six inches shorter than you. He could certainly drink, we didn't know where he used to put it. Despite his drinking though he probably weighed no more than ten stone with his clothes on. I see quite a few people like that in here, they drink for England but they don't put an ounce on. They say it is all to do with personal metabolism and family genetics.'

Senetti nodded three times slowly

'There is one other thing that you can chuck in the pot Danny and this is not from Magoo or anybody else, this is from me.'

'Go on.'

'I've been in this business over thirty years and in that time, I've seen a lot of drinkers and a lot of drunks. Drinkers come in all shapes and sizes but there are only two types of drunks. Phil, God bless him! My second partner after Billy Gardner, used to define them as amateur drunks and professional drunks.'

'Interesting, what's the difference?'

'Amateur drunks are the sort of people who usually drink occasionally. You see them out at Christmas, New Year's Eve, birthdays, major sports events, Friday nights, those sorts of occasions. They seem to have an objective, which is to get as drunk as possible as quickly as possible. They can take the amount but they can't take the effect. Their mood changes, as they get drunker, they start off being pleasant, agreeable, seemingly having a pleasant time, then gradually they become disagreeable, they squabble, swear, argue, sometimes even fight, they are the sort of people who you often speak to about their behaviour, they often force themselves into other people's company, people who don't want them. Extremely, you must throw them out, then when you do, they fall down in the street and you concern yourself with how they are going to get home.'

'And Professionals?'

'They are the opposite, they drink regularly, they wouldn't be in a pub on New Year's Eve. It's one of the few nights in the year that they deliberately don't go out. They consider nights like that to be amateur's night out. They understand the effects of drink, they are sociable and agreeable, they don't squabble, and they would never fight. You would rarely have to speak to them about their conduct, let alone throw them out. They are self-respecting. Oh, don't get me wrong, they are as drunk as the rest of us, they couldn't drive their car, well they wouldn't even try, whereas some amateurs would. Professionals are under the influence but they've not abandoned all control, when they've reached their limit, they know instinctively and they go home quietly.

They might totter a little on the way, but they would never fall in the street or for that matter anywhere else. When it comes to getting home, a sixth sense kicks in and they always make it safely.'

'What was Magoo?

'Oh, a professional most definitely.'

Senetti paused, he looked into Ava's eyes and she looked into his. Before he'd said it, he knew that he was going to deliver this question and so did she. She also knew the answer she was going to give and so did he.

'What about Jason Dunphy, Ava, was he an amateur or a professional?'

'Jason Dunphy, Danny, when it came to drinking was about as professional as they come.'

He didn't know why it should, but her comment chilled him and not for the first time in this investigation, he considered that he was dealing with something more than a trio of unusual incidents.

As he travelled back to Winton Kiss that evening, Senetti pondered. He reflected upon the events of the day. He thought about Jason Dunphy, he thought about Failsworth Station, he thought about Ava Gardner, the landlady at The Stonemasons Arms, he also thought about Bartholomew Topp. Not just about Bartholomew's mystery sighting, but also about him dying in his sleep. If Magoo's sighting wasn't a mirage and Senetti thought that the odds on that, were probably a 50/50 split, then what deduction could be made from that? Surely as Ava had suggested, they were the dogmatic beliefs of an eccentric drunk- or were they?

There was something else that kept flashing across Senetti's mind. He thought most of all about Ava's comments in relation to amateur and professional drunks and he wholeheartedly concurred with them.

As Senetti alighted his train at Winton Kiss, it was mid-evening and the brightness of the day was just about starting to ebb. He walked out of the station grounds, turned left and began the short walk down the hill to The Black Swan.

Chapter 11

Strategy Meeting.

Half-an-hour after she had made the allegation against Martin Kinder, Emma Luckhurst, lay on her bed in the Acorns Residential Unit and contemplated the interview that had just taken place between her and the two Social Workers, Max and Carol. She wasn't contemplating about her actions and their possible consequences. She thought she knew, but she couldn't be sure what those consequences would be, but she knew that there would be consequences. Emma's contemplation was more about self-assurance. She wanted to reassure herself that she had made the allegation as convincingly as she could. All in all, she concluded that she had.

She now felt that she no longer hated Bethan, she had gone past that. She didn't hate any of the other Trefor siblings and she certainly didn't hate Martin Kinder, but there were always casualties in these situations and he just happened to be in that place, at that time.

She knew that Safeguarding Children operations were all about procedures and protocols. There were manuals and guidebooks for everything. When something goes awry, the question which is often asked, is not 'could it have been prevented?' It is the question, 'have we followed procedure?' Because of *following procedures* and ensuring that every methodical letter *i* and *t* is dotted and crossed, Social Services professionals often operate at a grindingly slow pace. If you become involved with the bureaucracy of it all and you need a permission, authorisation, deviation or change of any kind, your experience will undoubtedly be that a long wait is required before a decision about your request returns to you. It often seems to the outsider that the simplest request, one which could be managed by the most junior individual, requires the most elaborate procedural authorisation by a mass of people who make up the chain of command. Such requests often require several authorisations and can take months to complete as they hop from desk to desk in search of a result which sometimes ends in oblivion. There is one exception to this circuitous, snail like, procedural tip-tap. When this exception occurs, Social Workers mobilise along a line that can go anywhere from swift action to blind panic. This exception is when an allegation is made concerning the sexual abuse of a child.

Under normal circumstances it would have been impossible to convene such a meeting within weeks, let alone days, but in less than two hours after Emma had finished making her disclosure, Max Edwards had achieved this almost impossibility and had convened an Emergency Child Protection Strategy Meeting. In attendance at this meeting as well as Max Edwards and Carol Tipley, were six other people: Mary Glynn, Jay Chopra, Clodagh Byrne, Yasmin Smith, Will Cunliffe and Laura Tobias. The first five were all qualified Social

Workers with varying degrees of experience and disciplines, Laura was there to record the minutes of the meeting.

Jay Chopra as chairperson opened the proceedings.

'We are here to consider a very serious allegation made by one of our looked after children, against one of our registered foster carers. Can I just remind everybody that although I am sure it will enter our discussions, this meeting has not been convened so that we can judge the validity or otherwise of the allegation. For one thing, we don't know enough about it, since we only have one version of events and for another, the voracity of the allegation will be the subject of another panel which will convene later when all facts and views have been established.'

Yasmin Smith, who was a newly qualified social worker asked, 'Why are we here then Jay?'

'Good question Yasmin, we're here to establish the situation in relation to any children whose safeguarding could be effected in any way by this allegation. If there are any such children then we need to have a plan and strategy for their care and protection. When I say children, I don't just mean looked after children, I mean all children, it could even be the foster carer's own children.'

He looked around the room.

Clodagh Byrne spoke, she was a seasoned Social Worker in her early fifties and for the last seven years she had managed the Family Placement Team for the City Council. The main responsibility of this team was to establish a pool of foster carers who would provide homes for looked after children,

'Jay is right of course to remind us of our responsibilities but the foster carers referred to here, no longer have any dependent children, therefore this is not an issue. The only consideration here, are the six looked after children. The five currently being looked after by the foster carer in addition to the child who has made the allegation.'

Jay spoke again.

'Has everybody read the brief statement taken from Emma L and produced by Carol and Max?'

Jay's question remained unanswered and as such was resolved in the affirmative.

'That statement in due course and as a matter of procedure will be passed on to the Police. The foster carers involved are Gerry and Martin Kinder. It is Gerry Kinder who holds the registration but she has not been referenced in any way in this allegation. As you all know, Clodagh Byrne is the Family Placement Officer for Gerry and Martin Kinder and Clodagh is going to give us some background on these carers.'

Clodagh said, 'I've prepared a small written synopsis.' She passed a single sheet of handwritten paper to each member. 'It's easy to follow but I'll take you through it anyway.'

Members looked at her "synopsis," as she continued.

'Geraldine and Martin Kinder, both retired now, were both long- term Teachers, Martin was actually a head teacher, both currently in their mid-fifties. Started fostering about five years ago. For the first couple of years they only took in short term placements, six months at the most. They've built a very good record and are particularly successful at rehabilitation and working with estrangement. They're fit, intelligent, eloquent and honest. You'll see listed, the courses that they've attended and graduated from. In short, they are easily in the upper echelon of our register of local authority foster carers. About two years ago after another successful placement, we placed Bethan Trefor with them. Bethan is the eldest of a five-sibling family, all of school age, all looked after children from birth, but by different authorities within the City Region. Three of the children have different surnames, taken from their respective biological fathers.

She paused and looked around the room for comments. There were none, so she continued.

'This will not be a new story to anybody in this room but Bethan has been around our system from birth. Over the years she has lived in a variety of foster homes and attended a variety of schools. There is one exception which has no relevance to the case but apart from that, all Bethan's placements ended in disruption. Eventually she established herself for three years in Acorns Residential Unit. Even though she was, as I say, established and settled there, the environment and its influences were not thought to be the best for her potential. Bethan managed the situation very well for one so young, but we all knew that the unit environment was just enough to prevent her being as successful, as we all knew she could be. It was just that for many years we had nowhere else suitable for her to go to. Her Social Worker, Rosemary Rowntree knew about the Kinders from a previous placement, she thought that Bethan would flourish there and she moved heaven and earth to place Bethan with them. So, we placed her with them, it must be said with some trepidation, at first, but the placement has exceeded all expectations. Bethan was always bright but she was troubled and distracted in the Unit and it took away some of her focus.'

'I know Bethan,' Mary Glynn, interrupted, I agree with what you're saying.'

'Then Mary, you will know how troubled she was, the Kinders have completely turned her around. Bethan always had the ability, that was never in any doubt but they seem to have crystalized it. She took her GCSEs last year, ten straight As, it's an absolute school record. She is taking her A Levels this year, top grades are expected and a place at Oxbridge is being mentioned. The Chief Executive of the City Council is involved here too. Bethan has now come to the minister's attention and is being held aloft as a shining example of what government can achieve for a Looked after Child. So, whatever we do here will be scrutinised at the highest level.'

'Yes, everybody has heard about Bethan Trefor, the whole safeguarding world will have its eyes upon us, whatever we do,' said Mary.'

Clodagh resumed, 'Last year the Kinders took Lowri in, Lowri is Bethan's young sister by eight years. Then over a period of several months and it must be said here against all advice from family placement, they accommodated the rest of the family. So, at the time of writing, living in household Kinder are all the Trefor siblings: Bethan aged seventeen; Dylan who is sixteen, Glenys, fourteen, Gethin twelve and Lowri nine. All very settled, all together as a family and all doing very well individually. There has been no previous allegations or even mild criticisms from any quarter, about the Kinders, the opposite is true and if we had a league table for foster carers, which thankfully we don't, at least not yet, although we've got one for everything else, then the Kinders would be seated squarely on top of it. If you want my opinion, I know Emma L, she's a damaged young woman and I also know Martin Kinder, he is of the utmost respectability, and I just can't see him doing anything like this. On the balance of probability, and in my opinion, Emma is making this up.'

'Why would she do that?' Max said.

'I don't know the answer to that Max, but you know as well as I do, that we get more complaints and allegations as each year goes by. We are in a complaint culture these days. You also know that many of these allegations that come through here are false, they are quite simply made up, for a variety of reasons, malice, histrionics, attention seeking, boredom, you name it. Sometimes, they even do it for a laugh, they just don't realise the gravity of such a course of action.'

Max said, 'You know yourself Clodagh that child abuse transcends all barriers of apparent respectability. Speaking of league tables which you were, all of us in this room know that if we had a league for sexual abuse then respectability would be seated squarely at the top of it. This is not about opinions, we all have them and they are all useless in these situations, balance of probability doesn't come into it here, following that formula only gets you deregistered. These situations are about what we can and can't do, in line with the protocols that we have at our disposal.'

Jay Chopra spoke again.

'Clodagh, even though you might be right, and I also know Emma, and she can make things up, so you might be, but we don't know that for sure and currently we've got five young children, two of them teen-age girls under the care and protection of a man who has been accused of a serious sexual allegation against another teen-age girl. We are not a court of law, we are a safeguarding panel. The accusation is enough here. Our foster carers aren't presumed innocent until proven guilty. Until we know different they are presumed guilty, just in case they are. What if you are wrong, what if Emma is telling the truth? What happens if Martin Kinder does something like this again. What do we say then, we backed our professional judgement based on our opinion and our view of the balance of probability? They won't accept that will they? We all know where the blame comes to rest in these situations, it's always the same place, the Authorities, the people who are paid to protect. In this instance, the Social Workers. We're the scapegoats here. This is the type of situation, where if it goes the wrong way, people lose their jobs. We, are the people, I'm talking about, we are the ones that get booted out for unprofessional conduct, negligence or whatever they're calling it these days, and once you're out for something like this this, you don't come back again, we all know that. It's even worse now the way things are going, politicians are going to put us in gaol. Can you believe it, they are going to gaol us for doing our jobs? Whatever the offence they are going to hold us responsible, not the perpetrator, not the victim, the Social Worker.'

'What are you suggesting we do then Jay?' said Clodagh.'

'I don't know what we do, I honestly don't have a clear view just yet, I don't know if this allegation can be substantiated or not, it might be true, it might be false, I wasn't there at the time, I wasn't in that car and nobody else in this room was either, so we just don't know. The only people who know what really happened, if anything did, are Martin Kinder and Emma L. We know what Emma is saying, we haven't even asked Martin yet, what if he admits it? Whether he does or whether he doesn't, it doesn't matter to us, that's a matter for others. There are six children, let's not forget Emma, involved here and two adults and our responsibility is primarily to the children. All I know now is one thing, that as chair of this panel my fingerprints are all over whatever happens here today, that is immovable. There is no possibility under these circumstances where I will support a decision that leaves five children in a house under the protection and care of an alleged perpetrator of sexual abuse, for more than one minute than they need to be there. No matter how good and respectable a foster carer he is seen to be.'

He paused, then turning towards Laura Tobias he said, 'And I would like what I've just said, exactly as I've said it, clearly recorded against my name in the minutes please.'

'What if we looked at them separately,' asked Carol.

'What, as six separate cases?'

'We will have to do that anyway, but I was thinking more of immediately. I was thinking more of Bethan as one case and the four siblings as another and Emma as another, and anyway as far as Emma is concerned, she is in the unit, she is safe, she has no contact with the Kinders, so we can take her out of the picture for this meeting, can't we, can we at least agree on that?'

Jay said, 'Yes I think we can support that, do you all agree? Let me put it another way, if anybody does not agree, speak now.'

They all nodded in silent agreement.

Carol turned towards Clodagh Byrne, she said;

'If we just leave Bethan where she is for the moment at least until we've spoken with Rosemary Rowntree, her Social Worker, then she can advise us. That leaves four children, what are the chances of finding a good foster placement in the next day or two for four siblings to stay together? By the way where is Rosemary, as the Social Worker for the family shouldn't she be here?'

Clodagh laughed, it seemed almost hysterically. 'Carol you've not got a hope in hell in the next year or two never mind day or two. We just don't own that variety and number of placements. Rosemary incidentally, is in Crown Court as we speak, I'll be meeting her later at some point.'

'What placements have we got then?'

'None of these are definite but I can possibly place Glenys and Lowri in a foster home together on a short-term basis but it is right across the other side of the city to where they are now. It would mean that they would either have a long journey to school or they would have to change school altogether to a nearer one. Also, the foster carers I have in mind are going to Jamaica for two months. It's all been arranged and agreed, so the children would have to be moved again at least until they return.'

'We're not dealing with children here, we're dealing with parcels,' said Yasmin.

Clodagh ignored the comment from the newly qualified Social Worker and continued.

'The two boys, Gethin maybe, in a different placement altogether on his own. I'll have to make some phone calls, again it would be short term. Dylan, six-teen-year-old boy, no chance. I don't have one single vacancy across the whole city for a sixteen-year-old boy. So, I'm afraid that he is back in Residential, for the foreseeable.'

'What, in Acorns?' asked Yasmin?

'No Yasmin, not in Acorns, Emma is in there, the situation is potentially too explosive. We'll have to place him in another Residential Unit, probably in another borough and at some astronomical cost, which no doubt the Director will constantly remind me of.'

'I thought that we had just done a massive recruit-ment drive in the city, for foster carers. How can we have just done that, yet we've got none?' asked Jay.

Clodagh said, 'We are always looking for foster carers, we are always doing recruitment drives, the insoluble problem is that we continually face a national shortage of good ones. Hardly anybody wants to do it in the first place and of those that are prepared to do it, only a few are acceptable. Then there is the registra-tion process, which can take anything up to twelve months. People lose interest, long before that. Of those who eventually obtain a registration very few will take teenage boys, teenage boys are just too difficult to manage. Foster carers just don't want some testoster-one, hormone charged, six foot plus young man charging around their house. I don't have one single foster carer across the whole city out of a fluctuating pool of four hundred who has a vacancy for a teen-age boy.'

Jay said, 'Clodagh, you've said that twice now. This is all very enlightening but we are going completely off the subject here. So, if I can just bring us back to it and Carol, before you became side-tracked with the endless and apparently insoluble problem of finding an optimum number of foster carers, was there a point that you were trying to pursue, before that?'

Carol said, 'Yes, there was.'

'Can we hear it?'

Carol responded, 'As far as the fate of the Kinders, they will have to go before the fostering panel to give their side of this allegation. Then, their registration and future as foster carers will be up to the Panel. That aspect of it, is completely out of our hands. Conflict of Interests will dictate that nobody on this Panel can sit on The Fostering Panel. We are all disqualified from doing so because we're on this Panel. So, any discussion about guilt or innocence is superfluous, agreed?'

There was common acknowledgement of this.

Carol said, 'As far as the children are concerned, Jay is right, we can't leave five kids with those foster carers in that potential situation. However, subject to discussion and agreement from Rosemary Rowntree and The Director, we can make the case and they can take the risk, we can find a way to leave Bethan in place. Providing of course she wants to be left there. We'll have to give her some information about the allegation, then she can make her own mind up. We can justify that through our protocols. She is older than the others and at a different level of responsibility. We have to find somewhere for the four youngest to go as a matter of urgency, like today or tomorrow at the latest and Bethan stays at least until after the fostering panel, by which time she will probably be eighteen anyway and she will be making her own decisions.'

'It might work,' said Jay, 'I don't see that we have a lot of choice here. Obviously, it will all have to be handled sensitively or it could come back to bite us in our sensitive areas. The family Social Worker will have to be at the forefront of it all. Is that agreed then?'

Almost in unison they all said, 'Agreed!'

Chapter 12

Hypothesis

Thursday came around and Danny Senetti and Alberta Curtis Brightland were in Alberta's newly allocated office which overlooked a small but well-tended garden within the grounds of Norford Town Hall.

Senetti said, 'How did you get this place?'

'Araminta telephoned me yesterday, she said that some office space had become available in The Town Hall and asked me if I was interested in taking it, simple as that really. So, I came here today and they just handed me the keys. Apparently, it's vacant for eleven weeks, previous tenant is in Australia on some council exchange scheme.'

'Is that how long you envisage us being on this case, eleven weeks, my heart sinks. What happened to your report about coincidence after twenty-four hours?'

She ignored his comment but responded with, 'Don't despair, I plan to be back in London, long before eleven weeks has gone by.'

'All the years I've been on the Council, I've never had so much as the offer of a share of a second-hand desk, even a chair, from anybody, let alone an office with a floor, walls and a ceiling and windows.'

'Well we can both use this place and we can both stand on the floor and we can both look out of the windows and there is more.'

'Don't tell me that they are going to put posh curtains up and paint the place a hint of blossom, or a hint of apricot or a hint of something. Why is it always a hint of, why is it never the actual colour but always a hint of it and why, when it is finished, does it always look like magnolia anyway?'

'No, decoration hasn't been mentioned, but they are going to give us a computer and bring in another desk and I can't promise but I think I can get you a whole chair which you can have exclusively for yourself.'

'I think that I've got used to working from my kitchen table or the nearest bar stool, I wouldn't know what to do with a whole town hall chair to myself.'

'Well, they will be here if you want them. How did you get on with Alma Alice Spain and Jason Dunphy?'

'They are both very interesting. I've looked at both cases, I've visited both scenes and I've spoken to some people, but do you mind if we try a little hypothesizing first.'

'No go ahead,' as she said this she sat down behind the desk while Senetti remained standing at the opposite end of the small room.

'Just tell me Alberta, have you ever hated anyone?'

'I don't know, it's a spontaneous question that deserves an unspontaneous answer.'

'Aren't all questions spontaneous?'

'Let's not start that again. I've just thought about your question. I don't think I've ever really hated anyone. Not real hatred, the nearest I ever got to it was Abigail Wilkins. I was the second prettiest girl in the class, and the second cleverest but she was the first at both. She beat me at everything she was always first.'

'But did you hate her?'

'I probably did at the time, yes.'

'Did you ever wish her dead?'

'Probably, in a school girl way.'

'Did you ever plan to kill her?'

'Are you serious?'

'In absolute earnest, yes.'

'No, of course not, look Danny, is this conversation going anywhere or is it just you trying to amuse yourself again.'

'I was thinking, what makes somebody deliberately and in a cold-blooded way, murder somebody else. Possibly somebody who they don't even know, possibly somebody who they've never even met?'

'I suppose that there are lots of different reasons, it all depends on the particular case.'

'We say that Alberta, and it would seem to be the intelligent and open view to hold, but is it true?

'What are you getting at?'

'Leaving aside, personal, practical gain?'

'Such as?' She interrupted.

'Such as you get to be with your lover after all, or you get all the insurance money or you inherit the throne, leaving those aside give me two reasons why people murder people.'

'Revenge, jealousy, hatred, insanity, a moment of madness!'

'Is that one, two, three or four reasons?'

'Five, I think'

'All right, Alberta let's have a look at them. I suppose a cold- blooded murderer, must have an element of insanity about him, but I would suggest that insanity is more a symptom of the murderer than a reason for the murder. Jealousy, again that element has been present in some murders but such murders have not always been cold-blooded and usually the murderer has had some involvement with the victim. It's what the French sometimes call a crime of passion. You were probably jealous of Abigail Wilkins and you also knew her, but you didn't plan to murder her.'

'Danny, where are we going with all this?'

'We're hypothesizing Alberta, that's what we are doing.'

'And where does your hypothesis take us?'

'Vengeance and hatred, can you have one without the other.'

'Yes, quite easily, you can hate somebody but do nothing more. As well as this you can be vengeful in a cold calculating way there doesn't actually have to be hatred involved.'

'Let's just look at vengeance for a minute Alberta, why would you be vengeful, I don't mean all the detail, but what must be present before revenge, the way I see it, it is almost a prerequisite of it.'

'Hurt, or pain, or are they one and the same thing, there is no revenge without hurt.'

'Hurt, it's not the word I was thinking of, it is a much better one, but you are right, if revenge is there, then usually hurt has made an appearance before it shows itself.'

'Danny, don't people who take revenge on others have to have known them first for the hurt to happen?'

'No, not at all Alberta, vengeance conquers all in these circumstances.'

'You seem surprisingly knowledgeable on criminal psychology for a local councillor. Is criminology some sort of hobby of yours.'

'No, I am a complete amateur. I was involved with a case a while back, which ostensibly started with a murder that same year, but the reason for that murder stretched back almost two hundred years. When the original hurt was done the present-day victim of the murder and the present-day murderer in this case, hadn't even been born. Everything was sourced in some hurt that was inflicted in an entirely different country in the 1840s.'

'I didn't know that you had been involved in the investigation of murder before, you didn't say anything about that to me.'

'Alberta, we've only known each other a few hours, I've hardly had the opportunity to say anything, about anything to you.'

'Have you investigated other murders? Have you had a lot of experience investigating murders?'

'Alberta, as you have just said, I'm a locally elected councillor, not a homicide detective, what do you think?'

'How did you get involved with the last one?'

'Somebody else involved me and I just got drawn into it gradually, then before I knew where I was, I was in it.'

'And in that case, you were on, the murderer, murdered somebody in the present day for something that happened two hundred years previous?'

'That's probably oversimplifying it a bit, but that's a good enough summary of it yes, that's what I said.'

'Has any of this got anything to do with any of our incidents?'

'I don't know, they may all turn out to be complete accidents. Anyway now, it's your turn, I've done all the hypothesizing up to now. I don't want to put ideas into your head.'

'All right, Danny, we've got two apparently unconnected and unusual deaths that have been the subject of a little investigation. They could be accidents, incidents, misadventures call them what you will. They could though quite easily be murders and as far as the scrutiny goes it was seemingly minimal, and if you weren't looking for anything suspicious then you would readily accept them as accidents. If you look for an accident then it is probably true to say that you will find one.'

'Then let's look at them differently, let's not look at them as accidents.'

'You mean let's look at them as murders.'

'There's only you and I here and as I said earlier we're only hypothesizing.'

'All right present the case, Councillor.'

'First, example one, the accident. Councillor Jason Dunphy, goes out St Patrick's night to a local pub, has too much to drink, that's not unheard of, an Irishman having one too many on St Patrick's night. He's waiting on the Metrolink platform to go home, it's dark, he's drunk, he passes out or stumbles, either or, straight into the path of a through tram, all very sad and tragic but very plausible.'

'Example two?' She queried.

'The same as has just been referred to, the only difference being, instead of falling onto the tracks he was pushed onto them by somebody else.'

'There is another possibility,' said Alberta.

'Suicide, I don't think so. No apparent reason, none that's found its way into the case. I made some calls and the feedback I've had is that suicide wasn't there.'

'So, you think its murder?'

'I think that it's murder before suicide, yes. As you may recall I've met Jason Dunphy on a couple of occasions. By all accounts a big drinker but despite that, he was only a little slip of a guy. About five feet and a bit and he probably weighed about ten stone, it wouldn't take much to push him onto the track'.

'Why don't you think like everybody else, that it was just an accident?'

'Who is everybody else?'

'The police, the coroner, anybody who has looked at it.'

'Your bosses at the children's commission obviously think something is not quite how it should be, otherwise you wouldn't be up here and we wouldn't be having this conversation.'

'Danny, they are looking at it from an entirely different perspective than murder or suicide.'

'Maybe they are Alberta, I don't know what their reasons are, you are the one who works for them not me, but the point is they are looking at it, aren't they, they are not just accepting these cases as they are said to have happened, are they?'

She gave a perfunctory nod.

'I've been to Failsworth Metrolink Station, it's a relatively new station, it's well-lit and its platforms are solid and with plenty of room. The one that Jason Dunphy was standing on was about ten feet wide. I can't think of any reason why he would want to be standing right at the platform edge. Why would anybody stand at a platform edge when they were waiting for a train, that's the last place you would stand, surely?'

'Why indeed but people do don't they, I've seen them do it, maybe because he was drunk.'

'That's another thing, Councillor Jason Dunphy by all accounts was a professional drunk'

'A professional drunk? I've never heard of that one before, you'll have to explain.'

'Gladly, there are professional drunks and amateur drunks. Amateurs don't drink regularly, they drink on their birthday or at Christmas or New Year's Eve or on holiday or worse when they've had a serious argument with somebody. They have no experience of the effect of drink and they basically don't know how to conduct themselves when they've had it. They are the ones who get thrown out of pubs, get into fights, fall into canals, get run over, and are unable to find their way home and so on.'

He was aware that he was reiterating, almost verbatim, what Ava Gardner had told him, but he carried on.

'Whereas professional drunks have experienced it all a thousand times. Sure, its effect slows them down, but they know exactly what they are doing because they've done it all before. As far as getting home is concerned, well that's the easiest bit, they just go on auto pilot. Jason Dunphy fell into the latter category, he had probably done that journey from the Stonemasons Arms to his own front door on countless occasions. He would know every sight, sound, smell, touch and taste of that journey and being drunk is no reason for him of all people to be stood at the edge of that station platform! If anything, it would have been a reason in his mind for him to stand further back. So, if he didn't fall and he didn't jump, that only leaves one other explanation.'

'That's quite a bit of criminal psychology Danny or should I say drunk's psychology. If what you are saying is right, then why would anybody want to do that to somebody else. Especially in our case, Councillor Jason Dunphy who never did anything but good?'

'That's a different question altogether, and as somebody said to me the other day in answer to the same question, I've got absolutely no idea. We'll have to look at that another time. Anyway, that's my hypothesis on Jason. Now we come to Alma Alice.'

'Are you suggesting that it's a similar situation for Alma Alice?'

'I'm not suggesting that Alberta, I know little about her, all I'm saying is that the police were not looking for foul play of any kind, whereas we might be.'

Senetti looked straight at Alberta.

'There is something else as well, but I don't know whether I'm making a forced connection.'

'What is it?'

'Do we know if Councillor Jason and Alma Alice knew each other, had they ever met, is it possible, is it likely?'

'Well, is it?'

'Everything is possible, yet I have no information to support this, but I'm working on it. In this instance and for the sake of my hypothesis it's also likely. She was a safeguarding social worker in Manchester and he was a councillor in Oldham. Both boroughs are next to each other. His speciality was safeguarding. He'd held the executive portfolio previously. Both those councils are autonomous councils but they are also part of the C.A.'

'The C.A. what's C.A?'

It's an anachronism, or is it abbreviation, I'm never quite sure what the difference is, do you know?'

'Danny!'

'Come on Alberta, you've heard of The Northern Powerhouse, *Devo Manc,* the devolution of power from Westminster to the Greater Manchester Authority? For the first time in a thousand years we won't have to doff our caps to our elders and betters, in London, before we clear the cotton dust from our throats. Or we won't have to ask permission if we want to take our kids on holiday for a fortnight's hop picking in Kent. It hasn't been out of the news for the last three years. Not up here anyway, but maybe that type of news doesn't reach the altitude of your ivory tower in Westminster.'

'I'm not actually in Westminster, anyway I do know about it yes.'

'C.A., it stands for the Combined Authority and oversimplified it is an organisation that has been set up to promote collaboration between ten local authorities in the North West of England and Manchester and Oldham are two of them.'

'Who are the other eight'?

'Alberta, don't make me recite them, not now, it's boring and it's irrelevant. However, what is not irrelevant, is that it's highly possible that Jason Dunphy and

Alma Alice Spain, knew each other, or at least had met, probably professionally.'

'I don't really understand the connection, even if they were sleeping partners, what is the implication?'

'I don't know myself but according to our information, she left her car at the office then walked a short distance, on a wintry night, to a remote address then gets herself run over, why?'

'What do you mean, why did she get herself run over?'

'No Alberta, I mean why did she walk that distance, why didn't she drive?'

'A million reasons, pick any one, she liked walking, she felt she needed the exercise, could be anything.'

'The way I see it, there could be some innocuous reason why she walked, you've just mentioned two of them. There could though be two others which are not furtive, no I wouldn't say that, but they do beg a question or two, I have just thought of them.'

'I am intrigued Danny, what are they?'

'The first is that she didn't want anybody to see her car parked up at Parkhurst Lane.'

'And the second?'

'This to me is perhaps the most likely. She was meeting somebody there and whoever she was meeting was arriving by car. Or it could be a combination of both. Yes, that's it, she didn't want anybody to recognise her car and the person she was meeting had one already and they were both going to use that.'

'Danny, she was a social worker not an undercover agent for an anti -terrorist agency.'

'Alberta, you don't have to be an undercover agent to be secretive. Anything that somebody doesn't want somebody else to know about can fall into the category of being clandestine and there are countless situations that are reconciled to such behaviour. So, no you don't have to be undercover, just, say for example, cheating on your partner would put you in that category. It may not even be about you. The secrecy could be about the person you're meeting.'

'She didn't have a partner.'

'We don't know that, she didn't have a husband anymore, but they are not the same thing. Anyway, I was only using that as an example.'

'What was the name of your local contact in Didsbury?'

'Jim Bigelow, Youth offending Team.'

'Was he able to shed any light on anything, did he tell you anything useful?'

'Useful?'

'I suppose useful is the wrong word. Anything that might give us a lead as to why Alma Alice might want to be apparently secretive about her car, that is of course if she was, but as you say we are just hypothesizing.'

'He didn't come up with much. All he seemed to know about her was that at one time she did online dating.'

'You hear some funny stories about people who meet online.'

'No, you don't Alberta, no more than anywhere else. You hear just as many funny stories about people who meet at a tea-dance or in the supermarket or in the library or at the bus stop. It's all a myth, like most myths it becomes perpetuated by the media. One out of five people, these days are in relationships that have started online. Are you in a relationship Alberta? Have you got a husband or a boyfriend?'

'Danny let us keep all our private lives out of this case. By the way how do you know this stuff, one out of five indeed?'

'I've told you before Alberta, because I'm a Councillor and I must attend these meetings and listen to this stuff. Most people would get up and leave the room but councillors can't do that and the people that present this stuff know this and they've got to have somebody listening to what they must say, so they just present and present for as long as they can get away with it.'

There was a lengthy pause as they both looked at each other. Alberta broke the silence. 'Where do we go from here?'

'I was just thinking the very same thing.'

'We could press on with Jason and Alma Alice.'

'You could take them Alberta, have another look, you might be able to come up with something, you know, a different pair of eyes.'

'No, I think you're coming up with an interesting hypothesis for both and I think you should stick with it.'

'Do I detect a slight wavering of enthusiasm for the case on your part?'

'No, it's just that I've not quite finished in London. It is taking longer than I thought and I'm going to have to go back down there, at least once maybe twice.'

'That's a bit disappointing, this whole investigation is turning into a full-time job, I wasn't planning on a full-time job when I agreed to help, I've already got one of those being a councillor. I haven't got the time to do two.'

'I understand, it hasn't gone unnoticed. I've thought of that and I've got you some help.'

'You've got *me* some help, Alberta, I thought that *I* was supposed to be the help. It's your case Alberta, not mine. Anyway, who is this help?'

'Be patient Danny, all will be revealed and very soon at that.'

He fished out Araminta's pink file from his brown satchel and studied it.

'I've been looking at this last one, Velma Vine, foster carer, another death on the tracks, in January last year. According to the file, she fell into the path of a freight train. This is becoming popular, at least it isn't another hit and run, they are the hardest to solve and they are becoming the hardest of crimes to investigate.'

'How do you know that Danny?'

'I think I read it somewhere.'

'Yes, but why is that, why should they be harder to investigate than any other crime?'

'What are most crimes solved by?'

'Detection I guess.'

'Detection sure, can you elaborate on detection?'

'Clues, evidence, witnesses.'

'As usual you are spot on, detection must have a bit of support, as you say in the shape of clues and evidence. Most crimes are solved by witnesses, recorded evidence or forensic science or at least one or two of them and all too often all these aspects are absent in a hit and run. There are no witnesses, especially if the spot is remote, no recorded evidence, usually because of that remoteness, as we don't put surveillance cameras where nobody goes and very little or no forensic evidence, because the weapon in the form of the car has been driven away, and there has been no direct contact between the victim and the perpetrator, so there is nothing left to examine, no clothing fibres, saliva specimens or the like. So, no witnesses, no cctv, no forensics, no weapon, where do you start?'

She seemed to him, to ignore what he had just said, in any case she made no response.

Just then there was a knock on the door. He strode over and opened it. Framed in the doorway was a young woman. She was dark-skinned, tall and trim, he thought her to be about thirty years of age.

She smiled and said, 'Hello I'm Lizzie Lambert and you are obviously Danny Senetti.' She held out her right hand in anticipation of a handshake, he obliged.

Alberta spoke from within the confines of the room, 'Welcome Lizzie, come in,'

The young woman stepped into the room. Senetti looked at her, he noticed how she seemed self-assured and confident. Alberta came from behind her desk. She and Lizzie hugged each other. Senetti pondered, why did everybody hug each other these days, they didn't used to do. Not so long ago, you just hugged your mother or your children or a close friend whom you'd not seen for a long time. Now complete strangers who had just met, hugged each other. It was taking over from the handshake as an opening or closing ritual and that's what it seemed to be to him, elaborate and ritualistic, almost fraudulent.

Alberta said, 'Let's do it formally. Lizzie Lambert meet Councillor Danny Senetti. Danny, Lizzie will be joining our team, she is the help we spoke about previously.'

'Welcome Lizzie,' said Senetti, 'We certainly need all the help we can get.'

Alberta thought about Senetti's reaction to the announcement. Most people would have been uncomfortable with the introduction of a third party in this way. They would have challenged Lizzie and asked her questions to establish her credentials. Senetti though didn't do that. It wasn't so much that he didn't do it, it was more that he *deliberately* didn't do it. It was more that he was conscious not to do it. Alberta thought that Danny Senetti didn't want to be seen doing what everybody else would do under those circumstances.

In that precise moment Alberta realised, she had grossly underestimated Danny Senetti. His 'hypothesizing' over the last hour had almost convinced her of that and now his reaction to Lizzie Lambert all but confirmed it. She had wanted a simple local leg man who she could despatch at her beck and call, an establishment figure who would give her investigation protocol and credibility on paper. Instead she had been given this renegade, this original thinker, who stepped outside the circle at will, his-will.

Senetti spoke, 'Lizzie, I take it you've had some sort of brief from Alberta, so I'll dispense with any introduction and you might as well come in at the deep end.'

Lizzie smiled, Senetti thought that she looked younger when she smiled. She had a perfect set of teeth which he decided were due more to the skills of an expensive dentist than to nature.

She said, 'I've had an initial brief yes and I've got some written information, she brandished Araminta's file, 'But that's about the extent of my knowledge.'

Senetti thought that she had a cut-glass accent, the kind of accent that some people came out of Oxbridge with, although they didn't necessarily have it when they went there originally.

'Don't concern yourself with that. If anything, it's a good thing. It means you won't clutter your mind with pre-conceived ideas. I wonder Lizzie, what are your initial thoughts on the case.'

Lizzie responded, 'I was looking at the incident concerning Velma Vine and I thought that I might visit the scene.'

It was Alberta's turn to speak, 'There's a coincidence, Danny and I were just discussing the case. That's a good idea Lizzie; so that you and Danny can get to know each other better as colleagues, why don't you both visit the scene together?'

Senetti looked again at his own file and he said, 'I notice that this incident took place at Trensis railway station.'

'Do you know Trensis station?' asked Lizzie.

Senetti replied, 'I do yes, it's not far from where I live. It's a remote station. The line runs between Manchester and Sheffield which is a busy line but few of those trains stop at Trensis. I know somebody who might be able to help us with this.'

'Who's that?' asked Alberta

'She's a police officer called Megan Rees Jenkins. I'll set up a meeting with her at Trensis Station. I'll try for Tuesday next week. It suits my diary what about you Lizzie?'

'I'd like to be at that meeting, yes Tuesday would be fine,' said Lizzie.

'All right, it makes sense,' replied Senetti.

'You gave me the distinct impression police officers weren't very high up on your respect list.'

'Like most occupations Alberta, it usually depends on the individual and not the body. Anyway, Megan is Transport Police and in the absence of any other kind of plan, she's the best idea, certainly the best I've got, so unless anybody has a better one, let's use her.'

'All right Danny, Lizzy, same process, we investigate the scene then we meet back here, when?'

'Sometime next week after Tuesday, when is it convenient for you, I am not sure of my own commitments next week, I'll be in touch, you're in London aren't you?'

'Yes, but I'm not sure when I'll be back or when I'm travelling back.'

Both Senetti and Lizzie nodded in approval. Senetti turned to Lizzie, 'Here's my card with contact details.' She reciprocated with her own.

'One more thing Alberta.'

'Yes?'

'As you are tripping down to London, what about a little investigation regarding Alma Alice Spain?'

Alberta looked puzzled, 'What do you mean 'our' Alma Alice Spain.'

This time it was Senetti's turn to look puzzled. 'Do we know of another?'

'No, of course we don't.'

'Kensington and Chelsea, that's in London, isn't it?'

'It is, why, what did you have in mind?'

'Do you remember I said that Jim Bigelow told me that Alma Alice was online dating?'

'I do yes.'

'Well, as they say, it's a bit of a long shot, but there is a woman called Jean Fortescue, she was a former colleague of Alma Alice's. Jim reckons that Jean and Alma were close. He told me that he overheard them talking about Alma's online dating. Apparently, Jean now manages a social work team for Kensington and Chelsea Borough Council. I thought that while you are down there, you might just look her up, see if she has got anything to say which might be of interest.'

Senetti wasn't sure but he thought he noticed a physical reaction from Alberta, after he had made, what he considered was a progressive yet harmless request. He thought that she appeared a little shaken and that just for a moment, she lost her usual composure.

She said, 'I'll do my best but I've got a bit of a schedule when I'm down there.'

Not content to leave it at that he said, 'We could always contact her by telephone but I thought it might serve us better if it was face to face. Anyway, see how your schedule goes. However we do it, she's a lead and we need to follow it up. We can revisit Jean Fortescue when you get back. I've got to go now, I've got a meeting, then I need to catch a Scrutiny Committee meeting this evening. Then I'm off home. Nice to meet you Lizzie. See you Tuesday hopefully, like I say, I'll be in touch.'

As Senetti walked along the corridors of Norford Town Hall, he pondered on the case. He was puzzled by it in general. Separate incidents apparently unconnected. All resulting in fatalities'. The deaths of three people, a councillor, a social worker and a foster carer. Hit and run and two deaths on tracks, surely Senetti thought, there must be a connection. If there was a connection what was it? If they weren't accidents and they weren't suicides what were they? There could only be one other possibility, you don't hit and run yourself over, they were murders! If they were murders, were they carried out by separate murderers, whereby victims were killed in different ways, by different people. He didn't think so. No, if they were murders and he now told himself, he thought that they were, then there was only one murderer. There were also other aspects to this case, one concerned the murderer and the other one concerned his investigative partners Alberta Curtis Brightland and now Lizzie Lambert. In relation to the murderer, how could this person be in the right place at the right time on separate occasions at different times, on different days? It was quite simply just not feasible. If you considered Jason Dunphy's case alone, the murderer couldn't just follow him around in the hope that an opportunity would present itself and that at some time the councillor would turn up at a deserted tram station on a dark night, with a through train due any minute, and that the murderer would then seize his opportunity. No, there was a certain level of planning here and before it could be executed a certain amount of information needed to be known. That information wouldn't be too hard to establish in Jason Dunphy's case. He was a councillor, he was a public figure and a creature of habit. It would be public knowledge he was attending the function at the Stonemasons Arms on Saint Patrick's night and a little bit of elementary research would have established his travel pattern home. However, the other incidents were a different story altogether. Alma Alice Spain was neither a public figure nor a creature of habit. How could you know that Alma Alice would be at that car park on that day at a certain time? It wasn't as if she was a regular visitor there, she had obviously not been there in her life before, as she had to ask Jim Bigelow for directions as to where Parkhurst Lane was. Although he hadn't taken any more than a cursory look at the case regarding Velma Vine, he was expecting the same question to leap out looking for an answer. Where did this person find this information, how did he know that Alma Alice Spain would be where she was, when she was. He couldn't come up with an answer, not even a ridiculous one.

Then there was the question of motive, why were these murders happening? What was the reason for them? Vengeance, yes, he thought that there was a strong element of vengeance running through the case, but vengeance for what. Safeguarding professionals were there to protect children. Why would anybody be vengeful against such people? He couldn't come up with any answers to any of these questions.

Then, there was Alberta's behaviour, it puzzled him. It was her case, after all she had come all the way up from London to take charge of it. It was her who had initiated it. Without her, he wouldn't even be pondering. Why then did she seem to have little enthusiasm for it? Why did she not seem to be taking any lead on it? Why was she all too ready to accept the easy answer to everything? Why was she ready to accept that everything was coincidence, when although it could be, it seemingly wasn't? Why did she not put in any kind of challenge against this coincidence? It was as if for some reason best known to herself she wanted everything to be over and done with, then she could return to London as soon as possible. Maybe that was it, and it was as simple as that, she just didn't want to be here. It was obvious that she had no interest for the case. It was obvious in her response to visiting Jean Fortescue in Kensington and Chelsea, she just did not want to go! Yes, there was a lot of unanswered questions about Alberta Curtis Brightland and her conduct in this case and it puzzled him.

Then there was Lizzie Lambert, who was she? Where had she come from? Where had she been and what was her connection to Alberta? There was a lot of unanswered questions there too. He recalled how when he'd first met Alberta she'd been insistent on confidentiality about the case almost to the point of obsession. Yet she'd just drafted Lizzie in without even having a discussion with him. He'd deliberately not quizzed her because he didn't want to appear churlish but there were some things about her he needed to know.

He was meeting Lizzie next week and he would ask her a few questions without being too interrogative.

Chapter 13

Disruption

Later that day, at just after 3:00pm, two greyish, nondescript cars pulled up simultaneously and parked quite deliberately around the corner from a large house in Chorlton-cum-Hardy. The driver of one, Rosemary Rowntree, left her car and joined the driver of the other Clodagh Byrne, in the passenger seat.

They had both known each other as colleagues for several years, Clodagh spoke first.

'I hate these situations, most things in this job seem to get easier with experience but no matter how many times you manage a disruption the one after it always seems to get harder instead of easier.'

'This is a particularly messy one for me, I fought hard to get this placement put together and now it's me that's tearing it apart. At times like this I hate this job.'

'It isn't you Rosemary, it is just a given set of circumstances, but it is still awful. I know I shouldn't say this but sometimes, I think that disruptions carried out in this way inflict more damage on the children than if we ignored the abuse and left them with the alleged perpetrator.'

'It's a view Rosemary, but the priorities in safeguarding have changed. When I first came into child protection, all those years ago, everything was about the children and everything went down the line to the child. It didn't matter if you took a risk as long as you could show that you were doing it in the best interests of the child. Now it is all entirely different, everything must go up the line, it's all about protecting yourself and your own boss and your own boss's boss. It's like this situation here, you and I both know what is in the best interests of this family and placement disruption, here and now-isn't it.'

'It's these politicians Clodagh, they don't care what the right thing actually is, they only care about what the right thing is seen to be and whatever it is at the time, that they are seen to be doing it. There will come a time when if some ill befalls a child, the first course of action will be to hold the social worker responsible. If it happens in school, it will be the Teacher, anybody as long as there is a professional to blame.'

The two women entered silence for a few moments.

'What's the plan then?' asked Clodagh.

'I spoke to Gerry earlier on the phone, she doesn't know anything, except that we need to speak to her on a matter of great urgency. Martin is out, I asked her not to bother him, and she said she can't anyway, he's out golfing.'

'Where are the family as we speak?'

'Today, so as I said, it is Martin's golf day, so he is out of the way, the words thankful and small mercies come to mind. He can be a bit forthright and assertive if he chooses, when he's got his headteacher's shirt on and we don't need any of that today. Bethan is in her room revising. The rest of them are all at school, they start trickling back about 4pm. Lowri is usually first, then Gethin and Glenys and finally Dylan. Only this time there is a complication.'

'What a surprise, what is it?'

'Dylan is playing football for the school, so he's not expected home until about 7pm.Which again might help us, providing Martin isn't back by then.'

'We don't know, he could be, Gerry said he usually gets back about eightish, but if Dylan is late and Martin is early, especially if Martin's been in the nineteenth hole, who knows, we could have a situation.' Rosemary shook her head as she said this.

'The nineteenth hole?'

'You don't play golf, do you?'

'No, I don't know the first thing about it.'

'Anyway, forget about the nineteenth hole, it doesn't matter. We could go to the school for Dylan, try it that way.'

'Yeah, I can just see the headlines now, Social Workers snatch star-teenage-striker during cup final.'

Rosemary said, 'All right then, this is my suggestion, we'll go and see Gerry in a few minutes. We'll tell her that an allegation has been made. We won't say who's made it or who it is against, or what it is about. We'll say, except for Bethan, we've got to move all the children on a temporary basis until the allegation has been investigated and resolved. Obviously, we want to keep everything as calm as possible and if there are any hysterics we can use Bethan's situation as a calming influence, saying that she is staying and we don't want her upset. We'll keep stressing that this is a temporary measure along the lines of, it's just procedure in these situations, it is all inevitable but it's important that it's all done as calmly as possible for the sake of the children.'

'Yes, I know the script,' Clodagh said wearily.

'We'll do two shifts, one for Lowri, Gethin and Glenys, we'll do those first, we'll use your car, it's bigger. We'll settle them in to their new placements, then we'll find a cup of coffee and come back here for say seven-o-clock, then we'll take Dylan. There needs to be the two of us together at all times. These are stressful situations, people can react in strange ways. We don't want to be fending off any allegations against ourselves, emotional abuse, rough handling, bullying or anything like that.'

'Surely.'

'Tell me a bit more about the placements you've got.'

'As I said over the phone, at such short notice Rosemary, there isn't much choice but the picture has changed a little even in the space of an hour.'

'I appreciate that Clodagh, just tell me what we've got.'

'For the three youngest there are two choices. One choice is I can place Lowri and Glenys together with a solo female foster carer in Fallowfield and Gethin with a couple in Northenden. That way they all get to stay at the same schools that they are already in

'Why can't we place all three in one or other of the placements?'

'We haven't really got time to discuss this, but briefly one placement only takes girls and she's adamant about it and the other will only do a single placement at a time. I'm fortunate to have the Rileys in Northenden, they'd stopped fostering for a while but they are back on the board now.'

'I know that you are doing your best, it's just a shame that we can't keep the three youngest together.'

'I've tried all the persuasions and all the permutations Rosemary and these are two good placements with good levels of care, way above minimum standards. If your overriding concern is keeping them together then you've got second choice.'

'Where's that?'

Clodagh paused momentarily, 'Ena and Tony Boswell.'

'No, not the Boswell's, are they still fostering? I thought that they'd been struck off years ago. Wasn't there some issue about his drinking and Ena washing the children's faces with a pair of old knickers?'

'It was all investigated and found to be unsubstantiated, unimportant and irrelevant.'

'Unsubstantiated? Unimportant? Unbelievable! We could drive to the Derby Arms in Ladybarn now and I'll bet you my pension, Tony is plonked on that stool in the corner of the bar, hardly able to speak, down with the dead men.'

'Yes, but we are not going to do that are we? We are not going to go to the Derby Arms. For one thing Rosemary, it isn't part of our job, and if we went sneaking around spying on our foster carers, especially those who take a drink and disciplining them in some way, then it wouldn't be very long before we didn't have any foster carers. Then where would all the children go? While we are thinking along these lines, if we disciplined all our social workers who drank a bit too much for their own and everybody else's good, then it wouldn't be very long before we didn't have too many of those either. As I said, we don't have the time for this discussion, we need foster carers of all kinds, from all backgrounds, diversity is the name of the game and Tony Boswell's drinking has no bearing on anything, lots of people drink, he just happens to be one of them. All we need to know about the Boswells today, is that they are all singing, all dancing, fully registered, highly experienced foster carers, who have, and this bit is important, availability, and are more than happy to take three siblings together.'

'More than happy to take three fostering allowances together. So that Mr Boswell can spend even more time in the Derby Arms.'

Clodagh ignored the comment, she knew that there was often professional disagreement between the Field Social Workers and the Family Placement Officers. The former thought that the latter didn't provide enough quality foster placements and that they compromised quality to get their numbers quota whereas the latter thought that the former didn't support the placements enough. There were many complaints about foster carers and many came from Field Social Workers themselves. They were often trivial and she recalled one where the Field Social Worker officially complained about the strength of the tea she was given during a visit. One of Clodagh's Family Placement Officer's had to journey out to see the foster carer and speak to her about it. Not surprisingly the complaint was met with ridicule by the foster carer. Nevertheless, all official complaints, against foster carers had to be investigated and this usually fell to the Family Placement Officers. These held views and complaints did nothing to endear one group of overworked Social Workers to another.

Clodagh said, 'You know the old saying, I provide, you decide.'

'What about Dylan, back to the unit I suppose?'

'No, not necessarily, there has been a late development there too.'

'Tell me.'

'Two brand new foster carers, received their registration last week, only went on the board today, looking to foster teenage boys.'

'What specifically teenage boys?'

'Exactly that.'

'Sounds tremendous, a lucky break, we don't get many of them, where do they live?'

'Winton Kiss.'

'Where is that, never heard of it?

'Neither had I until six months ago. It's out of borough, a small village on the edge of the Peak District.'

'Sounds charming.'

'It is actually, it's a bit 1950's but in a lot of ways that's a good thing.'

'Who are the foster carers?'

'Robert Lawton and Sven Russell?'

'Oh, I've heard of these two, aren't they a Gay couple?'

'They are yes, does that present a problem to you?'

'No, it doesn't present a problem.'

'Then why mention it at all.'

'Whereas it doesn't present a problem of any kind, it presents an extra consideration.'

'Rosemary, why does it? Why should a decision be based on somebody's sexuality any more than it should be based on the colour of their eyes or the length of their hair, or the size of their feet?'

'Clodagh, please spare me the homespun PC lecture, we've both been doing this a long time, remember. I've heard all these old responses a thousand times and I didn't say anything that remotely resembled a decision being based on sexuality, it was you who said that. Just to make it clear, a decision should not be based upon someone's sexuality, I agree. What I said, was that sexuality, can bring an extra consideration to a case, which it does, we shouldn't just ignore it, as if it is totally and completely insignificant, which it isn't. We are considering placing a teen-age boy here. The colour of the foster carers eyes, the length of their hair and the size of their feet are little more than cosmetic issues. Their sexuality is not, it is an important issue. Tell you what, let's put the shoe on the other foot, forgive the cliché, go along and ask Robert Lawton and Sven Russell if they consider their sexuality on the same level of importance as their shoe size or the length of their hair and see what answer you will get from them.'

Clodagh said, 'All right then, there is also the budgetary consideration, you know how it works, it's a fraction of the cost to place Dylan in foster care than it is to place him in residential.'

'Should money be a consideration here, shouldn't the child's best interest be at the heart of the matter? I'm a Social Worker in child protection not an accountant in finance.'

'So am I, but we can't protect anybody without resources and that means money and if you've got money, especially when it is somebody else's then you've got to manage it properly and that means some sort of budget. I don't pretend to understand them myself but surely you appreciate the need for such systems. Surely we also have to consider the big picture and money is a big part of that big picture.'

A brief silence ensued.

Clodagh broke it, 'Rosemary, in a few minutes we have to go into a potentially volatile situation and come out of it with three shocked children, we need an exit strategy and a critical part of such a strategy is where we exit to, so where is it to be?'

'What do you think Clodagh?'

'I don't think anything Rosemary, this is not my call, it is your call, you are the one who has the statutory responsibility here, it is you who has to sign it off, I provide, you decide.'

'All right, as far Dylan is concerned, he goes to Robert and Sven in Winton Kiss.'

'And the youngsters?'

Rosemary was pensive and anxious, then after a long deliberation she said; 'The Boswells, at least it keeps three siblings together, for the time being anyway.'

'Right, then let's go.'

Both front doors of the nondescript car opened at the same time and the two Social Workers, Rosemary Rowntree and Clodagh Byrne strode purposely, yet slowly towards the front gate of the large house in Chorlton-cum-Hardy.

Another placement disruption that would see a whole family rendered asunder was just about to take place.

Chapter 14

Archie Hamilton

M ost Local Authorities in the U.K. are, and have been for quite some time, governed by a two-tier system. An explanation of this system is to state that in the first instance all policy decisions are implemented by an Executive Cabinet. This cabinet normally consists of around eight to ten members. These members are all elected councillors and each member is responsible for a departmental portfolio. An example of this would be "The Executive Member for Education." Such a member would have ultimate responsibility for all business that would be deemed to fall into the portfolio under the heading of Education. Secondly, as well as the Executive Cabinet, there is also an additional tier of government, a secondary chamber as some call it. This second chamber is also made up of elected members. This membership, wherever possible, is usually cross- party and acts as a check and balance mechanism. In carrying out these checks and balances it scrutinizes the decisions made by the Executive Members for each portfolio. This committee is often known as The Scrutiny Committee.

The Scrutiny Committee for Children & Young People for the borough of Norford consists of

Councillors; Patrick Arness, Archie Hamilton (Chair), Wendy Morrison, Melanie Oxton, Christine Pringle, Ian Reynolds and Henry Zochonis. The committee also has an appointed officer as clerk. This committee convenes regularly. The meeting is a public meeting and as such is open to all. The reality though is to state that members of the public are usually en absentia at these conventions. Attendance is almost always confined to those who are summoned there and there is a stark absence of representation from anybody, who would appear by choice.

As the title suggests this committee scrutinizes all council business that effects children and young people, this of course includes the safeguarding of children in care. This committee had been sitting this evening and having debated and concluded its business, had just risen. The committee room, as is always the case, without exception, after evening meetings, had emptied quickly of both elected members and officers alike. Their exit was so hurried, it was as if instead of leaving the Town Hall they were fleeing the building. One councillor though, remained in the room, Councillor Archibald Douglas Forsyth Hamilton OBE. There was also a councillor who although not a committee member had been present in the public area throughout some of proceedings. He now approached the committee area; it was Councillor Danny Senetti. These two councillors had a personal connection, for up until seven years ago, Danny had been married to Charlotte, Archie's eldest daughter and as such they were the ex-in-laws of each other. As well as this the older man was and still is Grandfather to Danny's children, both of whom are students at different universities and both of whom live with their mother, when they are at home. The two men have had for many years a relationship which Charlotte once described as being one of 'teasing challenge.'

'Archie, have you got a few minutes.'

'For you Danny, my erstwhile son-in-law, always.'

Senetti sat down at the bottom end of the table and Archie remained seated in his chairperson's place at the head of it.

'Archie, how long have you been on this committee?'

'Danny, what possible interest could my tenure on this committee be to you?'

'Archie, just humour me for a few minutes and answer the question.'

'A few minutes you say Danny? I've been humouring you, for most of your life and come to think of it a large part of mine as well and where has it got me? Nowhere that's where, absolutely nowhere.'

'Think of it as being a gesture for your grandchildren Archie, or indeed in turn for their children. Think of it as being for future generations.'

'Tell me this, what have future generations ever done for me? The problem with future generations is that they don't know they're born.'

'I knew that this was going to be difficult, I can't imagine why it should be, it surely is the simplest of questions, but I knew it was going to be difficult to get an answer, and why did I know this Archie? I know this because everything and anything connected to you, in any way, has always been difficult and this side of the grave, mine or yours I can't see any alteration to it.'

'I've been on this committee, on and off, in its different guises for around thirty years.'

'Thank-you Archie.'

'Now why do you need to know?'

'I can't say a lot, I've been bound by others to a certain element of confidentiality. What I can say is I'm working on an investigation connected to incidents involving people connected to safeguarding children.'

'What investigation is this? Why don't I, as chair of this Scrutiny Committee responsible for safeguarding children know about this investigation? Everything connected to safeguarding children in the borough of Norford, should come through this scrutiny committee, A committee of which, I repeat, I am chair. What do I get, instead of being given this knowledge in an open and transparent way, without me having to ask for it? My own ex son-in-law, who is not even a member of this committee, investigating in my ignorance and informing me he is bound by a certain element of confidentiality.'

The older man's voice took on a mocking tone as he spoke the last four words.

'Archie, I'm not involved in this in any way, in my capacity as a member of any committee.'

'I'll be thankful for small mercies. Tell me then, in exactly what capacity are you involved in this investigation?'

'This investigation isn't being carried out exclusively in Norford, it also involves other boroughs across the city region. Perhaps a report will eventually find its way to this scrutiny committee, of which you are chair. I don't know the answer to that, for sure, but at this moment, this investigation has only just begun, so there isn't really anything to report. As well as this, it isn't your committee Archie, it belongs to the people of Norford.'

'Listen to yourself Danny, the people of Norford, oh how civic minded, how democratic you've suddenly become. What are you doing investigating anyway? You're not an investigator, you're a back-bench councillor and you are also Chair of the Airport Committee and you wouldn't be in that position if it wasn't for me. You are Councillor Senetti, Danny, locally elected member for Winton Kiss. With, if I may add a wafer-thin majority and with that Lib Dem harridan woman with the squinty eyes breathing down your neck at the next election, you might not be that for much longer, you're not sodding Hercule Poirot.'

'I was wondering when you were going to bring that up, the Airport thing. I'm sorry I took the job now. I only did it as a favour to you, because you told me you were standing down from the council and you needed the vacancy filling to smooth your way out. Of course, despite making two separate sleep-inducing, backside-numbing, sophomoric speeches, to the whole council, speeches that nobody understood a word of, allegedly giving your reasons why you were standing down, what did you do? I'll tell you what you did Archie, absolutely nothing! You're still here and both you and I know, you'll be here for a long time yet. As far as standing down is concerned Archie, you stood up and about-turned.'

'I didn't about turn Danny, I changed my mind that's all, it is as simple as that. A human being is entitled to change his mind. That's one of the reasons we have minds so that we can change them.'

'It is just that you seem to change yours Archie as often as you change your shirt and speaking of shirts, why are you wearing a bright red one, with gold arm-bands and a white string tie, you're a local councillor not Mark Twain.'

'It's all part of my natural flamboyance. The electorate these days are more sophisticated than they once were, their expectations are higher.'

'Natural flamboyance, what exactly are you talking about, is that why you are dressed as a Mississippi river boat gambler? It wouldn't surprise me if you had a derringer hidden in your shirt cuff.'

'Are you still buying your clothes from that charity shop on Norford Road, what is it called now, the one that donates all its takings to the donkey sanctuary in Mexico, or is it Bolivia? Or is it the Donkey Sanctuary that actually provides the clothes for the shop, I get mixed up. Anyway, forget clothes, you need to look at your anger levels Danny, start expressing yourself in a more diplomatic way and try to be more sensitive to the feelings of others.'

'You've completely distracted me now from the reason we are having this conversation.'

'You need to look at your concentration levels too. What have you got yourself involved in this time? I would have thought that after The Man of Insignificance affair, where you and that partner of yours almost got yourselves shot dead and even when you'd escaped that, you just about escaped gaol by a beard whisker. By the way where is she, that investigative partner of yours, she can't be far away, where is Doctor Maxine Wells?'

'Who was it who involved me in the first place in The Man of Insignificance? It was you Archie and what was your contribution to the case, you just nodded off for a couple of months. I wouldn't have even met Maxine if it hadn't been for you, anyway she is not involved in any way in this case.'

'I don't call being deliberately run over by a car, left for dead and being in a life-threatening coma for weeks, nodding off, as you put it. You will recall, it was me, who single-handedly cracked that case for you, within days of coming around whilst you and Doctor Glamour-puss dithered for weeks on end. The Man of Insignificance tried to murder me but I outfoxed him, even in my sleep? Would you like to know what annoys me?'

'No, I wouldn't like to know what annoys you, I have absolutely no interest whatsoever in knowing what annoys anybody and I don't understand why people keep trotting out that old question, as if it is some kind of talking piece. I went into Dermot's Patisserie last week, just for a cup of tea and a bun. There was only one spare seat in the whole place, at a table where this nice old lady was sitting. I asked her if she minded me sitting there, she said she didn't, so I sat down. I was drinking my Earl Gray tea and having a flick through the morning paper when for no apparent reason, she said ".... Do you know what annoys me....?' I thought to myself no, I don't and I don't really want to know either. Why can't you tell me what makes you happy or makes you laugh but no she wanted to tell me about what annoys her, so being the empathetic, considerate person that I am, I had to sit there whilst she launched into this tirade about what annoys her and you know what, I've forgotten every word that she uttered and it was only a week ago, so don't tell me what annoys you because I won't listen and even if I do, I'll just forget anyway.'

'You won't listen? I thought that you were an empathetic, considerate person.'

'I am, I always take the other persons feelings into account.'

'I think you're having an identity crisis, first you think you're a detective, then you think you're a counsellor, you're a coun-cillor Danny not a counsellor. I've got a question for you, listen to this.'

'Oh no, it's not another one of those childish conundrums, that you seem to have a never-ending list of, is it? The ones where you are the only person in the world who thinks they are funny.'

'Santa Claus, The Tooth Fairy....'

'I knew it.'

'Santa Claus, The Tooth Fairy, an empathetic and considerate Danny Senetti and an old drunk were walking down the street, when simultaneously, they all spotted a fifty-pound note lying in their path, who got the money?

'Archie, I've told you, I've got no time for these.'

'Come on Danny who got the money?'

'Oh! Santa Claus.'

'Why Danny.'

'Archie!'

'The answer Danny is obviously the old drunk. Would you like to know why?'

'I can't wait, I won't be able to do anything until I find out.'

'The reason it was the old drunk, is because the other three are all mythical creatures.'

Both men began to laugh.

Senetti said, 'Archie you might be able to help me out in this investigation.'

'What do you need to know?'

'I need some information on two people who you have probably worked with over the years.'

'Who are they?'

'One is a former councillor from Oldham, Jason Dunphy and the other is a social worker from Manchester, Alma Alice Spain.'

'I knew both, they are both dead. Weren't they victims of hit and run accidents. What are you getting yourself mixed up with dead victims of hit and run accidents for?'

'No, they weren't both victims of hit and run accidents, one was hit by a car and the other a tram but don't let's get distracted with any of that, we don't need to discuss any of that and I know they are both dead, I know quite a lot about their deaths. I want some information about them when they were alive.'

'What do you want to know?'

'I am mostly interested in their professional lives, are there any common denominators?' Did they know each other, would they have come across each other, at least professionally?'

'I'll tell you what I know; as you say, Jason Dunphy was a councillor in Oldham and Alma Alice was a social worker in Manchester. They were both roughly the same age, I'd say around forty. Jason was Irish, Alma was local. They have both been around safeguarding a long time, all their professional lives. It's highly likely they would have worked together at some stage, most council business across the city region is highly incestuous. If anybody is around for even more than a couple of years and they are involved in similar work to somebody else then they would usually come into contact in one way or another. It's all to do with the people, committee ratio, it is, at its most intense in children's safeguarding.'

'The people, committee ratio?'

'Aye.'

'What do you mean Archie, the people, committee ratio, this is not another riddle coming up is it?'

'Let me explain it to you Danny.'

'I'm looking forward to hearing it, but can you let me have the abridged version?'

'You'll have the version I give you or none'

'Go on.'

'It works like this. If somebody puts the roundabout in the wrong place, or puts double yellow lines around the car park, or gives an ambulance a parking ticket, then there is a bit of a hue and cry and the council might find itself in one of those daft newspapers, you've seen the headlines, barmy councils, public money, and all that stuff. The point is, it all dies down after a day or two.'

'Archie, I know all this, I may not be an elder statesman like you but I've been around long enough. What exactly is the point? This is like one of your council speeches.'

'The point is this, Councillor Senetti, safeguarding children is one on its own, it's an entirely different situation. If something happens to a child, there is uproar and it doesn't go away for a very long time. If it's serious, heads roll, politicians and directors can lose their jobs even end up in front of a judge.'

'Archie, everybody knows all this. Why do you always insist on telling everybody, everything that they already know. Why not just now and again tell us something that none of us know.'

The older man ignored him and just continued with his homily.

'So, what happens, is that everybody gets nervous, so very few decisions are made by singular people. They are all made by committees and panels and what do committees and panels breed Danny?'

'I knew that there was going to be a riddle in it. Go on tell me what committees and panels breed?'

'Committees and panels breed more committees and more panels. So, you end up with committees, sub-committees, panels, boards, sometimes even debating similar questions.'

'Isn't it a good thing for several people to have an input into one issue, and isn't that called collective responsibility.'

'It's called that by the people who support these committees and in fairness there is an element of that.'

'And in unfairness.'

'Well a lot of these committees are set up so that when a difficult decision is made and it all goes wrong, then no one individual can be held accountable. So instead of these committees sitting for scrutiny, they can become about self-preservation of the individuals who actually make up that committee. Also, where you have a committee of say seven members, which seems to be the optimum number these days, it takes that much longer to get them all together, reconcile their diaries and so on.'

'Aren't two heads always better than one and three always better than two?'

'No Danny they are not, not always, it depends on who's shoulders the head sits.'

Both men became pensive for a moment.

'Now we come to the people committee ratio that I mentioned earlier.'

'Oh! the people committee ratio, I'd completely forgotten about that. You know what Archie you have this ability and I use the word loosely, to make people forget about what's been discussed previously, it's a kind of amnesia that one contracts when one enters into a conversation with you.'

'You know Danny, sometimes you can just brighten up a room by leaving it. What sometimes happens is that in simple terms there are so many committees created with so many rules governing their membership, that in the end there are not enough qualified people to sit on them. So, people find themselves on two, three even four committees at a time. Nowhere is this more apparent throughout the council than in anything to do with safeguarding children.'

'Archie, I've got a question for you?

'Go on.'

'What has all this people committee ratio and all the rest of this lecture that you've just delivered got to do with Councillor Jason Dunphy and Alma Alice Spain?'

'Danny, you asked me would Jason and Alma have come into contact professionally and the committee to people ratio dictates that they almost certainly would have. Both Jason and Alma had been around a long time and as most committees are a tenure of at least twelve months, often longer, then they would have known each other professionally. At some stage of their professional lives they would have almost certainly, at some period, been members of the same committee or panel. Maybe more than one.'

'Hmm, that is interesting Archie. Which one, that's the question, do we know which one?'

'No, we don't know which one, I can't recall either of them being on any I was on and I'm assuming that they were never on any you were on, otherwise you wouldn't be asking the question. I don't know the answer to that and short of asking every single councillor who has held office in the City Region over a period, or trawling through every set of council committee minutes over the period, which would probably take you ten years to just collate, let alone read, then there doesn't seem to be any way of finding out.'

'Isn't there somebody, a person, who might be central to this, who might know? There is, isn't there, I can tell by the look on your face.'

'There might be, there might be, but I don't really see where you are going with this. So, they probably were on some board together, well what of it. What does that prove? What does it even suggest? I know that these conventions can be mind-numbing. Is that what you think, that Alma and Jason died of communal boredom? That their panel killed them?'

'Who is it Archie?'

'His name is Charlie Conway, have you ever come across him?'

'I've heard the name Chic Conway, but I don't know who he is or what he does.'

'They are one and the same person. Everybody calls him Chic because of his dapper turnout. He used to be the chief committee clerk for the city region which is where all the personnel for the safeguarding panels and committees are drawn from. He used to allocate places, compile all the lists of committee members, collate and distributes all the minutes. Anything to do with safe-guarding- committees and panels, that has happened in the last thirty years, then if Chic doesn't know about it, nobody does. If anybody can point you in the right direction then he can.'

'Where can I find him?'

'He retired last year.'

'Retired! then he's hardly...'

Archie interrupted.

'Danny, don't get excited, I know exactly where you can find him, you'll like this, it will be a little treat for you and near home too.'

'Where?'

'He's always liked a drink Chic, bit like you Danny. By the way how is your drinking these days?'

'Archie let's not go down that road again. We've both been down it so many times before and we both know that it doesn't lead anywhere. It's a dead-end Archie so let's just concentrate on Chic. Have you got an address for him or perhaps a phone-number?'

'No nothing like that.'

'But he's a council officer.'

'No, he's not, not anymore, he's a retired council officer and he's entitled to his privacy. Any way he's not going to be very informative, if you go around and knock on his door unannounced.'

'I wouldn't go unannounced, I'd telephone first.'

'No, that's not the way to go about it.'

'All right, then what is?'

'There's a pub in Malton town centre, I don't go in pubs, so I don't know the name of it. I'm sure it is next door to the bank. I've walked past it many a time, it's got five steps leading to the front door. When I've walked past it, I've seen people going in and coming out of it. The clientele I've seen look a bit crazy to me. The drama college students use it, sometimes they are in character. One day you'll see King Richard going in and another day you'll see Oscar Wilde coming out. Do you know the place I mean?'

'I do yeah, you mean Lulu's'

'No surprise there then, apparently and according to my information, Chic goes in there almost every week day. Gets in at two on the dot, leaves around four, not always on the dot.'

'How do you know these things Archie, you're not having people followed are you?'

Both men laughed.

'Danny, when you've been around as long as I have, you get to know about situations that others don't.'

'Right, I'll go and have a drink with Chic.'

Chapter 15

Panel

When a foster carer's registration comes under review because of a serious allegation, to the extent that this registration becomes in jeopardy of loss, then this review is undertaken by a formally convened panel. This convention is not open to the public, it convenes behind closed doors. However, some written information in the form of minutes is available at a later stage. The small membership of this panel is selected from a larger group of people who are actively involved in the safeguarding of all children.

It was before such a panel that Gerry and Martin Kinder were asked to appear, in order to answer Emma Luckhurst's previous allegation of sexual assault against Martin.

Immediately after the allegation was made and in accordance with its nature, which was of a sexual content and in accordance with protocol for such an allegation, it was referred to the local police. The local police had sought an interview with Emma but despite their overtures and assurances Emma had refused any such meeting. The message that came back to the police through Emma's guardians, was that she did not wish to press criminal charges and she would not support any such prosecution. Furthermore, she certainly would not sign anything and she most definitely would not appear in court. In the light of all this, the police had concluded, that there was no evidence to prosecute, no case to answer and they had dropped the matter altogether. Though the action of the police, or lack of it, concluded the matter regarding any criminal proceedings, it did not represent anything conclusive for the safeguarding professionals.

Prior to any police involvement, with breakneck speed and on the same day as Emma's allegation, four of the five Trefor siblings whom the Kinders were looking after in their capacity as foster carers were removed from their home and placed elsewhere. The eldest and the Kinder's long term placement Bethan, was allowed to remain until a resolution to the allegation had been found. This disruption and its execution was the cause of much upset and anguish within the Kinder household and amongst the Trefor siblings. Amongst both, this disruption would have far reaching implications.

Gerry held the view that she and her husband had been left unsupported by the professionals, that these professionals had been all too ready to believe the complainant, that their reaction had been knee-jerked and not thought through. Her arguments had been listened to by various managers with an apparent sympathetic ear but the situation had remained unchanged. What disturbed Gerry more than anything was the way in which the allegation had been totally embraced by Social Workers as if seemingly they had no choice whatsoever. She wasn't really concerned for her own future as a foster carer, she had decided for herself that she didn't have one. She had made the decision to foster through purely altruistic reasons. Her motivation was a simple one, to help young disadvantaged people. She didn't need the responsibility and she certainly didn't need the money. What also concerned Gerry more than anything, was that the stability of the Trefor siblings had been undermined, possibly forever and it had been undermined by the very people who were supposed to do the opposite.

Except for a small few, Gerry Kinder had lost all confidence in the 'so-called professionals' within the safeguarding children system. She concluded that at best, this system chugged along in a somewhat oblivious state, when things were going smoothly, but when things went wrong it floundered and panicked. It was a system that she no longer wanted to be part of and had it not been for the fact that Bethan Trefor's welfare was her most important consideration, she would have without compunction resigned her registration as a foster carer, forthwith.

Martin shared many of his wife's views as far as the conduct of the 'so-called professionals' were concerned and in what he believed to be the consequences of their spontaneous actions. It was after all him who was being accused. It was all to do with his own reputation within the community which he felt had been damaged by what he saw as their acts of self-preservation and recklessness.

Allegations of child abuse are meant to be handled by all concerned, with the utmost confidentiality. Nevertheless, information about them almost always leaks out into the community. The allegation against Martin Kinder was no exception in this respect.

Martin had spent all his working life in education. First as a teacher then as a deputy-head teacher then as a head teacher. His last position, for eighteen years before he took early retirement was as the head teacher of a nationally recognised blue-chip girls high school in South Manchester. A month after the allegation broke, he was due to return there, to officiate at an awards ceremony. Two weeks before the ceremony, he received a telephone call from the Chair of School Governors, a local councillor Eileen Quilligotti whom he had known for over twenty years. Councillor Quilligotti considered '.... Martin, I'm sure that it is all a horrible misunderstanding and that it will be resolved in due course. However, until it is and under the circumstances, for everybody's sake, it is probably wise if you don't attend the ceremony.'

There were other issues too. When he entered his local golf club, where he'd been a member for 24 years, as soon as he walked in, a silence fell upon the assembled members and when he went into his local pub for his regular Sunday afternoon drink the same happened. When he mentioned this to his wife, she had said he was, 'being a little paranoid,' but he knew, he wasn't being. In general, some people who previously had actively sought to engage with him, now sought to avoid him. In the last twenty-four weeks which had been the time between him being notified of the allegation and his attendance at panel to - day, he had overheard the muffled term 'child molester,' on several occasions. He had stopped attending the golf club and the pub altogether and had remained in his house. Most of the time in his study. The whole situation had depressed him and unknown to his wife he was being treated for such by his local GP.

Today the Combined Authority Fostering Panel convened. Members of the panel deliberated inside their meeting room. The Fostering Panel consisted of seven members. To draw in as broad a range of views as possible the membership was taken from different areas of the local Safeguarding Children's Provision. This panel today consisted of; Velma Vine, a foster carer (Chair), Dr Frank Delgado, a paediatrician, Councillor Jason Dunphy, Alma Alice Spain, a Social Worker, Inspector Deacon Bailey a Police Officer, Dean Holland, a Social Worker and Rachel Pimlott another Social Worker. Laura Tobias was also in attendance taking the minutes. The panel were listening to a submission from the Trefor family Social Worker, Rosemary Rowntree.

Rosemary said, 'Martin and Gerry Kinder are to be commended here, it would have been so easy for them, after their experience to look inwardly at this situation and to be consumed altogether by it. If they had done this, then it would have been to the complete detriment of Bethan Trefor. They knew this and they did the opposite. However, it has taken a monumental effort on their part, particularly Martin. They have been completely child-centred and although events since the allegation had upset Bethan and she did suffer a small blip which could have turned out to be a huge blip, she is now back on track. Bethan can do very well, she can genuinely be anything she wants to be, but the stability of this placement with the Kinders is crucial to any ambition. If this panel was to deregister the Kinders or they were to resign, then Bethan's whole future could very easily go right back to where it was four years ago, before she was placed with them.'

Velma Vine was an experienced foster carer, she had been fostering for twenty years, she had been a member of the panel for nine years and she had been Chair of the Fostering Panel since early in the millennium. She was a veteran of many such panel reviews. She had been listening intently to Rosemary's comments, she now spoke.

'Rosemary, many of us on this panel are aware of your long established professional relationship with this young person, your dedication to her well-being, does you credit, but as chair of this panel, I need to remind us all in this room, exactly what our remit is. We are The Fostering Panel and today we are here to look at the registration of these two foster carers Gerry and Martin Kinder. This review is not exclusively concerned with the allegation made against Martin which we have all had detail on. Nevertheless, it would be untrue not to acknowledge that this review has been precipitated by this allegation. We neither register nor deregister lightly, but we have a serious issue here which is to assess these foster carers continuing practice against the background of the allegation. It is not the role of this convention to say which young people should be placed with which foster carers, that responsibility lies elsewhere.'

Rosemary interjected, 'Yes Chair, but if the panel withdraws the Kinders' registration completely, then these foster carers will be disqualified from accommodating anybody at all, which of course includes Bethan.'

'Rosemary, with respect, you state the obvious, but what exactly are you suggesting we do?' asked Velma.

'Something that we never ever do in these circumstances.'

'What's that?'

'Take a risk, just for once, take a risk.'

'Would you like to elaborate on this risk, as you call it?'

'Certainly, if it will help. From my conversations with Gerry Kinder, I'm sure that she has no desire to continue as a foster carer. She has been very disappointed with the support she has had from the service since this allegation was made, I know this because she has told me as much. She is though greatly concerned for the future and welfare of Bethan. So, it's straightforward, leave the situation exactly as it is. Allow the Kinders to keep their registration exclusively for Bethan. Leave Bethan exactly where she is, leave her with Gerry and Martin Kinder.'

'Rosemary, we can't take risks with the safeguarding of looked after children. We have a serious sexual allegation made against the male foster carer by a female teenage looked after child and you want us to support a situation whereupon another female teenage looked after child continues to live with the same foster carer. What would happen if he assaulted her as well?'

'Velma, it's an alleged assault, let's not forget it is alleged, nothing has been even remotely substantiated, let alone proven. The investigation carried out by the police could find no evidence whatsoever to support this allegation and they dropped the charge. Even that's not true because there was no charge in the first place. It didn't even get that far. Martin Kinder didn't assault Emma Luckhurst, it's a malicious allegation made by Emma for reasons best known to herself. If you want my opinion it's sourced in malice, jealousy and vindictiveness.'

'Thank you, Rosemary, and even if we didn't want your opinion, we've certainly got it. This malice, jealousy and vindictiveness you speak of, you know this because?'

'I know this Velma, because Martin Kinder has denied that this allegation ever took place. I know this because I've been doing this job a long time and during that time, I've got to know a lot of looked after children and a lot of foster carers. I know Martin Kinder and I know Emma Luckhurst and I know who I believe. It's called supporting my professional judgement. As well as my professional judgement, I also know Gerry Kinder and Gerry believes Martin.'

'But Rosemary, he's her husband, she is his wife, what would you expect? All I'm saying is that you can't be sure. You can't know what you've just said is correct, you weren't there. The only people who know for sure what happened are Martin Kinder and Emma.'

'Yes, and Emma knows this, she's been in the system longer than some of us have, she knows it inside out. She knows that any allegation made by a solo person against another solo person is one word against another and can neither be proven nor disproven. In this instance, if it's good enough for the police and the criminal court system then it should be good enough for us.'

'We are not the police, we are not looking for evidence one way or another. We are not seeking to press charges or prosecute guilty people or even exonerate innocent ones, we are seeking to safeguard vulnerable children. The police work on burden of proof, if anything we work on balance of probability and balance of probability states that Emma's allegation could just as easily be true as it could be false.'

'But Velma, we are not working on balance of probability, it is complete hypocrisy to say that we are. If we were, we would say that Martin Kinder is a respectable teacher and headteacher of many years' experience who has been in an environment which has been populated by teen-age girls all his working life and in all those years there has not been one single suggestion or blemish against him from any quarter. On the other hand, we have Emma, a damaged child who has a history of saying things that are not quite right. She makes a solo allegation, which she knows the implications of. Then she just walks completely away from it.   When the police ask to interview her, she refuses. When she is asked to make a statement, she refuses, she refuses any course of action that supports what she has alleged. The balance of probability, if we were applying it, which we are not, is heavily stacked in favour of Martin Kinder and we should have the courage of our own convictions, to come out and say that it is. There was a time, not so long ago when we would have done this, but now when we come across an allegation like this, we just adopt the same old mantra.'

'And what same old mantra is that Rosemary, do tell?'

'The mantra that says the child will be believed no matter what.'

'Well I don't agree with you, I think in these cases we should always go on the side of caution. You know as well as I do people who commit sexual assault come in all shapes and sizes and it doesn't matter how seemingly respectable they have been in the past. Past respectability has absolutely nothing to do with present guilt or innocence. You know as well as I do, that criminal courts, indeed fostering panels the length and breadth of the land, see a constant stream of so called respectable people before them on a regular basis accused of sexual assault and they aren't all innocent, are they?'

'No, they are not, but neither are they all guilty either. I've appeared before this panel on many occasions over the years and with an allegation like this we never seem to make any attempt to find the truth. We always seem to act on what could or might have happened instead of trying to find out what has. In these cases of alleged sexual assault which are inconclusive, it is all too easy to make the foster carer the scapegoat and we must be seen to be doing something. Obviously, we can't deregister the child so we deregister the foster carer, it's the easy way out, because we have no responsibility to him and he's dispensable. Only this time if that's what this safeguarding panel does, then it is this panel who will not be safeguarding Bethan Trefor, it will be doing the opposite of that, it will be undermining her future. You say that we don't know anything for sure, but we do, we know that Bethan is innocent in this. Emma, and Martin Kinder, yes one of them has created this mess, albeit one of them unknowingly, we also know that one of them is telling lies, but putting that aside, you the panel have an opportunity to put this right. All you must do is allow Bethan Trefor to stay with the Kinders, a place where she already is anyway, and a place where she has been for the last four years and a place where she wants to remain. Oh, and just for good measure, Bethan believes Martin as well and before you ask me how I know this, I know it because she told me so.'

How does Bethan know about this, aren't these matters supposed to be confidential?' Said Doctor Frank Delgado.

Rosemary said, 'Doctor she isn't stupid, we are talking about a young person here who is being offered places at Oxbridge. Six months age she saw her brothers and sisters removed from their dream placement. As for confidentiality, for years now, these issues have remained confidential for about half-an-hour. As much as you try to keep them that way, they always leak out somehow. Foster carers across the city region are discussing this one, probably as we speak and most of them, I'm told, are coming down firmly on the side of Martin Kinder.'

Velma said, 'Rosemary I think that you've made your point and made it well. We haven't heard from Gerry or Martin Kinder at this panel and we won't be doing as they've chosen to stay away, which is of course their right. We do though have individual written statements from both, which I trust we've all read. Martin Kinder denies the allegation and says that it never happened and Gerry says that she supports her husband, which is of course exactly what we would expect them to say. Does anybody have any questions or comments to make about Gerry or Martin's written submissions?'

'I suppose what puzzles me,' said Inspector Deacon Bailey, 'is why an intelligent man and an experienced headteacher of teenage girls and an experienced foster carer like Martin Kinder would get in a car alone with a troubled female teen-age girl. Why didn't his wife go with him?'

'She did on the first occasion but not on the second,' said Velma.

'Yes, I already know that Velma but why?'

'We don't know,' said Alma Spain. 'We could say he engineered it that way so they could be alone together and this suited his purpose.'

'Or we could say that she engineered it that way for the same reason,' said Dean Holland.

'The same reason?' queried Alma.

'Yes, her word against his, no witnesses,' responded Deacon Bailey.

'Why wait almost two years to make an allegation?' asked Rachel Pimlott.

Deacon said, 'Time scales are a strange thing, I've worked on sexual assaults that have been five, ten, even twenty years old, I've even heard of them older than that, in the police. Victims have all kinds of reasons for the timing of their disclosure. In my experience, we can't really place any importance one way or another on the timing of it.'

Velma said, 'Spoken like a true policeman Deacon, but we're not the police, we are the fostering panel. The way I see it as chair of this panel is this.'

There was a lengthy pause before she continued.

'Albeit conditional at this precise moment, Martin and Gerry Kinder currently have a registration from this Authority to foster young people between the ages of five years and twenty-one years. Currently they have in placement an eighteen-year-old female. She has been with them around four years and by all accounts is doing exceptionally well. Regrettably an allegation of a sexual nature has been made against the male carer. We can talk about the veracity of this allegation forever, but the way things stand, there is a complete absence of any evidence from either side. It is a prime example of text-book, solo allegation. Basically, one person's word against another. The only way we might get to the truth, if truth is what we are concerned with, is if either the accused or the accuser says something different and so far, there is no indication of that. So, this panel can do three things. One, we can completely ignore this allegation and reinstate their registration in its entirety. Tell you what, let's get that one out of the way first. Who on this panel is for completely disregarding this allegation? It has after all as Rosemary has quite rightly pointed out been investigated by the police who have dropped the case. We could reinstate the Kinders registration in full. Such an action would mean that the Kinders and all the Trefor siblings would be eligible for rehabilitation. Who is for considering that?'

As she said this she looked around the room at each panel member.

'Jason, you've been uncharacteristically quiet on this, is that what you think that we should do?'

Jason Dunphy said, 'No, I don't think reinstatement is altogether an option that's available to us and as Rosemary has already explained, Mrs Kinder no longer wishes to carry on fostering. So, what would be the point in reinstatement? We would have an all singing all dancing foster carer, who wasn't prepared to undertake the task. As well as this, we would be sending out the message that we totally disbelieved the accuser and in the event of any future fallout from anywhere, what evidence do we have to support that view.'

Velma continued, 'Is there anybody in this room who disagrees with Jason on this point of total reinstatement.'

The room fell into silence.

'Right then, that leaves two other options. Either we deregister them altogether so they can't foster again and that includes disrupting their current placement. Or, we allow them to carry on exactly as they are and as Rosemary has suggested. So, who is for what, and briefly, please, Alma?'

Alma said, 'Anything else is too much of a risk and as Jason says there is a complete absence of any evidence either way. So, I'm for complete deregistration and moving Bethan.'

'Jason, we've had your submission but what is your vote?'

'Deregistration.'

'What about you Dean?'

'I think, that Bethan should stay in placement so I support Rosemary's idea.'

'What about you Doctor, what's your view on this?'

'I think the young person should stay in placement so I don't support deregistration.'

'Rachel?'

'Preserve their registration for Bethan.'

'Deacon?'

'Just in case the allegation is true, I support deregistration.'

'Right then, so that's three for preserving the Kinders' registration which would enable them to continue looking after Bethan Trefor and three for complete deregistration. Meaning that Bethan would have to be moved immediately, which probably means that she will be in residential care by to-morrow.   Not for the first time we're evenly balanced. It looks like it's me as chair with the casting vote. This is a very difficult situation I find myself in and I can honestly say I don't have a clear view about this. I think though that to discharge my obligations to the panel I'm going to have to vote for complete deregistration.'

'Disgraceful, no other word for it,' said Rosemary. 'Obligations to the panel indeed, what about your obligations to the people. The child and the foster carers. That's the problem when you give amateurs casting votes.' As she said this, she glared fiercely at Velma Vine, then she stood up and flounced out the room, slamming the door with a resounding crash as she left.

Chapter 16

Camille and Justine

In the Welsh county of Gwynedd, and extending thirty miles into The Irish Sea, is the highly regarded beauty spot, known as the Llyn Peninsula. Through the centuries, the relative isolation of the peninsula has given it an unspoilt air and both these attributes have served to keep the area comparatively separate from urban life. Sitting slightly inland, on the south side of the Llyn Peninsula, and lying roughly equidistant between the well-known, tourist popular, market and coastal communities of both Criccieth and Pwllheli, is the relatively unknown, small village of Chwilog. The village used to be on a railway line and at one time had its own station. The Railway was opened in 1867, and quietly prospered, particularly, in the nineteen-forties, when its vans, via a circuitous route, transported milk, in churns, to Liverpool. Unfortunately, both the line and the station were closed in1964, and the site is currently a bus station. Another of the village's claims is a little obscure, but nevertheless an endearing one, inasmuch as, in 1908, the local primary school was opened by Margaret Lloyd George who at the time was the wife of the then Chancellor of the Exchequer David Lloyd George. From 1916, until 1922, a period that contained most of World War One, David Lloyd George, who was raised and grew up in nearby Llamystumdwy, would go on to become one of the best known Prime Ministers in the history of the UK.

Chwilog is a tranquil place, with typical Welsh stone houses under Welsh roof slates, lined either side of its one main street, which runs through the middle of the village. At the last census, the village recorded a population of 640 inhabitants. At least a third of the inhabitants are recorded as being over sixty-years of age. The village presents itself as one which is respectful and welcoming yet minds its own business. Within the village boundaries are a butcher's shop, a post office-cum-general store and a pub, The Madryn Arms. If you were to pass through the village, via the B4354, keeping The Madryn Arms on your right-hand side, after about five hundred metres, on the same side where this straight road begins to meander, on a bend you will come across a twin entrance junction. Central to this junction is a raised pretty-flowered section, wherein you will find the sign for, "Ocean Heights Holiday Park." Opened in 1978, Ocean Heights is a well maintained, well managed caravan park and although this number fluctuates a little from year to year, placed strategically within its manicured lawns, on specially constructed hard standing areas, are approximately one hundred modern luxury caravans.

At the risk of stating the obvious, caravans today are decidedly not what they were yesterday. Long gone is the short narrow, dumpy, cold and draughty metal box that they once were. This offer has now been replaced by a spacious, sleek, handsome vehicle with all the modern inside conveniences and outside areas. In short, living in a caravan in Ocean Heights today, is tantamount to living in a mini luxury apartment, with double glazing, central heating, en-suite facilities, fridge freezer, satellite tv, Wi-Fi connection, et al. The caravans on Ocean Heights though, are not all year-round residential homes for local people. The park closes during the winter months and the people who occupy the caravans on Ocean Heights are holiday makers, mainly from North West England and the Midlands. They visit their caravans regularly throughout the year, some of them staying for months at a time, others only a few weeks, others only a few days at a time; from March to November, they come and go as they choose.

At the end of the central lane on the caravan park, sitting on a comparatively large plot is one such luxury caravan. Attached to a central post on the outside decking and befitting the location is a slate address plate which declares this caravan to be number '110.' This number is known by the site management as Caravan, One-One-Zero. Caravaners, often name their caravans and traditionally these names, like ships names are female. On the front of Caravan, One-One-Zero, is a uniform name plate. It is gold with black lettering and bears the inscription, "Diana."

Diana is a large caravan, being thirty-eight feet long by fourteen feet wide. It is liveried in white and crème. Wrapped around the front and side of the vehicle is a large decked area. On the decking is a table and four chairs.

Seated at two of the chairs at either side of the table are two young women, both in their thirties. One of these women is slightly older than the other. It is a glorious, summer early-evening and both women are attired in the summer holiday dress of shorts, vests and sandals.

The slightly older woman who is called Camille, asked.

'You didn't say how you found this place Justine?'

'I didn't Camille, really find it that is, if anything it found me. I wasn't even looking for a place of any kind, let alone a caravan. I didn't know anything about caravans, prior to buying this one, I don't think I've ever been in one, in my whole life. I decided I'd take a short holiday here. I hadn't even been in this part of Wales before. My only experience of the whole country was a conference in Cardiff. As soon as I arrived, I felt comfortable here. I was staying in a little B & B over in Caernarvon. I'd heard about the Llyn Peninsula and how beautiful it was. One day I was just wandering around the area aimlessly, going nowhere in particular, when I happened upon Chwilog. I was struck by its air of tranquillity and with what I think of, as its old Welshness, then I came upon Ocean Heights. I suppose my curiosity got the better of me. Then I saw this caravan and I knew that it was what I was looking for. Anyway, what do think of it?'

'Oh! I think it's perfect in every way. Do you get to come here much, with work and everything?'

'Not as much as I'd like to but I'm working on that.'

'Do you come here with friends?'

'It's funny you should ask that, because nobody apart from myself, absolutely nobody has ever set foot in this caravan. You are the first and only person to come here. You are the only person who I've ever invited.'

'I'm honoured and thank you truly for the invite, I feel very comfortable here, very welcome and I'm really enjoying myself.'

'You are welcome Camille, you are more welcome than anybody else I can think of.'

'Justine.'

'Yes, Camille'

'Have you given any more thought to the discussion we were having in the restaurant last night?'

'Any more thought? I think of little else, it occupies my thoughts at least half my waking life, do you mean any particular part of it?'

'Not really Justine, any part of it, all of it, some of it, I'd like to pick up the discussion where we left off. It is very important, for me at least, to have a clear view as to the reason why. It all came as a bit of a shock, or was it just the wine talking?'

'It wasn't as far as I'm concerned, I've thought about the whole story, quite a lot over for the last five years and the time has come soon to progress the thinking into action. Anyway, we only had a glass each.'

Both women laughed

'If you've thought like this for a good while, why do you think that you've left it so long before you translated your thoughts into a plan of action?'

'It is not easy to answer that Camille. First of all, I wanted to get through Oxford and be as successful as I could be. It was something that I had to do as much for my parents as for me.'

'Do you feel that you've done that.'

'Yes, I think that I've had as much success in that area as I need at the moment. It isn't easy to explain. It was more of what I didn't want to become. I didn't want to be the same as those belonging to me. I've learned that for people with my background, opportunity is a rare commodity. Once I had concentrated on my opportunity, then I could focus on my distraction.'

'Your distraction Justine?'

'I call it that yes, but it is more than that. The reality is, it is everything else, that is the distraction. The real mission is what we were discussing last night.'

'By those belonging to you, do you mean family members?'

'I do yes Camille, but it is important that I think of it in the context of those family members not being given the opportunity I was given or at least, when they did get it, it was taken away from them by others. It is very important that I never lose sight of that fact.'

'There are a lot of questions to be both asked and answered.'

The younger woman said, 'There were for me at the beginning, then somehow I worked through them. You see I always believed in the righteousness of it. That sounds religious and sacrificial and perhaps in a way it is. I suppose if you find aspects too difficult to reconcile, then perhaps you should not take the matter any further.'

'No, I don't want to stop Justine, it's so important. No, it's more than important, what's another word for important, only more so?'

'Vital?'

'Yes, that will do, it's vital.'

A brief silence ensued and the two women sipped from their coffee cups. It was the older woman who broke the silence.

'Do you miss your family Justine?'

'You are my family now Camille, you know that, and I am yours. We are all each other has now, each other. Though, you had your family much longer than I had mine and they were snatched away from you so cruelly, so finally and so unexpectedly. Mine were hardly together at all. You could even argue that we weren't even a proper family. We didn't live together, well not for any length of time and we certainly didn't grow up together in a house whereas, you grew up with your parents and your siblings.'

'There is much more to a family than all growing up together in the same place. They were your brothers and your sisters, of course you were a proper family. You may not have been as traditional as many families but you were certainly a family.'

'Thank you Camille, you are being very kind, your family, do you miss them?'

'I'll always miss them, I've adjusted to the loss now, the circumstances were tragic and yes almost unbelievable but they've happened. I've no right to expect that they couldn't happen to me and even if I did have, my expectations were dashed.'

'Do you blame anybody for your loss?'

'That's an odd question Justine and an odd word *blame*. No, I've thought about this quite a lot and there is nobody to blame, it was just a tragic accident.'

'I think that you are right to think that way, oh yes, much more than that, most definitely. My family weren't wiped out in an instant, sorry I didn't mean to use that terminology.'

'It's all right Justine, anyway that's what happened, it was a freak accident. There was nobody else responsible. That's exactly what happened. One minute I had a family and the next minute I had none. The only good thing about it was that there were no second generation, so there were no heartbroken kids in the wake of things.'

'It's a good word Camille, *responsible*. You see my situation is different. My family were apart all our lives. Then, when we had the chance to be together, that togetherness was denied us by others. It wasn't an accident, it was the opposite of an accident. It was a planned contrivance. It was even worse than that, even though it was lawful, it was a criminal offence. As far as I'm concerned, the people responsible are criminals.'

'You've never really told me the full story.'

'It's very complicated.'

'We've got time.'

'The full story Camille is really very complicated and if you are really interested it needs to unfold across time. If you are interested in the short version though, I'll tell you.'

'What is important to you is important to me Justine and I'm very interested.'

'All right then, the short version is this. Through what I can only describe as a malicious lie, which was sourced in petulance, envy and grievance, the object of which was to create and cause as much harm as possible to my family, a cumulative set of circumstances were created which enabled a group of so called professional people to arrive at a set of decisions, which over a period, indirectly caused the destruction of my family.'

Camille said, 'I hope you don't mind me saying but that's a bit of a mouthful'..." a cumulative set of cir-cumstances were created which enabled a group...."

'It does sound like jargon, I know, but the cold reality is...'

Tears began to well in the younger woman's eyes and the older woman gazed upon her sympathetically. The younger woman continued.

'As I say, the cold reality is that because a group of people were following procedure, a procedure which ordinary decent people don't fully understand, there's more jargon for you, my family were given a suspended death sentence, and in the end, that's what happened to them all, they all died.'

'Weren't these people just doing their job, you know following protocol, trying to protect others?'

Justine said, 'No, they weren't, well apart from following protocol, which they almost certainly were doing, they were enslaved by it. They weren't doing their jobs at all, they should have been, but they were doing the opposite of what their jobs were. Which as you rightly say was to protect others. Not just others but very vulnerable others, innocent others, who had no voice at all in the situation, no voice in the future of their lives, no voice in anything. What these criminals were doing was protecting themselves from the potential consequences of their own mistakes. Not even the consequences, but the potential consequences. Theirs was a conspiracy driven by their own craven instincts. In my eyes, they are little better than criminals, forget the little better, that's exactly what they are, criminals, murderers.'

'It sounds abominable, unbelievable.'

'It's sounds unbelievable, but it's not, it happens all the time, all over the country and there is worse to this story. As well as this, they undermined somebody who actually was trying to protect others and indirectly caused his tragic and premature death.'

'Why are these people such monsters?'

'They wouldn't recognise themselves as such Camille, they certainly wouldn't admit to it, but yes, in a way they are. How else can you describe a group of people who made no attempt whatsoever to seek the truth and who just followed the path of least resistance, who's actions caused the deaths of others, just because this group were so self-protective that they couldn't even challenge their own procedures?'

'Wow! that's quite a story.' The older woman leaned back in her chair and exhaled deeply.'

The younger woman also leaned back in her chair, she appeared drained by her divulgence.

'Can any redress be brought against these people Justine?'

'Not in the normal way Camille no, at least not in any way I can see. We can't discipline nor sue them. They can't be prosecuted in any way, at least not in the eyes of the law. They haven't committed a crime they haven't broken any laws. The opposite is true, they have carried out the law to their own letter and they are protected by it. As you said before, to all intents and purposes they have just been doing their job.'

Camille said, 'Do you know anything more about these people?'

'I know lots more about them. Did you have any particular information in mind?

'Do you know who they are, do you know their names?'

'I know exactly who they are, it's not a secret of any kind, it's all a matter of record, and I know all their names.'

'What, it is all out in the open?'

'No, it isn't quite that Camille. It isn't in the news-papers or anything like that. These criminals, claim that they operate, at least in theory, in an atmosphere of pro-tection and transparency but what they really do is hide behind a cloak of self - protection and confidentiality. Either way, their discussions and recommendations are written down in official minute form, it is all a matter of record, it is just a case of knowing where to look.'

'So, by knowing what they've said, you can sepa-rate the innocent from the guilty.'

'No not really, there are no completely innocent, they all bear a collective responsibility, an individual might express an opinion contrary to another opinion but in the end, they all play a part in the decision, so they are all guilty. However, there are varying degrees of guilt, just as there are degrees in most crimes.'

'What about this malicious lie that you mentioned, the one that started it all off, was this made by one of these professionals?'

'No, that has another source altogether, that despi-cable individual is more culpable than anybody else. The professionals were completely self – deluded in their righteousness and that's bad enough, but this indi-vidual knew exactly what was happening. It was all completely premeditated, planned and executed with deliberation. As well as this, this individual knew that it was all made up and that it was a complete lie.'

Justine responded, 'Why do people do that?'

'Envy, jealousy, anger, hatred, at least one of those things, perhaps a combination of all of them. It was all done with malice of forethought to cause as much misery and upheaval as possible and it was successful. There is though too much understanding of people's motivation. Sometimes it is as simple as you've done something wrong and your reason for doing it won't change the consequences.'

Camille questioned, 'Do you know this individual too?'

'I know her identity yes, although I've not been able to keep tabs on her as easily as I have on the others, so for the moment she has disappeared, but her where-abouts will be discovered once I set my mind to it. I've learned that she has surprisingly made a new life for herself, a comparatively successful one. Let her bask in her own security for the moment. If anybody deserves to have retribution visited upon them. Then it is surely her'.

'Have you been keeping tabs on the others?'

'Yes, as best as I could. For the last five years I've been two hundred miles away down there in London, but this will shortly change.'

'But why would you want to keep tabs on them, surely it is all in the past?'

'No Camille it isn't all in the past, it is as we were saying last night. It is in the past for some people, espe-cially those who are dead and those who are alive who have forgotten about it, but I'm neither and for me it is very much a part of my present. No, not my present, my future. Look, you are the only family member who I have left, you're all I have left in the world, if I confide in you then I might put you in a difficult position. So perhaps we should stop this conversation now.'

'You won't put me in a difficult position, whatever you are involved in then I want to be in it too. Why do you keep watch on them?'

'I keep watch on them because I need to know what they are up to. Where they live, where they work, where they drink, where they eat, who they associate with, their habits, their movements, anything I can find out about them is relevant to my plans.'

'Your plans?'

'Look, you've got one more chance, are you sure that you want to know any of this.'

'Yes, I'm interested and furthermore …' she paused.

'Furthermore?' The younger woman interrupted

'It excites me.'

'Yes, it excites me too Camille.'

The two women paused, their breathing reached an audible pitch and it could be heard by a third party both individually and collectively, had there been one present, but of course there wasn't any such presence.

'What are your plans Justine, are they complicated?'

'No, they are the opposite, they are really quite simple to draw up, but not so simple to execute.'

'I'm intrigued, keep going.'

'I have thought about it long and hard; for a period, I considered that the way to go was a campaign that was done through official complaint, possibly through private prosecution in the courts, maybe even seek media attention.'

'It sounds like you have decided against all that.'

'I have yes, too drawn out, expensive, takes over your life and twenty or thirty years later you are no further on and you look ninety years of age with the stress of it all. Then, the best you get is an apology from somebody who wasn't even there at the time. The people who were there, have died or rode off into the sunset with their impeccable service records and big, fat, local government pensions. No, my family were precious to me, they deserve redress, their lives have been snuffed out by officialdom, then officialdom just coughs and gets on with its life as if nothing important has happened, well not this time. This time it is nemesis.'

'Nemesis Justine - doesn't that belong in ancient Greek mythology?'

'It has its source there yes, but it is just as relevant today as it was in Ancient Greece.'

'Nemesis, righteous indignation, dealing out what is due.'

'Yes, retribution.'

'You plan to have them killed?'

'Just as they had my family killed, but I think that we should understand, it is not just having them killed, more executing them and so as not to shirk the responsibility or hide behind some protocol, we do it ourselves.'

'It's a grand scheme of an idea, I think that I've always wanted deep down to execute somebody. It would give me a feeling of absolute power. Is there a particular time and place when you plan to do it, a particular method that you would use?'

'No, Camille there is no common aspect to these executions. That really is the last thing that we want. We want as much variety as we can think of, it is the passport here. If you use common aspects you develop a modus operandi, a pattern, and once you do that, the chance of you getting stopped increases. If we get caught early on then the executions stop and there are a lot of them to be carried out.'

'Justine, what if we get caught late?'

'Being caught late is preferable to being caught early, but the best time to get caught is to not get caught at all and that's what I intend to happen. As far as method of execution is concerned it will be individual and will be one befitting my family as much as deserving to the criminal.'

'You've obviously given a great deal of thought to this and I agree we need to have variety with our methods and disguise the incidents so that they look like something else instead of an execution. Oh, and the criminal needs to be wholly unsuspecting.'

'Yes Camille, I like those ideas. We need to have a very long discussion about the whole history, names, places, dates, you need to learn every nuance of the whole case.'

'You know Justine, it really is amazing that after all those years, all that distance and all those people in the whole world, that we should by the merest of chances find each other.'

They both stood up from their chairs, they laughed, at first a soft girlish giggle which accelerated to an almost hysterical crescendo. Then for a few minutes they danced in a freestyle way, then they fell into each other's arms and as they hugged one another, tears streamed down their faces and fell onto the decking of Caravan One-One-Zero.

Chapter 17

Trensis Station

If you leave the town of Malton, heading towards the county of Derbyshire, the road meanders a lot, but sticks mainly to a westerly direction. After a relatively short distance, say a quarter of a mile you will cross the outer boundary of the village of Trensis. In medieval times, the site that the village now sits on, was a hunting wood which was part of The Forest of Peak. In the Elizabethan era, a few houses sprung up and as the village moved through history, more were added. These days the village's one arterial road, which is unsurprisingly called Trensis Road, has houses of all styles and ages, along both sides of it. Trensis is currently placed in Malton, Norford, Greater Manchester, but in the past, it has been in the county of Derbyshire. As you travel Trensis Road today, at its end you will arrive at a waterless confluence where three counties meet, Cheshire, Derbyshire and Greater Manchester. If you turn off the road at this merger, you will travel down a narrow but well made up tarmac lane which eventually turns to cobbles, along the way you will pass a medium sized pond which has a rather magnificent centrepiece in the form of a black and white dovecote surmounted by an ornamental weather vane. At the end of this lane is a bridge, this bridge is narrow with a headroom of 2.4 metres and it is part of the viaduct that carries the railway. Just before this viaduct is Trensis Railway Station and this station was exactly where Danny Senetti was heading for today. He was travelling in his 11-year-old maroon Mercedes Benz, with the registration plate ARC 70. The car had originally belonged to Archie Hamilton. Archie had purchased it as a life-long birthday gift to himself on the arrival of his 70th birthday, hence the number plate. With a massive touch of mordancy, a year or so after his purchase, he had suffered a short illness and even though he had made a prompt and complete recovery, a consequence of this illness was that his driving licence had been temporarily, revoked on medical grounds. He could have attempted to regain the document but he reasoned that he didn't use the car that much anyway and he could use the exercise that would come with walking instead of driving, so he decided against it. In an uncharacteristic bout of generosity, he had gifted the car to Danny Senetti, who at the time had been married to Archie's daughter, Charlotte.

As the maroon Mercedes moved along Trensis Road, Senetti listened to the music coming from his CD player. Although Senetti had been a young boy, a teen-ager and a young person in the 80s, and 90s his own musical preference was distinctly not of that era. The music that he listened to predated that and was written and recorded from around 1955 and through the 60s and 70s. He now listened to the lyrics being belted out from his system. A strong classical operatic voice gave out the introduction. Then the track burst into a fusion of blues and power pop as the lyrics came in...

"Just got back from the local palais
Where the music was so sweet
Knocked me right back in the alley
I'm ready, yeah, yeah, yeah, I'm ready."

Senetti pondered, he had always loved the music from this time, ballad, doo-wap, skiffle, rock n roll, blues all of it, as long as it came from that period. He wasn't sure why he was such a fan. It certainly wasn't music that was contemporaneous to him. It had been born, breathed, lived, died and some of it had even been resurrected before he had even been born. He couldn't quite remember when he had first heard it. He wasn't sure, so he settled for his self-suggestion that it was probably from the old 45 rpm record collection his mother used to have when he was growing up. He wondered whether she still had the collection and decided that she probably did.

She had often played some of her collection when he was a schoolboy growing up in the late 70s and early 80s. She had a cream and red leatherette Dansette record player which used to stack twelve 45 rpm discs at a time. He could see that record player now in his mind's eye, with its stack of black vinyl discs, waiting to drop to order on the turn table. The record player always seemed to be on, when he was trying to do his homework, on either a Saturday morning or a Sunday evening and when his dad was either at work or in the pub. The music would filter through from his mother's living room, up the narrow staircase and into his tiny bedroom. He knew all the artists, the bands, all the members of the bands and all their songs. He thought that if he ever found himself on one of those television quiz shows, where you had to answer questions on a specialist subject, then 1950s, 1960s and 1970s popular music would be the one he would choose. Senetti listened as the first song came to an end and another tune eased out of his car speakers.

'Can't we be sweethearts
Why don't we fall in love
Right from the start
You're the girl I'm dreamin of'

He was on his way to meet Sergeant Megan Rees-Jenkins, who worked for the accident investigation branch of The British Transport Police. She had been involved in the investigation into Velma Vine's accident last year. Senetti and Megan had worked together on several joint initiatives over the years. He knew her to be an original and intelligent investigator and he trusted her.

As he arrived at Trensis Station, he noticed a black, sports type, four-seater BMW convertible in the car park. Senetti's knowledge of cars was limited but he thought it to be a top of the range car, the type of car favoured by single female executives with no children. He knew it wouldn't be Megan's. The vehicle also had what was obviously a personalised number plate: LLA 111. He guessed that the three letters were meant to denote *Lizzie Lambert,* the front windows were tinted and he couldn't clearly see inside. Although he could discern that there was somebody in the driver's seat. As she opened the door and stepped out, he could see that it was, indeed, Lizzie Lambert.

'Councillor we meet again,' she said in a cheerful voice.

She smiled and showed Senetti those perfect teeth again.

'Good Morning Lizzie,' replied Senetti.

Senetti could see that Megan had not yet arrived. He observed that the station was small but immaculately kept. He had read somewhere buried in council papers of a 'Friends of Trensis Station Group' and he put the station's good condition down to their activities. He wandered through the white picket gate that was the public entrance to the place. There were only two platforms, both about one hundred metres long, one for the Sheffield train and the other for the Manchester train going in the opposite direction. A successful attempt had been made to spruce up the station and it was painted blue and white. On the Manchester bound platform was a small stone built waiting room. He stepped inside it and strangely enough to his surprise it contained a bench above which a public call booth was fixed. Out of curiosity he stepped inside the booth, sat down and picked up the telephone receiver. To his amazement he was met with a dialling tone, the phone actually worked.

'You've come to an obscure place to make a phone call Councillor, perhaps you should invest in a mobile phone, they seem to be popular these days.'

Senetti looked out from the waiting room and saw the tall, statuesque, rain-coated figure of Megan Rees-Jenkins.

'I hope we don't get the weather you're expecting,' he said.

'Lizzie Lambert meet Megan Rees Jenkins,' he indicated each woman to the other in introduction.

As he made these introductions he stepped out of the waiting room onto the platform and took Megan's outstretched hands in his own. Megan stepped forward, wrapped her arms around him and gave him a hug, then they separated and stood next to each other on the Manchester platform facing the Sheffield one.

'I know how much you love hugs,' said Megan.

'You've gone blond.'

'I've been blond for years. Senetti, you're hopeless when it comes to anything like cosmetics. What are you up to anyway with this Velma Vine case? The coroner recorded a verdict of accidental death. Since when did investigating death on the tracks come under the remit of the local councillor from what's the name of that place you represent?'

'Winton Kiss!'

'That's it yeah, Winton Kiss.'

'I'm working for the Children's Commissioner's Office and they are looking into it, Lizzie also works for them.'

Megan said, 'Looking into it with a view to what Danny?'

'There isn't really a held view, well not at this moment, it's one of those let's look at it and see if we can learn from it. This case is just one of several cases all of which are thought to be unusual. Was Velma Vine's case unusual, Meg?'

'In my opinion it was yes, it seemed to exist in a vacuum.'

'Why do you say that?'

'I say it because Velma Vine was a perfectly, healthy, respectable, fit, intelligent woman, waiting for the midday train to attend a regular meeting that she'd attended for years in Manchester, when for no apparent reason, she fell into the path of a through freight train that just happened to be hurtling through at the time.'

'An accumulation of circumstances eh?'

'Could it not just have been an accident,' asked Lizzie.

'Of course, it could, I mean anything can be an accident, that's often-what accidents are, just as the councillor says, an accumulation of circumstances. But looking around here, there is nothing obvious to suggest an accident. There is nothing to fall over or fall off.'

'Suicide?' Said Lizzie.

'I looked at that from all angles, we did extensive background checks on Velma, we spoke to her partner, her children, her colleagues, even the neighbours.'

'Did anything come of it?' Lizzie questioned.

'Absolutely nothing, there was no suggestion of unhappiness, stress, mental illness, depression. She was a moderate social drinker, no drugs, she was a settled, stable person, who seemed to lead a happy and fulfilled life.'

'What about murder?' asked Senetti.

'No reason for it, no apparent enemies, the woman was a saint. We did a fingertip search of this place, we found nothing, there's no CCTV, no witnesses at the station. No overlooking properties. Trensis Station isn't a busy station, it carries about sixty passengers a day and most of those are at the morning and evening rush hours. The train that Velma was waiting for, often doesn't pick anybody up at this station at that time, only her and then only once a month.'

'Once a month?' Said Senetti.

'Yes, this meeting she was attending convened once a month.'

'What was it?'

'I don't know, some dreary council gathering, they are all the same, aren't they? You know better than me on that score.'

'Saying all you've just said, why then weren't you satisfied?'

'How do you know I wasn't?'

'Because, I know you Meg and I can see the look on your face.'

'In the end, I was ordered off the case by my superiors, they said that there was nothing left to investigate. They said that there was an absolute absence of evidence for anything one way or another.'

'You sound as if you didn't agree with their decision.'

'Absence of evidence, doesn't always mean evidence of absence. I'll take you into my confidence Danny, but you've got to respect that this is exactly what I am doing.'

'This seems to be happening to me a lot these days, after years of being marginalised, I've suddenly become a confidante, I'll keep it close.'

'You've never been marginalised in your life Senetti. Do either of you know how many injuries are recorded on the railways and tramways in the U.K. each year?'

Lizzie said, 'Haven't got a clue!'

'Take a guess.'

'A thousand?'

'The latest set of figures released stated that there were on average 11,047 injuries recorded on the rail and tramways each year? Do you know how many of those were death on tracks?'

'What is this Meg, the great railway quiz? just tell us,' said Senetti.

Lizzie then looked on as Senetti and Megan entered into a dialogue.

'Out of 11,047, 354 were deaths on tracks and out of those 354, 304 were suicides.'

'Where is the connection with Velma ?' he asked.

'I've had an involvement with many deaths on tracks in the North west of England and over the years I must have investigated anything up to hundred and nothing about Velma Vine's death says it was suicide. Whereas, everything about it says it was murder.'

'What makes you say that?'

'All the circumstances and conditions point to it.'

'In what way? Asked Senetti.

'In this way, if you wanted to murder Velma, what easier way than to push her off a platform into the path of a through freight train. Somebody knew she would be at that same station on that same platform every month. What better place could you pick than Trensis Station? Even the freight train itself was a godsend.'

'Why was that?'

'Freight trains don't carry any passengers just one driver and a guard, one at the front and one a long way behind at the back. Both those operators would be concentrating on their duties, so there is little chance of there being any witnesses from the train. Whereas, if you've got a train full of fifty passengers, you've potentially got fifty witnesses.'

'I never thought of that. I thought I read somewhere that all freight is moved through the night.'

'You're right Danny most of it is but not all of it.'

'Are freight trains time-tabled? How would you know the timetable for a freight-train?'

'All trains are time-tabled with no exceptions. The information is out there, like most things these days, if you made it your business to find out, then you could find out.'

'There is a lot missing though Megan, in establishing this incident as a murder.'

'There is too much missing Danny, we've already spoken about witnesses and forensics so basically there is nothing to investigate.'

'There is something else missing too Megan, something that is needed at every murder.'

'You mean the reason why.'

'Well yes, why would anybody want to murder a lady, who as you said, was apparently a saint, where are the suspects, what is the reason, what is the motive?'

'We couldn't find an answer to any of those questions, so in the end I was forced to abandon the investigation.'

'This meeting you speak about, the one Velma was attending, who else was attending.?'

'I don't know, it was at Manchester Town Hall, something to do with safeguarding children, something to do with the council, we didn't really consider the meeting itself relevant, only the regularity of it, as I said it was probably just a typical boring council meeting. Does it have any relevance?'

'I don't really know, I suppose it's a straw, but we're clutching them right now. You said that it was a regular thing, same time, same day every month.'

'Apparently it was, yeah.'

Senetti said, 'If it was murder, then this murderer knew quite a bit about Velma, he knew about the meeting, exactly when it was, how Velma travelled to it, apparently all about Trensis Station and what time the freight train was coming. As you say he didn't just turn up at Trensis Station hoping that Velma Vine would be stood on the platform and at the same time a fast travelling freight train would come hurtling through. He would have to have done some research?'

'You're right Danny, he would, but none of the information he needed would be too difficult to establish. A simple bit of surveillance, a browse around the internet, a couple of telephone calls, would tell you all you needed to know. There was a slim chance that somebody might come along and witness the deed, there always is, but obviously he was prepared to take that chance and obviously nobody did. He would probably have had some sort of disguise anyway. Then all he had to do was disappear from the scene. Not very difficult around here.'

Senetti said, 'Would anybody want to murder somebody who they had absolutely no connection to whatsoever?'

'What you mean, two people who had never even met?'

'No, I mean even more than that.'

'You'll have to explain.'

'I'm not sure what I mean myself but suppose you were doing this because of something that had actually happened to somebody else.'

'Why would you do that?'

'It doesn't matter so much as why you are actually doing it.'

'I sense that there is an "as opposed to" coming along here.'

'As opposed to why you actually believe you are doing it.'

'All right Danny, whatever reason you are doing it, the question is why are you doing it?'

'I know, I understand Meg, I agree with what you're saying but I don't have the answer.'

'Nor me.'

'One more question Meg. Do you recall the Jason Dunphy case?'

'Yeah, local Councillor killed on the tracks last year. I wasn't involved in any way in the investigation, he was on the Metro, not my jurisdiction, but I know a little background information.'

'I appreciate that it wasn't your case but knowing what you know about both Jason Dunphy and Velma Vine, would you put those two cases together in any way at all?'

'It wouldn't be too hard would it, it would probably be harder not to, both killed on the tracks, both at remote stations both involved with local councils, you certainly couldn't discount it. On the other hand, it could just be plain and simple coincidence.'

'Coincidence, there's a word I seem to keep falling over recently.'

'Sometimes it just happens that way and you have to accept it.'

'Right Megan, I suppose that's it, see you in another three years.'

Just then Megan looked over at Lizzie intently, Lizzie had played the part of a bystander in the conversation. 'Have we met before Lizzie, I can't recall where when or why but for some reason I sense something familiar?'

'We may have done Megan, everybody seems to meet everybody else these days. If you've not actually met them in the flesh, then you've seen them on social media. If we have met, then please accept my apologies, because like you, I can't recall either.'

'It won't be on social media, I deliberately avoid that, where exactly did you say you worked?'

'I'm retained as a Consultant by the Combined Authority but currently, I'm working out of the Children's Commissioner's office at Norford Council.'

'I see, hence your association with my favourite councillor.'

'Yes, he's quite something isn't he,'

'He certainly is.'

'Thanks Megan, I'll see you around,' said Senetti.

'Not as much as I'd like to Danny.'

'Why is that then?'

'I'm being transferred.'

'Really, where to?'

'I'll be based in Bangor.'

'Bangor, Wales?'

'Is there any other.'

'Why is that then?'

'It's at my request, my mother has not been very well of late and my dad, although he's fit and well for his age, he finds it a strain to look after her. They are all I've got, in the way of family, so I've made the decision to be nearer them and after all these years in the north of England, I'm going back to God's country.'

'Where do they live?'

'They live in a place called Llanystumdwy.'

'Can't say that I know it. I'm certainly not going to attempt to say it.'

'Can't say that I'm surprised on either count. It's on the Llyn Peninsula about half way between Pwllheli and Criccieth, have you heard of either of those places.'

'I have, yes, both of them, what's more, I can pronounce both their names, when do you go?'

'I'm in transition now, just waiting for a house I'm buying in the area to be finalised, it's all gone through, I'm just waiting for the heads up from the solicitor, then I'm off. I'm on a week at the most, maybe even days.'

'Good luck with it, I'll miss you.'

'I've got to go too.' Said Lizzie.

Senetti said, 'Oh, I thought we might have a cup of coffee, discuss the case a bit more.'

'Sorry not today, perhaps later. We are meeting up with Alberta later in the week aren't we, do it then eh? See you Megan, nice to meet you.'

'I've got to go too, I'll walk with you Lizzie.'

Senetti watched the two women as they both walked together in silence. They walked back out through the white picket gate, crossed the gravel car park, and walked towards their respective cars. In his mind, their cars became metaphors for the individual women. One a new flash showy sports car and the other an older solid type saloon. As they both drove towards the cobbled lane, they individually passed Senetti's line of vision, and both smiled and gave him a hand wave.

He pondered on his view of both. One he knew well, or as well as he knew anybody. She was a sound person and he trusted her. He trusted both her integrity and her judgement. The other he hardly knew at all. It was unfair, he knew this, to pass judgement on her based on such short and limited acquaintance. Yet, he felt he didn't trust her, neither her integrity nor her judgement.

Senetti, went back inside the little waiting room and sat down. He pondered on his conversations about the case of Alma Alice Spain, Jason Dunphy and now Velma Vine. He thought about his conversations with Alberta Curtis Brightland, with Ava Gardner, the pub Landlady, and now with Megan Rees Jenkins. He was beginning to tire of repeating this to himself but once again he considered these three incidents. He couldn't see how any of them could be suicides or accidents. He now thought the three of them were murders. Another thought now came back into his head. Were these cases connected to each other? There was the obvious connection of the safeguarding aspect but was there another connection, perhaps one that had been overlooked or not yet uncovered. Then there was the methodology. It was true they weren't identical, two deaths on tracks and one hit and run in a deserted remote street, no they weren't identical scenes of crime but they were similar. There were no guns, knives, bombs or poisons involved, and why was that? Was it because the murderer wanted to make these incidents look like accidents so that he wouldn't be caught? He decided that it obviously was, but was there also another reason. There was also another question which was absolutely begging to be asked. If the murders were connected, then surely so was the murderer, was he one and the same person?

Finally, he considered his investigating colleagues. It was Megan's attitude and comments that had stirred him in this. He compared her challenging approach to the almost non- participatory approach of Lizzie Lambert's, who had stood there in silence throughout, barely asking a question, barely taking an interest. Then there was Alberta who obviously didn't want the case in the first place and just wanted to skip back to London on every occasion. He was convinced that she was just going to hang around for another two or three weeks, then submit some bland report that basically said, 'nothing to report.' She would use his name to give it local credibility. So that when people read the report it would say "....co-authored by Councillor Danny Senetti."

Well, that wasn't his way. Once he started something he did his best to finish it. Furthermore, three innocent, local people, maybe even more than three, had been murdered in Greater Manchester. These victims and their families deserved more respect. It was his part of the world, he lived here, he didn't live in London. He decided there and then he wasn't going to be the local help anymore. He was going to take the lead and there wasn't anything, anybody could do about it.

He knew what he needed to do. He was a bit of a loner in most things.He didn't have many people who he saw on a regular basis. He didn't, for example, meet up with the boys on a Friday night. Arrangements like that, didn't suit him. He always went into the pub alone. Once he was in though, he was in company, if he wanted it.

When it came to work though, he did his best work with a partner. He would bring his own partner in, just as Alberta had brought Lizzie in. That partner though had to be one he could trust and rely on and there just weren't many of those about. In addition to trust and reliability, this was murder and murderers are dangerous, so it had to be somebody who could hold their nerve too.

There was one person though, who had all those credentials. He only knew of one and he wasn't sure if she'd sign up with him again, after the case of *A Man of Insignificance* during which both him and her had almost ended up dead themselves.

Nevertheless, if you don't ask then you don't get. So, he was going to ask and see if she'd have him. That person was - Doctor Maxine Wells.

Chapter 18

Threesome

Charles Trubshaw (1840 – 1917) was born into an architectural family and it was therefore natural, that he should take up that profession, which unsurprisingly he did.

For most of his working life he was associated with the design and construction of railway buildings. Prior to building the Midland Hotel in Manchester he had only ever built Railway Stations. It was therefore inevitable that some critics of both him and the hotel building itself would say that it looked like a railway station and naturally some of them did.

The Midland Hotel was commissioned by the Midland Railway Company in their expectancy of coming to Manchester. This though was an expectation on their part that was not realised. Nevertheless, this grand Edwardian, 312-bedroom hotel was opened in 1903. The building now has a grade 2 listed status and is the oldest hotel in Manchester and arguably the best. The hotel's guest list is so illustrious, it is impossible to start it and completely impossible to finish it. Anybody who is anybody and has visited Manchester in the last hundred years plus, has stayed at 'The Midland' and is still doing so.

There are an endless number of stories and fables associated with The Midland Hotel. Some completely true, some false and some probably in the middle of both. Many of them connected to person or persons of fame. Probably the two most repeated one's concern two entirely different situations. The first story is that on the 4th of May 1904, an inaugural meeting took place between two gentlemen. These gentlemen were Charles Stuart Rolls and Frederik Henry Royce and because of the conversation that ensued between them that day, the company of Rolls Royce was later founded.

The second story concerns the footballing superstar, soccer genius and earnest carouser George Best. At the time George was out of favour with his club Manchester United and his career was experiencing a temporary lull. George had spent the evening, in the company of the then Miss World, winning heavily in a nearby casino. Later that night, a waiter, who apparently, was also an ardent Manchester United supporter, upon delivering champagne to George's hotel room witnessed thousands of pounds and the current Miss World displayed tastefully on the king-size bed. This prompted the remark from the waiter, 'Where did it all go wrong George?

It was a Saturday night and tonight Jay Chopra was staying at the Midland Hotel. It was his birthday and he had planned a special treat for himself. He had reserved a penthouse room on the top floor with a balcony that looked out onto the city of Manchester. From this balcony, he had an aerial view of all the city lights of Manchester.

The reservation of the room had been very expensive and even more expensive was the female company he had hired for the night. It was though, he told himself a once a year treat, it wasn't as if he did it regularly. Then he told himself, he did do it regularly, hire company that is, but not in such grand surroundings as a penthouse suite in The Midland. Anyway, what matter, he could afford it and what after all was money for, if it didn't buy you some pleasure now and again?

He was very well paid at the city council as Director of Social Services and so he should be, he was talented and he worked hard. He had worked his way up from a humble background, worked hard at school, put himself through university, gained the qualifications, then started on the bottom rung. On the personal front, he had remained a bachelor all his life, with no family responsibilities and what was more important to him, none of the costs associated with keeping one. In the main he led a modest moderate life and did nothing to excess.

Yes, there was no doubt, he deserved what was in prospect for him tonight and he was unashamedly looking forward to it.

Just then he thought about the 'fee' he had agreed to pay his escorts. He produced an envelope from his inside jacket pocket and placed it on the small table in front of him

Tonight, he was expecting two special guests, two ladies, their names were Camille and Justine and he was excited about the meeting. Camille and Justine weren't old friends, he didn't know them, he had never met them before in his life, well not in the flesh. He doubted that their real names even were Camille and Justine, but names didn't matter.

He had met them both online. No, upon reflection that wasn't quite accurate, he had met one of them online, Camille, the other girl he had not met in any way. When he had suggested to Camille that another woman would, 'enhance the experience for all three of them,' she had readily agreed. She had said that this 'could be arranged' and that she would fix it and bring along her friend, Justine, although obviously as there were two of them the price would now 'be enhanced,' that was the term, she had used.

He now looked at his wrist watch, 7.55pm. Camille and Justine were due at 8:00pm, he had his instructions from Camille, no texts, no phone calls, no emails no anything. She had told him quite firmly but politely that if he contravened any of this then there would as she put it be, 'no date.' Anyway, how could he do any of these? The only contact details he had for Camille were through the 'Courtesan' website. She had suggested a room number to him, which he had complied with and she had reliably informed him that she and her friend would arrive as close to eight-o-clock as possible. There was no doubt that Camille was controlling the whole situation but that was exactly what he expected from his dominatrix women. Now as he sat on the edge of the magnificent king-size bed he felt a combination of nervousness and excitement.

The intercom rang in his suite. 'Hello Jay, Camille and Justine here, can you buzz us into the penthouse lift?'

'Immediately, come up.'

Less than thirty seconds later the doors of the private elevator opened onto the penthouse suite and as they did, the two girls glided silently into the suite of rooms. They were both taller than him in their heels. He noticed that they both wore long black evening dresses and black velvet shawls with hoods and that they were both wearing black face masks in a kind of Marie Antoinette style, which covered the top half of their faces. Even under their disguises he could see that both women were elegant and ravishingly beautiful. Their dress code puzzled him, he was tempted to ask why, but he thought that he would postpone the query for the moment, then he realised that there was a masque ball taking place downstairs in the main hall and for some reason, possibly connected with concealing their identities, they were trying to appear inconspicuous by fitting in with that event. His mind concentrated on the situation for a few seconds, then he realised that it was something that he didn't really care about one way or another. If anything, he approved of it. He thought that he would concentrate on some initial pleasantries.

'I'm Jay, I just love the dresses and the masks,' as he said this he smiled then he leaned forward and kissed both women separately, on their cheeks.

They both returned his smile.

'I'm Camille this is Justine.' They both pushed back their hoods from their faces and smiled.

He walked across to the small table and picked up the envelope he had placed upon it a few minutes ago.

'This is yours Camille, as we agreed. Shall we get it out of the way first?'

'That will be O.K. Jay, just leave it there, let's not rush the matter, let's not rush anything. You're not in a hurry, are you?'

He studied her eyes behind the mask.

'Not in the slightest, leave the masks on, it's more interesting, it's not every day I get to meet two masked women. Would you like to eat?' As he said this he looked over towards a buffet tray which was placed on a table near the far wall and contained an assortment of caviar, and cold cuts.

'No thank you,' said Camille.'

'No thank you, said Justine.'

He said, 'What about some Champagne its vintage?' He looked over at the champagne, which was cooling in the silver ice bucket; there were also three crystal champagne flutes resting on a silver tray next to the bucket and a silver jug, some small bottles of water, a bottle of red wine and a bottle of white wine which was in a cooler.'

'I'll get it,' said Justine.

She walked over to the ice bucket and proceeded to pour three glasses. The keen observer would have noticed quizzically that the young woman only filled one of the glasses with champagne, the other two she filled with water, but of course there was no keen observer.

'Shall we get started,' said Jay.

'As we said, we've got lots of time, let's all enjoy ourselves,' said Camille.

'Sorry girls, it's me, I'm just feeling a little nervous.'

'It's understandable Jay, but there is no need, we'll look after you, won't we Justine.'

'Yes, we will, tell you what Jay, let's start at nine-o-clock. Let's have a glass of that vintage champagne, relax, talk awhile, what do you say, just a bit of a chat ? Oh, and we've brought all the equipment, would you like to see it?'

'No, not now, you're right girls, let's leave that for later. It's always better if we know a little about each other, not too much though.'

'Are you from Manchester, do you work for a living Jay.'

'I am originally from Manchester and I do work for a living yes, what about you Justine?'

She laughed, then she said, 'we do this Jay, what we're doing now Camille and I, we meet men for sex games, we're called call-girls, or hookers or hostesses, I call myself a courtesan but the name doesn't really matter.'

'What sort of sex games?'

'Any games,' said Camille. 'We don't mind, we don't make the rules, the client does, you do Jay, we're pretty easy-going within reason.'

Justine said, 'What we do is not really that interesting, until of course we are actually doing it then it is wonderful. It isn't though the same as a proper job. If somebody in passing, asked either of us what we did for a living, we wouldn't own up, we'd say something else. I've always admired people who are confident enough in the integrity of their occupation to own up.'

'That's interesting, I've not heard anybody say that before.'

'What do you do Jay? I bet you'd own up, I bet you've got a proper job. What is it teacher, banker or doctor maybe?'

'No neither of those. I'm a Director of Social Services.'

Camille said, 'I'm none the wiser Jay, what exactly is a Director of Social Services?'

'I'm directly responsible for looking after all the vulnerable people in the city.

'That's a big responsibility. I thought that was a social worker.'

He indicated his empty glass, Justine refilled it.

'It is a Social Worker but for want of another title, I'm the head social worker in the city.'

'Wow, you're a prize Jay. We've got ourselves a prize Camille.'

'Thank you, ladies. I wasn't expecting any of this but I must admit, the conversation is very pleasant.' He raised his glass in their direction.

'Aren't social workers like doctors and lawyers, don't they specialise. Did you specialise Jay?'

'You are very knowledgeable, yes I work with looked after children.'

'Camille said, 'kids in care?'

'Yes, do you know anything about them?'

'I can't say that I have any first-hand knowledge but Justine knows a little about it.'

'Really, is that right Justine?'

'I have some experience of it, yes.'

She refilled his once again empty glass.

'What is your experience, were you a social worker?' By now he was gulping the champagne down.

'No, I wasn't a social worker but for a time I was a kid in care.'

Camille said, 'Let's have another drink, it's only eight – thirty, we said that we'd start at nine-o-clock.'

'Fine by me.' said Jay. 'I'm enjoying the conversation.'

'I'll get them,' said Camille, 'Why don't we go and stand on the veranda, look out across the city.'

'Yes, let's go on the veranda. It's not often, that Justine and I get the opportunity to look out over the tops of a major city like Manchester.'

The man and the two women walked over to the large double-glazed door. Jay picked up the remote control, pressed the button and the door slid effortlessly and silently open. All three of them stepped out onto the veranda. The two women stood facing the outside and flanked the man who stood between them facing back into the room.

'That's an amazing sight,' said Camille as she looked out onto the city lights.

'How is it that you're such an expert on looked after children Justine?'

'I spent many years of my life being one.'

'Really, where was that?'

'You say it Jay, as if it is some sort of curiosity.'

'No, I didn't mean it to sound like that.'

'Well if you're really interested Jay.'

'I am Justine.'

'If you really want to know, it wasn't too far from here'.

'For how long?'

'All my childhood, until I reached independence.'

'Were you with foster parents?'

'Some of the time yes.'

'As we have talked about foster parents and you are a Social Worker, I've got a question for you Jay.'

'All right.'

'Did you ever have any experience of foster parents?'

'Oh yes all the time, most children who come into care are looked after by foster parents.

'Have you ever sat in any kind of judgement against a foster parent?'

'Judgement? That's a very odd question, I don't think that I have ever sat in judgement on anybody, not deliberately anyway.'

'Surely, people who are looking after other people's children must be absolutely beyond reproach.'

'When foster parents....' his voice trailed off in mid-sentence and then in what seemed one seamless choreo-graphed move, both Justine and Camille crouched down and as they did, their arms encircled Jay Chopra's legs, then simultaneously they heaved him over the balcony veranda. It all happened so fast that the man hardly knew that it had occurred. His screams could be heard for a few seconds piercing the still night air. Then they fell silent, as he landed, in a broken boned-heap, an ever-widening whirlpool of blood, seeped onto the tarmac from his body, as his life expired, in the street below.

As he plummeted to his death the two women didn't even look over the balcony.

They then came back into the room. Camille washed all three champagne flutes, then filled only one of the glasses with champagne, she placed the two empty glasses in her handbag.

Placing their hoods back on, they both left the room. Again, they took the private lift and descended one floor. This time they opened a large metal door marked 'fire exit,' They then quickly and expertly and in the darkness, descended the fire escape which brought them out around the back of the building at ground floor level. Once outside they removed their masks before climbing into separate black cabs which formed a queue at the taxi rank in the road, adjacent to the hotel, then in seconds, they were both gone from the scene, as if they'd never been there, in the first place.

Chapter 19

Doctor Maxine Wells

When Doctor Maxine Wells logged into her computer that morning, she received a techno surprise. For when she routinely checked her patient appointments throughout that day, she discovered a very interesting entry which she wasn't expecting. Scheduled for the midday slot was a name that she knew all too well; Danny Senetti.

She regularly heard of, but she had neither seen nor heard from Senetti himself for almost a year. She rarely admitted it and even then, only to herself, but she held a grudging affection for some reason, which she could not explain, for the jaded councillor. Senetti was the biggest doctor-dodger who she could think of, so why was he coming to see her? She certainly hoped that he wasn't ill in any way. She checked his medical record, nothing had been added nor subtracted since she had last looked at it over a year ago and apart from a few common childhood ailments, the record which had been transferred over from his previous doctor, was the same blank sheet it had always been. There was not even a record of a routine blood pressure check. Danny Senetti had been on her patients' register and her fathers before her, for over twenty years. Yet in that time he had not once visited the practice for any kind of consultation. So why was he making an appearance now, after all this time? Maybe, he had suddenly become health conscious. This often happened to doctor-dodgers when they reached a certain stage in their lives. Maybe he was looking for some help with his drinking, which was legendary in Winton Kiss and further afield. Somehow, she doubted either of these as the reason for his intended visit, nevertheless she was puzzled.

Unusually, her patient rota went to plan and at 11:55 am, she stepped out of her surgery and into the corridor to greet Senetti. He was sitting patiently in one of the grey plastic chairs that were placed around the practice. He was holding what appeared to be a paper file of some kind. When he saw her, he sprang to his feet. There were other patients in the corridor so he thought it was best to keep it formal.

'Doctor, how good of you to see me.'

He stepped inside the surgery-room and she closed the door behind him, as he did, he placed the file he was holding on a small side table inside the room.

'Danny, it's lovely to see you.' She said as she clasped him by the shoulders and looked into his eyes.

He returned her gaze. There had only ever been one way to describe Maxine Wells. He had thought that, when he had first seen her and the description still held true... tall, blond, beautiful and clever. Apart from his mother, she was probably his favourite person.

'You too Maxine, it's almost a year.'

She indicated the patient's chair and he sat down.

'How are you?'

'Never better.'

'You're not ill in any way?'

'Not as far as I know.'

'Are you sure?'

'Yeah, I think so, should I be?'

'Yes, you should be.'

'Why?'

'Because Danny, as you well know, I am a doctor, you made an appointment to see me and I'm working right now as a doctor and these time slots are for my patients' consultations and if you're not here for that purpose, then you are taking up the time of somebody who could be.'

'I am one of your patients Doctor, I needed to see you at short-notice and this is the only way I know of doing it, and didn't you once tell me Doctor, that even if one of your patients has nothing wrong with him either mentally or physically, the fact alone, that he needs to talk to you, is grounds for an appointment.'

'I seem to remember saying that, yes.'

'Well that's it.'

'What's it?'

'I needed to talk to you. If I have contravened your high moral and medical ethics, I apologise, but I do need to talk to you.'

'All right you're forgiven, but at least let's put some medical emphasis on the appointment. I'm going to check your blood pressure and when you leave this room the nurse will be waiting for you and she's going to put you through a well-man procedure. I arranged it for you as soon as I saw your name on the rota this morning.'

'Oh! Do we have to?'

'Yes, we do, anyway when did you last have any kind of medical check-up?'

'Not sure, oh yes, I remember now, it was about ten years ago. The council insisted that all councillors had to have regular medicals, it was to do with the pension fund, they were probably looking to expel us from it, if we were found to have any illnesses. It was also to do with a healthy living, work-life balance trend that was doing the rounds, it was good while it lasted, they brought in an outside caterer who made these healthy eating lunches. There was a beetroot and feta cheese flan that I grew particularly fond of.'

'Danny, the medical, what about the medical?'

'I can't remember the detail. All the councillors had to book an appointment with various consultants in Manchester. After we all had the first consultation, the council received the medical bill. Once they saw that, they sacked the caterer and cancelled the whole pro-gramme. They decided as human beings we weren't worth that sort of money. Only new bin trucks and com-puter systems are worth that sort of money to the council, not people. We all went back to Draught Guinness and pork pie and pickles in the Town Hall Tavern.'

'When was this?'

'As I said, about ten years ago, maybe less.'

'As your GP, I've got no record of it.'

Danny shrugged his shoulders, 'Maxine, it's The Council, what do you expect? I've got no record of it either and it was my medical.'

'No matter, anyway this just reinforces the idea that you are long overdue some medical attention, don't you agree?'

'If you say so Doctor.'

Maxine applied the blood pressure cuff with auto-matic expedience.

'Well?'

'Well what?

'Well, is it a secret? Do I need to start doing this or stop doing that?'

'Unbelievably it's normal.'

'So, I'm in the clear.'

'As far as your blood pressure is concerned, yes. How is your drinking these days? Have you ever considered getting some help with it?'

'Maxine, my drinking is fine, it's going well, now you've done your duty and I feel reassured. Your receptionist told me I only get fifteen minutes on this appointment and half of it has gone already. So, can I please explain?'

'Go on then.'

'I need your advice and assistance.'

'All right, what with.'

'A case I'm working on.'

'A case for the council? Shouldn't you be discussing it with your Director of Public Health?'

'It's not really a medical case.'

'No? What a surprise, it's not really a council case either is it?'

'Why do you say that Maxine?'

'I say it because you've never been near me in your life with any council business and I say it because I know you Senetti. So, what actually is it? What are you mixed up in this time.'

'It is connected to the council indirectly. It's a possible case of triple murder.'

'Triple murder! aren't you getting a bit confused here. You're the local councillor, you're supposed to get involved in Health and Well-being, Education, Planning,

Safeguarding Children, Finance, inconveniencing all of us with speed bumps, road works and double yellow lines, not triple murder. That's the job of the local detective.'

'Maxine, I haven't got time right now to explain it all, when is your next chunk of free time?'

'This evening, after surgery, I suppose.'

'This evening, don't you stop around now for lunch? That's why I booked this midday slot.'

'Danny, I'm a G.P. I start work at seven in the morning and on a good day I finish at seven in the evening. Often much later. My lunch as you call it, well let's see what cuisine treat is in store for me today.'

She delved into her desk drawer and came out holding a lunch-box. She took the lid off and showed him the contents. Inside the box was a plastic bag containing some salad, there was also an apple and a banana.

'The biggest decision I'll have to make about lunch today, is shall I eat the banana or the apple first. Here is my lunch for today and I'll have to eat it at my desk whilst I'm between patients; glamourous isn't it, the life of a G.P?'

'It's slavery, all right then, meet me in The Travellers Oak tonight at seven-thirty.'

'I don't know Danny, its short notice.'

'Maxine, it's on your way home, it's almost across the road from your house. You can park your car up and walk it, in a couple of minutes. Just one hour and I'll explain everything. You'll be back in front of the TV, by nine-o-clock.'

She looked at her wristwatch, 'you've got five minutes before my next patient comes in.'

'The leader of the council put me forward for this, she pressed me into doing it, I objected but I couldn't really refuse. I'm working with two other officers. We were investigating what was originally described as 'incidents' but the more I've looked into them, the more I'm inclined to think that they are murders.'

'Danny, if you've got two other people assisting you, why do you need my input?'

'Maxine, I'm trying to be concise.'

'Well be it, then.'

'It's not easy, when you're interrupting at every stage, I've got an issue with my two colleagues.'

'What, both?'

'You are doing it again.'

'Danny, you are not the easiest person to work with, are you sure it's not you?'

'Now, if you can you just let me speak uninter-rupted for two minutes and I'll explain.'

A brief silence ensued.

'Thank you, I'll carry on. No, it isn't me Maxine, it's them. For whatever reason, I've not figured it out yet, but they do not seem to be interested in what they claim to be doing. They have no energy for the investi-gation. I might be complicating the issue, I am prepared to accept that. It might be simple, they might both be just lazy. It could be as simple as that. All I know, is that in a very short space of time I've lost all confidence in them, I've come to mistrust them both and I can't hon-estly say any different. I genuinely wish I could, but I just can't.'

'I can see that you mean it. Have you got an example of this laziness?'

'One of them has shown no enthusiasm at all for visiting any scenes of any of these incidents. Apart from a couple of discussions in the office, she has made no contribution whatsoever. During the investigation of one of the incidents the name of a possible material witness came to light. I asked Alberta, she's the one, I'm talking about, if she would go and contact this witness and interview her. This witness is now working in London and Alberta was down there at the time.'

'What was the problem?'

'The problem was, she put up all kinds of objections against doing this.'

'Did she go and see the witness?'

'I don't know, but I doubt it. I'll find out later this week, when I meet her again and right at this moment, I'm not sure that there is much to be gained by doing so. Perhaps she did after all, but the point is she should have been jumping at the chance, not trying to find excuses for not doing it.'

'Anyway, I'd like you to meet them, see what you think, so I'm going to try and set up a date this weekend, perhaps a lunch, will you come and give me your opinion.'

'I'll think about it, but if I do, it will only be for you Danny, and as long as you understand and accept that I'm not taking any preconceived ideas with me, about anything or from anybody, including you.'

'Maxine, I wouldn't have it any other way.'

'What exactly is the case about?'

'Over simplified we are looking....'

She laughed, then she interrupted, 'Danny you've never over simplified anything in your life, over complicated yes.'

'We are considering three separate deaths of three professional adults who have all died in unusual circumstances and they all have a connection to safeguarding children.'

'What sort of circumstances, what sort of professionals, when was this?'

'No, don't let's discuss it now, it's a digression and you haven't got the time. I can tell you all this tonight at The Travellers Oak I'll give you the full briefing, I've got paperwork and all.'

'Now you are stretching the bounds of credibility, you've actually got paperwork!'

'That file I've put on your side table, it's your copy, that's my paperwork. It's a paper-thin file but it's informative. Please have a look at it before we meet this evening. Back to this lunch, so you can run the rule over these fellow investigators, what do you think?'

'When do you plan to do this?'

'As I said, I was thinking of setting something up this week-end. I thought perhaps an informal lunch in Manchester, which would seem to be the easiest place for all to get to. I need to speak to Alberta and Lizzie about it, see what their commitments are. Isn't it the Malton Golf Cup, this weekend? Is your dad still golfing?'

'Yes, more than ever.'

'You'll be off work and you won't be seeing much of him this weekend.'

'My life doesn't completely revolve around work and my father.'

Senetti knew that the statement she had just made was untrue. Nevertheless, he refrained from any challenge to it, instead he said.

'I know that Maxine.'

'Oh, all right then.'

'Good, then that's settled.'

'How long have I got now?'

'It's two minutes before you keep your appointment with the well-man nurse.'

'Maxine do I really have to, I've got a life-threatening situation, that I need to give my attention to this afternoon.'

'Senetti, you are lying, but that doesn't matter. What does matter to you, is no well-man appointment for you, no week end lunch for me and no Travellers Oak this evening, so make your decision. Oh, and you've got one minute now and I'll be looking for the nurse's report on you at five-o-clock today.'

'All right I'll attend, I'm looking forward to it. What's the nurse's name?'

'Her name is Lucy.'

'It's a good name.'

'Good, then that's settled.' She parodied his earlier statement.'

Almost immediately there was a knock on the door. Maxine Wells, rose from her chair, walked over to the door and opened it. Standing there was a woman in her early thirties, she had bright red hair, wore a cheery smile and a nurse's uniform.

'Mr Senetti, I'm Lucy, Lucy Lockett, I'm the well-man nurse.'

'Lucy Lockett, is that really your name? How absolutely wonderful.'

'It is my name, yes, and please, I've had this name many years and I've heard all the clichés about pockets and ribbon and so on.'

'You'll get none from me, I think it is a marvellous name,' said Senetti. 'I've been having a good time with names recently, only last week I met Ava Gardner.'

'Ava who?'

'It doesn't matter Lucy, you're too young.'

'We have a well-man protocol to carry out. It takes no more than half an hour and I think that you'll find it extremely beneficial to your general health awareness.'

'I'm looking forward to it,' said Senetti. As he said this he gave Maxine a glance that conveyed the opposite.

'Don't forget Lucy, can I please have a copy of your initial report on Councillor Senetti, before you send the paperwork to the lab?'

'Of course, Doctor.'

'Then follow me to the nurse's room Mr Senetti.'

Chapter 20

Chic Conway and The Bar of World Opinion.

If you were ever to find yourself in Malton Town Centre which, is about a mile from the village of Winton Kiss. If you walk into the pedestrianised shopping area, as you move away from the main road, half way down the wide footway, wedged between a bank and a building that keeps changing its uses, you will come upon a pub. This pub has a traditional pub name, but that name, although displayed outside on the wall, is rarely used and is almost forgotten. This pub for many years, for reasons which we do not need to go into, has been known as 'Lulu's for as long as anybody can remember. It is often described by Malton residents as a 'strange house,' but this is usually by the Malton residents who have never set foot in it. This is the clear majority of them, but there is much more to Lulu's than this dismissive description suggests.

From the outside, this pub is no different from many others and probably from the inside too. As you climb the five short steps, from the street that lead to the front door and enter the premises, you will enter an average size pub lounge. At the bottom of the lounge, on the right-hand side, running in a straight line then dog legging twice at about 45 degrees each time, is the bar. Bars are not unusual in a pub; a pub would not be a pub without one. Yet the bar in Lulu's is well known in the neighbourhood and is both irreverently and affectionately referred to as - *The Bar of World Opinion*. There is a good reason for this name which we shall touch upon shortly.

Unlike many other pubs these days, Lulu's does not offer food nor lodgings. It opens its doors from 11:00 am until midnight most days, closing perhaps a little earlier during the week and a little bit later at the weekend and during those times it serves little else, but drink.

It is though between the hours of midday and 5:00pm, and from Monday to Friday both days inclusive, when most pubs in such quiet locations are empty and many of them are not even open; this is when Lulu's is at its most busy and at its most interesting.

During these times, Lulu's enjoys a comparatively thriving trade. Except for Tuesday afternoon when the pub puts on a show of Bingo, the clientele who huddle around *The Bar of World Opinion,* and its immediate environs and pass through its doors between midday and 5:00pm is almost exclusively male. Although the gender is common, the clientele is vast and varied and is difficult to describe in general terms, but here is an attempt to do so and in the process, refer to the variety of people whom you would find there.

This clientele consists of actors who wander in from the nearby drama college, often they are in character and make up, but these are usually the 'pass-throughs' as they are known. The incumbent membership of *The Bar of World Opinion* itself, consists of a concoction of personnel, who include amongst many others; A Dubliner, gamblers, poets, scousers, wafflers, wags, two Welshman, an ex-detective who claims to have investigated the Lord Lucan case, a man who keeps falling into people's privets, the retired town 'gentleman's barber,' who is known as 'one eyed Jake,' a retired one-armed postman known as Wingy, and three men who are all called 'Ken.' All members of *The Bar of World Opinion* have an inherent, natural ability to compose the most elaborate lies, which they then present with verbose conviction as the most earnest truths.

Despite such a concoction within its ranks, this membership is open in disposition and is extremely knowledgeable and well read on any subject under the sun; there is not one solitary topic in existence that can be introduced to The Bar of World Opinion, without the whole membership holding views upon it, and there being at least one member claiming to be a world authority on its detail. These claims are often baffling to the onlooker as he strives to make a connection between the apparent claimant and a subject of world turning importance.

In example of this, a recent debate ensued around the *Bar of World Opinion* on the all-important question of whether the late singer, Johnny Cash, had ever actually been in prison or if it was just a piece of publicity put out at the time by his management. One of the Kens argued the case for, whilst the Dubliner argued the case against. The debate was finally settled when a local 'poet' known as 'Othellio,' claimed to have been Cash's cell mate in San Quentin Jail in 1967. His assertive boast was accepted immediately. For whilst this claim was absurd in the extreme, accepting it represented entertainment, whereas disproving it represented mundanity and The Bar of World Opinion has no such interest in either the truth or the mundane.

The lingual discourse in Lulu's can flit back and forth from warm friendly banter to down-right blatant insult. Oddly enough, when this blatant insult occurs, the recipient of it often greets the utterance with absolute delight and accepts the described mantle with perverse and joyful ownership. It is not openly discussed, but it is acknowledged within the membership that if you have not had the most extreme and abusive vilification heaped in abundance upon your personage, your immediate family, your friends, your sexual impotence, your physical features, the parentage of your children, the past associations of your mother/grandmother with American soldiers, the comedy of your garb, et al, the list is again truly endless; within three days of joining the *Bar of World Opinion,* then it is as nothing and you are a *nobody.*

With very small exception the members of the *Bar of World Opinion* do not have what can be deemed as traditional occupations. If an observer were to enquire quite simply and politely as to what somebody does for a living, then the enquirer would know no more at the end of the answer than they did at the beginning of the question. Apart from having it as casual reference, almost always, to do with somebody else, as in..." the *wife* is on the late shift at the hospital tonight," or..." oh yes *he* works for Oxfam in Africa..." None of the membership appear to be involved directly or even indirectly in the subject which places itself importantly, in today's society, to give it an everyday name, the subject of *work.*

Membership of the *Bar of World Opinion,* offers the following as reasonable explanation for not engaging wholly or even in part, in what it seemingly and collectively considers to be an immoral activity, and in an almost indignant attempt to justify why none of the members will ever do a whole weeks' work in one simple go. Individual members describe their current situation as being thus;

'Early retirement,' 'writing a novel,' 'helping my dad with his new mobility scooter,' 'training a new dog,' 'just married,' 'in dispute with the CSA,' 'waiting for a new hearing aid.' 'in love,' 'in arrears with the rent,' 'heartbroken.' There is also an abundance of what are known as 'offwiths,' as in: off with my; 'back,' 'leg,' 'nerves,' 'shoulder,' 'arse,' again the list is truly endless.

Another common trait that seems to prevail throughout the membership of The Bar of World Opinion is the universal ability of all to consume the most copious amounts of beer, lager, spirits and wine in the shortest possible time. This ability is only surpassed by the marked unwillingness and inability to make even the feeblest token gesture that resembles an attempt to pay for any of it.

Between the daylight hours, previously mentioned, the drinkers who hold residence around The Bar of World Opinion consider it to be inhabited by writers, poets, artists and philosophers whereas the remainder in Malton think that the inhabitants of The Bar of World Opinion are just a bunch of old drunks.

On this sunny Thursday afternoon at 2:02 pm, precisely, less than an hour since his well-man appointment with nurse Lucy Lockett, Danny Senetti climbed the five steps outside Lulu's, walked through the door and made straight for *The Bar of World Opinion*. Senetti, although not a frequenter to Lulu's, was well known in Malton, predominantly because of his activities as a local councillor. As he approached the bar the drinking thong fell silent.

'Councillor, we don't often see you in here.' said the pub landlord, Alfred (Hilda) Hilderbrandt.

'I do come in now and again Hilda.'

'What can I get you?'

'Hmm, have you got any red wine?'

'Yes.'

'What is it?'

'It's Luis Felipe Edwards Gran Reserva Merlot.'

'Where is it from?'

Hilda known throughout Malton for his paucity of wit and intellect replied, 'Asda, no Aldi.'

'No, I don't mean which supermarket Hilda, I mean which country.'

Hilda, lifted a bottle of wine to his eye line and squinted at the label, speaking in a slow and ponderous way, he said, 'Colchaqua Valley.'

'Where's that?' Senetti said.

'Where's that Ken?'

'Chile.'

'Chile, where's that Ken?'

'South America.'

'I'll have a small glass of it.'

'I'm looking for a man called Charlie Conway.'

'Chic!'

'That's him, is he in?'

'Yes, he's in the quiet room reading the Guardian on his laptop.'

'What does Chic drink?'

'Today, he's drinking a small glass of white wine.'

'I'll take a small glass of white wine then.'

'Don't you want to know where it's from Councillor?'

'Yeah, go on then.'

'It's from New Zealand.'

'Good.'

'What's up Councillor, are you up for election again? Is Chic going to put some posters up for you?'

Senetti ignored the comment. The Bar of World Opinion was well known throughout Malton, for its collective skittish observations. He walked over to the half glass green door with a glass of wine in each hand. He pushed the door open with his knee and entered the room. Once inside the room, he could see that apart from himself, there was only one other occupant.

The other occupant was a man. Senetti thought he was about sixty years of age. Even sitting down, he appeared thin and wiry. He was clean shaven and Senetti observed that he had skin like a baby's. He was wearing shiny black shoes with pink socks, an immaculate light-coloured suit with a black shirt. In the top pocket of his jacket was a silk handkerchief, the same pink colour as his socks. On his head was a brushed felt fedora hat, the same colour as his suit. The hat was encircled by a pink hat band. Senetti considered that it was not difficult to understand why he was known as 'Chic.' Chic was looking at a laptop.

As Senetti walked over to Chic's table, the seated man removed his hat to reveal a shock of silver white hair.

'Hello Charlie, I'm Danny...'

'I know who you are Councillor.'

'I bought you a drink.'

'That's very kind of you.'

Senetti placed both glasses of wine on the small table.

Chic looking up from his laptop said, 'Crossword question "hijklmno," can be running, still or deep, five letters ?'

'Water,' said Senetti.

'I considered that but I couldn't place, "hijklmno" what does it mean.'

'It's an alphabetical sequence of letters, it runs from the letter *aitch* to letter *o*, H2O, is the chemical symbol for water.'

'So it is, did you just figure that out; I'm impressed Councillor.'

'Call me Danny.'

'My name is Charlie, but everybody calls me Chic.'

'Which do you prefer.'

'I'm used to Chic now.'

'Chic, it is then.'

'Please sit down. Try this one, the clue is *Monday hub,* I know it's an anagram but I just can't get it.'

'Hmm, I'll have to ponder on that one. Are you enjoying your retirement?'

'I think so yes, it's good to have the freedom to go where you want, whenever you want. Though I guess you are going to put me back at work, at least in spirit.'

'Why do you say that?'

'Why else would you be here?'

'I need your help, I need your memory.'

'It's not what it once was.'

'I've heard different.'

'I'm trying to establish if two professional public servants ever served together on the same combined authority committee. If they did, which one and when, it could even be more than one.'

'Over what period?'

'I'm guessing, but going off the age frames of the people, I don't see it being more than the last twenty years at the most.'

'Occupations?'

'One was a councillor, the other a social worker.'

'That's a lot of people over that period. As I'm sure you know there are ten boroughs in the Combined Authority. Average number of councillors for each authority is around sixty, that's getting on for six hundred plus councillors, and that doesn't include different councillors coming in and going out. Over twenty years that could be three, even four thousand and we haven't even started on officers which would be a similar problem. That's a lot of permutations. Do you know any more!?'

'There is a strong possibility that this committee could be connected to children's safeguarding.'

'There is obviously a reason why you can't, but to ask the obvious question, why can't you just ask them? The Councillor and the Social Worker that is.'

'They are both dead.'

'What is the name of the councillor?'

'Jason Declan Dunphy.'

'And the social worker?'

'Alma Alice Spain.'

Chic, nodded silently.

'Senetti said, 'Do you know those names?'

'Yes, but more for the manner of their deaths than their attendance on committees.'

'You can't remember if they served together?'

'They almost certainly will have, but without scouring thousands of files, in the hope that we get lucky, it's an impossible task.'

'Could we gain access to these files.'

'No, not that many Danny, we can't ransack thousands of council files. Not unless you want to be suspended from the council whilst we are both investigated for gross misconduct and breach of confidentiality. If we could narrow it down to say ten files, twenty maybe, then we'd have a chance.'

'Chic there is a third person who may have also sat on the same committee.'

'Councillor or Officer?'

'Neither.'

'Who then?'

'Foster Carer.'

'Why didn't you say so?'

'Does it make any difference; doesn't the same obstacle apply?'

'No, it doesn't.'

'Why?'

'Let's concentrate Danny on children's safeguarding panels. First, it is decided what role is needed, then once that is established, if this role is best carried out by a group of people as opposed to an individual. If it's the latter. Then we need to select the personnel who will make up the membership of that body. Obviously, those committee members are expected to bring some expertise to the proceedings. That expertise can be either political or occupational, a bit of both would be ideal either way, but they are drawn from a larger pool of people.'

'I understand what you are saying Chic, it makes sense and I knew some of it anyway, but where are we going with it?'

'Councillors and officers are in great demand across the board to fill these positions. They are both professionals, with the political and occupational expertise needed. Foster carers though qualify in a different way.'

'What way?'

'Foster carers are invaluable in safeguarding children. The whole provision of looked after children would just collapse without them. However, when it comes to filling committee places, there are some exceptions, there always will be, but foster carers in the main only have one area of expertise.'

'Foster care!'

'Yes, what is the name of the foster carer.'

'Velma Vine.'

'Oh yes, Velma, she was long term chairperson of The Fostering Panel, a position she held for many years.'

'When exactly, do you know?'

'I do Danny yes.'

'When Chic?'

'I remember she took up the role immediately we entered the millennium, in January, the year two thousand and she was still doing it up to the time of her death. She was on her way to chair The Fostering Panel, when she had her accident. Another death eh Danny. You're investigating three dead members of the fostering panel?'

'Chic, I'll confide...'

'No please don't Danny, please don't confide in me, I don't want to know. I had forty years on various councils. The last thirty of them spent keeping confidences. Now I don't have to keep any, I feel liberated.'

'Fair enough Chic, what about Jason and Alma. Does this help us with them?'

'It certainly does. Now we know the specific panel, this information should be in the public domain. Tell you what Danny, you go and get two more drinks and while you are doing that, I'll have a little tap around this lap-top. See if I can find the answer to your question.'

When Senetti returned with another glass of red and one of white wine, Chic looked up from his lap-top with an unmistakeable look of triumph on his face, he said;

'Velma Vine, Jason Dunphy and Alma Alice Spain were all sitting members of the Combined Authority Fostering Panel from January 2002 until January 2005. At which point Alma stood down, Jason carried on until April 2007, and we know what Velma did.'

'Between January 2002, and January 2005, all three of them, sat on the fostering panel. If the panel met every month over a three-year period that could be approaching forty panels. That's a lot of panels to go through Chic.'

'No, it wouldn't be that many, that's not how it operates Danny. Panel members are drawn from a larger pool. They usually work on a three to one ratio If they did, there would have been a pool of twenty-one. They don't like to switch the chairs around too much so they will have had a chair and a vice chair alternating. They have to have a bigger pool than the number of members required to make the panel constitutional in case of sickness, holidays and other absences. One pool member will have probably sat on ten panels out of thirty plus, obviously when you bring another member into it that number is reduced even more. When you are looking for the number of panels that your three all sat on at the same time, you are probably looking at two or three panels, could even be just one do you understand?'

'I do yes, thanks Chic, that's really helpful.'

The both sipped their wine.

'Tell me Chic, what does The Fostering Panel actually do, why does it exist?'

'Good question, it actually has a vital but very narrow remit. It considers the official registration of foster carers.'

'What exactly is there to consider.'

'To be a foster carer, you have to undergo a very intensive and intrusive assessment. After this assessment, the fostering panel decides on whether you can have a registration or not. Think of it as a type of licence to practise.'

'Does the fostering panel have the authority to withdraw your licence?'

'Yes, that's the other part of its remit.'

'What happens if you lose your licence?'

'No licence, no practise, its known as deregistration.'

'A bit like losing your driving licence, eh?'

'No Danny, it's not like losing your driving licence. You lose your driving licence, you can't drive for a year or two maybe three. Then you get it back, your insurance premium goes up a bit, then it's all forgotten. You lose your licence as a foster carer, you lose your foster kids, they may have been with you since they were babies, could be sixteen, seventeen years, they are your

CHIC CONWAY AND THE BAR OF WORLD OPINION

children in almost every way and you're their dad or their mum. You don't get them back, ever and it's never forgotten, it can be absolutely traumatic.'

'Sorry, I didn't look at it that way.'
  'Most people don't.'
  'Why would you be deregistered?'
  'There can be a lot of reasons, internal disciplinary ones. The most common reason would probably be a complaint made against your practise.'
  'A complaint by whom?'
  'Anybody you can think of, foster parents come under intense scrutiny, much more than ordinary parents, sometimes the complainant is anonymous and sometimes the complaint is obviously ridiculous, but they all have to be investigated.'
  'What sort of complaint?'
  'Oh, they are too vast and various, could be absolutely anything, made by absolutely anybody.'

Senetti finished his wine and rose from the table. 'Thanks Chic, you have been a godsend. One more thing, would you mind if I had your phone number, just in case?

  The older man spoke out his phone number and Senetti put it in his own phone. He walked over to the door and as he reached it, he turned around and looked at Chic, 'Dynamo,' he said.

  At first Chic looked perplexed, then a smile spread across his face, 'Dynamo, Monday, hub, Dynamo,' he said.'

  Once outside Lulu's, Senetti checked his wristwatch: 3:02pm. He had spent precisely one hour in

Chic's company. He made a phone call to Christine Harris, she was his personal assistant at Norford Council, he shared her expertise with other councillors. She had worked for various councils during her so far, thirty-year career and there was very little that she didn't know about their various systems. She was a good woman, she knew his weaknesses and his strengths and she kept an eye out for him. He both admired and respected her and as far as he knew the feeling was mutual.

'Hello Christine, how are you?'

'I'm well Councillor and you?'

'I'm well, you won't mind if I'm brief will you Chris?'

'No, not at all.'

'What can we find out about the Combined Authority Fostering Panel that convened regularly between January 2002 and January 2005?'

'It depends, fostering comes under the remit of children's social services and as such, some of it is confidential, however some of it is easily accessible through various websites and some of it will even be in the public domain.'

'Which will be which.'

'I've been down this road before, it's all a bit blurred. It's a very rough rule of thumb, but take a case, any case in example. It's usually quite easy to find out any information about formal conventions as they are almost always minuted and the minutes filed. It used to be in filing cabinets now it's all on the internet. It isn't so easy to find out information about the children. I worked in child protection for four years and any information on any children, names, dates of birth, addresses and so on was always edited out and just for the eyes of a few.'

'I need to know the identity of all the panel members during that three-year period.'

'That should be fairly straight forward information to obtain. When do you need it by?'

'Five-o-clock.'

'You don't change much do you Danny?'

'I'm under pressure Chris.'

'I'll have a look, if I find anything, I'll email it over to you.'

After speaking to Christine, as he began the walk across the park to his house, his phone rang, he ignored it. It rang again, he checked the screen, it was Archie Hamilton. Archie never rang anybody. Danny wasn't even sure that Archie was aware that the phone had been invented; he took the call.

'Archie.'

'Danny, answer your sodding phone will you!'

'I am answering it. I've just left Chic Conway, very interesting man.'

'Yeah, I thought you and he would see reward in each other.'

'Is that what you are doing Archie, checking up on me, making sure I'm following your leads?'

'No, I've got some information that might be of interest to you.'

'Oh.'

'Jay Chopra, have you heard of him.'

'Yeah, he's Director of Children's Services for the City Council.'

'Not any more he isn't.'

'Archie, I can't believe you've rung me up, you of all people, to discuss resignations, hirings and firings.'

'What? No, he's not been fired, he's not resigned, he's dead. He fell off the penthouse balcony at the Midland Hotel on Saturday Night. He comes into the category of the people you're looking at, safe-guarding official who has died in unusual circumstances.'

'Did he fall or did he jump or was he pushed?'

'Obviously I don't know the answer to that.'

'You said it was on Saturday.'

'Yes, about 9pm.'

'Today is Thursday.'

'You never lose it Danny. It's a kind of inherent sharpness that you seem to have.'

'What I mean is, why the delay in breaking the news?'

'Well, it's for reasons best known to others, but they've kept it quiet until now. I think that they've been waiting on reports and obviously there is a police investigation.'

'Is that all we know?'

'It's all I know.'

'Can you find out anymore, through you contacts in the Police Authority.'

'I might be able to but not today. Let police activity settle down a little. If it's being classed as criminal, they might have a suspect or even have made an arrest. We should at least be able find out the classification. I'll revisit it in a day or so and get back to you.'

'Thanks Archie.'

Senetti thought about Jay Chopra. He didn't know whether Chopra should be added to his own list or not.

As far as Jason, Alma and Velma were concerned, he was now convinced that they had been murdered and by the same person. As Alberta would probably say, Jay Chopra could just be coincidence and he could well be; but if he wasn't and he was a victim like the other three, then the killing hadn't stopped and the killer was still here, somewhere in the city region. Hiding out as the old cliché said, in plain sight.

Chapter 21

The Travellers Oak

As Maxine Wells looked out of her lounge window, she could see The Travellers Oak. She also saw the single decker bus pull up, it stopped on the other side of the road opposite the pub. Two male passengers alighted, they both crossed the road and entered the little pub. One of them she recognised vaguely, the other was Danny Senetti.

Maxine took the sighting of Senetti as cue to leave her house and make the short walk to meet him. As she entered The Travellers Oak, she noticed that it was quite busy with about a dozen or so mid-week drinkers, corralled into its small lounge. She saw Senetti stood at the bar.

'Would you like a drink Maxine, what is it, mango tango?'

'No, I'll have a glass of Prosecco.'

'Oh.'

'Do you think that we could have them outside in the beer-garden? It seems a shame to squander all this evening sunshine. Especially when I've been incarcerated in my surgery for most of the day. Would you mind also Danny, if we stand up, I've been sitting in the same chair in the same position for most of the day.'

'Good idea, why don't you find a chair-less table and I'll bring the drinks out?'

A few minutes later they were both standing around a small round table in the evening sunshine.

Senetti smiled, 'You put your all into that job.'

'What else can I do, it's my life?'

'Exactly, how old are you Maxine?'

'None of your business Senetti.'

'Have you ever thought of finding yourself a nice husband, having a couple of beautiful children, and settling down. You could still be a doctor. Only your perspective would be wider.'

'If I feel the need to look for a life organiser, I'll call you. Maybe you should find yourself a nice wife.'

'I've been married, remember, and it didn't suit.'

'You mean it didn't suit Charlotte. You didn't settle down. It didn't bother you, you probably didn't even realise that you were married. My guess is that you just went to the church, then carried on with your life, the same as before. Anyway, are you proposing? You've only bought me one glass of Prosecco, I'd want at least a bottle. Even you Senetti, as cheap as you can be, can't believe that one glass of cheap wine buys you a wife.'

'It was a registrar's office.'

'What?

'I was married in a registrar's office, not a church.'

'Tell me about your case.'

'Did you read the file?'

'Yes, you were right, it was paper thin, but I think that I've got the general idea.'

'Karen Spencer volunteered me. She summoned me to a meeting at the Town Hall at ten-o-clock on a

Monday morning, can you believe ten-o-clock of all times on a Monday of all days.'

'You've said yes, now the case, what about the case?'

'I'm assisting an officer from The Children's Commissioners Office. She has been sent up from London. She is re-examining three cases. People who died in unusual circumstances. The official version is this; there is a Councillor from Oldham, Jason Dunphy who got himself drunk and fell off the metro platform into the path of an oncoming through tram. Then there is Alma Alice Spain, she was a social worker from Manchester who was the victim of a hit and run in a car park. Then there is a foster carer, Velma Vine from Stockport who fell into the path of an oncoming freight train in the middle of the day. All these incidents took place over a recent twelve-month period.'

'You've got the City Region connection of Oldham, Manchester and Stockport. The narrow timeframe and the fact that all three had an involvement with safe-guarding children.'

'Yes, and there has been a possible late development.'

'Go on.'

'I only heard about it a few hours ago. Jay Chopra the Director of Children's Services for the City Council fell from the penthouse balcony of the Midland Hotel on Saturday night.'

'Then, it could be four, is foul play suspected in any of these cases?'

'Chopra isn't confirmed yet, there may be no connection. The police officer who looked into the foster carer's death was suspicious, but it was all circumstantial, there was nothing evidential and her superiors made her drop the case, before she could put any proper investigative time into it.'

'What about you and the children's' commissioner's officer, did you both have suspicions?'

'Well, that's just it, no. Alberta said that she was keeping an open mind, but from what I've heard, she has been putting everything down to coincidence. I don't think she really wants the case, she has just had it foisted upon her by her superiors in London. As for me, I had no suspicions at all until I started my own investigations.'

'Alberta, that's the officer?'

'Alberta Curtis-Brightland, do you know her?'

'No, never heard of her.'

'What about Lizzie Lambert.'

'Who is she?'

'She is the other officer I mentioned. She's just appeared from nowhere. Alberta brought her in, she said it was to help me.'

'Never heard of her either, there is no reason why I should. My involvement with Children's' Commissioner's Office is totally peripheral. I do meet safeguarding committees, most GP's do, but it isn't a regular occurrence. Over the years I've carried out medicals for a few of my patients or residents who had applied to be foster carers but that's it. In addition to which our practice has an appointed children's safeguarding liaison officer and she looks after anything like that, her experience in that area was one of the reasons we took her on.'

'Who is that?'

'Lucy Lockett, you met her earlier today.'

He nodded.

'Very nice lady, yes and very professional too.'

'It's good to have positive feedback. Lucy has done very well. Came from   a disadvantaged background to top graduate in her year. We are all very fond and proud of her.'

Senetti, then went on to give Maxine Wells a resume` of his investigations. He related his visits to the separate scenes, the metro station, the pub, the car park in Didsbury, the train station in Trensis. He also told her about his meeting with Jim Bigelow, his conversations with Ava Gardner about Bartholomew Topp and also Meg Rees-Jenkins and her suspicions. He told her about his discussion with Chic Conway, he repeated the news about Jay Chopra and related what Christine Harris had told him about obtaining information about child protection and finally he gave her a brief resume on the role of the Fostering Panel.

'That's it. Now you know everything I know. There are a lot of nuances, some common denominators and a lot of questions that remain unanswered.'

'Such as what Danny? People do sometimes die in unusual circumstances.'

'I understand that, but this is more than that.'

'You're not providing any evidence of more than that Danny.'

'If you take the locations, even though they are all in the City Region, they are all remote, with very few people going there.'

'That's one thing, yes.'

'It was known and easily established that the councillor and the foster carer were going to be at these locations on these dates and times.'

'What about the social worker?'

'I think she was lured there.'

'Is that why you are suggesting these incidents are murders? Safeguarding connection, remote locations and so on, why would that happen?

'What, why am I suggesting they were murdered?'

'No, you are closer to it than I am and you've got an instinct for these situations, so I'm not challenging your theory, I accept it. What I mean is, for what reason were they murdered?'

'I don't know for sure Maxine.'

'No, you don't know for sure but you've got half a guess, haven't you?'

'How do you know that?'

'Because I know you and I can tell.'

'I think that it was something to do with the victims' occupations and it is revenge for something they've done in their line of work.'

'So, we've got, somebody in the city region going around murdering safeguarding professionals.'

'Yes.'

'But safeguarding professionals protect people, they keep children safe and you would have had to do something very bad to deserve being murdered.'

'That's all in the eye of the beholder, always is.'

'Very true.'

'We know Maxine, that Jason, Alma and Velma all served together, that's the key word together, on the Fostering Panel between January 2002, and January 2005.'

'You think that these murders are connected to that panel.'

'They didn't know each other personally, in their day to day business they all worked for different councils. The Fostering Panel is the only connection between the three of them that I've been able to establish.'

'What about Jay Chopra, was he on the Fostering Panel.'

'No, he's not in the pool.'

'Where does he fit in?'

'I haven't been able to work that out yet.'

'Do we know who else was on the Fostering Panel at the same time as the three suspected murder victims?'

'Now you are thinking with me Maxine. No, we don't, but I've got a list of people the panel was drawn from. There are twenty-one names on it. I know some of them and I've discounted them for various reasons. Some I don't know at all. I've made you a copy of it. I've also annotated their particular interest and what councils, if any they represented. What else? Oh yeah, panel numbers are always seven in number, for the casting vote, which the chair has.'

He handed her a single piece of paper.

'The casting vote?'

'Yes, as with any convention, members from time to time will disagree on a course of action. That's when the majority rules. On occasions though, there is no majority and it's a tie, that's when the chair has the casting vote. It's common council procedure.'

'Do you recognise anybody on the list?'

'I know two, Councillor Neil Derbyshire and Frank Delgado. Councillor Derbyshire is a little eccentric, he used to cycle with dad, and Frank he's a retired consultant paediatrician who used to practise over in Rochdale.'

'Oh yes, I know Councillor Derbyshire too, I'd overlooked him, a little eccentric? He's as mad as King Lear! What about the Doctor?'

'What about him?'

'Well is he alive, for a start?'

'He has dementia but he is very much alive.'

'If he's got dementia, he isn't going to remember much, at least not about conventions that took place years ago.'

'Dementia doesn't necessarily work like that, but let's try him anyway, he might be able to contribute in some way, leave Frank to me.'

Maxine became pensive, 'Let's have a look at this Danny, let's be analytical here. As I said I accept your hypothesis. Let us step into the murderer's mind a little. Let's suppose again, that your life was affected so much by what these three people did on this panel between January 2002, and January 2005, that you decided to murder them.'

'All right Maxine.'

'Here is a question for you.'

'I'm listening.'

'You said that these murders happened recently over a twelve-month period, yes?'

'Correct.'

'Why would you wait all those years to act?'

'People often do, don't they?'

'They do Danny, but why? There could also be another reason, a practical reason, an entirely different one than just biding your time.'

'You'll have to explain Maxine.'

'Let's say the Fostering Panel convened between those dates and in this particular case that we have yet to identify, they deregistered the foster carer. What are the consequences of that action and who bears the brunt of it?'

'The consequences are that you cease fostering,' he said.

'What about any children who are living in your home.'

'They are removed.'

'What if they've been with you for years and you're like the mother or father that they've never had. What if you love them and they love you.'

'The system doesn't take that into account, Maxine.'

'To repeat myself who bears the brunt of this deregistration?'

'The foster carer.'

'Yes, that's true.'

'Anybody else?'

'Hmm?'

Danny, 'What about the child ?'

'Yes, I understand what you're saying, I'd over-looked that.'

'Permit me some conjecture of my own.'

'Most definitely.'

She said, 'You are the child of a deregistered foster care, not a very young child, you would have to have been old enough to be aware and you would have had to have been with your foster carer long enough to form an attachment. Let's say, just for the sake of the argument you're a teenager. You may even have been in the foster home with a brother or sister. Your whole family is torn apart and your whole life is turned upside down by this deregistration, how might you feel?'

'Hurt, maybe vengeful.'

'Yes, but you are too young to execute your vengeance.'

'It's a good theory Maxine, go on.'

'You wait until you're older, wiser, stronger, better resourced. Maybe even to see if your thirst for vengeance goes away, but it doesn't, if anything it gets stronger, you blame the faceless professionals who did not support you and who have torn your world apart and you make it your business to find out who they are. You discover that three of them are on that Fostering Panel and you murder them.'

'Velma, Jason and Alma.'

'There's something else Danny.'

'You're doing great Maxine, go on.'

'You mentioned a casting vote.'

'Yes?'

'It says on this list that Velma was chair of the panel, so presumably that vote was hers. Therefore, the vote must have been a tie, let's say three for deregistration and three not for it. That's three members plus the casting vote. We also know that Jay Chopra was not on that panel and anyway, he may yet turn out to be nothing to do with this. Yet, we've only got three murder victims and one of them is the casting vote.'

'There is a murder missing, or a potential murder about to happen, there should be four.'

'There should be, three for deregistration plus Velma.

'Maxine you're a marvel.'

'Danny, that's our current position.'

'The Fostering Panel sits every month, we know it draws its membership of seven from a pool of twenty-one. We need to look at every panel that Jason, Alma and Velma were on together. Then we probably need to look at all the cases that panel looked at during that sitting, that could be a lot of cases. If we could find the fourth victim, that's if there has been one and place him or her on the same panel then that should drastically reduce the possible permutations.'

'I'll speak to Frank Delgado, see if he can contribute, I am not optimistic, but you never know, he may remember something.'

'Just one more thing Maxine, Alma Alice Spain.'

'Yes,'

'There's two really. There's this friend of hers in London, Jean Fortescue, but I suppose we'll have to give Alberta the benefit of the doubt on that one for the time being and see what she reports back with. Did you know her?'

'Who, Jean Fortescue?'

'No, Alma Alice.'

'I don't think so, should I have done?'

'Her husband, sorry her ex-husband. I say ex-husband on two counts, one because she is dead but also because they were divorced some years before she died. He is a G.P., over in Bury. Just thought you may have come across him. His first name is Alexander.'

'Oh, Alex Spain, yes.'

'You do know him then.'

'Yes, not very well, her not at all, never met her, heard a bit about her though.'

'Why would you hear about her?'

'From Alex, I was on a training-course with him a few years back. He was going through his divorce at that time. She was perturbed about her sexuality, and she and Alex couldn't reconcile it, so they separated, then they divorced. He was upset about it at the time.'

'Perturbed about her sexuality, couldn't reconcile it, Maxine what does that mean. What does it actually translate as?'

'Its Doctor speak Danny.'

'Well that's great and I'm sure you need your own language, when you are with all these super brain medics, but can you give it me again. Only this time can you say it in plain old simple councillor speak? Then I can understand exactly what it is that you are talking about.'

'Councillor Speak?'

'Yeah, it's easy, it's a simple plain language. Basically, you just dumb down to the lowest possible level you can think of. Just imagine that you are talking to some old lady who is in her eighties. She doesn't have a mobile phone and she has never logged onto a computer in her life. Let's call her Marjorie, she left school when she was fifteen and worked in a shop. Then when she was twenty-one, she got married. Her husband went out to work and she had the children. She did home and family and he did work and money, then they both retired. Now she has just lost her husband, let's call him Arthur. Marjorie is as deaf as a dumb-bell and as mad as a snake and she's just had a letter about her council tax, from the council. She doesn't understand it and doesn't know what she is supposed to do about it. She has brought it to you, her local councillor and you are trying to explain it to her in terms that she understands-councillor speak.'

Maxine laughed, she'd missed Senetti's cynical little homilies, she wouldn't admit it but she had.

'In my best interpretation of councillor speak, Alma Alice decided she was a lesbian and she didn't want to be with Alex anymore.'

'Was this common knowledge?'

'Was what common knowledge?'

'The fact she was a lesbian.'

'I don't really know about Alma Alice, as I say, I didn't know her, but as far as Alex was concerned, no it wasn't. As I recall, he told me in confidence. I'd be guessing but I'd say they wanted to keep it private.'

'I thought everybody came out these days. I thought that as soon as you even remotely suspected you were gay or lesbian, even if it was only for a week, no not a week, a day, you contacted one of those shiny magazines.'

'No Danny, that's only if you are a "Z" list celebrity or a retired sportsman. Ordinary people tend to behave with as much dignity as their situation will allow and very often they don't want their private sex lives discussed in public, so they only tell those closest to them.'

'You would have to tell your husband though, wouldn't you and your mother and your best friend ?'

'Not necessarily, no, people can lead complicated lives. They often decide to keep their own counsel. I've known patients with lesbian feelings stay in marriages with children for life.'

'Aren't those people bisexual.'

'They could be yes, but not necessarily. Is Alma Alice's sexuality relevant to your case?'

'I don't know, I didn't even know about it until you mentioned it a few minutes ago.'

A brief silence ensued

'Maxine, you've never married and I've not heard of you having a boyfriend.'

'We are back on that one are we. Is there a point to be made here?'

'Are you a Lesbian?'

'Not that it's any of your business Senetti but no I'm not.'

'Are you bisexual then?'

'When it comes to asking intrusive questions in an ungracious way, I must admit you've got a gold medal in it.'

Chapter 22

Phone Day

Delilah Donegan announced. 'Two Eggs Royale; toasted muffins topped with wilted spinach, smoked salmon and coddled eggs and a colour topping of hollandaise sauce.' With a flourish she put the plate down on the kitchen table, where Danny Senetti was seated.

'It looks and smells delicious Delilah.'

'It will do you more good than Marmite and toast for sure.'

'There is nothing wrong with Marmite and toast.'

'There is Danny when you have it every day and when you have nothing else, except perhaps, as much cheap drink as you can pour into yourself.'

'There is nothing wrong with cheap drink either, some would say, the cheaper the better.'

'If you want to find yourself a nice wife, you need to cut down on your drinking and smarten yourself up a bit. You've still got your own hair and your own teeth and you're not bad looking in an acquired sort of way. You're obviously overweight, but things can be done in that area. If you put the effort in, you could make something of yourself before it's too late. You could start a little diet and exercise programme. Why don't you go to the shops at the weekend and buy yourself some nice new clothes and whilst you are at it, get shut of that old dressing gown you're wearing and find yourself some proper adult's slippers instead of those toddler's shoes you've got on your feet. God forbid if you had to answer the door wearing goblin's footwear.'

'Delilah, as you well know, I'm not looking for a wife of any kind, nice or otherwise, these slippers were a present from my mother and I'm quite happy in the clothes that I have. It's all part of my casual image.'

'Image? Danny, when you walk down the street in those clothes you wear, people don't see image, they see an hallucination and as for not looking for a wife, I was in the Travellers yesterday evening, you didn't see me, I was with himself and you were too preoccupied with that young doctor. and I saw the way you looked at her.'

'That young doctor, as you call her, and I, have nothing else other than a professional relationship and just because I admire the way she looks, which I do, it doesn't mean that I want to marry her. Those two aspects Delilah, are unconnected and a million miles apart.'

'That's exactly my point, of course all you have is a professional relationship, that's all you are going to get, you've got no option. Why would a beautiful, educated, wealthy young woman, like her, have anything else with a skint, scruffy, old politico, drunk, like yourself? Now if you were to have her as a wife then you would have some standing in the community.'

'Delilah, I already have standing in the community. In case you've forgotten I'm the locally elected councillor, how much more standing do you want me to have?

Danny, the only person in the community who thinks that the local councillor has any standing in the community is the local councillor. Everybody else knows that all politicos are liars and cheats and they are so low that they could walk under a snake's belly with a guardsman's busby on. That would be all right if they achieved anything for us, but they don't. Himself says that when politico's see the light at the end of the tunnel, they send out for more tunnel.'

That's because Delilah, in this country anyway, we are too preoccupied by a party-political system.'

If that's the case Danny; why is it, that whatever political party we vote for, the government always seems to get in?

'You know that's the trouble with you Delilah, you're too mealy-mouthed, you're not straight-forward, you don't speak with any candour. You skirt around subjects and you don't get to the point.'

'That's because I'm too concerned with other people's feelings and I don't like to hurt them. I've got too much apathy with other people, it can be a big fault sometimes.'

'That's too true Delilah'

She looked out of the kitchen window at the soft rain that was falling, and said, 'Do you think I'll need an umbrella?'

'There's a couple in the hall, in that stand, take one of those.'

'Umbrellas are ok, they keep the rain off you right enough, but the trouble is you have to carry them. Right, I'm off now, I'll be back on Tuesday morning and don't leave that plate for me to face when I return.'

She put her coat on and umbrella-less, went out the back door.

Senetti sat at the table eating his Eggs Royale. When he'd finished he put the empty plate to one side. He was attired in his usual, well-worn black and white dressing gown and the red slippers Delilah had referred to. On the table in front of him were his phone, his lap-top and a writing pad and pen. Today he was going to have a phone and lap-top day. He didn't really want one, these two items were his least favoured methods of communication. Nevertheless, he had a list of unresolved issues, mainly concerning his constituents but some concerning the case and the only way he could move them on was by telephone calls and emails.

His CD player was emitting tunes. He listened to the twin set fuzz guitars, one playing high note, the other playing low, and then the commencement of the falsetto tones of Frankie Valli and The Four Seasons;

'*Let's hang on*
To what we've got
Don't let go girl
We got a lot
Gotta a lot of love between us
Hang on, hang on…'

Senetti turned down the volume and as Frankie sang in the background, Senetti made his first call, to Christine Harris.

'Hello Christine, thanks for the list yesterday, it was very helpful.'

'That's all right Danny.'

'I need a bit more in pursuant of that list.'

'Go on.'

'I am interested in three members of the fostering pool. I need to know how many panels these three were on together. All three members must have been present on the same panel. I also need to know the date each panel was convened. I also need to know what was discussed at those panels. Finally, I need to know the names of the foster carers and any children who were involved.'

'I am looking at the email I sent you yesterday, which three members are you interested in?'

'Velma Vine, Jason Dunphy and Alma Alice Spain. Is that information available?'

'As I said yesterday, some of it will be and some of it won't. It won't be easy. The children will not be named in full in any documentation.'

'There must be somebody, somewhere who knows who they are.'

'There probably will be, but we would have to find out who that somebody is, let's not forget this is all ten, maybe fifteen years ago. People move on, even die. Then there is the small matter of getting them to tell us. Confidentiality is a central issue in child protection and breach of it is not done readily.'

'There is one more possible connection, it's a bit tenuous and may not even be there at all.'

'Well, come on Danny, let's have them all at once.'

'A man called Jay Chopra, I need to know if he has any connection to this Fostering Panel at all. He isn't on the list of Fostering Panel pool members that I've got.'

'Jay Chopra, I know of him, he's a director at City Council. Didn't I hear somewhere that he'd had an accident recently?'

'You did, he fell off a balcony. He wouldn't have been a director at the time we're considering, he would have been in a much junior position at that time. Nevertheless, he's been around a long time. At least as long as I've been on the council.'

'The best way to do this is to find out what information is readily available and see what else comes out in the process.'

'As always you are right, I really appreciate this, speak to you later.'

For the next hour and a half, Senetti made numerous calls in relation to his council business.

After this he decided it was time to speak to Alberta.

'Hello Alberta, it's Danny Senetti.'

'Hello Danny, it feels like a long time.'

'It's been a week or so.'

'Did you get to speak to Jean Fortescue?'

'Sorry, Jean Fortescue?'

'Yes, the friend of Alma Alice Spain. The one who works for Kensington and Chelsea.'

'No, I left a couple of messages but she didn't get back to me, what about you, any developments?'

Senetti pondered, he tried to be rational about it, as he considered the integrity of her reply to his question about Jean. He concluded that it didn't have any. He also thought that Alberta was trying to stop him pressing her on Jean Fortescue, by pushing him onto the back foot with her question about, '…any developments?' Nevertheless, his immediate prime concern was to bring about the lunch with her and Lizzie, whereupon Maxine would be in attendance. He said, 'I've not really had any opportunity to move things on much, but there have been some developments that we need to discuss. While you've been in London, I've been unexpectedly swamped with council caseload and I've had to concentrate on the day job.'

'I understand, but what are the developments?'

'Are you in Manchester or London this weekend?'

'I'm in Manchester on Sunday.'

'How about Sunday lunch, bring Lizzie, there's somebody I'd like you both to meet. We can discuss the case then.'

'Who is it?

'She's a friend of mine, she's a doctor. Like I say, you'll meet her on Sunday.'

'Did you have anywhere in mind?'

'I don't mind really, we could all meet up in Manchester, if you find that easier.'

'Actually, I'm a bit fed up with London and Manchester. It would be a pleasant change to sit somewhere, where the traffic is not whizzing past you at breakneck speeds. It would be nice to gaze upon some trees and some open fields instead of being surrounded by urban life on all sides.'

'I know just the place, it's no more than thirty minutes on the train from Piccadilly. If the weather is good we can sit outside. I'll email the details.'

'All right, I'll be there.'

Having obtained her agreement he said, 'Alberta, sorry about this but I'm under pressure to take this incoming call, you let Lizzie know and as I said, I'll email you, see you Sunday, bye.'

No sooner had he hung up than his phone rang, it was Maxine.

'Danny, I'm about to have a working lunch which incorporates a partners' meeting.

'A partners' meeting sounds riveting, what's on the menu, what is it today Maxine, a conference pear and a Kiwi fruit?'

'Today Danny is Friday, Friday is when I treat myself in the lunch stakes. I've sent out to Dermot's for some posh sandwiches.'

'Well, enjoy them.'

'They haven't arrived yet, so I've got a few minutes.'

'You've discovered something.'

'Perhaps, when I got home last night, I rang Frank Delgado to ask him what he remembered about his time on the fostering panel.'

'And what did he remember?'

'He half remembered being on it, during that period and he half-remembered Velma and Alma and Jason. But he couldn't remember any specific dates and he couldn't remember if he'd ever sat on a panel with all three of them and he couldn't really remember any of the cases that were discussed, when he was in attendance.'

'Is there anything he could remember?'

'Danny, have a little patience eh, this may be of interest. The point is this. He asked me a few questions about the case. Just to humour an old man really, I thought I'd answer them, it was just chat and anyway, I reasoned that he'd forget everything I'd told him by tomorrow, so where was the harm?'

'Yeah, fair enough.'

'I told him about the deaths of Velma, Jason and Alma and he asked me this, he said,' "Was the death of the Inspector by fire, connected in any way to the case?'

318

'Was he rambling?'

'A little, he seemed to be and that's exactly what I thought, but let's remember, before Frank Delgado was hit by dementia, he was a brilliant paediatrician and he deserves some respect. He at least deserves to be listened to.'

'What did you do?'

'I listened and he told me this story about somebody who he kept calling "The Inspector" who *exploded,* that was the word he used, who was burned to death in a back alley in Manchester.'

'It doesn't mean much to me, Maxine.'

'It didn't mean much to me Danny, but when I'd finished the call, I felt a bit saddened by Frank's condition and more out of regard for him than anything else, I thought that I'd have a browse on the internet. I wasn't expecting to find much. Then very quickly I came across an article in the Evening News about a former police inspector who had been burned alive in a back alley in Manchester on the evening of March 8th this year.'

'Go on, this is starting to look interesting.'

'The police inspector in question, according to the newspaper, is called Albert Bailey. If you fish your list of pool members out, the one you gave me a copy of, you'll find a **Deacon** Bailey.'

'Not the same name is it, but it's half right.'

'Exactly, it's half right. Let's be open here and use our initiative. Lots of people change their forename, they don't like the one they are given, so they pick one they do like, or they use their middle name or another altogether. Maybe he didn't like Albert. The point is when I referred Frank Delgado to a panel that he was on, he mentioned *an Inspector*. From what I've learned about these panels, a police inspector would be a good fit and a police inspector, with the same surname as one of your panel pool members was burnt to death in a back alley in March.'

'He could be the fourth victim, Maxine, the one we are looking for.'

'He could yes, so let's look at that.'

'You're right Maxine, sorry I'm having a bit of a phone day today. It numbs your brain after a bit. What did Frank mean by exploded?'

'The newspaper article referred to spontaneous combustion but that's a whole new conversation.'

'Right Danny, my sandwiches have arrived, French brie, Sicilian grapes and rocket salad with plum toma-toes. What are you on?

'I've had a late breakfast, Eggs Royale courtesy of Mrs Donegan.'

'Really.'

'Yeah, I know how to look after myself.'

'Shall we have that conversation another time?'

'Maxine, that lunch we spoke about with Alberta and Lizzie, I've arranged it for two-o-clock on Sunday, at The Kiss, can you meet me there an hour earlier? I'm sure by then we'll have things to discuss and you can explain spontaneous combustion to me.'

'Yes, I'll be there, see you then Danny.'

His phone rang again almost immediately, he looked at the number, it wasn't named on his screen so he decided to ignore it.

Just then he stretched his arm out and he knocked Delilah's plate off the table onto the floor, amazingly it broke into what seemed four equal parts. He wondered whether he should pick it up; he decided he'd do it later.

His phone rang yet again. He concluded that he really was having a phone day today. This time a name flashed up, Meg Rees-Jenkins. He was surprised, he took the call.

'Meg, you're the last person I was expecting, how is the house moving?'

'It's this weekend.'

'I can't help with the move Meg, I've got a full weekend.'

'No, that's not what I want Danny, it's all being done by professionals anyway.'

'How can I help then?'

'Your colleague, the one I met the other day at Trensis train station, how well do you know her?'

'Lizzie, I only met her last week myself, in total I've probably spent two whole hours in her company.'

'There is something odd about her.'

'Meg, that assertion applies to virtually everybody.'

'Remember, when I said to her she seemed familiar.'

'Yeah'

'I've just realised it's not her who is familiar, it's her car.'

'Why do a lot of the people I know speak in riddles and conundrums?'

'Back to my house move to Wales, for the last three months, I've been going back and forth, solicitors, surveyors, insurers, carpets, curtains, all the usual stuff, it can't all be accomplished by phone and email.'

'No.'

'I've got an old friend over there, I went to school with him, he manages a couple of caravan parks on the Llyn. One of these parks is in a place called Chwilog. It's about two miles from the house I've just bought. He's been letting me use one of the rental caravans when I've been overnight and sometimes at the week-end, mate's rates and all that.'

'Sounds helpful.'

'When I'm staying on the camp, I often go for a little jog in the morning around the area, I run around the camp and into the village. That's when I noticed the car, LLA 111. I noticed the plate, I've got an eye for stuff like that. I've seen it on more than one occasion parked up on the drive of one of the caravans. Then I noticed it, at Trensis Station, the other day but it didn't register until now.'

'Perhaps she owns the caravan Meg, or she was vis-iting, or something else, there could be a lot of reasons.'

'Yes, I realise all that. I also made some discreet enquiries and you're right, she does own the caravan. The point I'm trying to make is that when we were dis-cussing the Llyn Peninsula and Criccieth and Pwllheli, at the station the other day, why didn't she say some-thing about her connection to the place?'

'Maybe she has got a secret lover out there and she doesn't want anybody to know, or maybe she just wasn't listening to us. As I said, I hardly know her and going off recall she didn't say much about anything.'

'No, Danny she was definitely listening. I remember thinking how she listened intently to everything we said. Maybe I've been in this job too long, after a while you don't take anything at face value and you look for hidden meanings in what people say.'

'Or in this case what they don't say.'

'Most people would have said something, if only a passing reference to the area but she didn't say anything at all and when you withhold like that, it's usually because you've got something to hide. It may not necessarily be about the subject in discussion, but you've got something to hide about something, so in order not to give anything away, you don't say anything about anything, especially yourself.'

'It's a point well-made and an interesting piece of criminal psychology Meg.'

'Anyway, I wouldn't trust her.'

'All right Meg, I'll put it in the mix. I'm meeting her on Sunday, I'll throw a few probes out, see what comes back, what is the address of the caravan park and what was that place called again, the one where the caravan park is?'

'It's called Ocean Heights and it's in a place called Chwilog. I've got a post code, its LL53 6NQ.'

'Chwilog, yeah, good luck with the move. Oh, and keep in touch Meg, don't disappear. Remember you're moving to Wales not Wagga Wagga .'

'Thanks Danny, I won't.'

Senetti, leaned back in his chair, he pondered on what Meg had said. He also pondered on Albert Deacon Bailey, whoever he was. If Bailey was the fourth panel member then where did Jay Chopra fit in? That is if he did at all. He thought about Chic Conway and what Chic had told him about the possible trauma of de-registrations. He also thought about complaints and allegations. Surely all complaints weren't treated in the same way. Trivial complaints couldn't be managed the same way as serious ones. You couldn't convene The Fostering Panel every time some thirteen- year-old-kid complained about the time he had to be in for. On the other hand, you couldn't wait for the date of that panel to come around if the issue was grievous and urgent. So, there must be another mechanism, perhaps another type of Panel.'

His phone rang yet again...Christine Harris.

'Hello again Councillor, this is all in an email which I've sent over to you. The Fostering Panel doesn't convene at all in January and December, so that means that there were ten panels a year, panels in that period you are interested in, thirty in all. I've attached all the minutes for every panel, about four hundred pages in total. Page one of each set of minutes lists the panel attendees on that day.'

Senetti groaned, 'four hundred pages!'

'Councillor, as a sign of how much I hold you in regard. I've done a little exercise and separated the panels that your three panellists sat on together, there were three panels in all.'

'Thanks Chris, I don't know what I'd do if you weren't here. There is also a panellist called Bailey, Deacon Bailey, you know your way around this paper-work now. Are there any panels where, Alma Alice Spain, Jason Dunphy, Velma Vine and Deacon Bailey were all attendees on?'

'Just let me see now, just bear with me a minute or so, yes just one. A panel that convened in February 2004, had the attendees; Velma Vine as chair, Doctor Frank Delgado, Councillor Jason Dunphy, Alma Alice Spain, Inspector Deacon Bailey, Dean Holland and Rachel Pimlott.'

'That's the one I want Chris, Eureka!'

'Do we know any more about that panel?'

'The minutes for that panel Councillor are only seventeen pages, you'll need to read them.'

Chapter 23

Names and Initials

Senetti went upstairs and when he emerged fifteen minute later, he was fully dressed. He resumed his study of The Fostering Panel minutes. He studied Christine's email again and made some notes.

On the Panel of February 2004, there was only one case for consideration that day. Two foster carers with an impeccable record. One of the carers was accused of sexual abuse by a third party. The third party was referred to as 'EL.' There were a lot of forenames in the minutes but all surnames and addresses had been redacted out in thick black ink. For identification, the foster carers were called by their forenames, 'Gerry' and 'Martin' and they lived at a redacted-out address in Chorlton-cum-hardy. Senetti had the electoral role for the city region but electors were listed by surname and initial. The local councillor would have information on local forenames.

Senetti looked through his address book on his phone, Councillor Emile Sukarno.

'Emile, it's Danny Senetti.'

'Danny, how are you?'

'I'm well and you?'

'I'm all right.'

'Emile, I've got a little cross-boundary issue and I'd be grateful for your input.'

'Ask away Danny.'

'I'm trying to identify two people who were living in your ward in February 2004.'

'What have you got?'

' It's all I've got Emile, their forenames, which are Gerry and Martin.'

'February 2004, you said. My electoral role for the period shows...bear with me... it's whirring up now, damn computers! Let me put this in, Gerry and Martin? Yes! I've got a Geraldine and Martin Kinder living at number 12, Elm Grove. I remember him, he used to drink in the Beech on a Sunday afternoon. He was a teacher, so was she. He died a while back and not long after, she went to live in Canada. I think that she has some relatives out there.'

'Were they ever foster carers Emile?'

'Yes, I think they were.'

'When did she move to Canada?'

'I'm not sure, about seven, maybe eight years ago.'

'Thanks, Emile, catch up with you another time.'

The minutes of the fostering panel, referred to looked after children who had previously been in the Kinder's care; "Bethan T, Dylan R, Glenys G, Gethin J, and Lowri T. It referred to a previous *Emergency Strategy Meeting* whereupon it had been directed that; Dylan, Glenys, Gethin and Lowri be removed from the, "accommodation of The Kinders."

What did those names say to him? Nothing!

There was also another name that featured heavily in the recorded minutes, that of *Rosemary Rowntree*. She was the social worker for Bethan on the Kinder case. She had spoken at length during the panel, her comments were recorded. She didn't agree with the outcome of the panel. If anybody knew chapter and verse about this case it was her.

He checked the Social Workers' Register, online, but there was no entry with the name, Rosemary Rowntree for the whole of England and Wales. Maybe she had retired or died or maybe she didn't work in England and Wales anymore.

He checked the time 2:22pm

Once again, he turned to his phone.

'Hello Chic, it's Danny Senetti, have you got a few minutes?'

'For you, Councillor today yes, tomorrow who knows?'

'Chic, do you recall a social worker called Rosemary Rowntree?'

'I do yes.'

'Then why can't I find her on the Social Workers Register.'

'There are two possible reasons. The first is, about ten years ago she married. So, she has very possibly adopted her husband's surname. As well as that, I heard that she dropped out of field social work. She now lectures in it, at Salford University. So perhaps she has lapsed her registration.'

'Do you know what her husband's name is or where I can find her?'

'I don't know her husband's name and I don't know her address, I think she used to live over in South Manchester somewhere, Withington or that way, but that's a big area to comb. I've got a suggestion if you're interested.'

'Chic, it's far superior to the one I've got now.'

'If you log on to Salford University's website, their Health and Social Sciences Faculty. It's not a huge faculty and it will probably give you the names of the staff. I'd be surprised if there is more than one social work lecturer called Rosemary and you just might be able to get her married name from that.'

' Chic, I love you.'

I need all the affection I can get Councillor.

He did as Chic had suggested and found a Doctor Rosemary Gilmartin PhD, who lectured in Social Work.

He rang Maxine, she didn't answer.

His further investigations revealed a James and Rosemary Gilmartin at a Withington Address - St Martin's Drive.

His phone rang, it was Maxine.

'Danny, be quick.'

' Maxine, I've sent you an email, it's a copy of the minutes of a fostering panel from 2004. That panel is the reason for these murders, I know it is. Frank Delgado's policeman was on the panel, he's the fourth victim. Will you please read it and come back to me?'

'Danny, I've seen it. It's pages and pages. I can't read that, not now, I'm working and I just don't have the time today. I'm taking the weekend off, so I'll have a look at it tomorrow.'

'Maxine today is Friday.'

'I know that Danny.'

'You finish early on Friday.'

'Five o clock yes'

'Maxine, there is more I need to discuss. Meet me in the Travellers, at six. That gives you an hour to read my email'

'Senetti, you're turning me into either an alcoholic or a workaholic.'

'Maxine, you're already on your way to being a workaholic without any help from me and you are not going to be an alcoholic on two glasses of Prosecco twice a month. We can stand up in the beer garden, it will be good for you after sitting down in your surgery all day and the rain has stopped now and the sun is shining.'

'All right, I'll see you later.'

Three hours later, the early evening sun shone brightly in the beer garden of the Travellers Rest. Danny and Maxine stood at the high table at the bottom end of the garden.

'So, this is what happened Maxine. Two foster carers were looking after a group of children, when one of the children made an allegation of sexual assault against the male carer. As a result, the foster carers are deregistered and it all starts from there. Then, years later the people who recommended deregistration are tracked down and murdered. Oh, and the murders are made to look like accidents, obviously so the murderer can avoid detection. The big question for us, is who is the murderer? We know it's not one of the foster carers.'

'I'm not saying that it didn't happen. It is though a gigantic leap from deregistration to multiple murder.'

'It depends on the consequences of the deregistration.'

'They would have to be fairly catastrophic.'

'It's not conclusive but my enquiries have revealed that Martin Kinder died and Gerry went to live in Canada, years before these killings started. We are left with the children, who by now, will all be adults.'

'Point of correction, it wasn't one of the children who made the allegation Danny, it was a third party altogether. The accuser is only referred to once and she's given the initials "EL" for the dual purpose of identifying her in the panel's deliberations but keeping her real identity confidential. We know the forenames and the initial of the surname of the foster children and none of those children have the initials E or L. The alleged victim is somebody else entirely. There is another thing about the names of the foster children. It doesn't mention it in the minutes but I think that they are a sibling group.'

'Why do you say that?'

'Look at the names, what have they got in common?'

'Not much Maxine, if anything the opposite is true, if the initials are anything to go by they are all different. Why would a sibling group all have surnames that begin with a different initial for each one of them?'

'They are all different surnames, yes it's true. Just think of their forenames, Bethan, Dylan, Glenys, Gethin and Lowri, what is the common denominator?'

'I don't know.'

'Come on Danny, think.'

'They've all got two syllables.'

'Yes, that is true, but that's not what I'm referring to. What about the origin of their names?'

'Their origin? I don't know Maxine. They just seem like kids' names to me. I'm not very good on names.'

'Danny, they are all names of Welsh origin.'

'Oh yes, I can see that now. How does that establish them as a sibling group?'

'Unless the Kinders fostered children with Welsh names, to the exclusion of all other names, what other explanation could there be? It's parents who give names to children and you often find families, where all the children have nationality forenames. I've got a Spanish, an Iraqi and a Swedish family on my register and the children have all got Spanish and Iraqi and Swedish forenames.'

'What about the different surnames?'

'My theory would be that they all had the same mother but different fathers.'

'Why not different mothers same father?'

'If they all had different mothers it's unlikely that the authorities would remove five different children from five different women, all five can't have been unsuitable mothers. What's the odds on that? Anyway, It's the women who keep the children Danny, not the men. No, it's definitely same mother different fathers.'

'Points well-made again Maxine, did you notice the name Rosemary Rowntree in the report?'

'Yes, she was Bethan's social worker.'

'If she was Bethan's social worker and your theory about them being a sibling group is correct, then it is likely that she is the social worker for the whole family. It follows then that she knows more about the family than anybody.'

'You need to find her Danny, you need to speak to her before somebody else ends up dead. You know much more about this than anybody.'

'I'm fairly sure that I've traced her. If I've got the right one, she's not a practising Social Worker any more. She now lectures on the subject at Salford University. As well as that she's since married and now goes by the name of Rosemary Gilmartin, I've got an address for her in Withington, South Manchester.

Perhaps it was once true that I knew more about this case than anyone but now you know almost as much as I do and please don't misunderstand me Maxine, I'm grateful that you do. When it comes to getting information from people, it's horses for courses. Ava Gardner the landlady from the community pub and I are a great match. Conversely, when it comes to a retired female social worker who is no longer practising and is now working as a university lecturer, it's obvious that you are the better fit. You're a woman, she's a woman, she's a professional, you're a professional, you're a doctor, she's a lecturer, she'll trust you. Shame to say it, but people who have worked for local authorities for a long time, don't always trust councillors.'

'When?'

'Tomorrow.'

'Why so soon?'

'I want to know what she has to say before we meet Alberta and Lizzie on Sunday.'

'You mean just turn up at her house and introduce myself.'

'It's not the best way, I admit but we've got no other way of doing it. Tell her you are working on a case for The Children's Commissioner's Office, which is true anyway. Use the old charm, you know, bedside manner.'

'I'll do what I can.'

'At least Maxine we haven't got the pressure of concerning ourselves with the possibility of discovering another murder, or even worse discovering that there is another potential victim out there who is at risk of being murdered.'

'We can't be sure of that Danny, we have still not established the situation, one way or another regarding

Jay Chopra. If he is connected then he could be the start of a whole new thread.'

'That's true and there is something else that has just occurred to me. Somebody else who could be in danger. Somebody who we have yet to identify.'

'Somebody else?'

'Yes, if you're prepared to murder four people because of something that happened almost fifteen years ago. What is your motive for doing that?

'Hatred, revenge all those kinds of harmful aspects of human nature.'

'Very well put Maxine, but who might you hate most of all, more than anybody. Who would you feel vengeful about more than anybody else.'

'The person who started it all, the one who made the allegation in the first place.'

'You're right again Maxine, the one referred to as EL in the panel minutes. We need to know all about this family because one or more of them is probably a multi murderer and we also need to know the identity of this person who made the allegation, because she may be about to be murdered herself and whether this allegation is true or false, it was made a long time ago by somebody who was little more than a child at the time and probably a misguided and damaged one at that and nobody deserves to die for what they've said when they were a vulnerable child. The answers to all this could well be with Rosemary Gilmartin.'

'I'm shocked by your empathy and compassion Danny.'

'I have my moments Doctor. What about Rosemary?'

'I'll go tomorrow.'

Chapter 24

Rosemary Gilmartin

Maxine Wells, turned into the smart cul-de-sac that is St Martins Drive, Withington, a small suburb in South Manchester. There were seven detached houses dotted around the little hammerhead. She soon spotted the house she was looking for. There was a long drive leading to a double garage and there were two cars parked on the drive. She parked her own car, walked down the path, passed the two cars and found herself at the front door, which was ajar. On the right-hand door frame jamb was a bell push, she pressed it twice and instantaneously, she heard rapid, light, footsteps, approaching. The front door opened wide to reveal a petite slim lady who Maxine thought was probably about fifty years of age. The woman was bespectacled and had dark, brown hair which was tied back in a bun. It was a sunny morning and she was dressed in shorts, tee shirt and light canvass shoes. She gazed upon Maxine with a quizzical yet friendly look. In turn, Maxine smiled, as she did, she said;

'Hello, I do apologise for visiting you uninvited and unannounced. My name is Doctor Maxine Wells and I'm a medical doctor in general practise. My practice is over in Norford and here is some identification.'

'Thank you, Doctor Wells, don't worry about being unannounced. If the truth is known my husband is away for the weekend and I'm glad of the company. I left the front door open, hoping some company would turn up and here you are, providence indeed. Would you like to come through, I was sitting in the garden, perhaps you'd like to join me? I've just made some green tea; do you like green tea?'

'Very much so.'

She led the way through the hall into the lounge and out of some open patio doors into a well, tended, medium sized garden. On a small patio was some garden furniture, a table and four chairs, surmounted by a large, pastel-blue umbrella. She sat down on one chair and beckoned to Maxine to sit down on another.

'This is very kind and trusting of you,' said Maxine.

'Oh, I just back my judgements Doctor, you know they are usually right.'

'Please call me Maxine.'

'Please call me Rosemary.'

'I need to ask you Rosemary, are you and Rosemary Rowntree former city council social worker, the same person; I'm going to feel very foolish if you are not.'

'Oh, then you've not just accidentally dropped by? I am pleased to tell you Maxine that you don't in any way have to feel a fool. Rowntree was my maiden name, as they call it, but when I married James, I took his name. The irony of it was and still is, my husband and I weren't so concerned to follow that tradition, we just did it to please both sets of parents who are getting on a bit and are rather on the old-fashioned side, which is exactly how all parents should seem to be to their children.'

Maxine smiled. 'I'm currently working on a case for the Children's Commissioner's Office and we'd be most grateful for your help.'

'I'll do my best.'

'It concerns a family who were being looked after by The City Council from a period in the 1980s, 90s and later, probably until around 2010. I need some information on them.'

'What was their family name?'

'There were five people involved, and they had four different surnames between them, but their forenames were....'

Rosemary interrupted, 'Bethan, Dylan, Glenys, Gethin and Lowri.'

'You remember them very well after all this time.'

'I couldn't really forget them, they were part of my professional life for a long time. We used to call them the Trefors, which was technically incorrect as it was their mother's name and it was a name used by the mother and only two of the siblings.'

'What were their full names?'

'There was Bethan Trefor, Dylan Riley, Glenys Grant, Gethin Jawando and Lowri Trefor.'

'Do you mind if I take notes Rosemary?'

'No, not at all, write away.'

'What of their mother?'

'Angharad or Ann as she was known, was actually a few years younger than me. I met her briefly on a few occasions when I was a newly qualified social worker. In a way, she was a kind of surrogate mother. She wasn't involved much with any of the children after they were born. She conceived them, carried them through the pregnancies, gave birth to them and then handed them over to whatever social services department she was living under at the time. In the early days, my involvement was minimal, I used to arrange visits between Ann and Bethan the eldest child, but mum either didn't attend at all, or if she did, she was under the influence of drugs or drink. Initially and for most of the time, as far as the children were concerned, I only had responsibility for Bethan.'

'Why was that?'

'Ann was itinerant, she was always changing her address, she moved around a lot. Dylan, Glenys and Gethin were born in different local authority boroughs so initially they became the individual responsibility of those boroughs. Later, Lowri became my responsibility and ultimately they all did.'

'Look Rosemary, I don't want to put you into a situation whereby you are compromising your professional ethics or breaching any confidentiality.'

'Oh, don't worry about any of that. I'm past all that stuff now. For one thing, I left field social work behind years ago and for another it's all on public record anyway. Instead of doing it for a living, I now talk about it for a living and if I can't discuss what happened in my own life who can? Ask anything you need to ask.'

'Where is the Welsh connection with the Trefors?'

'The Trefors were a matriarchal family who went back three generations. Grandmother Diana or Gwendolyn as she initially was, moved from Manchester to Prestatyn in the late 1960s and Ann was born in Bangor Hospital in 1971, before moving back to Manchester at the age of five. We have no family history before Diana but there has always been that north-west England, North-Wales connection. They both died young, Diana in the early seventies and Ann in nineteen-ninety-six, I think. Both deaths were drug-related. They were known as problem kids in their day. Today they would be called looked after children and victims.

'Is that why all the children had Welsh forenames?'

'The children didn't know and Ann didn't say, but probably, yes.'

'What about their surnames?'

'According to reports, Ann in one of her more lucid moments claimed that, except for Bethan and Lowri she gave them all their individual father's names.'

'Why were Bethan and Lowri different?'

'Apparently, the identity of Lowri's father was uncertain to Ann. Although she knew exactly who Bethan's was.

'Why didn't she give Bethan her father's name?'

'We don't know and it was never an important issue. It wasn't really any of our business. As far as I know, there was some information left by Ann for Bethan, regarding her father's identity. It was to come into Bethan's possession when she was eighteen and was for Bethan's eyes only. I didn't actually see it, but I know that Bethan did. I also know that she showed it to Gerry Kinder. Gerry told me that it gave Bethan's father's name and some information about him. Of course, by the time Bethan got it, this information was probably out of date, but presumably his name would have remained the same. There was a story at one time that Bethan's father was a Canadian Diplomat but that might have been some flight of fancy on Ann's part.'

'Rosemary, you just mentioned the name Kinder. A major part of the case we are looking at, concerns the

Trefor's relationship with two foster carers, Martin & Gerry Kinder, how well did you know them, did you know them?'

'Oh yes, I knew them both very well. All the Trefor children moved around the city region's safeguarding system for years with all the implications that this has for children in that situation. Bethan, was naturally and academically gifted but she had travelled around the system in a very unstable way, all her life. At the time the Kinders appeared, she was languishing in a Residential Unit, just really waiting for her eighteenth birthday and her discharge as a looked after child. It was decided, probably as a last throw of the dice, that she would move in with Martin and Gerry Kinder who were academics themselves. All foster placements are a gamble but the results in a very short time were amazing. She settled immediately and her first set of exam results were incredible and even then, Oxbridge was being openly spoken about.'

'What happened next?'

'Over a period, all the Trefors gradually moved in with the Kinders and despite some misgivings the situation became relatively settled, then it happened.'

'The Allegation.'

'You know about it?'

'More of it, than about it.

'It was an allegation of a sexual nature made against Martin Kinder. It was made by a young woman called Emma Luckhurst, she'd been in the unit with Bethan and was still there when she made the allegation. A lot of people thought that it was a false, malicious allegation, which it probably was. Though now with hindsight, it was made by somebody who was little more than a child and it was probably motivated more in causing mischief than misery.'

'Is that what ultimately happened?'

'Unfortunately, the consequences of it and the knock-on of the disruption it caused were tragic, but in my opinion, this was due in a large way to the handling of the situation by professional management. It was obvious to anybody that it was a malicious allegation and the futures of five young people were at stake, but management was cowardly and reacted, they wouldn't take any risk whatsoever.'

'What actually happened Rosemary.'

'A few hours after and on the same day the allegation was made an Emergency Strategy Meeting was convened. The outcome was that Dylan, Glenys, Gethin and Lowri were moved out of the Kinders immediately and within hours.'

'What about Bethan?'

'Bethan stayed.'

'Who made the decisions at the Strategy Meeting.'

'It was a collective responsibility, but the main force on it was a man called Jay Chopra. I couldn't attend the meeting on the day, I was in court. I telephoned him later but he couldn't or wouldn't, take the call. By the time I got to speak to him the following day, everything had disrupted and it would have been impossible to turn the clock back.'

'You said the consequences of disruption were tragic.'

'Initially, there were a lot of tears, the cynical might call them histrionics. I suppose there were two stories here running at the same time. There was Bethan's story and then there was the other siblings and although that's five-different people, it all became encompassed in one story.'

Maxine, thought that she noticed the glisten of tears in Rosemary's eyes; at this juncture Rosemary excused herself and then returned a few minutes later.

Rosemary resumed her story;

'After the initial disruption of Dylan, Glenys, Gethin and Lowri, Bethan stayed with the Kinders. Six months later when the Fostering Panel deregistered Gerry and Martin, Bethan refused to leave the foster home. The Kinders instructed solicitors and before the legal argument had made any progress at all, Bethan passed her eighteenth birthday. After this milestone, safeguarding management were powerless and they had to leave her with the Kinders.'

'Did Bethan ever get to University?'

'Bethan did eventually go down to Oxford. She graduated with a double first. I went to the graduation ceremony, Gerry and Martin were there. Martin looked ill and he died shortly after. I attended his funeral and it was obvious that Gerry and Bethan held the Fostering Panel responsible for his premature death. Bethan told me that she had been robbed of the only father she had ever known.'

'This is awful,' said Maxine. 'Are you all right to continue with this Rosemary?'

'Oh yes, I've lived with this a long time now, all the hurt has long since gone away, shall I continue?'

'Yes, please'

'Shortly after Martin's death, Gerry went to live in Canada. I expect to be near her son, who at that time was a doctor in Vancouver. I lost touch with Gerry after that and I have not heard from her since.'

'What about the Trefors, did you hear from them?'

'About a year after Martin's funeral and after Gerry went to Canada, it was summer 2009, Bethan would have been in her early twenties by then. I'd left field social work and I was working at the University. I received a letter, it was completely unexpected, it was from Bethan. It was a brief letter. It struck me as a goodbye letter. She thanked me for my "support through-out the years," that's how she put it. She said she was also living in Canada and that she was making a life there for herself. There were Canadian air mail stamps on the envelope but no return address. That was the last I heard from her or of her and I've heard nothing since.'

'Do you think, she was looking for her father.'

'Who Knows?'

'Do you by any chance have a photograph of Bethan.'

'No, I don't have one.'

'So that was it.'

'As far as Bethan was concerned yes, but not as far as the other siblings were concerned.'

'What happened to them.'

'I suppose the unbelievable but true answer is that they all died prematurely, in tragic circumstances and in quick succession and over a short period of time.'

'What, all four of them?'

'Every one of them, yes.'

'That's unbelievable, how, when?'

'After the disruption at the Kinders, except for Lowri who stayed with the City Council, the Trefors all went back to their individual boroughs and resumed their old lives. Lowri was the first one, it wasn't long after I'd received Bethan's letter, a few months. Lowri was still in care, she was fifteen. I didn't know anything about it. I went into a store in Manchester and found myself stood next to an ex- colleague, you know how you do, she told me about it. Lowri had gone downhill since the disruption. She was mixing with all the wrong company. She was in a stolen car with some other kids. They were driving at speed and they turned the car over two of the kids died, one of them was Lowri.'

'And Dylan, Glenys and Gethin?'

'Over the next few years, first Gethin then Glenys and finally Dylan all died in tragic circumstances.'

'What were the circumstances?'

'Gethin committed suicide by throwing himself under a train. Glenys fell off the balcony from a tower block and Dylan perished in a house fire. Unbelievable but absolutely true.'

'You've certainly been through it Rosemary. I've just got one more question.'

'Ask it.'

'Did any of the Trefors have any children themselves?'

'I don't know about Bethan but as far as the others are concerned no, there wasn't one single offspring between the four of them.'

'Rosemary, was there a final opinion about the whole situation. Was there a held view.'

'Held views change back and forth Maxine. You know that, you're a Doctor and medical opinions change all the time. There was an opinion within the city region's safeguarding agencies that some of the Trefor's deaths were fallout from the allegation and that had it been managed differently and the Trefor family placement been kept together, then some of these deaths may have been avoided. But of course we will never really know.'

'What a story Rosemary, I feel as if I've been through the wringer and I've only had to listen to the story, you've had to live it.'

'Yes, there is no doubt that it leaves a scar, but it's all thankfully in the past now. There is a little addendum to the Trefor story, would you like to hear it?'

'It's not more tragedy is it.'

'It depends how you look at it, I found it quite heartening.'

'I'm in the mood for a bit of heartening.'

'In the summer of 2010, I accompanied a friend of mine to Leeds University to attend her son's graduation, from the Nursing Faculty. As you probably know Leeds is arguably the top University in England for graduation as a nurse. At this ceremony, all the graduates are handed their degree certificates. At the beginning of the proceedings, the top graduates of that year are given special awards. I was dumbstruck as the award for the top nurse of that whole intake was presented. The name wasn't familiar to me and I can't remember it now, but the young woman who was walking across the stage to collect this award was.'

'Don't tell me, it was Bethan Trefor.'

'No, Maxine it certainly wasn't Bethan Trefor.'

'She was calling herself something entirely different and as I said, I can't remember the name. However, there was no doubt about her identity, she was a little older but it was Emma Luckhurst.'

Chapter 25

Sunday Lunch

As you travel through Winton Kiss, along River Street, towards the county border of Derbyshire, less than a mile before you arrive at the sign, that reads "Derbyshire" and just before you come into open country, where the already narrow road, narrows even more, you will come upon a pub. This pub is not remarkable for the area or for that matter any area. It is mainly a straight up and down, stone built structure. The name of the pub itself, comes from the name of the village, "The Winton Kiss" known as *The Kiss* to locals. On the "A" board that stands outside it's frontage, the written proclamation boasts to serve "Fine Ales and Home Cooked Foods." It was where Danny Senetti had arranged to meet Maxine, Alberta and Lizzie for Sunday lunch.

Senetti was sitting alone outside in the sunshine, in the beer garden. He was at a table for four, he sat in one of the outsize wooden chairs that *The Kiss* was famous for. He saw Maxine's car pull up outside the front entrance. She got out of her car and entered the bar. She was dressed in a black vest, cream shorts and had a cream coloured bag slung over her shoulder. He thought that it was simple clothing, yet Maxine managed to look elegant, cool and beautiful wearing it. Having first paused at the bar, she entered the beer garden with a glass of iced orange juice in her hand. She smiled at Senetti then sat down at his table, in the chair next to him.

Senetti said, 'I've arranged for a taxi to meet Alberta and Lizzie off the train, so they should be here about ten past two.'

'That gives us about an hour then.'

'How did you get on with Rosemary Gilmartin, did she have any revelations?'

'She had nothing but.'

Maxine took Senetti though the detail of her meeting yesterday with the family social worker. She was very careful to leave nothing out; he listened intently without interruption.

'That's quite a story Maxine, do you believe it all?'

'I do, every word.'

'Let's just summarise, tell me if you think I've got anything wrong, left anything out or put anything in.'

They looked at each other in silence.

Senetti said, 'So this is the case of...The Looked After Child. A family spanning three generations, the Trefor family with connections in Wales and North-West England and going back to the 1950s, are all looked after in care by what we term these days the corporate parent. Grandmother dies in the 1970s and mother dies in the 1990s. Both in tragic and sad circumstances. How am I doing?'

'Good Danny, keep going.'

'As we approach the end of the 1990s and after a lifetime in care, the family consists of five siblings, same mother different fathers. Some siblings are doing better than others, but they are all in drift, under the auspices of different local authorities. Then the eldest sibling Bethan is taken out of Residential Care and placed in foster care with Gerry and Martin Kinder. Bethan is academically gifted and the placement is an immediate success in every way. Then gradually over a period, the other four siblings move in and the whole placement becomes relatively successful. Again, how am I doing?'

'Again Danny, so far so good.'

'Then in 2003, an allegation of sexual abuse is made. An Emergency Strategy Meeting is convened and the decision is that the four youngest siblings are moved out of the Kinder's home immediately. Then six months later, The Fostering Panel deregisters the Kinders and tries in vain to move Bethan out, but she and the Kinders resist. You do the next bit Maxine, you've had it from the horse's mouth.'

Maxine began to speak.

'Bethan eventually goes down to Oxford and does well. Martin Kinder dies around 2007. Bethan blames the decisions and actions of social services managers for his death. Gerry goes to live in Canada and the last we hear of Bethan is in 2009, when she is also living in Canada. We don't know though if she's living with Gerry Kinder or not. Meanwhile, back in England, the four younger Trefor siblings over a comparatively short period, all die in tragic and unusual circumstances.'

'Just remind me how the Trefor Siblings died Maxine.'

'I'll have to refer to my notes.' As she said this she produced a small notebook from her bag.

'Lowri was killed in a car accident. Gethin

committed suicide by throwing himself under a train. Glenys fell off a tower block balcony and Dylan burnt to death in a house fire.'

'Quite a catalogue of tragedy for one single family, wouldn't you say.'

'I would most definitely.'

'Obviously, we see the connection in the way our victims died and the way the Trefor siblings died. Jason under a tram, Velma under a train, Alma under a car, and I think we can bring Jay Chopra into the equation now, who fell off a balcony, and Deacon, who we'll say for the sake of our understanding, spontaneously combusted in a Manchester back alley. The question is Maxine, is it all coincidence and circumstantial or is it deliberately contrived and symbolic?'

'Danny, it can't be accidental, there are too many matches.'

'I agree Maxine, there are, all these matches and all this information that we've now learned which throws out several questions.'

'Go on.'

'Well, in view of the death of Jay Chopra, his connection to our case and also my understanding that his death is still the object of a police enquiry, perhaps we should consider handing over the file to police.'

'Danny, you're funny you are, what file? We don't have a file.'

'Maxine, this is no time for pedantry.'

'I don't really think that we have any evidence that isn't circumstantial. We can hardly say that Jay Chopra fell off a high balcony last week and so did Glenys Trefor, seven years ago so there is a connection.'

'It's a bit more than that Maxine.'

'It is Danny and you and I know it's all true, but it is going to be difficult to convince others and you have to admit that if nothing else, it is far-fetched. In addition to this, apart from Jay Chopra, we would be asking the police to re-open four old cases and the police don't like doing that. You end up in a battle with them whereupon you often come under suspicion yourself. There may come a time in this, when we must involve them. Right now, I think the police would take an onerous stance towards us. I personally, don't have the time to give to them and I'm just not in the mood for them, not now.'

'I agree, I just wanted to hear your view. All right then, we pursue our own investigations.'

'Who is the murderer, do we have a suspect?'

'We have a prime suspect.'

'Bethan Trefor, Danny, she is the only suspect. Let's just think about this now. Your brothers, sisters and your foster dad all die prematurely, let's put aside for the moment whether they are accidents, suicides or natural causes. You blame the authorities or some members of it. You find out who these members are and years later you set out on a quest for vengeance. Is it realistic?'

'It is Maxine, it is a little wild and not the norm but it is wholly realistic. It all fits in with what we know, with what we've found out.'

'You would have to know certain information. When Jason Dunphy was at the tram platform, which one, stuff like that.'

'Oh, that's all too easy to find out these days.'

'You would also have to know identities of panel members, minutes, outcomes, who said what, all that.'

'Same applies Maxine, it's all out there, once you

know where to look. Just consider what we've been able to find out, with a few internet searches, some phone calls and a handful of visits. I don't see discovering any of that being anything else other than a formality. There is though, another looming question.'

'A looming question?'

'Yes, I am going to have to do something about it, in the next few minutes.'

'Explain Councillor.'

'I'm allegedly working in full partnership on this case with Alberta Curtis-Brightland and Lizzie Lambert, who are due at this very table any moment, what do I tell them? How much of what we've discovered do I divulge? I use the term allegedly working, because I've hardly seen either of them since the case started, also as I've said, I don't trust either of them and if I did tell them what we know, who is to say that they won't decide to go to the police themselves?'

'Danny, you're on your own there. I'll back up and support whatever you decide to say, probably by silence, but on this occasion, I'm playing a passive role. As we speak, I've not even set eyes on either woman, so I'm going to have to leave the big decisions entirely to you. What did you say their surnames were, Curtis-Brightland and Lambert?'

'Yeah, Alberta Curtis Brightland and Lizzie Lambert!'

'Sorry, the surnames must not have registered, I've just been thinking of them as Alberta and Lizzie.'

Just then a cream coloured taxi came to a stop outside the beer garden. Two female figures alighted. Maxine noticed they were both tall, trim and dark-skinned. They were both dressed for the sunshine, in the obligatory shorts, vest and sandals. She observed how similar they both looked to each other and how similar their poise and posture was; she was also struck by their similarity of movement as they walked side by side and approached the table.

Danny stood up, 'Hello Alberta, Lizzie, pleased you could come. Lizzie Lambert, Alberta Curtis-Brightland please meet Doctor Maxine Wells.' The three women smiled at each other and shook hands.

Alberta eyed the surroundings and said, 'What a lovely pleasant and tranquil, rural change from all that excitement and traffic in London and Manchester.'

Maxine said, 'I'll get some drinks and menus, any preferences?'

'I'll have a white wine and soda,' both women said almost in unison.

When Maxine returned, Senetti was talking about the investigation. Maxine listened as he made no mention of the most up to date discoveries. He made no reference of any kind to: The Trefors, The Kinders, The Strategy Meeting, The Fostering Panel, Jay Chopra, Deacon Bailey or Rosemary Gilmartin. He confined his whole conversation almost in its entirety to Alma Alice, Jason Dunphy and Velma Vine.

He turned to Lizzie, 'We've not spoken since our meeting at Trensis Station with Megan. I wondered did you have any view on the incident involving Velma Vine. What did you think in relation to what Megan said?'

Lizzie said, 'Obviously, Megan is an experienced officer and her opinion must be respected. Saying that, that's all it was, little more than her opinion, there wasn't much in the way of evidence about anything, was there? She even cited absence of evidence as the reason her superiors closed the case.'

Senetti didn't respond directly he said, 'Funnily enough, I had a telephone call from Meg, a couple of days ago she's moving to some place in Wales I can't pronounce the name. It's somewhere near Phwelli, she asked me to say hello.'

Maxine watched intently as Senetti mentioned all this. She couldn't really see the relevance of the comment, but she knew Senetti well enough to know that there would be some, somewhere. She could also tell, that he was in anticipation of a reaction from Lizzie. Despite his anticipation, Lizzie listened to what Senetti said, she smiled but didn't respond.

Alberta asked, 'Where do we think we are with this case now Danny? We've been on it a few weeks and apart from some hypothesis, to use your own word and some opinion, we haven't really made any new discoveries, would you agree with that?'

Once again Senetti remained silent.

As the quartet ate and drank its way through lunch. Senetti and the two women entered into a discourse about the case. Maxine seemingly listened to their conversation, occasionally making a small contribution. In the main though she remained silent. What she was really studying was the physical appearance of the two women who were seated opposite her. They were both dark skinned with dark hair. Their facial features were neither similar nor dissimilar but it wasn't these that intrigued Maxine. It was in their bodies where Maxine found similarities. They were now both seated but Maxine had observed, to within fractions, that they were both the same height and they were of identical build. Maxine considered that they were probably the same weight to within half-a-kilo of each other, also their hands were very similar, almost identical. She glanced under the table at their feet. She could see both pairs clearly, barely encased in their brief summer sandals. They rested in front of her, underneath the table as if awaiting inspection. Maxine was not a foot expert. She knew that there were many permutations of feet and she also knew a little about their characteristics. Loosely, it wasn't a common consensus but it was a held view by many that there were thought to be five types of feet and they were often classified as being; *Egyptian, Roman, Greek, Germanic and Celtic feet*. She observed that Alberta's and Lizzie's feet were both Roman type. She considered, she was with two women, apparently not genetically connected, who were the same shape, weight, bearing, who had the same poise and posture and who had identical feet and hands. She was a little perplexed by this presentation.

An outsider listening to the conversation between Senetti and the two women, would have concluded that there wasn't really any more to investigate. Alberta said that she would get the report 'collated' and then she would contact Senetti about it in a 'couple of weeks.'

The afternoon went by and eventually Lizzie said, 'I think that's our return taxi that just pulled onto the rear car-park.'

Senetti said, 'I'll walk you over to it.'

'Lovely to meet you Maxine,' said Lizzie.'

Maxine smiled, 'It is indeed lovely to meet you both.'

Then the man and the two women walked over to the awaiting taxi.

As the three of them chatted outside the cab, Maxine took the short walk to where her car was parked. She pressed her key fob and her boot-lid opened. Inside the boot was, amongst other things, a brief case. From the case, she extricated eight paper envelopes, six relatively small ones and two larger ones. Having done this, she returned to the table. She could see that Alberta and Lizzie were being driven off in the taxi. Senetti was stood in the car park waving them off. Maxine began to pick up various objects from the table where the women had been sitting. She placed these objects in the small envelopes. She placed a teaspoon in one and a tissue in another. Then she found a small hair-grip and put that in an envelope. Then she placed three of the small envelopes in one of the big envelopes; then she placed the remaining three small envelopes in the remaining large envelope. After this she sealed the large envelopes, returned to her car and placed them in the boot. As she resumed her seat at the table, Senetti was just arriving there.

She smiled at him as he sat down. 'That was a very one-sided meeting.'

'It was, did you detect any enthusiasm from either of them?'

'I detected that you didn't tell them anything. You've told me more at our first meeting than they know. How can they show any enthusiasm when you keep them in ignorance and don't trust them?'

'Maxine, you are just being gracious towards them. You know more than they know because you've made it your business to know and as far as keeping them in ignorance, you are our right I don't trust them. I've said it before, I wish I did but I don't.'

'What now?'

'Tomorrow is Monday, I'll see if I can find out any more about Jay Chopra. The Police have had the case over a week now, it must have moved in some direction, they must have found out something.'

'Yes, but will they tell you.'

'I'm not going to ask them, not directly anyway. I'll take it through Archie, he's got good contacts with the police.'

'The way I see it now Danny, is that it comes down to two issues. The first one is Bethan Trefor. She is our prime suspect, as we said, she is our only suspect. We need to know where Bethan Trefor is. She could be back in Canada for all we know.'

'She isn't in Canada, Maxine, she's here, I know it. What's the other issue?'

'The other one, is Emma Luckhurst. We need to know where she is.'

'What about Rosemary, does she know anything?'

'Rosemary doesn't really know Emma and the last time she saw her was at Emma's graduation and that was years ago. We need to find two women before one of them murders the other. That's if it's not already been done. We've got no idea whatsoever as to their individual whereabouts. The last news we have of one of them is that she was living in Canada and the last news we have of the other one is she graduated as a nurse nearly ten years ago. She could be anywhere now. She could be married with six kids and living in South America. We don't know anything about them. We don't even know what either of them looks like.'

'She isn't in South America, Maxine, trust me. The answer to this is on our doorstep somewhere.'

'So, what are we going to do Danny.'

'I don't know Maxine but I'm certain that something is going to develop.'

'Well it needs to; can I drop you off anywhere?'

'Yeah, you can drop me off at The Swan, if it's not taking you out of your way.'

'No, I've got some business in Norford, I'm going past the front door of The Swan, but wouldn't you be better off going home and watching the derby game on the TV?'

'Sport on the TV on a Sunday afternoon, what are you trying to do Maxine, kill me off altogether? One of the reasons I go in The Swan is because they don't have a television.'

'At the risk of saying something I've said before. Have you ever thought Danny that you might need some help with you drinking?'

'Thanks for the offer Doctor, but I can manage perfectly all right on my own. Anyway, what business can you possibly have in Norford on a Sunday afternoon?'

'Yes Danny, business on a Sunday. Now do you want the lift or not?'

Chapter 26

Sisters under the Skin

The portable door chime rang in the kitchen of the terraced house in Winton Kiss. Senetti got up from his seat, walked across the room, down the hallway and opened the front door. Standing there smiling in the sunshine was Archie Hamilton.

'Come in Archie, would you like a cup of tea?'

'I'm not planning on staying long, but yes a cup of tea would be welcome.'

'Well, this is an unusual event Archie.'

'I have some personal business over here and knowing your Monday habits and the nice weather we are having, I thought you'd be in, so I caught the bus over. May as well get some use out of this concessionary travel pass.'

Danny led Archie through the house into the kitchen.

'Sit down Archie.'

'I've also got a bit more on Jay Chopra. It's not much but you may as well have it. I spoke to Alan Collier this morning, he's the Divisional Police Commander for Manchester City Centre. He wouldn't say much, but what he did say was that they are treating Jay Chopra's death as suspicious. He also said that they were looking for two young women, probably both in their thirties. Collier used that old cliché about, "eliminate them from our enquiries," and it might be true but it might not either.'

'Did he say anymore?'

'Apparently these women have been picked up on The Midland Hotel's security system. They are not very identifiable though, as both women wore masks.'

'Masks?'

'Yes, on the night in question, there was a charity ball at The Midland and most of the women who attended and there were three hundred people there, wore masks.'

'So, if nobody knows what they look like, it won't be an easy task to find them.'

'That would seem to be the way of it Danny, yes.'

'This case seems to get harder by the minute.'

'There is a bit more. The two women are black and I've got possible names; Camille and Justine but they are probably aliases.'

'Not much for the police to go on, is it?'

The two men drank their tea and talked. Their talk was mainly about council business. Archie left after about half an hour and Senetti went upstairs to change into some day clothes.

Downstairs again, his phone sprang to life on the kitchen table.

'Danny, it's Steve, Steve Fedeczko.'

'Hello Steve, I certainly wasn't expecting to be speaking to you again so soon.'

'It's just a small thing, but I thought that you should have it anyway.'

'I'm grateful that you would think of me.'

'Coleen and I were watching the TV last night.'

'It wasn't the derby-game was it?'

'What, oh no, I'm not interested in that. It was a programme about the Bermuda Triangle and it reminded me of something. Some time ago when Coleen was freelancing, she did a series of articles about scientific phenomena and The Bermuda Triangle featured in one of them. In one article Coleen referred to a family who disappeared completely. Their light aircraft was flying somewhere near Puerto Rico, when all contact was lost. A father his adult son and adult daughter were never seen again. It was in the news because he was a high ranking Canadian diplomat. Guess what the family name was Danny?'

'I give up Steve.'

'Curtis-Brightland, Danny that was the family name. That's where I'd heard the name of your colleague before, it was in my own wife's article. Michel, Sydney and Rio Curtis-Brightland. They all disappeared with their aeroplane and were never seen again. That's where I know the name from. Just thought that there might be a connection to something. Although I don't know what.'

'When was this Steve?'

'What the article or the incident?'

'The incident.'

'About seven years ago, it's got nothing to do with Jason Dunphy, but I just thought that you should have it.'

'Thanks Steve, appreciate it.'

After the call, Senetti sat there gormless and perplexed. He recalled Alberta had mentioned her father to him. She'd also mentioned a sister and a brother. She didn't mention any names, or if she did he couldn't recall them, but she said her parents named the children after places they'd been in at the time. Fedeczko had said Rio and Sydney, Rio de Janeiro and Sydney Australia, it had to be the same family. So, there was no doubt whatsoever that it was the same Curtis-Brightland family who had disappeared over the Bermuda Triangle. Alberta hadn't mentioned any of that stuff that Fedeczko had just told him about. It struck Senetti as a very deliberate and unusual omission. He couldn't understand why she had mentioned half of it and left half of it out. Such an omission could be none other than a deceitful one.

His doorbell rang again, this time it was Maxine.

'I'm getting more visitors today than I've had all year.'

'Thanks for the warm welcome Danny. I thought you'd be in, Monday after Sunday and all that.'

'Come in Maxine, I'll make you a cup of tea, I'm getting good at this. Sorry I didn't mean to sound ungracious, I mean it's lovely to see you, especially on a Monday, though why aren't you chained to your surgery desk?'

'On police advice, we've had to close the surgery for the day. Duncan had a visit from them this morning. Lucy Lockett has gone missing. According to her husband she went out with a friend last night although he doesn't know who that friend is. Anyway, she didn't come home. She's not answering her phone. It's all very much out of character. The police think that she may have been abducted.'

'Sorry Maxine, who is Duncan? Why would anybody abduct Lucy?'

'Doctor Duncan Wordsworth, he's my partner in the practice and as for Lucy, we don't know but that seems to be the way the Police are thinking.'

'Looks like we are both having a morning of it. I have just had a very strange telephone call about Alberta and before that, Archie came to see me. He said the Police are treating Chopra's death as suspicious and that they are trying to locate two young black women who have shown up on the security system at the Midland Hotel. Their names are Camille and Justine.'

'What was the strange call about Alberta?'

'It was from an old contact of mine. He told me that her father and her siblings had disappeared in an aeroplane accident some years ago.'

'Danny, do you know what the difference between a step-sibling and a half-sibling is?'

'Yes, a step-sibling is by a connection, often marriage and a half-sibling is a blood-tie.'

'That is correct.'

'Do you know what a uterine sibling is, do you know what an agnate-sibling is?'

'No Maxine, I don't.'

'Uterine siblings have the same mother whereas agnate siblings have the same father.'

'You're doing your doctor-speak again aren't you? I don't know where you are heading with this Maxine but I'm going to be patient.'

'Thank you, Danny, how are your languages, French and German?'

'Easy question, failed the first one at GCE, didn't go anywhere near the other, at any level. Although I did go to Berlin in 2002, with Kevin Malpas and we seemed to get by.'

'Does Kevin speak German?'

'It's hard to say really, as very few, from any country, seem to understand what Kevin's talking about.'

'Where's he from originally?'

'County Longsight.'

'County Where?'

'It doesn't matter Maxine.'

'Let's take the name Lambert, as in Lizzie Lambert. It is a name of German origin which has been assimilated into French. Originally it comes from the words *Land* and *Berht*. In English it roughly translates as *Bright Land*.'

'So, what you are saying Maxine, is that Brightland and Lambert are the same name in different languages'

'Yes.'

'And your point about uterine and agnate siblings?'

'When we were having lunch at the pub yesterday, I was struck by some of the physical similarities between Alberta and Lizzie.'

'Really Maxine, I don't think that they look anything like each other.'

'It's not so much facially, more to do with their physique, their bearing, their hands, feet. Anyway, I took some stuff that the women had been using off the lunch table, a tissue, a spoon a hairgrip, that sort of stuff. I took them to a friend of mine after I dropped you off at the Swan. He runs the DNA testing unit in Norford. He ran some speedy tests on them for me as a special favour. The results of these tests are not conclusive but they are fairly reliable, reliable enough for me, anyway.'

'So, you've carried out a DNA test on Alberta and Lizzie.'

'Yes.'

'And what have you discovered ?'

Alberta and Lizzie may not have been brought up together, they may have had entirely different backgrounds, they may have lived in different countries for most of their lives, but they are genetic sisters. Same father, different mothers. They are called Agnate Sisters. They are sisters Danny and why are we not aware of this? What does it all mean to this case?'

Senetti said wistfully … 'The Colonel's Lady and Judy O' Grady are sisters under the skin.'

'Raja Varma?'

'Rudyard Kipling!'

'It sounds appropriate but as I say what does it mean to this case?'

'It means Maxine, that from the onset both individually and collectively, Alberta Curtis Brightland and Lizzie Lambert have been trying to hide the most basic information from anybody and everybody, especially me.'

'Why?'

Senetti remained quiet, then he said.

'It's about deceit, guile and trickery. Instead of trying to progress this investigation, both Alberta and Lizzie have been trying to thwart it.'

'Why Danny, for what reason?'

'For the reason Maxine, that without Alberta and Lizzie, there wouldn't have been anything to investigate. You see, instead of being the investigators, they are actually the murderers and as such they couldn't afford any kind of connection between themselves and reality to be made. It's all a bit wild and fanciful, I know. You'll just have to suspend reality for a while, whilst I explain.

In addition to this, I haven't got all the pieces to fill the blanks in, so some of it is supposition on my part.'

'Well, will you explain it to me.'

'Let's start with Alma Alice Spain, killed accidentally and apparently by a boy racer in a remote area, do you remember?'

'I do, yes.'

'Alma Alice, that's where I came in. Only it wasn't a boy racer, in fact it wasn't a boy anything. This is how I see it now that I've had chance to think about it. Alma Alice was lured there, through an online date. Probably somebody she had met at least once before. The only thing is, it was a woman she was meeting not a man. She thought that they would both go off in the other woman's car, that's why she didn't bring her own car. Then shortly after she arrived at Parkhurst Lane, she was murdered and left for dead in the car park.'

'It's horrible, Danny.'

'Maxine, it all fits now. Do you remember I told you about Magoo from the pub, Bartholomew Topp?'

'Yes. I remember all of it yes.'

'Bartholomew thought he saw two black men, but what he really saw was two black *women*. However, the rest of Bartholomew's assertion was correct. It was just that he was a half-blind eccentric drunk, who nobody took seriously. One of the central points of these incidents is that everybody thought the murderer was a man. If you think of the victims; Alma Alice Spain, Councillor Jason Dunphy, Velma Vine, Deacon Bailey and Jay Chopra, they were all murdered, but not by a man Maxine, by two women.'

'Yes, I can see it now.'

'Try this Maxine, thirty-odd years ago, one man had two daughters by two different women. One of these daughters he stayed with and the other one he abandoned. Both those daughters were raised in entirely different backgrounds. We don't know the detail so let's just say that one grew up privileged with her father in Canada and the other grew up disadvantaged in England and Wales. They both grew into adults, unaware of the other's existence. We know all about the Trefors and the panels and meetings, so we don't need to go into that. Both women had tragedy in their lives in terms of their families. Again, we know about the Trefor's premature deaths. The only survivor of the Trefor family was Bethan Trefor. I've checked and Bethan is Welsh for Elizabeth and Lizzie is a shortened version of that name. Lizzie Lambert is Bethan Trefor. What I also learnt this morning was that Alberta's father, brother and sister disappeared in a plane accident five years ago.'

'It's incredible.'

'It is Maxine but it isn't as incredible as the next chapter.'

'Lizzie blamed professional management for the deaths of her siblings and her foster father, she vowed revenge at a young age.'

He paused and then continued, 'Lizzie went to Canada, we know this. Incredibly Alberta and Bethan as she probably was, found each other. We don't know for sure how and when, but they did. They realised that they were sisters. They were in fact the only family each other had. They were, for the want of a better description, Orphan Siblings.'

'Lizzie had a hurt and a vengeance inside her and at some stage Alberta came to be of the same mind as Lizzie. So, they set out on a vendetta, murdering those who they considered were to blame.'

'Lizzie and Alberta or Justine and Camille were here in England murdering people and then a fluke happened and Alberta found herself assigned to the case whereupon she was investigating her own murders. We know the rest.'

'The question is where are they now?'

Their discussions were interrupted by Maxine's telephone.

Maxine took the call. Initially, she didn't speak but she listened intently, then she said, 'Are you sure about this Duncan?'

She finished the call and turned to Danny.

'It seems there is yet a final twist. That was Duncan, all surgery calls are being paged through to him until the surgery re-opens, hopefully tomorrow. He's just received a call from Rosemary Gilmartin. She was trying to contact me and was diverted to him. The early edition of the Evening News has just published a photograph of Lucy Lockett under the heading, ..."Have you seen this nurse." Rosemary says it's a photo of Emma Luckhurst. Danny, Lucy Lockett is Emma Luckhurst.'

'What we need to know at this moment are the whereabouts of Alberta Curtis-Brightland and Lizzie Lambert.'

Maxine nodded in agreement.

She said, 'Do you think that they've abducted Emma?'

'I'm beginning to hope so Maxine, because the alternative doesn't bear thinking about.'

'They are hiding out somewhere, they could be anywhere.'

'I think I know where they are. Is your car outside?'

'Yes.'

'Let's take it, mine is known to Lizzie. There shouldn't be much traffic around this time, we should be able to make it in just over two hours.'

'Where are we going and what are we going to do when we get there?'

'Come on Maxine, I'll explain on the way.'

Chapter 27

Diana

Councillor Danny Senetti and Doctor Maxine Wells dashed outside and were quickly inside Maxine's silver Mercedes. It moved off silently from the kerb, picking up speed with the motion.

'Where are we going?'

'Straight ahead.'

'I'll need a bit more than that if I'm going to drive for two hours.'

He produced his small notebook and flicking over the pages he announced; 'I've got a post code, let's put it in the satnav, it's LL53 6NQ.'

He tapped the post code into the navigation system. The screen flashed up a distance of one-hundred and twenty-one-miles and a travelling time of two-hours and four-minutes.

She said, 'That's North-Wales, isn't it?'

'A place called Chwilog. On The Llyn Peninsula. It's a privately-owned caravan, one of those posh ones, it's on a camp site there, goes by the name of Ocean Heights.'

'I know the type of caravan you mean. Jo Westinghouse an old school friend of mine has one in Caernarfon, a place called Dinas Dille. I stayed there once for a weekend, like a little luxury flat.'

'You always seem to have up to date information on your school friends Maxine. Do you keep in touch with all of them?'

'As many as I can yes. Obviously, you can't keep in touch with every one of them, but there is a small group of us, about ten in number, who meet regularly about three times a year. Well school days are part of one's heritage aren't they? You don't bother with yours, do you? I think you told me that once before.'

'I certainly don't, they were nothing less than a bunch of immoral misfits, bullies and blackguards and if I never see any of them ever again, that will be too soon. There are three or four of them that I am compelled to speak to on a professional basis, but I'm working on a plan to get rid of at least one of them, if I'm lucky I might even take three down.'

'Do you at least go to the reunions? I always ensure I know when the reunions are and I always go'

'We've got something in common there Maxine. Like you I always ensure I know when and where our reunions are.'

'So, you at least go to them?'

'No, I ensure I'm miles away whilst they are taking place.'

Maxine said, 'You know Senetti before I met you, my life was straight forward. Go to work, look after people, come home. Everybody was who they seemed to be, they were all straight forward and honest, you knew what was what and who was who.'

'So, what's changed?'

'What's changed? Now, people are all contrived, pretending to be honourable, when they are really murderers. How do you get from Bethan Trefor to Lizzie

Lambert or Emma Luckhurst to Lucy Lockett, do you know Danny?'

'As the man said Maxine, it's life's tapestry. Bethan is a story of a looked after child, one that went wrong, sometimes they do. Emma is a different story, same subject but one who in the end, went right. The transition of Lucy's name is easy enough to imagine. First you are Emma Luckhurst then you marry a man called Lockett and become Emma Lockett, then perhaps Luckhurst becomes Lucky. Then you are Lucky Lockett. This naturally in time because of that nursery rhyme eventually converts to Lucy Lockett.'

'What about the transition from EL, looked after child who makes a false allegation, to Safeguarding Angel, Nurse Lucy Lockett.'

'That's a bit more complicated and takes a lot more effort. Nevertheless, it is to be greatly applauded. You're not against people changing are you Maxine?'

'No, not at all Danny, in fact the opposite but that change should be for the better.'

'In Emma's case it is. You said a few days ago that you were all fond and proud of her. Just keep the faith Maxine. Let's change the subject. The satnav says we're an hour and fifteen minutes away from this caravan.'

What are we going to do when we get there?'

'Don't worry I've got a plan.'

'That's exactly what does worry me, the last time you had a plan somebody ended up dead, it was almost you and me.'

'Maxine, trust me I'm a Councillor.'

'Just tell me that when we get to Ocean Heights we're not going to go charging through the caravan door.'

'No Maxine, we're not, we need help on this one.'

'Help from whom?'

'The authorities.'

'That's a new one, Danny Senetti looking for help from the authorities.'

'Every second is precious. We have to hope that Lucy is in there and that she is still alive and that she stays alive. If we are right and I'm sure we are right. Alberta and Lizzie or Camille and Justine between them have already killed five innocent people. We don't want to put them in the position of having nothing to lose and of another murder making no difference.'

He took his phone from his pocket and tapped a number. Hu turned toward Maxine and said, 'I'm calling Megan Rees Jenkins. I'm putting it on loud-speaker so you can hear the conversation.'

'Hello Megan, it's Danny Senetti.'

'Hello Danny, how are you?'

'I'm well myself but I'm anxious. We're in Maxine's car, on our way to Ocean Heights Caravan Park. We're currently just over an hour away, we've got an issue and we need your help.'

'What sort of issue?'

'At the moment we think that it's an abduction but it could be heading for a murder which is what we are trying to prevent.'

'An abduction, that could turn into murder? Danny is this live as we speak?'

'It isn't a hundred per cent Meg, but if I'm right, it is live yes.'

'Danny, this is serious, hundred per cent or one per cent, it doesn't matter. It's a police issue and can I just remind you, I'm a police officer.'

'Meg, trust me on this, there could be a life at stake. Although we do have a small advantage.'

'Damn, Senetti, I came over here for a quiet life, I've not even unpacked a box yet and my past life has followed me from my old doorstep to my new one. I'm apprehensive about asking this, but what exactly is this help that you need and what is this small advantage that we've got?'

'The help that we need is your involvement and the advantage is that they don't know that anybody is onto them.'

'They soon will Danny, when you tell me who they are and where they are.'

'They are Alberta Curtis Brightland and Lizzie Lambert you were right about Lizzie, she's got plenty to hide. We're fairly sure that they have abducted somebody called Lucy Lockett a local nurse and that they plan to kill her. I can't explain any more we're running out of time. Meg, you need to trust me. I just need you to do one small task and then you can raise your alarm. You can have, cops, firefighters, ambulance crew, dogs, cats, helicopters whatever you like swarming all over the scene. None of this though is going to do us any good if our abductee is dead, is it?'

'What do you want me to do?'

'Right, Megan this is the plan. Put your jogging outfit on and drive over to Ocean Heights Caravan Park. Then go for a jog through the park. See if Lizzie's car LLA 111 is there and if there is any evidence of occupancy at her caravan. If there is anything else you can glean, then do so, but don't forget Lizzie Lambert knows you and she's seen your car so under no circumstances must you be seen and identified otherwise it might panic them and then we'll lose any control of the situation that we have altogether.'

'You mean we've actually got some. I knew Lizzie Lambert was a bad one, I told you...'

'Meg we can discuss all this when Lizzie Lambert and Alberta Curtis Brightland have been arrested and when we know that Lucy is safe. When you've had your jog and as soon as you've seen what you've seen, find a bush to hide behind and call me immediately on this number. We'll be waiting for your call.'

'Shouldn't we just contact the police and leave it all to them?'

'All in good time Meg, how long will it take to mobilize them?'

'Why do I feel my pension slipping out of my grasp.'

'How long Meg?'

'They have alert squads for this type of thing now, they are trained to act very quickly. The helicopters are just over The Menai Straits, a matter of fifteen minutes maybe.'

'Right that's all for now Meg, speak to you soon.'

Maxine had sat through Danny and Megan's interchange in silence, she remained so. Danny too was silent, they looked at each other awaiting Megan's call.

Twenty minutes later Danny's phone rang. It was Megan. She seemed a little breathless.

'I've been to Ocean Heights. The car is there, there are also three people in the caravan. Two in the lounge and one in the bedroom at the back.'

'Did they see you?'

'They may have seen me but they won't have recognised me, I was all wrapped up.'

'The person in the back bedroom is asleep. Perhaps she is sedated I don't know. I could clearly see Lizzie and another woman who I presume is Alberta.'

'Well done Megan.'

'What next.'

'You set up your SWAT team or whatever they are called these days. Tell whoever is in charge that after you and I have finished this call, Maxine is going to call Alberta on her phone and engage her in conversation. The object being to distract them from your rescue operation and keep Lucy alive.'

'They might not like that and if you are going to do that Danny, wouldn't that call be better coming from you?'

'They might not like it Megan but that's what is happening. As for me making the call, I don't think so. I'm probably the last person she wants to speak to right now. If Alberta recognises my number she might not take the call. If they see Maxine's number, they won't recognise it. They'll be nervous anyway, they'll want to know who's calling them so they'll take the call, at least I hope they will. Ring me back on this number when you've got an E.T.A. for the police.'

Fifteen minute later Maxine's phone rang out, Senetti picked it up.

'Hello Danny, it's Megan again. Police team will be outside the caravan door in eleven minutes. If you are going to make your call I'd make it now.'

Maxine pulled the car over into a side road in the village of Chwilog, she switched the engine off and looked across looked at Senetti.

Senetti said, 'Remember Maxine say anything as long as she is distracted and engaged. Don't us one word when you can use two.'

Maxine tapped the phone number in'

'Hello,' said a female voice.'

'Hello, is that Alberta, Alberta Curtis-Brightland.'

'Yes, who is this?'

'We met on Sunday at the pub, we had lunch together at the Winton Kiss pub with Councillor Senetti and your colleague Lizzie Lambert.'

'Oh yes, it's Maxine isn't it. Sorry I didn't recognise your voice nor your number. Look Doctor, it's all a bit inconvenient at the moment. Can I call you back, tomorrow perhaps? I'm in my London office and I'm just about to go into a meeting.'

Maxine looked across at Danny, she raised her hand and shrugged her shoulders in a gesture that said...what should I say?

Senetti took his notebook out and hurriedly scribbled something on it and then held it up to Maxine. It read, **"mention the caravan."**

'Did you say you were in London.'

'Yes.'

Maxine waited for a moment, every second was precious

'That's odd.'

'Why is it odd?'

Again, Maxine waited before answering. 'Because Councillor Senetti seemed to think that you would be at your caravan today.'

There was a long pause at Alberta's end of the line, then she said;

'What caravan?'

'You know the one in North Wales.'

'How did you know about that.'

'Councillor Senetti told me about it.'

'As far as I'm aware Councillor Senetti doesn't even know of the existence of this caravan. So, I don't see how he could have mentioned it.'

'Clearly he does know about it. Otherwise I wouldn't know about it and clearly, I do. It doesn't matter, does it? It's not a secret of some kind, is it?'

'How exactly can I help you?'

'Did you say *this* caravan Alberta as opposed to *the* caravan or *that* caravan.'

'I don't really remember, does it matter.'

'The word *this* implies close-proximity. You are at the caravan, aren't you?'

'This is becoming a little tedious. As I said Maxine I've got to go into a meeting.'

'Councillor Senetti asked me to give you a message, it's about Jay Chopra.'

'Who is Jay Chopra?'

'Don't you know.'

'I wouldn't say so otherwise.'

'He was a Director at City Social Services.'

Alberta Said, 'Where is Councillor Senetti.'

Again, there was a long pause before Maxine said; 'There has been a suspected terrorist attack in Norford and Councillor Senetti is heavily involved with the emergency operations.

Just then Senetti's phone rang, he leapt out of the passenger seat to take the call.

Megan's voice said; Danny 'The Police are going in now as we speak.'

Back inside the car Maxine was still speaking to Alberta she said; 'Councillor Senetti, says that Jay Chopra's death is now being investigated as suspicious, the police have cctv images and they are looking for two women called Camille and Justine...'

Then, in the background, Maxine could hear the sound of tearing metal, breaking glass and raised voices. Obviously, the police had arrived. As if in confirmation of this a cavalcade of emergency services vehicles, lights flashing and siren's wailing now dashed past her in the direction of Ocean Heights. Overhead she could see and hear the police helicopter as it hovered above the caravan park. As Senetti returned to the passenger seat in Maxine's car she disconnected the call to Alberta. She started the engine up and drove the short distance towards Ocean Heights. Senetti remained motionless and silent beside her. He read Maxine's mind and she read his. They were both concerned for the welfare of Lucy Lockett. They raced to the envisaged chaotic scene at caravan, one-one-zero and were met, quite surprisingly by relative calm. There were uniformed, armed police, cars, firefighters, a fire engine and a helicopter around the caravan but they were all operating in an eerie silence.

Alberta Curtis-Brightland and Lizzie Lambert were being led away in silence and in handcuffs into the back of police custody van and uniformed officers were sealing the immediate area off with red and white tape. As Alberta got into the van she turned her head and her eyes momentarily met Senetti's. They hung together for a second then she was gone, locked away.

Lucy Lockett was sitting in one of the chairs on the elevated decking, she appeared ghostly pale, but alive and well. Maxine walked over to the policewoman who stood in front of the decking on apparent guard duty. After a brief exchange with the officer, Maxine joined Lucy and sat beside her.

Senetti and Megan stood side by side outside Maxine's car.

He looked at caravan one-one-zero. The door had been ripped from its hinges and lay on the ground. Every window was flung open. At that precise moment, in what Senetti considered to be a touch of ethereal irony, the music system in caravan, one-one-zero came to life and from within its confines came a musical refrain.

The lyrics could be heard clearly, as the audible male baritone voice sang out;

'I'm so young and you're so old
This my Darling I've been told
I don't care just what they say
Cause forever I will pray
You and I will be as free
As the birds up in the trees
Oh, please stay by me, Diana.'

Senetti pondered, he looked across at the nameplate on the front of the caravan, "Diana." It was as if the song was paying some kind of retrospective homage and lost lament to the name of the woman who started this whole saga just by being born, all that way, back in 1951. If only she could reappear and turn the clock back to the way things might have been then. Senetti thought, if only we had the chance to start all over again, what would we do that was different? If only everybody had known then, what they knew now. Then the road travelled may have been an entirely different one for the story of The Looked After Child.

THE END

Lightning Source UK Ltd.
Milton Keynes UK
UKOW04f1856110118
315984UK00001B/22/P